BY CURTIS SITTENFELD

Show Don't Tell
Romantic Comedy
Rodham
You Think It, I'll Say It
Eligible
Sisterland
American Wife
The Man of My Dreams
Prep

SHOW
DON'T TELL

SHOW
DON'T TELL

STORIES

CURTIS
SITTENFELD

RANDOM HOUSE

NEW YORK

Published in the United States by Random House,
an imprint and division of Penguin Random House LLC, New York.

RANDOM HOUSE and the HOUSE colophon are
registered trademarks of Penguin Random House LLC.

The following stories in this collection have been previously
published, sometimes in a different form: "Show Don't Tell" and
"A for Alone" in *The New Yorker*, "White Women LOL" on
The Oprah Magazine website, "The Richest Babysitter in the World"
in *The Atlantic* (online only), "Creative Differences" in *The Cut*,
"The Tomorrow Box" and "Giraffe and Flamingo" by Amazon Original,
and "The Hug" in the *Financial Times*. In addition, "The Marriage Clock"
was originally published by Audible Originals as "Atomic Marriage."

LIBRARY OF CONGRESS CATALOGING-IN-PUBLICATION DATA
Names: Sittenfeld, Curtis, author.
Title: Show don't tell / Curtis Sittenfeld.
Other titles: Show do not tell
Description: First edition. | New York, NY: Random House, 2025.
Identifiers: LCCN 2024035569 (print) | LCCN 2024035570 (ebook) |
ISBN 9780593446737 (Hardback) | ISBN 9780593446744 (Ebook)
Subjects: LCGFT: Short stories.
Classification: LCC PS3619.I94 S56 2025 (print) | LCC PS3619.I94 (ebook) |
DDC 813/.6—dc23/eng/20240809
LC record available at https://lccn.loc.gov/2024035569
LC ebook record available at https://lccn.loc.gov/2024035570

International edition ISBN 978-0-593-97851-1

Printed in the United States of America on acid-free paper

randomhousebooks.com

2 4 6 8 9 7 5 3 1

First Edition

Book design by Elizabeth A. D. Eno

For Sarah Coyne Sittenfeld
for so many reasons

CONTENTS

SHOW
DON'T TELL

SHOW DON'T TELL

At some point, a rich old man named Ryland W. Peaslee had made an enormous donation to the program, and this was why not only the second-year fellowships he'd endowed but also the people who received them were called Peaslees. You'd say, "He's a Peaslee," or "She's a Peaslee." Each year, four were granted. There were other kinds of fellowships, but none of them provided as much money—eighty-eight hundred dollars—as the Peaslees. Plus, with all the others, you still had to teach undergrads.

Our professors and the program administrators were cagey about the exact date when we'd receive the letters specifying our second-year funding, but a rumor was going around that it would be on a Monday in mid-March, which meant that, instead of sitting at my desk, I spent the majority of a morning and an early afternoon standing at the front window of my apartment, scanning the street for the mailman. For lunch, I ate a bowl of Grape-Nuts and yogurt—Monday nights after seminar were when I drank the most, and therefore when life seemed the most charged with flirtatious possibility, so I liked to eat light on those days—then I brushed my teeth, took a shower, and got dressed. It was still only two o'clock. Seminar started at four, and my apartment was a ten-minute walk from campus. I lived on the second floor of a small, crappy Dutch Colonial, on the same street as a bunch of sororities and the co-op, where I occasionally splurged on an organic pineapple, which I'd eat in its entirety. I was weirdly adept at cutting a pineapple, and doing so made me feel like a splendid tropical queen with no one to witness my splendor. It was 1998, and I was twenty-five.

I was so worked up about the funding letter that I decided to pack my bag and wait outside for the mailman, even though the temperature wasn't much above freezing. I sat in the mint-green steel chair on the front stoop, opened the paperback novel I was in the middle of, and proceeded to read not more than a few sentences. Graduate school was the part of my life when I had the most free time and the fewest obligations, when I discussed fiction the most and read it the least. But it was hard to focus when you were, like a pupa, in the process of becoming yourself.

My downstairs neighbor, Lorraine, emerged from her apartment while I was sitting on the stoop, a lit cigarette in her hand; presumably, she'd heard my door open and close and thought that I had left. We made eye contact, and I smirked—involuntarily, if that mitigates things, which it probably doesn't. She started to speak, but I held up my palm, standing as I did so, and shook my head. Then I pulled my bag onto my shoulder and began walking toward campus.

Lorraine was in her early fifties, and she had moved to the Midwest the same week in August that I had, also to get a master's degree but in a different department; she told me she was writing a memoir. I'd moved from Philadelphia, and she'd moved from Santa Fe. She was dark-haired and wore jeans and turquoise jewelry—I had the impression that she was more of a reinvented Northeastern WASP than a real desert dweller—and was solicitous in a way that made me wary. I wanted to have torrid affairs with hot guys my age, not hang out with a fifty-two-year-old woman. In early September, after sleeping at Doug's apartment for the first time, I'd returned home around eight in the morning, hungover and delighted with myself, and she'd been sitting on the front stoop, drinking coffee, and I'd said good morning and she'd said, "How are you?" and I'd said, "Fine, how are you?" and she'd said, "I'm thinking about how the English language lacks an adequate vocabulary for grief." After briefly hesitating, I'd said, "I guess that's true. Have a nice day!" Then I'd hurried inside.

It was likely because I was distracted by Doug, and our torridness, that I hadn't paid much attention at first to Lorraine's smoking. I could smell the smoke from my apartment, and one day I even pulled out my lease, to check if it specified that smoking wasn't permitted either inside or out—it did—but then I didn't do anything about it.

In the fourth week that Doug and I were dating, his work and mine were discussed in seminar on the same day. Mine was discussed mostly favorably and his was discussed mostly unfavorably, neither of which surprised me. The night before, while naked in Doug's bed, we'd decided to give each other feedback ahead of time. As he lay on top of me, he said that he liked my story, except that he'd been confused by the beginning. I then delivered a seventeen-minute monologue about all the ways he could improve his, at the conclusion of which he stood up, went into the other room, and turned on the TV, even though we hadn't had sex. I believed that a seventeen-minute critique was an act of love, and the truth is that I still do, but the difference between who I was then and who I am now is that now I never assume that anyone I encounter shares my opinion about anything.

The next night, most people went to the bar after class; it was only eight o'clock when Doug said that he had a headache and was going home. I said, "But getting criticism is why we're in the program, right?" He said, "Having a headache has nothing to do with the criticism." Three hours later, after leaving the bar, I walked to his apartment. I knocked on his door until he opened it, wearing boxers, a T-shirt, and an irked expression. He said, "I don't really feel like company tonight," and I said, "Can't I at least sleep here? We don't have to do it. I know you"—I made air quotes—"have a headache."

"You know what, Ruthie? This isn't working."

I was astonished. "Are you breaking up with me?"

"Obviously, we jumped into things too fast," he said. "So better to correct now than let the situation fester."

"I don't think 'fester' is the word you mean," I said. "Unless you see us as an infected wound."

He glared. "Don't workshop me."

It's not that I wasn't deeply upset; it was just that being deeply upset didn't preclude my remarking on his syntax. I walked to my own apartment, and I spent a lot of the next week crying, while intermittently seeing Doug from a few feet away in class and at lectures and bars.

Also during that week, I knocked on Lorraine's door and told her that I could smell her cigarette smoke in my apartment and was respectfully requesting that she smoke elsewhere. She was apologetic, and later that day she left a card and a single sunflower outside my front door—when I saw the sunflower, I was thrilled, because I thought it was from Doug—and, judging from the smell, she continued to smoke enthusiastically. I left a note for her saying that I appreciated the flower but would be contacting our landlord if she didn't stop. On Saturday, I returned home at one in the morning to find her sitting outside in the mint-green chair, enjoying a cigarette; I suspect that she'd thought I was asleep. She giggled and said, "This is awkward," and I ignored her and went inside. The next day, I emailed our landlord. After that, I'm pretty sure that Lorraine neither smoked as much on the property nor completely stopped, and I continued to ignore her. That is, I said no actual words to her, though, if she said hello, I nodded my head in acknowledgment.

Another month passed, and one afternoon a commercial airplane crashed in North Carolina, killing all forty-seven passengers and crew members. The next day, Lorraine was sitting in the mint-green chair reading the newspaper when I left the apartment, and she said, "Have you heard about the plane crash?" and I said, "Yes," and kept walking, and I had made it about ten feet when she said, "You're a fucking bitch." I was so surprised that I turned around and started laughing. Then I turned around again and walked away.

Once more, a single sunflower appeared outside my door, along with another note: *That outburst is not who I am. I admire you a lot.* I had already repeated to my classmates the story of my middle-aged turquoise-jewelry-wearing neighbor telling me I was a fucking bitch, and the note left me queasy and disappointed. In the next five months, right up to the afternoon that I was waiting for my funding letter, I interacted with Lorraine as little as possible.

It was, obviously, a reflection of how agitated the funding had made me that I'd sat on the stoop. As I walked to town, I began composing in my head a new email to my landlord. I would, I decided, use the word "carcinogenic."

Because there were still ninety minutes before seminar, I stopped at the bookstore. I ran into a classmate named Harold, who had recently said in seminar that everything I wrote gave off the vibe of ten-year-old girls at a slumber party. In the store, Harold told me that the funding letters weren't arriving today. His mail had already been delivered, and so had that of a guy named Cyrus, who lived next door; neither of them had received letters, and the newest intelligence was that the letters would be sent on Wednesday and probably arrive Thursday. Then Harold held up a paperback of *Mao II* and said, "If DeLillo isn't the ombudsman of American letters right now, I'm at a loss as to who is."

"I've actually never read him," I said. Harold's expression turned disapproving, and I added, "Lend me that when you're finished and I will."

"It's not mine," Harold said. "I just come in here and read twenty pages at a time. But seriously, Ruthie—not even *White Noise*?"

* * *

ON FRIDAY, A GUY in his forties who wasn't famous to the general population but had a cult following among my classmates and me—a distinction I didn't then understand—was coming to speak, and some second-years who lived in a house across the river were hosting the after-party. The funding letters still hadn't arrived, or at least this was what I thought when I met my friend Dorothy for dinner at five-thirty at a Thai restaurant; we were eating early so that we could get good seats at the event, which would take place in a campus auditorium. But, when I sat down, Dorothy said, "I got a Franklin. Did you get a Peaslee? I'll set aside my jealousy and be happy for you if you did."

In fact, I hadn't received any mail at all, after another exhausting day of stalking the mailman. When I told Dorothy this, I added, "Or do you think Lorraine stole my letter?"

"Yeah, probably," Dorothy said.

"No, really," I said.

"No," Dorothy said. "I bet it's there right now. Should we skip dinner and go see?"

Even though I'd left my apartment fifteen minutes before, I considered it. Then I said, "I've wasted this entire week waiting, and I'm sure I didn't get a Peaslee, anyway. But if I don't check I can pretend I got one until after the party tonight. Like Schrödinger's cat."

"Ha," Dorothy said, then her features twisted, her eyes filled, and she said, "I don't mind teaching Comp next year, but the past few weeks have just been such a mindfuck. It's like a referendum on our destinies." I adored Dorothy, and her eyes filled with tears in my presence several times a day, and probably several times out of it, too. A lot of the people in our program were nakedly emotional in a way that, in childhood, I had so successfully trained myself not to be that I almost really wasn't. Before entering grad school, I had never felt normal, but here I was competent and well-adjusted to a boring degree. I always showed up for class. I met deadlines. I made eye contact. Of course I was chronically sad, and of course various phobias lay dormant inside me, but none of that was currently dictating my behavior. I also didn't possess a certain kind of feral charisma or mystery, and I didn't know, though I wondered a lot, if charisma correlated with talent. That's why Dorothy was right, that funding did feel like a referendum.

In the auditorium, Dorothy and I found seats toward the front, next to Jay and Bhadveer, whom we referred to, unbeknownst to them, as our fake boyfriends. Jay was tall and plump, and Bhadveer was medium height and skinny, and the four of us were all single and hung out often. In lieu of a greeting, Jay said, "I'm not going to ask what funding you guys got, and I don't want you to ask me, and, if it's something you feel compelled to discuss, go sit somewhere else." Dorothy had entered the row before me and she glanced back and raised her eyebrows, and I mouthed *Rhetoric?* and she nodded. This was the worst funding, besides none, which a handful of students did in fact receive. Or maybe Rhetoric was even worse than nothing, because, if you got nothing, you could find another job, but with Rhetoric you had to teach five days a week for sixty-four hundred dollars a year. Aloud, Dorothy and I said "Sure," and "No, that's cool."

The auditorium filled, which meant that about five hundred people turned out to hear the man with the cult following, who was a graduate of the program. He was wearing an untucked shirt, baggy jeans, and beat-up hiking boots, and halfway through his reading, when he stumbled over a line he had written a decade earlier, he said, "Fuck, man, I need a drink," and about seven minutes after that a guy from my program passed a six-pack of beer up onto the stage, and the man yanked off a can, popped it open, and guzzled. He said, "That's the stuff," and the audience applauded enthusiastically. I found the man brilliant and wrote down three of his insights, but the beer bit made me uncomfortable in ways it would take between two days and twelve years to pinpoint.

After the talk, in the building's crowded lobby, I was standing with Jay when I spotted Lorraine about twenty feet away. "Eek," I said. "Can I hide behind you? I see my weirdo neighbor."

"The smoker?" Jay asked.

"Yeah, it's that woman in the black leather trench coat."

"The smoker is Lorraine? She tutors with me at the Writing Center. She's kind of bonkers."

"Exactly."

"You know about her daughter, right?"

"Should I?"

"She had a teenage daughter who died of anorexia. And not even that long ago—like two years?"

"Jesus," I said. "Maybe I am a fucking bitch."

"After that, I'd smoke, too."

"I already said I feel bad." There was a pause—the lobby was still crowded and buzzing—and I said, "Obviously, that's a horrible tragedy. But aren't her daughter's death and her blowing smoke into my apartment completely separate?"

Jay shrugged. "Maybe not to her."

THERE HAD BEEN SOME question as to whether the after-party would still happen, in light of so many people mourning their second-year funding, but word circulated in the auditorium lobby that it was on. Before we walked over, Dorothy, Jay, Bhadveer, and I stopped at a convenience store.

"I'm not drinking tonight," I told Dorothy.

She was closing the glass door of a refrigerator, and she frowned and said, "Why not?"

It was the way that the man with the cult following had opened the beer onstage combined with my new knowledge of Lorraine's daughter, and I would have told Dorothy this under different circumstances—I told her everything—but it seemed like too much to get into, with Jay and Bhadveer waiting at the cash register. I said, "So I don't throw myself at Doug."

"But if you don't drink you won't throw yourself at anyone else, either."

"Let's hope," I said. Doug and I had barely spoken since the first week of October. Following our breakup, we'd communicated only through typed critiques of each other's work—our professor required the critiques to be typed—and Doug's to me were one intellectually distant paragraph under which he wrote, *Best, Doug,* which always made me think, *How can someone who came inside me sign his critiques "Best"?* My critique to him after our breakup was three single-spaced pages, and, in the sense that my comments concerned his story, they were impersonal, but in the sense that his story was autobiographical and he knew that I knew this—he'd told me about the fishing trip with his stepfather that it was based on—they were not impersonal. (*I think this would be a lot more compelling if the protagonist showed greater self-awareness and took responsibility for his role in the boat sinking.*) After that, I didn't write him any critiques. I wasn't going to knowingly give him bad advice, but I didn't want to bestow on him another act of love. Or I did want to bestow on him acts of love—all I wanted was to bestow—but it was too painful to do so when my ability to edit his work was probably the thing he liked and hated most about me. Also, he'd begun dating an undergraduate named Brianna.

It was dark out, and on the bridge across the river I ended up walking next to Bhadveer, about fifteen feet behind Dorothy and Jay. "Can you fucking believe it about Larry?" Bhadveer asked.

"Wait, is Larry a Peaslee?"

"Yeah. Remember that piece of shit he wrote about the Nazi soldier?"

"And who else is one?" I asked.

"You mean besides the guy who has two thumbs and loves blowjobs?" Bhadveer had made fists and was pointing with his thumbs at his face.

"You got one?" I said.

"If you're trying to conceal your surprise, try a little harder. Did you get one?"

"I haven't actually seen today's mail, but I doubt it."

"I bet you were in the running," he said, which seemed both chivalrous and like something he wouldn't have said if he weren't a recipient.

"Thanks for the vote of confidence."

"Well, at least one Peaslee has to be female, right?" he said. "And there aren't that many of you." This was true. Of our cohort of twenty-two, seven were girls or women or whatever we were supposed to call ourselves and one another—I myself was inconsistent on this front.

I said, "So you, Larry, and two we don't know."

PROGRAM PARTIES WERE OFTEN weird—sometimes they took place at a farmhouse that a group of students rented a few miles out of town, and sometimes attendees did acid, so it wasn't that uncommon for, say, a twenty-three-year-old poet who had grown up in San Francisco and graduated from Brown to be found wandering in his underwear in a frozen cornfield—and I could tell as soon as we arrived that this party was going to be extra weird. A second-year named Chuck was standing at the front door, holding a Pez dispenser topped by a skull, and as people entered he offered them a candy, saying, as it landed in their palms, "Memento mori." By some mixture of intuition and strategically looking around, I knew immediately that neither the man with the cult following nor Doug was there.

In the kitchen, as Dorothy waited to set her six-pack in the refrigerator, the girl-woman in front of her, whose name was Cecilia, abruptly whirled around and hissed, "Can you please get the fuck out of my space bubble?"

Dorothy and I joined a conversation in progress among five people, and it soon emerged that one of them, Jonah, was the third Peaslee. Jonah's mother had starred in a popular nighttime soap opera in the eighties, and, to a one, Jonah's stories featured autoerotic asphyxiation, which I'd been unfamiliar with and had to have explained to me by Dorothy. But Jonah's autoerotic-asphyxiation descriptions were artful, and the news that he was a Peaslee didn't offend my sense of justice.

The group of us speculated about who the fourth Peaslee was, and the consensus was Aisha, who was one of two Black people in the entire program, and who was in her late thirties and had formerly been an anesthesiologist. She rarely came to parties, which I respected. I couldn't stay away from them—what if something juicy happened and/or Doug was in the mood to reunite? It was also technically possible that the fourth Peaslee was a woman named Marcy, who was in her early thirties, married, and had a two-year-old kid who was always sick. However, it was widely understood that Marcy was a terrible writer; more than once, I'd heard the suggestion that her acceptance into the program had been a clerical error.

I was in the living room, perched side by side on a windowsill with Bhadveer, when three girl-women converged in a group hug that lasted, and I'm not exaggerating, five minutes. These were the only women in my year besides me, Dorothy, Aisha, and Marcy. There was a fair amount of space around them, so that everyone along the room's periphery bore witness to the hug, which I assumed was part of the point. In the first few seconds of the hug, I thought, *Okay, for sure none of you are Peaslees,* which gave credence to the Aisha theory—or could it be me? Was there any chance? Should I leave to go check my mail?—and as the hug approached the thirty-second mark I thought, *For God's sake, we get it, you're strong females who support one another, even when the system has screwed you,* and after a full minute I was grimacing and I hated all three of them, even though under normal circumstances I hated only one, who was very performatively virtuous and often insisted on telling you about the meaningful conversations she had had with janitors or about the healthy, nourishing whole-wheat bread she'd baked that afternoon.

Bhadveer said, "I'm trying to determine whether observing group hugs makes me more or less uncomfortable than participating in them."

"If you were participating, at least you could cop a feel," I said.

"I like the way you think, Flaherty." Bhadveer always called me by my last name. Then he said, "Are Genevieve and Tom in an open marriage?" Genevieve was a second-year poet, and Tom was her husband, who worked a normal-person job, possibly in IT.

"Not that I know of," I said. "Why?"

"Because she's totally macking on Milo tonight. Look." Now that Bhadveer pointed it out, I saw that, across the room, Genevieve and a first-year named Milo were sitting extremely close together on a couch, talking intensely.

I said, "Is her husband here?"

"By all indications, no."

I scanned the room, and beyond it the front door, which every minute or two opened to admit more people.

"Doug isn't here, either, if that's who you're really looking for," Bhadveer said.

"Have you heard that everyone thinks the fourth Peaslee is Aisha?"

Bhadveer made a scoffing noise.

"Why not?" I said.

"Other than because her work sucks?"

I was genuinely surprised. "Aisha's work doesn't suck. Anyway, Larry's work sucks, and they gave him a Peaslee."

"I'm not saying she's dumb," Bhadveer said. "She got through medical school. She's just not a good writer."

I furrowed my brow. "Is the subtext of this conversation racial?"

"It wasn't, but it can be if you want. Enlighten me, oh suburban white girl." He took a sip of beer and added, "Aisha is gorgeous, right?"

I nodded.

"Great literature has never been produced by a beautiful woman."

I stared at him for a few seconds. "That's ridiculous."

"Name a book. I'll wait."

"Virginia Woolf was a babe." Of the many foolish things I said in graduate school, this is the one that haunts me the most. But I didn't regret it immediately.

Bhadveer shook his head. "You're thinking of that one picture taken when she was, like, nineteen. And it's kind of sideways, right? To obscure her long face. Why the long face, Virginia?"

I named a writer who had finished our program two years before we arrived, who was rumored to have received a half-million-dollar advance for her first novel. "Have you seen her in real life?" Bhadveer asked, and I admitted I hadn't. He said, "She does the best with what she has, but she's not beautiful." Then he added, "Don't take this the wrong way, but there tends to be an inverse relationship between how hot a woman is and how good a writer. Exhibit A is George Eliot."

"That's literally the dumbest idea I've ever heard," I said.

"It's because you need to be hungry to be a great writer, and beautiful women aren't hungry. Go ahead and contradict me."

"Joan Didion," I said. "Alice Munro. Louise Erdrich." But providing counterexamples felt distasteful rather than satisfying. I stood. "I could pretend that I'm going to refill my cup, but really I just want to get away from you."

As I walked out of the living room, the group hug finally broke apart.

THE MAN WITH THE cult following had arrived and was surrounded by a crowd in the dining room. I stood near a platter of program-sponsored cheese. I could get no closer to him than eight feet, not that I would have tried to speak to him directly, anyway.

"It's tin lunch pails at Yaddo," he was saying. "The picnic baskets are at MacDowell."

Someone nudged me. "I heard he likes getting blown by young women," Bhadveer murmured. "Maybe you should volunteer."

"Why would I do that?" I murmured back.

"Because then he'll help you get published."

"First of all," I said, still murmuring, "I would never give a blowjob to a man in his forties. Well, not until I'm in my forties. Or at least my late thirties. Second of all, you seem really obsessed with blowjobs tonight."

"Flaherty, I'm always obsessed with blowjobs."

I rolled my eyes. "You should thank me for setting you up for that."

Bhadveer tapped his beer bottle against my plastic cup of water. "Thank you."

Was I imagining it, or had the question just arisen of whether I'd ever give a blowjob to Bhadveer? Was he semi-ineptly flirting or simply sharing his sincere thoughts?

I said, "Are you already hammered?"

"Yes," he said, but it was hard to know which narrative this information supported.

We were quiet, and I began listening again to the man with the cult following, who was describing a recent dog-sled trip in Alaska he'd written about for a men's magazine.

"Wait," I murmured to Bhadveer. "Clarice Lispector."

Bhadveer looked momentarily confused, then shook his head. He said, "Clarice Lispector was nothing special."

"DOUG ISN'T COMING TONIGHT," Dorothy said. "I just heard from Harold that he's afraid you got a Peaslee, and he doesn't want you rubbing it in his face."

"Wow," I said. "How flattering and insulting."

"I was on my way to tell you it's okay for you to drink after all when I suddenly realized how to fix my story. I should shift it all to the omniscient point of view. Don't you think? Then I can include the innkeeper's backstory, and people won't be distracted wondering how the servants know all those details about him." Dorothy had been working on the same story since August. It was set in Virginia in 1870, it fluctuated between twenty and twenty-six pages long, and every sentence in it was exquisite. As a whole, however, it lacked momentum. Several times, she had revised it significantly, and it always turned out equally exquisite and equally lacking in momentum.

"Sure," I said. "I don't see why not."

"I'm going to go try."

"Now?"

Dorothy nodded.

In another life—if I were still in college—I would have protested. But here it was understood that work, in whatever fashion and on whatever schedule you managed to produce it, took precedence over everything else. This is the lesson of graduate school I am most grateful for. "Want to get breakfast tomorrow?" I said. "You can tell me how it went."

"Definitely," Dorothy said. "But call me tonight when you get your mail. No matter what time it is, call me."

"Bhadveer said he thinks Aisha is too beautiful to be a good writer," I said. "He was just expounding on how great literature has never been written by a beautiful woman."

Dorothy made a face. "Aisha's not beautiful," she said.

THERE WAS A LINE outside the first-floor bathroom, so I went upstairs and opened the door to one of the bedrooms that I knew had a bathroom. A standing light in the bedroom was on, and atop the mattress Genevieve and Milo—the married second-year poet and the first-year who wasn't her husband—were lying with their limbs entangled, making out. If I'd been drinking, I probably would have apologized and backed away. But being sober when everyone else seemed increasingly drunk was like wearing a cape that made me invisible. Surely it didn't matter if I quickly peed adjacent to Genevieve and Milo's foreplay?

Indeed, they barely looked up, and insofar as they did I'm not sure they recognized me. Genevieve and her husband soon got divorced, and eventually she and Milo married, and later they became born-again, and now they have six—six!—children. Although

I haven't seen either of them for years, I have the sense that I was present at the Big Bang of their family, except for the fact that I'm guessing their family doesn't believe in the Big Bang.

At the bottom of the staircase, I saw Bhadveer again. "Arundhati Roy?" I said. I no longer had any idea if I was joking.

His expression was dismissive. "Don't pander."

AROUND MIDNIGHT, THE PARTY started dwindling. Some people were dancing to "Brick House" in the living room and a participant in the group hug was crying in the kitchen, but a steady stream of guests were leaving. The knowledge that I wouldn't be hungover the next morning was so pleasing that at intervals I actively savored it, like a twenty-dollar bill I'd found in my pocket. Really, why did I ever drink?

I was talking to Cecilia, she of the space bubble, when one of the people who lived in the house, a woman named Jess, approached me and said, "Is it true you're sober?"

When I confirmed that I was, she asked if I'd drive the man with the cult following to his hotel. She said, "You can take my car, and I'll pick it up tomorrow."

In the living room, she introduced me to him. She said, "Ruthie will be your chauffeur."

He bowed clumsily.

Jess's car turned out to be a pale blue Honda sedan with a plastic hula-girl figurine hanging from the rearview mirror. I wondered, of course, if the man would try to elicit a blowjob. But from our first seconds alone together I could tell he wasn't going to, and I was both relieved and faintly, faintly insulted. Other than the fact that I was driving, the situation reminded me of when I was in high school and got rides home from dads after babysitting.

"Are you a first- or second-year?" the man asked as I turned onto the street that ran along the park.

"First," I said.

The man chuckled a little. "Dare I ask if you're a Peaslee?"

Because I didn't want to bore a successful writer with the details of my un-received mail, I said, "I'm not. Peaslees didn't exist when you were in the program, did they?"

"No, they did," he said. "It was only fourteen years ago that I graduated from here. And I was a Peaslee. Not to boast." The man had written six books, more than one of which had been nominated for major prizes. His work had been translated into many languages, and he was a tenured professor at a prestigious school in California. As we crossed the river, he chuckled again and said, "Fourteen years probably sounds like a long time to you, doesn't it? Someday, it won't." The car was silent—I did and didn't believe him—and he said, "Do you like the program?"

"I love it," I said. "I mean, some people are annoying. But even the annoying ones—they're usually annoying in interesting ways."

"Are you familiar with the narcissism of small differences?"

"I can probably infer what it is, but no."

"Freud stole the concept from an English anthropologist named Ernest Crawley. It explains the infighting among groups whose members have far more in common than not. I've always thought that if any two students in the program were co-workers at a big company, they'd become close friends. They'd be thrilled to find another person who cares about what they care about, who thinks about things instead of just sleepwalking. But when you're in the program there's such an abundance of kindred spirits to choose from that those same two people might be mortal enemies."

I thought of the performatively virtuous woman from the group hug and then of Bhadveer. After tonight, was Bhadveer on my shit list or were we about to start dating?

"Are you a good writer?" the man asked.

I laughed. "That's a totally subjective question."

"Do you think you're a good writer? Would you enjoy your work if someone else had written it?"

"Yes," I said. "I would."

"That's important. Hold on to it. Oh, and don't marry anyone from the program. If you do, you'll both end up cheating. Hell, if you're a writer, you'll probably cheat on whoever you marry. But you might as well decrease your odds."

Being the driver was making me feel like a kind of program ambassador, and it was in this capacity, as I stopped at the last light before the hotel, that I said, "Is there anything you need that you don't have?" I meant a toothbrush, but as soon as I said it I wondered if I'd offered him a blowjob.

He seemed sad, though, and not lecherous, when he said, "Sweetheart, there aren't enough hours in the day to tell you all the things I need and don't have."

SINCE I DIDN'T OWN a car, it felt strange to park in front of my own apartment; it was distracting enough that there were maybe three seconds when I wasn't thinking about my funding letter. But by the time I unlocked my mailbox, which hung on an exterior wall of the house, my hands were shaking.

The envelope was by itself, the only mail I'd received. It was white, with the address of the program embossed in black in the upper left corner. "Dear Ruth," the letter started. "For the 1998–99 academic year, we are pleased to offer you a Ryland W. Peaslee Fellowship in the amount of $8,800."

I screamed, and then I realized what I'd done, which was to scream at one in the morning. Also—really—I thought that now I'd probably never give Bhadveer a blowjob. Giving a blowjob to a Peaslee, it turned out, wasn't the best I could do, the closest I could get.

In the almost twenty years that have passed since that night, I have written—have had published—seven novels; all except the first two were bestsellers. As it happens, my novels are considered "women's fiction." This is an actual term used by both publishers and bookstores, and means something only slightly different from "gives off the vibe of ten-year-old girls at a slumber party." Several times a year, I travel to speak to auditoriums of five hundred people, no more than a handful of whom are men. On occasion, none are men.

While I'm sure I've sold more books, it's Bhadveer who has attained the status we all believed ourselves to be aspiring to back then—his novels are prominently reviewed, he wins prizes (not yet the Pulitzer, though no doubt it's only a matter of time), he's regularly interviewed on public radio. He's the kind of writer, I trust, about whom current students in the program have heated opinions; I'm the kind of writer their mothers read while recovering from knee surgery. To be clear, I'm mocking neither my readers nor myself here—it took a long time, but eventually I stopped seeing women as inherently ridiculous.

A few years ago, by coincidence, Bhadveer and I both gave readings on the same night in Portland, Oregon. His was at an independent bookstore, and mine was at a library, and we were staying at the same hotel. We hadn't kept in touch, but I'd asked my publicist to reach out to his publicist to see if he'd like to get a drink, which we did in the hotel bar. Bhadveer had grown into a handsome man—he was no longer skinny but seemed very fit and also trendily dressed—and I found his company almost intolerable. He name-dropped the magazine editors who courted him and the famous people who were fans of his work and the festivals he'd attended in China and Australia. (I didn't say that I, too, had been invited to the international festivals, though I hadn't gone, because my children were still young then.) He went out of his way to convey that he hadn't read my books, which is never necessary; writers can tell by a lack of specificity. I felt sad at how much I disliked him. I also felt sad that he called me not Flaherty, not even Ruthie, but just Ruth.

At the end of an hour, during which he consumed three Old-Fashioneds and I had one glass of red wine, he said, "It's funny that no one other than us is at all successful, isn't it? Besides Grant, obviously."

Both Bhadveer's career and mine are overshadowed by that of

someone who was a virtual nonentity in graduate school, a very quiet guy who went on to write screenplays for which he's twice won an Oscar. He then started directing movies as well, movies that are violent, stylized, and enormously popular; if there are any women in them, they're usually raped and often decapitated. This is all bewildering to me, because in graduate school I was under the impression that Grant admired my writing, my slumber-party fiction, more than any of my other male classmates did. Though we almost never spoke, his typed critiques were unequivocally complimentary and encouraging. It's for this reason that, despite his misogyny-flavored mega-success, I wish him well.

In the hotel bar, I said to Bhadveer, "Well, Harold has that collection, right? And Marcy has two novels."

"That have sold, what, twelve copies combined? I gave Harold a blurb out of pity, but I couldn't get through the first story."

I tried to decide whether to be nice or honest, then said, "Yeah, neither could I."

"Think about it," Bhadveer said. "Jay's not a writer. Dorothy's not a writer. Your boy Doug's not a writer. Aisha's not a writer."

"You know the experiment in the seventies with the blue-eyed and brown-eyed students?" I said. "I sometimes wonder if we're like that."

"But Jonah and Larry were Peaslees with us, and neither of them is a writer."

As I said, this was a while back. It took months to determine how I wish I'd replied, which is: Yes, you can say whether people have published books. But you don't get to say whether they're writers. Some of them are probably working on books now that they'll eventually finish and sell; some of them probably haven't written fiction for years and might never again. But the way they inhabit the world, the way they observe it—of course they're writers.

* * *

ON THAT LONG-AGO NIGHT when I opened the letter at one in the morning, perhaps thirty seconds passed between my scream and Lorraine's door opening. She hurried out in a white silk slip and matching bathrobe and said with alarm, "Ruthie, are you okay?"

I extended the letter toward her. "I got a Peaslee! I'm a Peaslee!"

Lorraine hesitated, and I was startled. Was it possible that even inside our university, across the small divide of two similar programs, the significance of the Peaslee didn't translate?

"The fellowship!" I added. "I got the best kind of fellowship for next year!"

"Oh, Ruthie, how wonderful," she said, and she stepped forward and hugged me tightly.

THE MARRIAGE CLOCK

Heather's flight out of LAX will leave at six A.M., meaning she set her alarm for four, and it's a little past midnight when Maya vomits. Heather is the one who hears her on the monitor, enters the room, and knows from the smell, before turning on the light, what has happened. Given the circumstances, Maya appears unfazed. She is three. "There was some spit-up in my mouth," she says in an earnest voice.

Heather calls for Nick and tells him to bring the thermometer, which reveals that Maya doesn't have a fever. While Nick changes the sheets, Heather gives Maya as quick a bath as possible. "Is it morning?" Maya asks as Heather fills the tub, and Heather shakes her head. Within half an hour, Maya is back in bed with the light off, and so are Heather and Nick. But where Nick seems never to have fully awakened, Heather is wired. "I wish I weren't going to Alabama," she says.

"I doubt she's sick," Nick mumbles. "It was probably just something she ate."

"But we didn't have anything out of the ordinary for dinner."

Nick had grilled sausage on the deck, and Heather had made salad and rice.

"Worst-case scenario, she *is* sick. I can handle a puking three-year-old."

"So you do think she's sick?"

"For fuck's sake," Nick says. "Can I just go to sleep?"

Heather lies awake until two-thirty; sleeps from two-thirty to three-forty; wakes before her alarm goes off; checks on Maya (she's sleeping normally and her forehead doesn't feel hot); takes a shower; dresses; returns to Maya's room; sits in the armchair in the dark; cries but only for two minutes; orders an Uber; stands and places her hand on her daughter's sternum, above the quilt; then goes downstairs. Her suitcase is already packed and waiting by the front door.

HEATHER'S TITLE AT THE studio is Senior Vice President of Film Production and Development. Once or twice a year she speaks at women's leadership conferences where she describes her career path and current responsibilities. The trip she is taking today, she thinks as she fastens her seatbelt on the plane, surely is not one she'll ever describe to the aspiring female leaders of America.

She is flying to Mobile, Alabama, by way of Houston, to meet with the author of *The Marriage Clock*, a self-help book that has, since its publication four years ago, sold twenty million copies and been translated into forty-two languages. Although the author has a divinity degree and the book exudes a Christian scent—or so Heather has heard, though she has not yet read it and is planning to do so on the plane—its popularity has transcended its churchy origins and found traction in the mainstream. Heather's studio optioned the book last year, and a well-known director and a respected screenwriter are now attached. The plan is for the film to be about three married couples who all live on the same street and in various ways embody the book's advice, which is to say that the plan is to make a relatively inexpensive, innocuous romantic comedy that cashes in on the *Marriage Clock* brand. Heather's objective, the reason for her trip, is to convince the author, whom she has never met, to permit one of the three fictional couples to be gay; thus far the author, who retains creative approval rights, has diplomatically but firmly expressed unwillingness. (His creative approval was something Heather opposed at the time of purchase, but two other studios were also making offers, and she was overridden.)

Ironically, it was through her sister, Tracy, that Heather first heard of *The Marriage Clock*. Tracy lives in Boston with her wife, Sue, and their eight-year-old twins and recommended the book during one of the long phone conversations she and Heather have on the weekends when Maya is napping and Nick is playing Ultimate Frisbee. "It's corny," Tracy said. "But the suggestions make a lot of sense, and you can read the entire thing in under an hour."

However, Heather still hadn't read it when her studio entered into negotiations to option the book. At that point, she read the book's so-called Clock Doctrine, which took up two pages. The author, whose name is Brock Lewis, borrowed the premise of the book from the Doomsday Clock created by scientists in the 1940s. But instead of Brock Lewis's clock representing how close the human race was to nuclear war, instead of the minute hand approaching or receding from midnight based on technological developments or incidents of international tension or accord, this minute hand approaches or recedes from divorce based on the behavior of the couple. If you follow the Doctrine, Brock Lewis promises, your marriage will remain intact.

After Heather learned of Brock Lewis's opposition to including a gay couple in the film, she texted her sister, *He sounds pretty gross & conservative.*

Of course he does, Tracy texted back. *Doesn't he have a megachurch in Mississippi?*

Another text from Tracy followed: *That doesn't mean he's wrong about preventing divorce.*

In fact, Brock Lewis has never led a congregation; also, he lives outside Mobile, Alabama. For the last year, Heather and her assistant have—though only to each other and only aloud, not in emails—referred to *The Marriage Clock* as *The Homophobic Clock*; they refer to Brock Lewis himself as the Homophobe.

AFTER THE PLANE TO Houston takes off, Heather realizes that she forgot her hard copy of *The Marriage Clock* at home and downloads a digital version. Tracy was correct: It takes fifty minutes to read. Heather then reads Brock Lewis's Wikipedia page, then several newspaper and magazine articles about him emailed by her assistant. Then she rereads the Clock Doctrine.

The Doctrine has been widely mocked, including in a sketch on *Saturday Night Live*. In all its cringey specificity and euphemistic prudery, its fat-shaming, fart-fearing, heteronormative reductiveness, this, verbatim, is what it says:

1. Spend at least one hour a week alone, awake, and clothed with your spouse during which your phones aren't with you.

2. Express your physical passion for your spouse a minimum of once a week. If you and your spouse experience different levels of passion, compromise. Husbands should not practice self-gratification more than once a week, and wives should not decline physical passion more than once a week.

3. Embrace your spouse every time one of you leaves or returns to your home.

4. Once a day, put into words something you appreciate about your spouse.

5. Once a month, engage with your spouse in the divine—pray in church, hike in nature, attend a concert, or otherwise honor your spiritual life.

6. Once a year, either on your anniversary or your spouse's birthday, write him or her a letter describing the reasons you love them.

7. Eye contact is like Vitamin D. At meals, especially if you have children, always make a point of sitting across from your spouse.

8. If you have young children, do not allow them to sleep in your bed.

9. If you have children of any age, continue to address your spouse by his or her first name rather than calling them "Mom" or "Dad."

10. Do not engage in any form of self-grooming in front of your spouse that you wouldn't perform in the boarding gate area of an airport.

11. Do not use the toilet in front of your spouse, and do not break wind in front of your spouse. If after using the toilet you've left residue in the bowl, wipe it away immediately.

12. Unless you have a medical condition, do not gain more than ten pounds above the weight you were on the day you married. If you are already more than ten pounds over-weight, embark on a regimen of healthy eating and exercise.

Addendum: If you have not yet had children, there are strong advantages to the man not being in the room during the delivery. At a minimum, he should stand at the woman's shoulders. Many women find that their sisters or mothers are a preferable source of support during this time.

* * *

THE MOBILE AIRPORT IS tiny, and as Heather is riding down the escalator to the baggage claim area, she catches sight of a man holding a sheet of paper with her first and last name written in black capital letters. Heather is staying for just one night and will sleep in a guest house on Brock Lewis's beachfront compound; because she isn't planning to drive anywhere on her own, her assistant arranged for a town car to meet her.

"Hi," Heather says to the man and gestures to the paper. "That's me. I just have a carry-on."

"Hi, me," the man says and sticks out his right hand. "Welcome to Mobile."

With a start, Heather realizes that the man is Brock Lewis himself. "Oh! Sorry! I didn't expect—wow, how nice of you to come get me. Heather Theisen."

"Brock Lewis."

She knows from Wikipedia that he's forty-eight—six years older than she is—but in pictures he looks more middle-aged, or maybe just cheesier, than he does in person. He is trim, wearing a light blue polo shirt, khaki pants, and Top-Siders. He's a very different physical and sartorial type from, say, Nick—Heather's husband is the bassist in a rock band and favors skinny jeans and a blond man-bun—but Brock Lewis doesn't, as Heather expected, seem to occupy a different generation. He seems like her peer.

"Aren't we at least an hour from where you live?" Heather says.

"Depends on traffic, but, yes, we'll head across the Jubilee Parkway. You ever visited Mobile Bay before?"

"As a matter of fact, it's my first time in Alabama."

"I wondered if that would be the case." His voice is warm as he adds, "And I figured if you were coming this far on a fool's errand, the least I could do was show some Southern hospitality." He says this, of course, in his Southern accent.

In spite of herself, Heather laughs. "No beating around the

bush, huh? I appreciate your candor. But I have to warn you that I can be very persuasive."

"I don't doubt it." Brock Lewis smiles. "And I can be very resolute. Nevertheless, it's flattering when a big-city businesswoman flies all the way to our little backwater."

Is the Homophobe—Mr. Marriage Clock—*flirting* with her?

"I sense that I'm being mocked," Heather says. "And that's how I can tell already that you and I are going to get along."

This is so weird—truly, it's the last thing she expected—but is she flirting back?

HE DRIVES A WHITE Porsche SUV with creamy leather seats. Though for her own icky satisfaction she wanted him to be playing church hymns or maybe some kind of Christian rock, the music that emerges from the SUV's speakers is Johnny Cash. (If she's being honest, it's also for her own icky satisfaction, in the hope of being maximally appalled, that she had her assistant accept the invitation to stay at Brock's house rather than in a hotel.)

After Brock pays a parking attendant through the window, while Heather texts her assistant to cancel the town car, they head east on the highway. It's late September, the temperature in the mid-eighties, the sky blue and cloudless. "Let's get this part out of the way," Brock says. "I personally don't have a problem with gay folks. I'm a theologian of the love-the-sinner variety. But my base, my true audience, would see including a gay couple as a betrayal of *The Marriage Clock*'s core values. And those folks are the ones who'll stay with me for the long haul, for the other books I write. To secular readers, I'm a flash in the pan."

"I have about seven rebuttals for you," Heather says. "I'm just trying to figure out in what order to deploy them." Again, this is not the tone she expected their conversation to take; she expected to be speaking not as her real self but rather to rely on a professional cajolery, a feigned patience for his point of view.

Brock chuckles. "Fire away."

"First of all, gay people aren't sinners. There's nothing for you to forgive. Do you know any gay people?"

"Of course," Brock says. "It's 2015."

"Who?"

"Just off the top of my head, there's a young lady who's the daughter of a neighbor."

"And you truly think her life is sinful?"

"I know our Creator didn't intend for women to be with other women and men to be with other men. It's damaging to families and the institution of marriage. God meant for physical passion to be an expression of His love, a means of procreation, and not just a casual thing between two people who see each other's pictures on the internet."

Wow, Heather thinks. Aloud, lightly, she says, "If God has an opinion about the internet, what do you think are His favorite websites?"

Brock is silent, and she wonders if she went too far. Then he says, "I'll bet He enjoys looking at Bleacher Report every now and again."

Heather laughs. "Since you obviously have compassion for all kinds of people, why not give your base the benefit of the doubt and assume they have the capacity to grow? Isn't a Hollywood film from a major studio an amazing opportunity to give a voice to this marginalized population?"

"What a silver tongue you have, Miss Heather."

"I'm serious. It's a chance to be on the right side of history."

"There's a story we tell in our family," Brock says. "When my younger daughter, who's now fourteen, was in preschool, my wife was trying to get her to put her shoes on one morning, and my daughter was refusing. Finally, with all the confidence of a stubborn four-year-old, my daughter said to my wife, 'Let's disagree to disagree.' And that's what you and I might have to do today."

"We might," Heather says. "But so far we're only through two of my seven arguments."

"Onward then. We do have a long drive ahead of us."

"*The Marriage Clock* has sold twenty million copies, right? On top of which we paid you handsomely for the option, and you'll get more when the film is made. At which point, obviously, your book sales will spike. The film will be like a huge international multi-month advertising campaign for the book, and neither you nor your publisher will pay a dime for it."

"That I like the sound of."

"Forgive me if this is gauche, but I can't imagine you've made less than thirty or forty million off the book so far. So let's say your assumption that your base will desert you if the film includes a gay couple is correct, and I don't think it is, but for the sake of argument—even so, haven't you earned enough money for several lifetimes?"

Is it because they're in Alabama that she's making this particular argument? If he lived in L.A., would she ever imagine that the thirst for cash, or power, or influence could be quenched by forty million dollars?

"After my book hit the bestseller lists, I'll tell you what I did. I established a charity that funds missions to all corners of the globe. Say you have a teeny-tiny church here in the States. You apply, we give you a grant, and off you go to Haiti or Ghana. If your question is do I have enough money for myself and my family, I absolutely do. But the more books I sell, the more we can spread the word of Christ."

Right—of course he's not just in it for the money.

"What kind of books are you planning to write next?"

"Detective novels."

She looks at him. "Seriously?"

He seems amused by her skepticism. "Is that so unlikely?"

"I guess I just assumed you'd write more advice books."

"Well, the detective novels will have a message of morality."

Although she is tempted to be sarcastic—to say *How enticing!*—presumably he's just as sensitive about his creative endeavors as the writers she meets with in L.A. Instead she says, "That sounds intriguing." There's a silence, then she adds, "What if the gay couple in the film are churchgoers? Then it's the best of both worlds."

He chuckles. "Miss Heather, I'm going to take you out on my boat this afternoon. Would you like that?"

"That's very hospitable. On top of you picking me up, I mean. Do you always pull out all the stops for visitors? I'm sure a fair number of TV crews and journalists come to see you."

"You know what I did before *The Marriage Clock*? I was putting in sixty-hour weeks in the health care industry, and now I'm like Santa Claus—I work about one day a year."

"Should I continue my charm offensive or will it be more effective if I let you have a break?"

"I suppose you did come all this way."

"Really and truly, this is my number-one reason. I'm being completely honest, more honest than I probably should be. We want to make a wonderful romantic comedy out of your book, a new classic. That's ambitious, but we have an A-list director, an A-list writer for the script, and we're talking to some of the very biggest actresses and actors. I never want to overpromise, but I think we can make the kind of movie that becomes part of people's lives, that they watch over and over with their families, or on Christmas, or when they're sick or just feeling low. But if there's a stipulation that no characters can be gay, it's going to be hard, if not impossible, for the studio to get entirely behind the film either emotionally or financially. First, there's always a danger of that information leaking, which would be a publicity nightmare. There could be boycotts and protests. Even if there aren't, very few people in the industry will feel comfortable with the restriction. So, consciously or not, from cinematographers to publicists, they'll have trouble throwing their hearts into this, and heart is the X factor of what distinguishes an adequate project from a magical one. We don't want this to be an apple with a worm at the core. I'm asking you to trust us to make a film that captures the spirit of your book and celebrates marriage and love and doesn't have a secret proviso of exclusion. You don't need to answer me now. But I hope you'll know I'm being sincere. I want this to be a movie that reminds me why *I'm* married, that makes *me* hopeful and grateful."

"How long have you been married?"

"Seven years."

"Kids?"

"A three-year-old daughter. Not quite to the disagree-to-disagree stage, but I bet we'll get there before long."

"I can tell you're speaking from the heart," he says. "And I want you to know I appreciate it."

"Is that a diplomatic way of saying I haven't persuaded you?"

"I promise to think about what you're saying." When he turns his head to look at her, she can't see his eyes because of his sunglasses, but she notices that on his right wrist, he wears a thin multicolored string bracelet that she'd guess is South American in provenance. "That's the best you're going to do for now."

THE COMPOUND IS TEN acres, which Brock told Heather as they pulled into a white shell driveway, and the grassy western edge slopes down to the bay with a private dock jutting into the water. The main house is a Creole cottage—"Creole cottage" is the term Brock used, though Heather would estimate it's eight thousand square feet—with a porch that runs the length of the front. On the porch are several rocking chairs, large spiky plants in porcelain containers, and overhead fans. There's a freestanding four-car garage (Brock does not pull into it) and, separated from the main house by a kidney-shaped pool set in a flagstone terrace, the guest house where Heather will sleep.

She suspects the guest house is furnished with the Lewises' cast-offs. The patchwork quilt on the bed looks handmade, and atop a coffee table is a cellophane bag, tied with a rustic brown string, of seashell-shaped soaps and a note that says in feminine-looking cursive *Welcome, friend!*

Heather and Brock are meeting on the dock at 3:45, which is only a few minutes away. She texts Nick to ask if there's been any word from Maya's preschool. When, from the Houston airport, Heather had texted, *How's she doing?* Nick texted back, *Just did dropoff, she seems totally normal.* Did he know he'd violated the preschool policy, which is to keep children home for twenty-four hours after they vomit? Instead of commenting on the violation, Heather wrote, *What u give her for breakfast?*

Waffles and applesauce, Nick had texted back. *All fine.*

Now Nick texts, *Nope no word.*

I'm in Alabama, Heather texts, and Nick's reply is the thumbs-up emoji. There was a time when he would have asked *How is it,* then there was a time when he wouldn't have asked but Heather still would have been surprised that he hadn't, and now she'd be surprised if he did. When they met, Nick was, in addition to being in a band that was quite possibly about to be signed by a major label, working for a mortgage lender, and his and Heather's incomes were roughly equal. Eight years later, he quit his job to stay home with Maya and focus on music. For a while, the arrangement made sense, but these days the band gets far fewer gigs than it did when Nick was working full-time, and Maya goes to preschool six hours a day.

Heather's phone buzzes with an incoming text, and for a second she thinks she was wrong, that Nick *is* asking how things are in Alabama. Instead, the text is from her assistant.

BROCK TAKES HEATHER'S HAND as she climbs from the dock into the motorboat, using one of the seats as a step, then he unties the rope—apparently called a *line*—from a piling and hops into the boat himself. Heather sits on a padded white bench, and Brock stands at the steering wheel. He has changed from khaki pants into khaki shorts and from Top-Siders into flip-flops, though his pale blue polo shirt is the same. Heather also has on the same shirt from before, a sleeveless green silk blouse, and the same flats, but has replaced her pants suit with jeans, which she's rolled up. Again, they both wear sunglasses.

She has decided that she should indeed temporarily lay off the persuasion in the hope of making it more effective later. Instead, after they're out on the open water, she asks him, over the sound of the motor, about himself. He tells her he grew up in Birmingham, the son of a lawyer and a homemaker, and attended Auburn University. His parents still live in Birmingham, and so does his younger sister, a caterer and mother of five. "So is she a great cook?" Heather asks.

Brock grins. "You'd think she would be, wouldn't you?" This makes Heather laugh, and Brock adds, "She's a great *person,* let's put it that way." He is quiet before adding, "We had a brother, too. Duncan. He died in college, in a car accident with some of his frat brothers, although they all survived."

"I'm so sorry," Heather says.

Brock says he was newly married at the time, working as an analyst at an investment banking firm in Atlanta, and he suspects he would have gone on to business school, but instead he went to divinity school in Dallas. Upon graduating, he was offered a job as a deacon at a church in Fort Worth and was unsure whether to accept it or return to the business sector; he decided to split the difference by taking a position with a Christian health care network. Then he and his wife hit a rough patch. They ended up separating— they didn't have children—and eventually divorcing. A few years later, he met and married his second wife, Ginny. They had two daughters, and he climbed the ladder at the health care company. By all appearances, his life was successful and fulfilling, but it was difficult for him to enjoy because, once again, he'd become estranged from his wife. Just as he and his first wife had, he and Ginny separated. Brock moved into a high-rise apartment in Dallas. One day while watching television alone, he had the realization that if they divorced, he'd likely keep repeating this pattern for the rest of his life. Or else, he thought, he could make this marriage last; what did he have to lose by trying? All of this was a decade ago.

He drew up a list of the five couples he knew who had the strongest marriages, two of whom lived in Dallas and three of whom didn't, and he drove to see each of them, holding soul-searching conversations about what had allowed them to not only stay together but also continue to respect and enjoy each other when so many other couples couldn't. He took notes, not because he was planning to write a book (Heather isn't sure she believes this part, though he himself might believe it) but because he wanted to make sure he remembered their advice. At the conclusion of his road trip, he moved back in with his family. (Listening to him, Heather wonders if this narrative would make a better film than the one about the three neighbor couples. Or perhaps if the first one does well, this could be a prequel?) Instead of bickering with his wife or snapping at his children, who were then four and seven, Brock thought about what the couples he'd visited would do in these situations. The improvement in his marriage was dramatic and swift—in fact, the shift was so notable that soon friends were seeking *his* advice on how he and Ginny made their marriage work. He wrote up the Clock Doctrine as a document for these friends, though he didn't call it the Clock Doctrine; he called it Brock Lewis's Marriage Checklist. The Doomsday Clock metaphor didn't occur to him for another five years, when he happened to see a documentary on the subject. At that point, he took three weeks' leave from his job, wrote a first draft of the book, and sold it for a thousand dollars to a Christian publisher in San Antonio. It came out only in paperback, and the original print run was five hundred copies; it's now in its 370th printing.

Everything Brock has just told her, with one exception, is part of the public record, familiar to Heather from the articles she read on the plane; the exception is that Heather didn't know about his brother. But there's another surprise, which is that most of the questions she asks him, he asks her back—before they move on to the next topic, he says, "What about you?" This is surprising both because he's famous and because he's a man.

When he asks Heather if she has siblings, she says she has a sister who's two years younger. He asks if they're close, and Heather says, "Yes, very. She lives in Boston, but we talk on the phone two or three times a week."

"Is she a working mom like you?"

"She's a nurse practitioner, and she has twins who are eight." Heather wasn't planning to tell him that Tracy is gay—she thinks it implies that her arguments about the film arise from personal bias—but, given that he told her about his brother's death, it seems weird to withhold this detail. She adds, "And my sister's wife's name is Sue."

"Ah." He says it neutrally, and for a minute neither of them says anything else. Finally he says, "Best shrimping you're likely to find anywhere is in this bay. Plus crabs, flounder, oysters—just about anything you'd want for an out-of-this-world seafood stew. See that island up ahead?" He points to land that looks to be about a quarter of a mile in diameter, with a few trees and no buildings. "I once spotted a gator sunning himself there. I'll be darned if he was less than ten feet long."

"I didn't think alligators lived in salt water."

"Ah, but, Miss Heather, sometimes God's creatures go astray."

A minute later, he cuts the motor and ties the boat to a dock piling. He jumps out, and when he extends his hand to help her, in just the way he helped her into the boat, it's the first time she wonders if they're genuinely attracted to each other. The energy between them up to now, the flirting that kicked in from their initial moments together—it wasn't personal or specific. It was a reflexive acknowledgment that they both possess good social skills, but it didn't have to do with recognizing anything particular in each other. However, isn't it awfully unlikely that the author of *The Marriage Clock* would participate in person-specific flirting?

And then, as they are walking up the almost white sand toward a grove of cypress trees and discussing a juggernaut film produced by her studio, he touches her bare left forearm with the tips of two fingers and says, "Did you put on sunscreen?"

"I didn't," she says. "But it's pretty late in the day, right? And I don't burn that easily." Oddly, as she is speaking, he has not removed his fingers from her arm.

"Being on the water, I'd recommend it," he says. "Hold that thought." He walks back toward the boat, and as she stands there, she abruptly has a feeling she hasn't felt for a long time: of lying in a bed with a man you're not yet sick of, when your clothes are partly or completely off, you've been kissing, he gets up to quickly do something or retrieve something, and you're sure that when he returns you'll have sex; it's that rare experience of waiting for an imminent good thing you know for certain will happen.

Which, given the circumstances, is a preposterous comparison, except that as Brock approaches, holding a tube of sunscreen, instead of passing it to her, he squirts some onto his fingers. When they are standing close enough to kiss, he says, "Look at me." He proceeds to spread the sunscreen on her cheeks, nose, forehead, and chin. What he's doing, what she's allowing—isn't this shocking? But, behind her sunglasses, she has closed her eyes, which helps her pretend it's not. There was when he touched her forearm some capitulation followed by a desperate flare-up of want, and his fingertips on her face are rapidly intensifying it; she feels like an animal lying on its back with its belly exposed, purring. *What* is happening?

Actually, she knows what is happening in the technical or factual sense. She once took a meeting with the co-authors of a book about proxemics, or body language and cultural norms of space; the book would have been even more of a stretch to develop than *The Marriage Clock,* and the studio didn't end up optioning it. But Brock has just entered her so-called intimate zone, which for Americans is between zero and eighteen inches. However, what he is doing symbolically, what he believes himself to be doing—she has no idea.

"That should take care of you," he says in a completely normal voice and steps back.

She opens her eyes and says, "Thanks." In a voice she can't imagine is normal but tries to make so, she adds, "I feel like I have the energy to look out for one person. You know, make sure one person has a water bottle, one person has a snack, one person has on sunscreen. It's just that since I became a mother, even when I'm traveling, that person is never me."

His expression, especially with his sunglasses, is hard to read. She hopes it's not pity. He says, "Keep in mind what they say on planes about putting on your own oxygen mask before helping others."

They revert to their earlier conversation about the juggernaut film, but now everything either of them says seems false and superficial, or at least everything she says does. She is completely self-conscious. Are they going to kiss? Have sex? If so, will it be here, on the island? In the last eleven years, she hasn't been with anyone other than Nick.

She and Brock do not kiss or have sex on the island. They discuss Heather's job and local fauna and a Civil War battle that occurred nearby, after the Civil War had already ended. She doesn't lobby him about the film. He takes her hand again when she climbs into the boat, then he drops it.

Back on the dock at his compound, he confirms that she will join him and his wife at six o'clock for dinner in their kitchen.

IN THE GUEST HOUSE, when Heather FaceTimes with Nick and Maya, Maya repeatedly kisses the screen of Nick's phone. To Nick, whom she can't see, Heather says, "Can you not let her do that?" This isn't the first time they've discussed the topic. To Maya, Heather adds, "Sweetheart, blow me a kiss." She demonstrates.

Once when Maya was a few months old, Heather was sitting at the dining room table pumping breast milk. As Nick walked by,

Heather pointed to her suctioned nipples and said, "Look—now I'm your literal cash cow."

"Fuck you," Nick replied.

She apologized—three times, in fact, the first of which was immediately—and she thinks maybe the moment she gave up on him was after he didn't accept her third apology. Is the moment he gave up on her when she made the comment, or had it happened at some earlier moment, or did it happen gradually?

Although, surprisingly, they don't not have sex. Not not-having sex happens about every ten days and only ever in the middle of the night, when one of them who's half asleep initiates it with the other who's completely asleep. They never kiss, and they never talk about any of it—about hating each other, about sleep sex, about not kissing. When Tracy tells Heather that she and Nick should try couples therapy, Heather always says, "The only thing worse than being in my marriage would be paying someone two hundred and fifty dollars an hour to discuss being in my marriage."

While FaceTiming, Maya says, "I have a question. Cats say meow."

Heather waits a few seconds before realizing this *is* the question. "Yes, they do," Heather says.

GINNY LEWIS, BROCK'S WIFE, greets Heather at the front door of the main house, which Heather walked around to although she could see the back door, off the kitchen, from the guest house. Ginny, whose Southern accent is even stronger than Brock's, is an attractive brunette wearing workout leggings, a tank top, and trendy gold jewelry of the sort L.A. actresses in their twenties favored a year ago; her arms are tan and toned. Her manner is friendly but preoccupied, and it soon emerges that after dinner, she and their older daughter, Tiff, are going to work on a Candyland-themed homecoming float at the home of another mother-daughter duo named Marcy and Madison. It also becomes clear that Ginny is not sure, professionally speaking, who Heather is. After Heather has followed Ginny to the kitchen, which is enormous, full of gleaming white marble surfaces, and contiguous to an equally enormous great room full of new-looking furniture, Ginny pours Heather a glass of rosé. "Now remind me what magazine you write for," Ginny says.

Brock enters the kitchen from a rear staircase. "She's from Hollywood, hon. She's from the studio." He holds up one hand in a wave. "Greetings, Miss Heather. I hope you brought your appetite." At the sight of him, goose bumps rise on Heather's arms, and she has so thoroughly lost her bearings that it's no longer surprising that the Homophobe is giving her goose bumps. Brock adds, "I'm comfortable promising that our meal tonight will be very tasty because it was prepared by the indefatigable Bertha. If there's a woman on the Gulf Coast who makes better baked scallops, I haven't met her."

They soon sit—just the three of them, with no sign of the Lewis daughters or of the indefatigable Bertha. Brock is at the head of an oval table, and Ginny and Heather are on either side of him. They all three join hands before Brock says grace, and Brock's hand in Heather's makes her heart hammer. The baked scallops are in a rich, creamy casserole that Heather can barely eat because she's so worked up and confused. She doesn't do much better with the salad, though she does successfully down two large glasses of rosé.

Heather asks Ginny about homecoming at the Lewis daughters' school, which leads to a discussion of local football, which leads to a discussion of Auburn football; Ginny is capable of citing various players' stats. As Ginny segues to the topic of Tiff's upcoming driver's test, Heather wonders if Brock and Ginny express their physical passion a minimum of once a week. Do they put what they appreciate about each other into words once a day, do they avoid performing any grooming rituals in front of each other that they wouldn't perform in the boarding gate area of an airport, do they wipe away residue from the toilet bowl? Though given the size and style of the house, Heather doubts they share a bathroom. They do not seem strikingly affectionate, nor does there appear to be any particular discord between them.

Ginny says she's worried Tiff isn't ready to take her driver's test on Monday, and Brock says, "She has all weekend to practice."

"Practice?" Ginny makes a skeptical expression. "Practicing for anything is anathema to that girl!" She pronounces it *anna-theema*, emphasizing the third syllable in her Southern accent. Heather takes note of Ginny's pronunciation without interest.

Brock, however, repeats the word, pronouncing it correctly. "Anathema."

"Really?" Ginny's expression of skepticism deepens. "I don't think that's right."

Mildly, Brock says, "I'm pretty sure it is."

Ginny glances across the table at Heather. "I'll bet *you* know all about words."

"She's not a journalist. Remember? She's from the studio."

There's an edge in Brock's voice and it's because of this edge that Heather can't bring herself to side with him. She says, "That's actually one of those words I've always been confused by." When she and Brock make eye contact, she can tell he knows she's lying.

"It must be an interesting lifestyle, working with famous actors." There's an edge to Ginny's voice, too, and Heather wonders if she's a person who believes Hollywood is a den of iniquity.

Heather says, "It's so kind of both of you to open your home to me."

Unconvincingly, Ginny says, "Our pleasure." She looks at her watch. "Tiff and I need to get a move on." Ginny carries her plate to the sink, then walks toward a built-in desk in the corner of the kitchen, presses a button on an intercom panel in the wall, and says, "Tiff, step lively."

Two minutes later, Tiff appears—she is similar in appearance to Ginny, down to her stylish, apparently un-sweated-in workout clothes—and Heather stands to shake Tiff's hand. Before leaving the kitchen, Ginny says to Brock, "Babe, the pie is on top of the microwave." Then both Ginny and Tiff are gone, the front door audibly closing behind them. Ginny and Brock did not, Heather notes, embrace before Ginny's departure.

The first thing that either she or Brock says in Ginny and Tiff's absence seems important; it seems tone-setting, behavior-influencing. And Heather doesn't trust herself to choose what it is. (She wonders, is Brock's younger daughter in the house?) Heather takes a sip of rosé and looks at Brock. He is looking at her. Neither of them speaks, and she smiles a small and slightly embarrassed smile. She looks away, she thinks, *I will sleep with you, I will sleep with you and never tell anyone* (she will, of course, tell her sister), then she looks back at him and it's almost unbearable. Then he says, "Got room for some cherry pie?"

Is this a rebuff or just a delay? When he sits again, he positions his chair several inches farther from the table, from *her,* than it was before. Plus, he quits joking around—his earlier jauntiness is replaced so completely with an earnest solemnity that it's as if he doesn't have a sense of humor. As they eat the pie, he tells a long story about an eleven-year-old boy at their church whose lemonade stand raised five thousand dollars for orphans in Malaysia.

"That's impressive," Heather says. "When I was eleven, I'm afraid I devoted my energy to things like buying lip gloss and having crushes."

He looks at her with distaste, and she can feel him continue to retract, making less of an effort conversationally. Even so, when they've finished their slices and she says, rather showily, "My flight's early so I guess I should turn in and give you your night back," she thinks he might contradict her. And she definitely thinks—just as a matter of chivalry, even if they don't lay a finger on each other—he'll walk her to the guest house.

Instead he says, "I'm going to clean up in here, but let me give you a flashlight. And you've got a car coming in the morning, correct? Alas, a six A.M. airport run is a bit much for a man of my advanced years."

"No, of course," Heather says as they both stand. "You couldn't have been nicer. I mean, you couldn't have unless you want to take this moment to officially give your blessing to the more inclusive version of your film."

Although she wasn't exactly making a joke, it doesn't land. Whatever openness is in his face, whatever possibility exists between them, shuts entirely. She is reaching for her plate, to clear it, and he shakes his head. "Leave it," he says almost coldly. Without acknowledging her remark about the film, he walks to the desk and, from a drawer, pulls out a large black and yellow flashlight and passes it to her. The flashlight, rather than a handshake or hug, is their farewell, she understands. And it immediately seems like a humiliating consolation prize because when she steps out the back door, the pool is aglow with underwater lights. It's a humid night, and she can simultaneously hear the gurgle of the pool and the lapping of the ocean against the shore behind her. She enters the guest house, flips on the overhead lights, uses the bathroom, then sits drunkenly on the couch in the front room. Maybe he'll still come for her? After the dishes are clean?

She glances out the window that faces the kitchen of the main house, across the pool, and, because no shades are drawn, she can see Brock's back as he stands at the sink. She walks to the door of the guest house and flips the two light switches off. Then she walks to the window, crouches on her knees, and raises her head so her eyes are just above the windowsill. Fleetingly, there forms in her brain an image of herself standing behind a podium at a women's leadership conference, wearing a navy skirt suit, dispensing advice. In the last ten years, she became convinced that was her real self.

How long does she skulk and spy? Perhaps a couple minutes. He turns, disappears from view, reappears in profile in another window, and disappears again. To continue tracking him, she must stand. She steps to the right side of the window and leans her head to the left. He has taken a seat on a sectional sofa in the great room—now only his shoulders and the back of his head are visible—and he turns on the television. Truly, if he starts watching porn, she'll go back; she'll re-enter the house and climb on top of him. But he watches a football game. She stands there for maybe four more terrible minutes.

Eventually, without ever turning on the lights, brushing her teeth, or changing into her pajamas, she lies down on the patch-work quilt. She thinks of herself in this moment as continuing to wait rather than going to bed, though just before she falls asleep, she remembers to set her phone alarm for 5 A.M.

After the alarm goes off and she has showered, dressed, and brushed her teeth extra vigorously to compensate for skipping last night, she opens the front door of the guest house. It's just getting light outside. Even though Brock told her he wouldn't be taking her to the airport, she hoped he might be in the driveway; presumably, she hoped this because of how he unexpectedly met her at the airport the day before. Instead a town car's motor is running, and a driver stands beside it in a maroon uniform, smoking a cigarette.

But then she *does* see Brock. She sees him twenty yards away, in the direction of the beach but before the sand starts, standing near a large and many-branched oak tree. He is wearing running shorts and a gray T-shirt, and he appears to be stretching, although she assumes what he's really doing is witnessing her departure.

She says to the driver, "Can you hold on for a second?"

She walks briskly toward Brock, and when she's a few feet from him, she can see that his face has that puffy morning vulnerability; maybe hers does, too, or maybe it was washed away by showering. "Sleep well?" he says in a friendly tone.

"I have to ask," she says. "What was your endgame? Were you trying to show me that even evangelical Christians can be naughty? Is this how you inoculate yourself against real adultery, with the tiniest taste of it? Or is this stuff more recreational for you?"

They are still making eye contact. He says, "I'm not sure that—"

When he doesn't finish the sentiment, she says, "You're not sure what? If you're about to say you don't know what I'm talking about, I'm about to say I don't believe you."

He is quiet for at least ten seconds. His expression has become

spooked, in a way that's just as evocative, albeit depressingly evocative, as waiting for him to retrieve the sunscreen was yesterday. At
some point, every man she dated looked at her like this; eventually,
by being herself, she spooked them all. The one person it never
happened with was Nick, which was why she married him.

"Here's the thing," she says. "You've become this magnet for
people who want marital advice, which means people who are un-
happily married. I'll bet you could sense *my* marital unhappiness.
And the fact that what you chose to do with it—on the island—"
Now she is the one who hesitates, though only briefly. "I may not
be religious," she says, "but I would never toy with someone else's
emotions for sport. Never."

"I shouldn't have touched your face," he says. "You're right. I
apologize."

"Is applying sunscreen your signature move?"

"It's not. No."

She wants to ask if he's done it before with other women, but is
asking too needy? *Fuck it,* she thinks and says, "Have you done it
before with other women?"

"If you're wondering whether we made a genuine connection,"
he says, and he seems less spooked now and more irritated, "let's
not forget the reason you came here. You're a studio shill."

She is taken aback. "Sure," she says. "But I'm a human being,
too."

They both are quiet, and he sighs. "The funny thing about being
the guy who wrote *The Marriage Clock* is that my struggles are
hiding in plain sight. I've never tried to conceal that I think marriage is a tough enterprise. I get treated like some kind of guru, like
I've got it all figured out, when really I was so confused I had to
write a book to get my head on straight." He pauses again before
saying, "No. I haven't put sunscreen on other women."

On the ride to the airport, in the back seat of the town car, at
first she thinks the reason she can't stop smiling is this concession,
its implied flattery. But crossing the Jubilee Parkway, below a light
gray sky and above dark gray water, she realizes what it really is:

When she was younger, in her twenties, she'd have confronted him drunk rather than sober. Or she'd have called him a bigot; she'd have lashed out about the subject easiest to lash out about, rather than the more embarrassing thing bothering her. That instead she admitted the truth—isn't that, in its way, a form of women's leadership?

HEATHER SLEEPS THROUGH THE first flight, reads scripts during the second flight, lands at LAX before eleven A.M., Ubers to her office, works until six, then attends a premiere. It's after ten by the time she gets home and Maya is long asleep. Leaving her suitcase by the front door, Heather climbs the stairs and walks straight to her daughter's room. The fact that Maya looks exactly as she did when Heather departed more than forty hours ago contributes to Heather's sense that everything with Brock Lewis happened not to her but to a character in a movie she saw.

When she enters the master bedroom, Nick is lying under the sheets, propped up on his two pillows, shirtless, his man-bun still in place. He's holding a book in his hands, and the book is *The Marriage Clock*. Even before she says hello, Heather laughs.

Nick says, "What?"

"You just—" She pauses. "You look like you're in an ad."

He lifts the book toward her. "I think we should do this."

Is he kidding? Still standing near the door, she folds her arms. "What page are you on?"

"I know the guy's a douchebag, but if a bunch of monkeys sitting in front of typewriters could eventually write *Hamlet,* an evangelical hatemonger can write a book about marriage that contains good advice. I'm twenty pages from the end."

She's surprised he knows Brock Lewis is a hatemonger; she doesn't think they ever discussed the reason she went to Alabama. Nick adds, "Want to try it?"

"You can't be serious."

"We have nothing to lose."

Heather hesitates—this is just so bizarre—then says, "True." She recalls the Clock Doctrine item about kissing hello or goodbye, and she thinks that if she and Nick really were in a movie, they'd kiss now. But as real people, as themselves, there's no way; the idea of kissing him is repellant. Also, he doesn't particularly seem like a person who wants to kiss *her*. She says, "When would we start?"

He shrugs. "Tomorrow?"

THE FILM DOES NOT get made before Heather accepts another job, a promotion, at a different studio. The reason it doesn't get made isn't the impasse about the gay couple but general logistics. The A-list actress who's interested isn't immediately available, so the A-list director starts shooting something else, though the studio does renew the option when it expires.

Meanwhile, she and Nick adhere to the Clock Doctrine. Not one hundred percent, but not so far off. It's like a fitness regimen, with a regimen's requirements and rewards, its incrementalness giving way to a large improvement that feels more sudden than it is. Every day, they both try. On her birthday, he writes her a letter that contains the sentences *You are an amazing mom* and *I am so proud of how hard you work and how successful you are,* both of which stun her— she'd long assumed Nick found the way she handles her job and the way she is with Maya to be her most irritating qualities. Over time, the misery she was gripped by before she went to Alabama lifts like a cloud cover. On weekends when they are with Maya—both of them holding one of her pudgy hands at, say, the farmers' market— Heather feels their good fortune, their sweetness as a family. Whereas before, she was aware of it, but she never experienced it.

One Sunday a year after she visited Mobile, Heather is talking on the phone to her sister while Nick is at the hardware store and Maya plays in the other room. Although there's less to say now that Heather is no longer actively fantasizing about leaving Nick, she and Tracy still revisit the same handful of topics so frequently that it's like they're having one lifelong macro-conversation.

Heather says, "Sometimes I think about Brock Lewis, and I think how weird it is that the method I'm using to stay married is built on a foundation of bullshit and hypocrisy."

Tracy, who knows what did and didn't transpire on Heather's trip to Mobile, says, "Really? Hypocrisy I get, but why bullshit?"

"I just feel like Brock Lewis gets credit for being optimistic in his belief that marriages are worth saving, but isn't it pessimistic to think that saving them is so hard? His premise is that marriage is at best a compromise and at worst a total grind."

"Oh, Heather." Tracy's tone is warm, not mocking. She says, "You're such a romantic."

WHITE WOMEN LOL

Kiwi the Shih Tzu gets loose on the Thursday before the schools in the district let out for winter break. This means everyone knows, in a way they might not if he got loose after break had started. Regardless, everyone knows Kiwi. He weighs maybe eight pounds, and the plentiful white fur around his face accentuates his dark eyes and dark little nose. (Do dogs have faces? Jill isn't sure.) But Kiwi is both yippy and cute, and though Jill—who is not particularly a dog lover—has never sought to pet him, he's the only dog at the elementary school drop-off whose name she knows.

Aside from his cuteness, there are probably two other reasons Kiwi is a celebrity: The first is that he belongs to the Johnson family, and Vanessa Johnson herself is something of a celebrity. She's an anchor on Channel 8 evening news, is widely agreed to be the most beautiful mother at Hardale East Elementary School, is Black, and lives in the tree-lined, large-house-filled neighborhood adjacent to the school, which allows her to bring Kiwi on a leash when she walks with her children to school in the morning; meanwhile, almost all of the school's other Black families, whose children account for under ten percent of the student body, live miles to the north, and ride the bus to campus. The second reason for Kiwi's celebrity is that, for kids, including Jill's own son and daughter, "Shih Tzu" is fun to say.

The way Kiwi escapes is that the Johnsons' house cleaner, who has been working for them on a weekly basis for years, carries a bag of garbage outside to the trash bin, leaves the back door open, and doesn't securely close the storm door. Apparently, while the house cleaner is despondent, Vanessa Johnson doesn't blame her; Kiwi is wily, and such a thing could have happened on anyone's watch. But, as Jill hears from her best friend Amy, whose other best friend is Vanessa, it isn't the first time the house cleaner has let this happen. However, in the other instances, Kiwi didn't make it out of the backyard.

It's from Amy that Jill learns about Kiwi. At 9 P.M. Thursday, Amy texts her, *Kiwi has been missing since noon!*

This is the first text Amy has sent Jill in weeks, and Jill immediately replies, *Oh no what happened?*

Amy explains the situation, and Jill expresses concern, which she does feel, though perhaps not as much as an actual dog lover would and not a concern totally separate from her own concerns about her strained friendship with Amy and her—Jill's—recently tarnished standing in the community. Jill initially thinks she's learning about a dog's imminent death rather than its escape; she thinks she's feeling a conclusive sorrow rather than the agitated hope of the unresolved. Their neighborhood is a grid of quiet, stately residential avenues bound by significantly busier streets. Additionally, in their part of the Midwest, a cold front is expected for the weekend and the temperature will likely fall to the single digits.

Jill and Amy engage in a thirteen-text volley, and the last text between them, from Jill, is *Wow I feel so bad, keep me posted*

She refrains from adding:

Does everyone at school hate me?

Is it too soon for me to come back to dropoff?

Are we still friends?

* * *

ALMOST THREE WEEKS PRIOR, Amy's husband, Rick, hosted her fortieth birthday party in the elegantly appointed back room of a trendy
downtown restaurant. There was a fireplace, a bar, and many high
round tables where guests could congregate first for drinks and
then for the buffet dinner. Instead of flowers, there were willow
branches and white lights.

About four dozen people were in attendance, the majority of
them Hardale East Elementary School parents. Jill drank two
glasses of wine and participated in several enjoyable conversations: one with Joanna Thomas and Wendy Upson about whether
Mrs. Pogue, who was all of their daughters' first grade teacher, was
pregnant; one with Sarah O'Dell about who they thought the mur-
derer would turn out to be in a series they both were watching; and
one with Scott Nowacki about the candy-cane-patterned pants he
was wearing. Scott Nowacki was Jill's go-to for harmless married
flirtation, and when she'd learned that he was also her friend Rose's
go-to for harmless married flirtation, it had enhanced rather than
diminished her own flirtation with him because then she and Rose
could jokily compare notes as well as speculate about whether
Scott and his wife, Megan, still had sex. Jill didn't speak to Vanessa
Johnson, though she did end up at the bar at the same time as Vanessa's husband, Tony; as was often the case at such gatherings,
Vanessa and Tony were the only Black people present. Jill and Tony
warmly exclaimed about how hard it was to believe that the busy
month of December had arrived already.

The birthday cake was exceptional: hazelnut-almond topped
with dark chocolate ganache and white chocolate truffles. The
party was just winding down, with a third or so of the guests having departed, when Jill emerged from the restroom and noticed a
table of five people who hadn't been there when she'd entered the
restroom. They were Black.

They were Black, and they were stylish: two women and three
men, all probably a little younger than Amy and Jill. One woman

wore a floral silk blouse with a maroon background, and the other wore a black shrug over a beige camisole. Of the men, one wore a coat and tie, one a coat without a tie, and the third an orange cravat.

They weren't Amy's friends—they weren't guests—because Jill would have known them if they were. It was impossible that Amy would have friends close enough for inclusion at her birthday party whom Jill had never met. Jill also knew they weren't Amy's guests because they weren't mingling. And did she know because they were Black? Sure, of course—also that.

She approached their table. In the time since, she has vacillated between attempting to re-create her own mindset and to permanently erase it from her memory. She thinks she was trying harder than usual—harder than she would have with a group of white people—to seem friendly and diplomatic. Though her first words to the group were not recorded, what she had said was "I realize this might not be obvious, but there's a private party going on in this room. A birthday party."

The two women and three men looked at her with varying degrees of amusement and irritation. Jill added, "You're not friends of Vanessa and Tony, are you?"

After a pause, the woman in the floral blouse said, "No. We're not friends of Vanessa and Tony."

"If you wouldn't mind taking your drinks to the main room," Jill said, and, though she was unaware of it in the moment, the recording had started, "I think that would be best."

With undisguised contempt, the man wearing the cravat said, "Oh, really? Is that what you think?"

"I'm not trying to be—" For the first time, Jill faltered. "It's my friend Amy's birthday, and her husband rented this room. That's all."

The woman in the blouse said, also contemptuously, "Do you feel unsafe? Are you going to call the cops?"

"Am I going to call the cops?" Jill was repeating these words, she is certain, in bewilderment at the escalation. But she concedes that, in the video, if one is inclined toward such an interpretation, her tone might come off as more contemplative. "This isn't—" she began, but expressing herself had, abruptly, become very challenging. She said, "This isn't political. I just think you'd all be more comfortable in the other room."

"Bless your heart," the man in the cravat said. "Bless your heart for not making this *political.*"

One of the other two men, the one not wearing a tie, said, "Your friend's party is over. The room was rented until ten o'clock." He held out his left arm, and on his wrist was a steel and white gold watch, which was, as it happened, the same watch worn by Jill's husband, Ken. The time displayed was ten-twenty.

In a mocking voice, the woman in the blouse said, "Sorry!" And, with fake cheer, the man in the cravat said, "So that's why they're letting in the Negro riffraff!"

"That's not at all what I meant," Jill said.

One of the men hadn't spoken, and one of the women hadn't, either; the woman was the one using her phone to record the encounter, as Jill subsequently deduced from the angle of the camera. The man with the watch said, "Just like you, we're trying to enjoy an evening out. Could you leave us alone?" His voice contained no note of sarcasm, and later Jill wished she had taken her cue from him.

Instead she folded her arms and sighed, and even she must admit that, in the video, the sigh is peevish, not compassionate or repentant. But the man in the cravat and the woman in the blouse were being so rude! Over a sincere misunderstanding! Jill said, "Well, I didn't realize what time it was."

The woman in the blouse laughed mirthlessly. This is where the recording ends.

BY LATE FRIDAY AFTERNOON—THE last day of school before winter break, more than twenty-four hours after Kiwi's escape—flyers blanket the neighborhood. There is one on the lamppost outside

Jill's family's house, which Jill spies from her living room window, and, though she's still mostly hiding indoors almost three weeks after Amy's birthday party, she walks out to examine it.

In big letters at the top, the flyer says LOST DOG, then there's a phone number, then there's a large color photo of Kiwi looking particularly adorable, his tongue hanging out, then in smaller print it says: *Our beloved Kiwi has been missing since 12/21. Please call if you see him!! He loves dog treats, especially Doggy Did brand turkey liver flavor and might approach if you shake a container of them. Call any time day or night!!!*

Already, Jill has received a mass email from Vanessa containing all the same information, with the additional hopeful tidbit (this is how Jill realizes that they are not exactly on a canine death watch) that Kiwi was spotted early this morning in a yard on Goodridge Lane, though he ran away when the person tried to read his tags, and the additional factual tidbit that live traps are being set up at three locations. The email, which was forwarded to Jill four other times after she received it from Vanessa (Jill takes it as a positive sign that she still makes her acquaintances' forwarding cut), ended with an appeal to repost or at least reply to Vanessa's posts about Kiwi on Facebook and Nextdoor so as to make them appear more prominently in people's feeds.

As Jill re-enters her house, she can hear the competing sounds of her children's iPads in the kitchen; her daughter, who is six, is watching YouTube videos of a tween singer, and her son, who is ten, is watching YouTube videos of other kids playing video games. She would repost Vanessa's Facebook posts, Jill thinks, if she were still on Facebook. But almost three weeks ago, she deleted her account.

IT WAS THE MAN with the cravat—it turned out his name was Ronald William Fitzsimmons IV, and he was a curator at the contemporary art museum—who posted the video on Facebook the day after Amy's party. His comment read *Committed the crime of* *drinking $16 cocktails while black last night . . . white women LOL.*

By the time Jill learned of the post, the video had been up for two hours, been viewed 937 times, and shared 201. The responses included:

Ronald so sorry you had to endure this, that woman is idiotic garbage

White privilege is a hell of a drug

Internet, do your thing, let's find out who Vodka Vicky is

There was a long comment that started, *As a white woman who has been doing a lot of soul-searching lately . . .* and the rest was so tedious that, even under the circumstances, Jill skimmed it. There was a GIF of a fair-haired white man blinking (posted by a Black man) and another GIF of a cartoon rat shaking his finger in disapproval (posted by a Black woman) and another GIF of a baby spitting out what looked like pureed peas in abject disgust (posted by a white woman).

In response to the exhortation to find out who the woman was, there was a comment from Joanna Thomas, one of the people with whom Jill had speculated about whether their daughters' teacher was pregnant. *I was at this party and I know this woman,* Joanna had written. *She is not a bad person and it's sad to me we live in such divisive times.*

Under Joanna's comment, another mother from Hardale East Elementary School, a woman Jill knew in passing, had written, *Your silence will not protect you, Joanna.* Obviously, that's Jill Gershin.

The woman had tagged Jill, which was how she found Ronald William Fitzsimmons IV's original post and also, presumably, how strangers began to denounce her directly by tagging her when they shared the video. The first message began *Lady you should of minded your own damn business* . . . The second, which was where she stopped, said in its entirety *Ha ha Vodka Vicky, did you buy that dress at Talbots?*

ON SATURDAY MORNING, JILL'S alarm goes off at six-thirty, an hour later than she sets it during the week; ever since the incident, she's preferred to get her workouts in while her neighbors are sleeping. It's still mostly dark, and a not terrible thirty-eight degrees, when she leaves the house, running west on Vista Boulevard. In her earbuds, she listens to an economics podcast; prior to the incident, she usually streamed pop mixes during runs, but is she still allowed to listen to Rihanna and Beyoncé?

Jill has been jogging for twenty minutes, and the sky is more light than dark, when, shockingly, she sees Kiwi. Kiwi! Out of nowhere! So small and white-furred, and so surprisingly fast. He's fifteen feet away? By this point, Jill is on Tyler Drive, which is a half-mile loop off Vista Boulevard. Kiwi is scampering across the sprawling front yard of a sprawling brick Colonial house. Within seconds, he's forty feet away. Jill is filled with adrenaline. What should her strategy be?

"Kiwi!" she cries just as the dog disappears around the side of the house. Jill darts over the frost-covered grass, tracking Kiwi's path onto the driveway, under a porte cochere supported by Ionic columns, and into the backyard, which features a brick terrace and no sign of Kiwi. This is crushing. Jill doesn't know who lives here. Should she knock on their door? It's just after seven. If only she'd procured a container of turkey liver treats!

She turns in a circle, scanning the backyard. The grass beyond the terrace abuts a wooded area of a dozen or so acres—Tyler Drive is the fanciest street in the neighborhood, with a stone arch marking its only entrance—and Jill assumes Kiwi is somewhere in there. She pulls her phone from the thigh pocket of her leggings and, with trembling fingers, texts Amy, *Just saw Kiwi!!! On Tyler drive. What's Vanessa number? Couldn't catch him ynfortunateky*

Amy takes seven minutes to respond. By then, Jill has started to feel weird about her presence in a stranger's backyard, so she returns to the street and, still confused about a course of action, continues jogging.

Amy's first text is a blue bubble containing Vanessa's contact information. Her second is *Great!!* Her third reads, *You know about change of plan? Kiwi runs away whenever people see him.* Her fourth text is a screenshot of a Facebook post from Vanessa. *Update on our precious pup: The animal rescue experts are telling us he's now "in flight mode" so if you see him, it's VERY likely he will run away from you. You have 2 choices, 1 is do the opposite of what I said before (smh)—Don't chase him, don't call his name, don't do anything except call me or Tony ASAP. Choice 2 is—Lay down on the ground acting like you're hurt, moan and whimper, get in fetal position, and he might come over to "help" you. This doesn't sound crazy at all, right? Thank you friends <3*

Jill stops jogging to read the post twice. She texts back, *Yikes.* Then she texts Vanessa about the sighting—*It's Jill Gershin, I saw Kiwi less than 10 min ago at 27 Tyler Drive but he ran northwest*—and Vanessa texts back, *Oh wow many thanks Jill! Tony and I are about to go looking so we will start there.* She includes the emoji that Jill thinks of as either praying hands or gratitude, though maybe it's both.

Amy does not reply.

A FEW YEARS EARLIER, in order to be more present with her family, Jill had turned off her push notifications for Facebook. Thus, it had been her friend Rose—the one with whom Jill shared the harmless crush on Scott Nowacki—who, semi-inadvertently, alerted Jill to the video. Around 3 P.M. that Sunday, the day after the birthday party, Rose texted, *Jill I think that thing on FB is so unfair to you. Hope you're hanging in there.* Immediately, uneasiness flared up in Jill, or maybe it was more that a bad feeling had been coursing through her body since the birthday party. Jill texted back, *Um . . . what thing on FB?* But she checked without waiting for Rose's reply.

She watched the video and read the comments while perched on a small antique rocking chair in an alcove of the upstairs hallway, a piece of furniture it was possible that no member of her family had ever used; she'd received Rose's text on her way to grab a basket of dirty laundry. Sitting on the rocker, Jill wondered if she might faint. This was horrifying. It was horrifying in several different ways. Did the video really show what it purported to show? Would she be fired from her job? (She was a senior project manager at the corporate headquarters of a chain of regional supermarkets.) Were her children now in danger? Did her family need to move to a different state?

She texted Amy, *Can u call me?*

When Amy didn't call within forty seconds, Jill went to find Ken, who was in the kitchen boiling water for a priming solution for the beer he brewed at home. Ken did not have a Facebook account or otherwise participate in social media and tended, as a point of pride, to feign incomprehension about its vernacular. In this instance, however, perhaps due to Jill's agitation, he did not showily request a definition of terms. "This is the kind of thing that could end up on *Good Morning America*," Jill said.

As they watched the video together, she again felt that she might faint. On second viewing, she knew she didn't come off well. But surely she didn't come off as officially racist, like those white people in Target or at delis yelling at immigrants for wearing turbans or speaking Spanish. Did she?

She said to Ken, "How bad do you think it is?"

Mildly, he said, "If you thought they were crashing Amy's party, it would have been better to ask the restaurant manager to talk to them."

"Yes, obviously," Jill snapped. "Should I time travel back to last night and do that instead?"

Ken shrugged. "Don't viral videos blow over in a day or two?"

"I'm not sure," she said. "This is my first time starring in one."

When Ken didn't respond, she added, "Are you worried about our family's safety?"

Still mildly, he said, "In what sense?"

"Forget it." She went back upstairs, texting Amy as she climbed the steps. *Are u around? Really need to talk. Kind of freaking out.*

When Amy still hadn't responded within half an hour, Jill texted, *Where are u? Is everything ok?* An hour later, she texted, *Seriously I'm getting worried.*

Amy called her just after 8 P.M., following a five-hour stretch in which Jill had not left the house. Instead of accompanying Ken and their daughter to their son's basketball game, Jill had stayed in, and rather than meeting her family for dinner afterward at the pizza place they often went to on Sundays, Jill had had the pizza delivered to their house. When Jill answered Amy's call, she said, "Thank God. Where have you been all day?"

Amy sighed. "Yeah, this really sucks."

"So you've seen it?"

"Yes," Amy said. "I've seen it."

"I mean, when people go looking for evidence of something, of course they'll find it."

"Well, it's not like they had to look that hard."

Jill was shocked. "Wait," she said. "Do you think I'm some kind of white supremacist?"

"I think the whole thing is just awkward and embarrassing." Jill assumed Amy meant embarrassing to Jill, until Amy added, "I wish you hadn't mentioned that it was *my* birthday."

For several hours, Jill had been imagining that, in her best friend capacity, Amy would say something wise and comforting and, ideally, exculpatory. To encounter the opposite from Amy was far more upsetting than from Ken.

"It also might have been nice to have a heads-up that it happened," Amy was saying.

"I had no idea they were recording it," Jill said. "I didn't know it would have an afterlife. Honestly, I thought I was doing you a favor. If one of the bathroom stalls had run out of toilet paper and

I'd seen a roll nearby, I'd have replaced it myself instead of bothering you at your own party."

"You might want to give some thought to that comparison," Amy said. "Black people and a roll of toilet paper—that's really problematic."

Jill considered pointing out that, as problematicness went, until the previous year, Amy had referred to the Black students who were bused to Hardale East Elementary School as "deseg kids," as in *desegregation*. Amy had attended Hardale East in the 1980s, and that was the term she'd grown up with; Jill, who had grown up in a different city, delicately said one day, "I think these days we call them transfer students."

On the phone, Jill said, "Have you talked to Vanessa about the video?"

"Yes," Amy said.

"And?"

"What do you want me to say? It's not a good look."

"Was she extra offended?"

"I didn't ask."

"You don't think she'll bring it up on the news, do you?"

"If you're stressing, call her." Amy sighed again. "I can't believe that all the people I didn't invite know about my party now."

THE JOHNSON FAMILY—VANESSA, TONY, and their twin seven-year-old sons—were supposed to fly to Sarasota for Christmas with Tony's extended family. They were to leave Saturday morning, December 23, but they delayed their departure; apparently, the boys are inconsolable. Tony and the twins did fly out Sunday morning—Kiwi has now been missing for three days—and Vanessa has stayed behind in the hope of catching Kiwi in time for them all to be together on Christmas day.

Jill learns this when she runs into her neighbor Eileen on Sunday afternoon at a pet products megastore, where Jill has gone to buy Doggy Did brand turkey liver treats and finds Eileen doing the same. Other dog treats are sold at her usual grocery store, Jill discovered, but not the Doggy Did turkey liver kind. Jill isn't even sure that the recommendation to shake a treats container at Kiwi stands, but she dreamed last night that she caught Kiwi, and what if the dream was a premonition? When she awakened, it seemed imperative she do *something*. Also, the predicted temperature plunge has occurred, and now it's ten degrees outside.

Jill additionally learns from Eileen that a fox was caught yesterday in one of the three live traps set for Kiwi, then the fox was freed; and that, as enticement, the traps contain hot dogs and Vanessa Johnson's pajamas.

"How's Vanessa holding up?" Jill asks.

"I heard she hasn't slept since Thursday."

"Is it because she doesn't have any pajamas to wear?" Jill says.

Does Eileen not laugh because she doesn't think it's funny or because of Jill's status as a pariah? "Because she's so worried," Eileen says.

"Right," Jill says. "Of course."

She was not fired from her job. But when she returned to work after the incident, she was summoned to a meeting with her boss, the director of human resources, and the assistant general counsel, and told that she was being suspended with pay until January 2, while an investigation determined whether she'd violated company policy by engaging in "racial misconduct." Although Jill wasn't sure she should be signing anything without a lawyer of her own, she did so, agreeing to the terms, which included no media contact—an unnecessary stipulation. The entire meeting was an out-of-body experience. The director of human resources was named Suzanne, and, for God's sake, when Suzanne had been pregnant, Jill had given her her own maternity clothes. Also, perhaps not coincidentally, Suzanne and Jill were Facebook friends.

During the two hours Jill was at work that day, three colleagues said something to her. A white man named Bruce said as they waited for an elevator, "They sure have gotten entitled, haven't they?" Jill was horrified and changed the subject. A white woman named Paula said as Jill returned to her office, as if this were a compliment, "Jill, you're famous!" Jill was horrified and fake-smiled. And another white woman named Helen stopped by Jill's office and said, "My church has started hosting a monthly dialogue between the races. I met an African American grandma named Mother Bernice at one of them, and she's not angry at all. She's not about assigning blame. She's all about love, and she's become like family to me. I want to invite you to the next dialogue."

"I'll keep that in mind," Jill said.

There were, in Jill's sixty-person division, two Black employees, one named Sheila and one named Peter. She did not work closely with either of them, and neither of them said anything to her.

After the HR meeting, she managed to make it to her car before bursting into tears, and, after a few minutes, she pulled herself together enough to call Ken.

"Suspended *with* pay?" he said. "Not without."

"Yes," Jill said. "With."

"Well, hey," he said. "You get an extra month of vacation."

AT HOME IN HER kitchen, Jill does not think Ken is paying attention as she unloads bags from the grocery store and the pet product store, but when she sets the clear cylinder of dog treats on the counter, he says in a wry tone, "Wow."

Jill says nothing.

"I hate to be the bearer of bad news," he says, "but you know that even if you're the one who catches Kiwi, it doesn't offset what happened at Amy's birthday, right?"

Jill still says nothing.

"It's interesting how Kiwi has mobilized people," Ken says. "If our neighbors paid a fraction of the attention they're giving a dog to inequities in public education, what could be achieved?"

"You know what?" Jill says. "Maybe if you joined Facebook, you could find a like-minded community who'd be interested in discussing this topic."

* * *

IN THE END, THE video seemed to have gone local-viral more than viral-viral. It did not end up on *Good Morning America,* or even on the local news—not on Channel 8 with Vanessa nor on the other stations—and strangers did not come to Jill's house.

But at dinner, on that Monday after Ronald William Fitzsimmons IV posted the video, Jill's daughter, Becca, who was in first grade, said, "Mommy, why don't you like people with brown skin?"

Jill and Becca were seated on one side of the kitchen table, and Ken and their son, Josh, who was in fourth grade, were on the other. Jill made frantic eye contact with Ken. She swallowed her bite of the meatloaf she'd had abundant time to make that day after being sent home from the office and said, "Of course I don't not like people with brown skin. People who are Jewish like us know that it's very important to speak out against all forms of prejudice."

"Then why did you yell at them?" Becca said.

"I didn't," Jill said. "There was a misunderstanding."

"Did a teacher say something to you or did a student?" Ken asked Becca.

Josh said, "Mom, why are they calling you Vodka Vicky when your name is Jill?"

That morning, instead of Jill walking with the children the two blocks to school drop-off, Ken had driven them, and in the weeks after, he continued to do so. Instead of lingering at drop-off, as was Jill's habit, he'd drive on to work without emerging from the car to chat with the other neighborhood parents—mostly mothers, some holding coffee or dog leashes, congregating outside for a few minutes before the ones with jobs went to work and the ones without jobs went to do Jill didn't really know what. This was how and where Jill had made Kiwi's acquaintance.

Ken also was now the one to get the children from aftercare. Because of Jill's job suspension, aftercare was not currently necessary, but she decided it was best for the kids to maintain their routine.

IT'S BITTERLY COLD ON Christmas morning. During her run, Jill turns from Vista Boulevard onto Tyler Drive and sees Vanessa squatting by an empty cage just behind the stone arch. This is the fourth day of Kiwi's absconsion.

So as not to startle Vanessa, Jill says her name when she's still several feet away. When Vanessa looks up, she says, "Oh. Hi, Jill." Vanessa stands.

It's only when she gets closer that Jill realizes she has never before seen Vanessa without makeup. She's seen her with TV makeup, when Vanessa attends school events directly after delivering the news, but Jill didn't realize until now that Vanessa wears subtler makeup at morning drop-off. On this morning, Vanessa still looks beautiful—she has almond-shaped eyes, smooth skin, and long loosely curled hair over which she wears a red fleece hat—but she's palpably weary and anxious. Steam emerges from both their mouths.

Jill says, "Did you decide not to go to Florida?"

"I'm headed to the airport after this," Vanessa says. "I come back tomorrow at noon."

"I can check the traps while you're away. We don't celebrate Christmas so I'm not busy."

"Dave Duncan organized a Google doc with different shifts. I think it's full, but if you tell him you're available for backup, that's great in case people forget. And Dave's the one to call if Kiwi *is* in the cage—he'll take Kiwi to his house. We're not supposed to get him out of the cage outside because if he gets loose again, we're really screwed."

"Got it," Jill says. Dave Duncan's son is on the same basketball team as Jill's son, and she considers Dave an asshole because of the way he yells from the sidelines at games. Does she need to revise this opinion?

"And I'll be back in twenty-four hours." Abruptly, Vanessa looks like she's about to cry. In a breathless voice, she says, "Jill, there's only one present I care about giving my kids this year."

"I know," Jill says. "We all want it for them." When she steps forward and hugs Vanessa, there are easily eight layers of parka, fleece, and long underwear between them. Does Vanessa mind being hugged by the person in the video? Have the events of the last week buried the video? As a choked sob escapes from Vanessa, Jill thinks for the first time about why it is that they're not close. The most obvious reason is that Vanessa is intimidatingly beautiful; also, doesn't Vanessa's friendship with Amy establish some minor rivalry between Vanessa and Jill? But does the latter explanation hold, when Jill and Amy share other friends? They're still hugging when Jill says, "Maybe in the new year, we could have a drink sometime. And hopefully celebrate Kiwi's safe return."

"I'd like that," Vanessa says as they pull apart.

"The video from Amy's birthday," Jill adds. "That's not who I really am."

Vanessa's expression changes. It changes from distraught and open to impatient and closed.

Jill says, "I mean, not that having a drink would be racial at all. It would just be like neighbors—"

Vanessa holds up one gloved hand. "Jill," she says and shakes her head. "I don't have the bandwidth now."

TWO YEARS AGO, AFTER an unarmed Black seventeen-year-old boy in their city was fatally shot by a white police officer, Jill marched downtown while carrying a sign that said, IF YOU WANT PEACE, WORK FOR JUSTICE. Around that time, she made a donation to the NAACP. Well, she thought of making a donation to the NAACP. She can't remember if she actually did. But if she didn't, it was because it slipped her mind, not because she chose not to.

She knows the things white people aren't supposed to say: *Can I touch your hair?* and *I don't see race* or, even worse, *I don't care if a person is Black, white, green, purple, or polka-dotted.* She would *never* say those things. She knows what a micro-aggression is.

But also: After her cousin Maureen's divorce from her terrible husband was finalized, Jill texted her, *Free at last, free at last, thank god almighty ur free at last.*

Also also: One weekend last summer, Jill drove her children forty minutes to a state park to swim in a river she'd always heard was nice, and when they got to the beach, there were three other families there, all Black, and Jill said to her kids, "Wait, don't get out of the car," and her son said, "Why?" and Jill said, "Just hold on, there's something I need to check." She group-texted two friends: *Have u ever been to Redbird State Park? Would u let your kids swim there?* As she waited for responses, she googled *Redbird River clean,* then *Redbird River polluted,* then *Redbird safe to swim.* It wasn't that she didn't want her children swimming with the other families, and it wasn't that she was unacquainted with the fraught history of race and swimming. It was that could this be a Flint situation, where the water was dirty but no one in charge cared because it wasn't supposed to affect white people? Her Google searches turned up various touristy descriptors: *A beloved spot for fishing and canoeing, with gorgeous views.* Then Amy texted, *Never been but heard it's awesome* and Rose texted, *Ted and I were there a LONG time ago, before we had kids.* Jill's daughter said, "Why did we drive all the way here just to sit in the car?" and finally Jill said, "Okay, you can swim."

It *had* just been the Flint question, hadn't it?

Also also also: Once on a work trip to Louisville, she rented a car at the airport. She had to wait in line for twenty minutes. She told the agent, who was a white man, that she wanted satellite radio, and the agent said it would be an extra fifteen dollars and Jill said that was a small price to pay for the pleasure of Beyoncé's company and then she and the agent told each other their favorite Beyoncé songs. (Jill's was "Crazy in Love," and the agent's was "Irreplaceable.")

In the garage, she found the car, stowed her suitcase in its trunk and her purse on the passenger seat, and pulled into the line to exit. There was another wait, of about eight minutes, during which Jill fiddled with the radio and couldn't get the satellite stations to work. When she pulled up to the booth to present her rental papers, she said to the attendant, who was a Black woman, "I asked for satellite radio, but they didn't give it to me."

With a notable lack of sympathy, the woman said, "It doesn't work in the garage."

But it also didn't work when Jill pulled out of the garage. She circled the entire airport and re-entered the rental car area. She bypassed the lanes where one was supposed to return cars, parked, and approached the booth on foot. She said to the same woman from before, "I really don't think the satellite radio is activated in my car."

"Go inside, and they'll give you a different car."

"Can't you just make it work in the car I already have?" Jill said.

"You need to go inside," the attendant said.

"I don't want to go back inside," Jill said. "I just waited in line for twenty minutes to get this car. And I specified that I wanted satellite radio."

"Then call the 1-800 number in your rental agreement."

"I don't *want* to call a 1-800 number!" Jill shouted. "I want to be helped by a real human being!"

There was a silence, and then, in a withering tone, the attendant said, "Ma'am, I am a real human being."

She and Jill looked at each other. The attendant wore a red polo shirt with the icon of the rental car company stitched into the fabric above her left breast; her hair was in cornrows, and she was probably about Jill's age.

"Yes," Jill said, "I realize that."

Another silence ensued.

"Do you?" the woman asked.

* * *

JILL CAN'T FIGURE OUT how to access Dave Duncan's Google doc without contacting Dave Duncan himself, but she checks the live cages, all three of them, twice more on Christmas Day. She drives by them once before she and her family leave for the movie theater and once after dinner. The cages are all empty. According to Jill's phone, the temperature has fallen to two degrees.

It's on the morning of the twenty-sixth, around 7 A.M., while jogging, that she sees Kiwi again. He's in a yard two doors down from the yard where she saw him before, on Tyler Drive. He's sniffing the base of a tree. This time, Jill suppresses the impulse to call out his name. She stops running when she is still twenty-five feet away. She takes a step onto the wintry lawn closest to her and stands there for a few seconds, then, slowly, she drops to her knees. The ground is so cold! (This morning, the temperature is twelve degrees; she is wearing two pairs of leggings and, on her torso, long underwear, a fleece sweatshirt, and a thick jacket.)

She considers pulling out her phone and looking at the recommendations from Vanessa that Amy texted her, but Jill is pretty sure she remembers them: *Act like you're hurt. Whimper and moan.*

She lowers her bottom against her heels then lies down on her left side, keeping her ear a few inches off the ground. If Kiwi is aware of her, he gives no sign of it. She whimpers, first briefly and quietly, experimentally, and it comes out sounding, of all things, sexual. She focuses on injecting pain into the whimper—genuine sorrow, real remorse. She grows louder. She draws her knees up, into the fetal position.

How, at Amy's birthday party, did she know they didn't belong there? How did she *know*? And would answering this question be tolerable or intolerable? What would happen next?

In the winter dawn, she continues whimpering, and at last, Kiwi glances in her direction. He seems nonchalant, possibly disdainful. She whimpers again. She waits to see if he will try to help her, or if she will have to help herself.

THE RICHEST BABYSITTER IN THE WORLD

During the interview, I realized almost immediately that the woman was pregnant—I guessed she was about halfway along—but she didn't remark on it, and of course neither did I. Over the phone, we'd discussed only her three-year-old daughter. The woman, whose name was Diane, was looking for a babysitter for the girl, whose name was Sophie, two mornings a week from 9 A.M. to noon, for ten dollars an hour. This was in late January 1997, my senior year at U-Dub—the University of Washington— and I'd seen the job advertised on an index card pinned to the bulletin board outside the career center, the information in tidy blue cursive.

We met for the interview at a café near campus, after describing ourselves over the phone. She'd said, "I'm five-four, and I have tortoiseshell glasses and light brown hair cut in a bob."

Having never previously described my appearance to a stranger, I hesitated before saying, "I'm five-nine, and I have light brown hair too, but curly. And no glasses."

When I entered the café, I looked around, and a woman with light brown hair and glasses waved. When I reached the table where she sat, she smiled. "Kit?" I nodded, and she held her hand to her chest and, in a quiet voice, said, "Diane." Still quietly, she thanked me for coming and asked if I'd like something to drink. "My treat," she added, and it was when she reached for her wallet and passed me a five-dollar bill that I noticed the hard swell of her belly beneath a loose black sweater.

I went to the counter and ordered a cappuccino, and back at the table I dropped the dollar bill and change in front of Diane more gracelessly than I'd intended. Then I sat down again.

She asked, then apologized for asking, whether I knew what I was doing after graduation (moving to Tucson with a friend, and, as soon as I was eligible for in-state tuition, applying to law school at the University of Arizona); whether I was from Seattle (no, but Olympia, so not too far); and whether I had brothers or sisters (when I said yes, seven of them, she seemed so startled that I added, as I did whenever people found this fact distractingly surprising, that they all were younger half-siblings from my parents' remarriages to other people). Only then did Diane inquire about my babysitting experience. After I described working informally for families in my mom's neighborhood starting at the age of thirteen and officially nannying the previous summer for twin infants and the summer before that for a five-year-old and an eight-year-old, she said, "You sound more than qualified to watch Sophie. I'm trying to finish up my dissertation for a doctorate in art history. I did the coursework when we lived in New York, and now I just need to write the last two chapters. Sophie goes to preschool Monday, Wednesday, and Friday, but you'd come the other mornings and, if this works with your schedule, the occasional Saturday night. Not every week, though. My husband usually works on the weekends."

Was the job mine? I hoped so. The job I already had, which was fifteen hours a week in the office of a vice provost, mostly involved transcribing letters dictated by the vice provost on mini cassette tapes. I listened to the tapes via headphones connected to a machine made for this purpose, whose main body sat on a desk with a foot pump down below that I could tap to rewind the tape sev-

eral seconds. To indicate formatting, the vice provost, whom I
never spoke with directly, would say, "Period, paragraph," and the
words *period, paragraph* often accompanied me through the other
parts of my life, as did the smell of the office, which was a combination of copy-machine ink, coffee, and the fake rose perfume of
the secretary to whom I reported, who'd worked there for more
than thirty years. The secretary was nice, and I hated transcribing,
hated the office's smell, and earned $5.80 an hour, after annual
raises on the $4.75 I'd been making when I'd started as a fresh-
man. Even if Diane hired me, I'd hold on to the administrative
job—I needed to buy half a car by June—but the babysitting position seemed tantalizingly, almost suspiciously lucrative.

Then Diane said, "Did you bring a résumé? I'd like to call your
references as soon as possible."

"Oh, I don't have that on me." I chose not to mention that I
didn't have a résumé anywhere else, either. "But I can get phone
numbers to you later today."

"Do you have a car?"

Buying the car was the reason I'd started checking the career-
center bulletin board. Together with my housemate Kevin, who
was not exactly my friend and also unfortunately not my boyfriend, I was, for two thousand dollars, going to purchase from a
third housemate a navy blue Ford Taurus with eighty thousand
miles on it. Kevin and I would drive it to Tucson, where he was
from, and share it once we got there, which seemed to me to be
thrillingly like something a married couple would do, as if we were
simply vaulting over the dating phase. To Diane I said, "I have a
bike."

Diane's brow furrowed briefly, but then she said, "I think that
should be fine. We live close to campus, in Ravenna. Would you be
free to come over tomorrow morning to meet Sophie, so we can
see if it's a good fit? It could just be for half an hour, but I'll pay
you for two hours."

A good fit? I thought. *For a three-year-old?* Several times I'd
been left to look after kids whose families I'd never met until a few

minutes prior. At the same time, it seemed obscene—in a good way—to receive twenty dollars for a half hour of work. "Sure," I said. "I can do that."

I'D WONDERED IF THEIR house would be huge, but it wasn't. It was pretty, though, the wooden exterior painted pale green, with a pitched roof and a front porch. Though it was overcast and only forty-five degrees out, Diane and Sophie were waiting on the porch when I arrived. As I climbed off my bike and walked it up the brick path to the porch steps, Sophie called to me, "Ava has two guinea pigs."

"Wow," I said. "Lucky Ava."

Making eye contact above her daughter's head, Diane said to me, "Sophie's friend from school. Sophie, this is Kit. Can you say hello?"

"They eat carrots," Sophie said.

"You know what?" I was, by this point, squatting in front of her. "*I* eat carrots. But I'm pretty sure I'm not a guinea pig."

Sophie grinned. "If you have one, you have to have another so they don't get lonely."

"Hmm," I said. "Carrots or guinea pigs?"

Sophie then shrieked—apparently with happiness—and I hoped again that I'd be hired. Inside, they gave me a tour. The rooms were all tidy, and the furniture was simple but somehow expensive-looking: a rectangular sofa with a gray linen slipcover, a coffee table of light wood that matched the wood of the bookshelves. At the rear of the house, off the kitchen, was a sun porch they'd made into a playroom, where picture books lined a small shelf, and toys were stored in canvas bins. Upstairs, of the four bedrooms, one was Diane's office and one was a guest room with a double bed; none was a nursery. When Sophie and I returned to the playroom, Diane stayed on the second floor.

Sophie turned out to be obsessed with the movie *The Little Mermaid,* and she wanted to act as Princess Ariel while I was Scuttle the seagull. Approximately fifty times in a row, we re-created the moment when Ariel brings Scuttle objects from a shipwreck.

"Scuttle," Sophie-as-Ariel said, "look what we found!"

"Oh, look at this," I replied as Scuttle, holding aloft the dinner fork she'd passed me, which had a yellow resin handle. "Wow. This is special. This is very, very unusual." Sophie had taught me my lines, and when I used only one *very,* she always flagged the omission.

"What?" Sophie-as-Ariel asked. "What is it?"

"It's a . . . *dinglehopper*! Humans use these little babies to straighten their hair out." Then I'd use the fork to brush my hair.

Each time we got to the dinglehopper part, Sophie laughed boisterously, then leaned her face in close to mine and, as herself, whispered, "It's a fork." Then she'd take the utensil from my hand and say once again, in her Ariel voice, "Scuttle, look what we found!"

We were still doing this—it was all we'd done—when Diane reappeared after about twenty minutes and said, "It sounds like you two have had a lot of fun. Sophie, would you like it if Kit comes back to play for longer?"

It had occurred to me that she was listening from the second floor, and although I didn't think of myself as a person who did well under pressure, I was optimistic.

Sophie scowled at her mother, the first sign of petulance I'd seen in her. "That's not Kit," Sophie hissed. "That's Scuttle."

I knew I was in.

IT WAS TRUE ENOUGH that I planned to apply to law school, although going to law school was not the main reason I was moving to Arizona. I was moving to Arizona because one night in December, Kevin had said, "You should move to Tucson with me."

"Really?" I'd said.

"Yeah," he'd said. "We can be roommates."

When he said this, we were lying fully clothed above the covers on the futon that was my bed, him on his back, me on my side, with about two feet of space between us. We'd just finished watching an episode of *The X-Files*—I owned VHS box sets of all the available seasons—and the credits were rolling, accompanied by that spooky music. Kevin and I had never kissed, and we'd known each other only since moving into the same run-down six-person house in August. For the first month, we hardly interacted; our rooms were at opposite ends of a long hall. If my friend Cath, who'd told me about the opening in the house, was around, she and I usually made spaghetti for dinner and ate it in the kitchen, but otherwise I ate meals in my room. If I was hungry, I bought a burrito for dinner, and if I wasn't that hungry, I ate a bowl of Corn Pops, which was also what I ate every day for breakfast. While I ate, I read copies of the UW *Daily* and *The Seattle Times* that I'd taken from the recycling bin in the vice provost's office.

Once, in early October, just after two in the morning, I'd been watching *The X-Files,* and someone knocked on my slightly open door, and then Kevin asked, "Is that the one where Mulder finds out why his sister was taken?" We proceeded to spend half an hour discussing which episodes we liked best, by which point my face was burning because of how much I enjoyed talking to him. I gathered my courage and said, "We could watch another one now?"

"Yeah, for sure," he said, then clambered knees-first onto the futon, lay on his back, and settled his head against one of my two pillows. At his approach, I'd instinctively scooted a few inches away, which I regretted within seconds. But scooting in again felt too obvious. So I stayed where I was but turned on my side, curling my body toward his as I fast-forwarded to the next episode. I proceeded to absorb none of it, which didn't really matter, because I'd already watched it several times. This pattern—the physical configuration, the viewing of the program—repeated itself several times a week from that night on. It often occurred to me that the way our bodies angled complementarily in each other's direction without touching at any point was similar to the Earth's continents. If pushed together, I thought, our contours would fit perfectly, as if, like the ancient supercontinent Pangaea, we'd previously been attached.

In those first couple of weeks, I frequently wondered if Kevin was about to become my boyfriend, until the time he brought home another girl and I passed both of them in the hall as I returned to my room after brushing my teeth. "Hey, Kit!" Kevin said in a friendly voice, and the girl, whom I'd never before laid eyes on, said in the exact same tone, "Hey, Kit!" I went into my room, closed the door, and cried so hard that I had to change my pillowcase.

Back then, I believed that incidents or moments or words people said were proof of one thing or proof of another; I believed in proof over ambiguity, even when the proof supported a disappointing outcome. When Kevin hooked up with that girl, it was proof that he didn't want to be my boyfriend, but then, when he suggested that I move to Tucson with him—he was moving back to work for his father's property management company—it was proof that the secret love between us was mutual.

He added, "Theresa is going to sell me her car for two thousand bucks, but we could split the cost and both use it. And we wouldn't have to pay rent, because we'd live in one of my dad's units. Are you thinking of becoming a lawyer? The U of A law school is really good."

The logistics of life after college baffled me. How did a person know what to do with herself? I didn't want to return to Olympia, because my parents' houses were crowded and, inside them, someone was almost always sick or crying, or two people were squabbling.

"Well, I wasn't thinking of becoming a lawyer," I said. "But it's a good idea."

IN THE THIRD WEEK of my babysitting job, it rained as I biked over, and, because my clothes got soaked, Diane lent me a T-shirt, a hooded sweatshirt, and sweatpants. The sweatshirt was gray, with maroon letters spelling out HARVARD, and when I emerged from the bathroom after changing, I asked, "Did you go to Harvard?" I had never, to my knowledge, met someone who had.

"Yes, but that's actually Bryan's sweatshirt."

"Did he go to Harvard, too?"

"He was the year ahead of me. I wanted to ask: Would you be free to babysit this Saturday? I know it's late notice." In general, Diane was both more formal and more considerate than anyone else I'd babysat for. She'd ask, rather than instruct—Would I like to take Sophie to the library today? Would it work to bake cookies with Sophie?—and when I'd pulled up in front of their house on my bike that morning, she and Sophie had been waiting outside in raincoats. "I feel terrible," Diane said. "I tried calling you, but I think you'd already left. When it next rains, we can pick you up." She also told me to help myself to whatever food I wanted when it was Sophie's snack time. Almost all their food, I'd discovered, was organic.

"I can babysit on Saturday," I said.

INSTEAD OF MY BIKING on Saturday evening, Diane picked me up. When we walked together into the kitchen through the garage, Sophie sat with a plate of macaroni and cheese, cut-up chicken, and steamed broccoli in front of her; across the table sat a short man with receding brown hair and round-lensed wire glasses. "I don't think you've met Bryan, have you?" Diane said to me.

"The famous Kit!" Bryan exclaimed, and his voice was warm. "My rival!" I must have looked uncertain, because he added, "*I* used to play the role of Scuttle, but apparently I'm not nearly as good as you." He grabbed Sophie's fork off the table, inspected it, and said, "It's a . . . *dinglehopper*." Then he laughed uproariously.

I glanced at Sophie and then Diane, who was at the sink squeezing dish soap into a pot, and neither of them seemed surprised by Bryan's ebullience.

"Seriously," Bryan said, "thanks for all your help. I've heard nothing but raves."

"Oh," I said. "Sure."

From the sink, Diane said, "Sophie goes to bed at seven-thirty, so if you head upstairs at seven, there should be plenty of time for bath and two or three books. The restaurant we're going to is called Buongusto, and I left the number on the message pad by the phone. The reservation is under our last name."

"We're going to have such a crazy Saturday night that we might even stay out until ten P.M.," Bryan said. He again laughed that laugh that seemed to dramatically exceed its cause yet came off as endearing rather than annoying. He possessed some palpable intelligence and confidence that made his friendliness feel optional, as if he was a good guy by choice rather than by requirement. Or maybe I just thought that because I knew he'd gone to Harvard.

"Kit, I drew a tornado," Sophie said as I took a seat next to her at the table.

"Awesome," I said.

"I *drew*," Bryan said.

"The lotion for after the bath is on top of Sophie's dresser," Diane said.

"Tornadoes form because warm and cold air mix together," Sophie said.

"Although luckily, they almost never happen around here," I said. "After you finish eating, I'd love for you to show me your picture." I pointed to her plate. "Your dinner looks delicious."

"I'll let you take over this uphill battle." Bryan stood. "Diane, you ready?"

They both embraced Sophie, and after they were gone, she and I did our usual activities—she had a family of clothed cotton mice figurines we often played with, then we drew pictures, then we acted out the dinglehopper scene a dozen times—plus the bath, during which she pointed between her legs and said, "It's not called a *b*agina. It's called a *v*agina."

"Yes," I said. "That's true." After I'd read her a few books and tucked her in, I sat for a while at her request on the floor in the upstairs hallway outside her room. When I was sure that she was asleep, I went to the kitchen, fixed myself a bowl of organic vanilla ice cream with organic hot-fudge sauce, ate it, cleaned up those dishes and the ones from dinner, and sat in the living room reading the magazines on a side table: *Time,* then *Scientific American,* then *Harvard Magazine.* Although I knew that Diane and Bryan's last name was Woley, I wasn't sure how old they were. I guessed thirty-one and thirty-two, but when I looked at the alumni notes for people who'd graduated in 1987 or 1988, and then in the years before and after, there was no mention of either of them. There were, however, many sentences so strange and specific that I had to reread them multiple times before even partially decoding them: "Anders McFadden writes in from Alexandria, VA, 'In March, my wife Izzie and I had the pleasure of catching up in Gstaad with Pete and Katherine "Weewee" Horstman. Fabulous skiing and plentiful libations!' "

The Woleys returned at ten on the dot, and Bryan gave me a ride home. He drove a Jeep Grand Cherokee—it was much bigger than Diane's Volvo sedan—and as I buckled my seatbelt, he asked, "You're a senior, right? What's your major?"

"Sociology."

"Meaning Engels and Durkheim and those guys?"

"Well, they're the foundation, but I take classes more on modern stuff like the legal system and health care."

"What about the legal system and health care?"

I hesitated—being asked about myself was almost disorienting, and by an adult male even more so—before saying, "My last paper was about how we define health, like 'we' meaning 'society.' "

"So why is a sociology major going to law school?" His tone remained warm, and I noted with some surprise that Diane must have told him of my plans. "Do you really want to be a lawyer, or are you one of those people who goes to law school because they have no idea what else to do with their life?" He then exploded with laughter, then quieted down, but when I said "Both," he exploded with laughter anew. When he'd settled again, he said, "Graduating from college is incredibly confusing. It's amazing to have so many options, and it's terrifying to have so many options. I double-majored in computer science and electrical engineering, and I use both and neither every day. The former I use more practically, but the latter underpins a lot of the way I see the world."

"What's your job?"

"I started an internet sales company," he said.

"Oh," I said. "Cool."

"Do you ever look at the web?"

"I have before."

"What kind of things do you look up?"

"Well, I only looked once, but do you know who Jewel is? The singer? There's a song of hers, and I wanted to know the words, but I couldn't find them."

"Yeah, totally." Bryan was nodding. "A start-up is a lot of long hours, which isn't ideal in this stage of our family's life, but you've got to strike while the iron's hot." Surely this was an allusion to Diane's pregnancy, but he didn't elaborate. My theory was that perhaps Diane had had troubled pregnancies in the past and was superstitious. "Here's a dilemma for you," Bryan said. "Has Sophie ever told you she really wants a Barbie?"

"Yes."

"Diane's adamant that we shouldn't get her one, for the reasons you'd imagine—the sexism and whatnot. But my take is, don't elevate Barbies by forbidding them. Just give her the damn doll and let her see it's not that great."

I had, in my youth, owned Hawaiian Barbie, Astronaut Barbie, and Loving You Barbie (her dress had puffy sleeves and a pattern of hearts). I said, "Well, Sophie is definitely the smartest kid I've babysat for. She told me that we couldn't have a Triceratops play with a Plateosaurus because one of them lived during the Cretaceous period and the other lived during the Triassic, but I don't even remember which was which. I think she'll be okay either way, though—if you do get her a Barbie or if you don't."

"Kit, maybe you *should* be a lawyer," Bryan said. "Because that was an impressively evasive answer." As we turned right onto Twentieth Avenue, he explosively laughed before saying, "You know what it is?"

I glanced across the front seat in confusion. "What what is?"

He said, "It's a . . . *dinglehopper*!"

THE NEXT TUESDAY, WHEN Diane appeared on the first floor in the way that meant it was almost time for me to leave, she said, "I have a question, and you can think about it and answer on Thursday. You've probably noticed that I'm—" She swept her hand in front of her torso, as if saying the actual word was embarrassing. "I'm due April twenty-second. We don't have family here, and I'm wondering if you're willing to be on call for when I go into labor, to come watch Sophie. Obviously, it could be in the middle of the night, but you wouldn't have to bike—Bryan would come get you. My labor wasn't crazily long the first time, so I don't think you'd need to be here more than twenty-four hours, and I'd pay you a flat fee of five hundred dollars for the first twenty-four hours and twenty-five an hour after."

"Yeah, I'll do that," I said.

"You really can think about it. It could mean missing class, depending on the timing."

I'd also potentially need to call in sick to my job in the vice provost's office, but I was pretty sure I'd never mentioned that job to Diane. And besides: five hundred dollars for twenty-four hours? For a large chunk of which Sophie would be asleep, for all of which I'd have unfettered access to organic popcorn and pistachios and cheddar cheese? "No, I'll do it," I said. "It's fine."

So Diane was further along than I'd thought, less than two months from her due date. I was relieved for her pregnancy to finally be acknowledged, and, in a different way, relieved at this request that made the job make sense. I even wondered if all my babysitting up to that point, including the previous Saturday night, had been an audition for the role of Sophie's caretaker during the delivery—if it had been necessary for me to go from being a stranger to being trusted via the steps of babysitting Sophie with Diane in the house, meeting Bryan, babysitting solo. As far as I could tell, Diane really was working on her dissertation (sometimes Sophie and I passed her office, where she sat with her back to the open door, a laptop computer on the desk in front of her), but I knew well that concrete tasks and ulterior motives weren't mutually exclusive. In fact, it was probably because I was a person regularly unable to say what I thought or meant or wanted that I perceived Diane as circumspect. Much later, after I myself became a mother, I perceived her less as incapable of expressing her wishes and more as both very careful and very private. I also wondered about her prescience—whether she'd cultivated care and privacy early, anticipating the eventual need for them.

ONE THURSDAY IN MID-APRIL, just before I left the Woleys' house, Diane handed me a business envelope and said, "I'm going to pay you now for when I have the baby. It's cash. Is that okay?"

Did she mean that five hundred dollars was inside the envelope? If so, it was by far the most money I'd ever had in my possession. "You can pay me after the baby comes," I said.

Diane's expression was strange—it took me a few seconds to realize that it was probably an expression of self-consciousness—as she said, "Bryan and I don't see eye to eye on how much a babysitter should be paid. I try to pay on the higher side, because what's more important than the well-being of our child? When Sophie was two, I once came back from the grocery store and her babysitter had gone to the bathroom and given her a plastic bag to play with to keep her busy, and I just thought, The fact that I even need to explain why this is unacceptable . . ." Diane trailed off. "If it comes up with Bryan, you can tell him I already paid you without specifying the amount. He's a great person, a great dad, but he's frugal."

I hadn't previously known if she realized that she was overpaying me in general and vastly overpaying me for the delivery. In the moment, however, I was most struck by her trust—by how flattering her confidence was that I wouldn't just take the cash and disappear. The five hundred dollars would push me over the thousand I needed to buy half the Ford Taurus.

The very next day, a few minutes after 11 P.M., a housemate named Jessica knocked on the door of my room to tell me that I had a phone call. When I walked to the kitchen and lifted the receiver, a female voice said, "Kit, it's Diane. Am I waking you up?"

"No, I was watching TV."

"I'm—well, I'm in labor, actually. Can Bryan come get you?" She sounded no different, no less calm, than she usually did, and I thought of the times I'd observed my own mother on the cusp of having a baby. Once, at four in the morning, when I was eight and my mother was about to have my sister Sherry, I'd awakened to her yelling up the staircase to my stepfather, "Fucking hell, Doug, my pink hairbrush, not my comb."

When I climbed into Bryan's Jeep, he said, "It begins again," then burst into laughter. While we rode back to their house, he was warm and chatty, thrumming with even more energy than usual, and as we pulled into the garage, he said, "Diane's channeling her nerves into making sure she's written down every last thing for you about how Sophie will want her morning oatmeal with twelve blueberries instead of thirteen, so our objective here is to reassure her that it's all going to be fine."

"Sure," I said.

Inside, we walked up to the second floor and into Bryan and Diane's bedroom, where Diane was zipping a small duffel bag set on an ottoman in front of a matching beige armchair. "Thanks for coming, Kit," she said. There might have been something embarrassingly intimate about being in their room with both of them, with Sophie asleep in her bed, except that the significance of the impending baby overrode everything else.

Diane said to me, "Would you mind setting the alarm clock in the guest room for six o'clock and then coming in and sitting there?" She gestured toward the armchair. "Sophie wakes up around six-thirty, and she'll run into our room and be confused if no one's here. You can give her oatmeal for breakfast, and for lunch, a PB&J and fruit, and if you're still here for dinner, there's cash in an envelope on the kitchen table to order pizza. She likes just plain ch— Oh God." Abruptly, Diane turned, pressing her forearms against the wall and her head against her forearms.

Bryan approached and rubbed her lower back. "You're doing great, sweetie."

"Oh my God," Diane whispered. (*Fucking hell, Doug, my pink hairbrush, not my comb.*)

Again, I felt like either I was seeing something I shouldn't or I was so unimportant that it didn't matter. Bryan and I made eye contact. "We're leaving now," he said. "We'll go out the back door, so come down in a few minutes and lock it again."

JUST BEFORE 10 A.M., hours earlier than I'd expected, Bryan called the house to say that Diane had given birth to a healthy, seven-pound girl whose name was Emily Jane. He was going to come home, pick up Sophie and me, drop me off, and take Sophie to meet her sister.

Sophie drew a picture of Ariel and Scuttle, above which I wrote the words *Welcome Baby Emily*. Presumably, Bryan had barely slept, but he was in high spirits, picking up Sophie and spinning her around the kitchen. "You're going to be the *best* big sister," he said. As we pulled out of the driveway, with me in the passenger seat and Sophie in the back, he said, "I know it's a cliché, but the miracle of life is pretty damn miraculous. This actual human being exists where once there was no one. And she's perfect!"

"I like the name," I said.

"Then there's the mind-bending question of what changes she'll see in her lifetime," Bryan said. "It's totally conceivable that she'll live to the age of a hundred and fifty or two hundred and travel to other planets, not as an astronaut but as a regular person."

"My great-grandma was born in 1895, and she's still alive," I said. "Sometimes I can't believe she experienced the 1800s, even if it wasn't for that long."

"Yeah, exactly," Bryan said. "Think of everything she's witnessed. At the turn of the century, cars and light bulbs barely existed, and now people have their own computers." He glanced across the front seat. "Are you still planning to move to the desert for law school? If you decide to stick around here, I'll be making a bunch of hires in the next six months."

"Well, I don't really know anything about the World Wide Web." An internet sales company sounded even more boring than the vice provost's office (*period, paragraph*), but, so as not to seem ungrateful, I added, "Thank you, though."

"Have you ever heard the expression 'Hire for talent, train for skills'?"

"Now I have."

Though I hadn't been joking, when he laughed his uproarious laugh it sounded slightly different than it always had before, as if, perhaps unprecedentedly in our interactions, it was sincere rather than generously fake. "Besides," he added, "in a company like mine, there are plenty of positions beyond programming—there's customer service, writing copy for the website, et cetera, et cetera. Are you a good writer?"

"Not really."

He laughed intensely. "At least you're honest. But seriously, you're a solid, reliable person, and, believe it or not, that's rare. There are a lot of flakes out there."

From the back seat, Sophie said, "Daddy, what's a flake?"

"In this instance, I mean someone who says they'll do something and doesn't do it. But it can also mean a little piece of something, like cereal."

I turned around and said to Sophie, "I'm glad that I'm not a little piece of cereal! Are you looking forward to seeing baby Emily's toes?"

Sophie held up both hands and rubbed her fingertips together, as we'd practiced; in my experience, the feet were a good place for toddlers to touch a new sibling without manhandling them. In an earnest voice, Sophie said, "So tiny and so precious."

This time, when Bryan laughed, so did I.

BABYSITTING FOR THE WOLEYS didn't change that much after Emily's arrival; Diane usually kept the baby in the upstairs bedroom, or occasionally ran errands with her, so it was mostly still Sophie and me hanging out, walking to the park or the library. Emily cried sometimes, of course, but she was good-natured, and Diane still seemed calm and self-contained. The main differences were that there were purple circles under Diane's eyes and more takeout containers in the refrigerator. And her parents came from Delaware to visit for a long weekend, but, though I heard about the visit from Sophie, I never met them.

One early morning around this time, Kevin and I watched the episode of *The X-Files* in which, while on a case in rural Alaska, Mulder and Scully needed to examine each other's bodies for a possible extraterrestrial-worm infection. As Kevin and I lay in our Pangaea posture—complementary, untouching—he said, "Would you rather fuck Mulder or Scully?"

Immediately, my face was aflame. I didn't look at Kevin as I said, "Mulder." That this was the correct answer seemed obvious—Mulder was male, and Scully was female—but then Kevin said, "If both of them wanted to fuck you at the same time, would you do it?"

I snuck a peek at him, but he was looking ahead at the TV.

"I don't think that's going to happen," I said.

Kevin didn't respond. I sensed that we were on a fulcrum, feared messing up, and suspected that not really answering would be the worst mistake of all. I blurted out, "I don't get why threesomes are supposed to be that great, because I think the thing about sex that would be fun would be feeling really close to another person." Immediately, I wanted to retract the words; I was humiliated by my use of conditional verbs, not to mention my sheer corniness.

"But if the other people in the threesome are both hot," Kevin said, "then wouldn't that be fun too?"

It did not occur to me until hours later, as I lay awake ruminating, that I could have asked him the same questions he was asking me.

A WEEK AND A half before my graduation in mid-June, in a copy of *The Seattle Times* that I took from the vice provost's office, I was surprised to see a tiny photo of Bryan Woley on the front page. The article, which had the headline "Pangaea to Go Public," started, "Online bookstore and internet sales upstart Pangaea will publicly offer shares of its stock as soon as August, according to founder Bryan T. Woley . . ."

Discovering that Bryan's company was called Pangaea was even more astonishing than reading about him in the newspaper; the name felt like a good omen for moving to Tucson with Kevin, an affirmation from the universe. The next day, as Diane was letting me in the front door and Sophie cheerfully lay on the living room floor with her legs in the air, I mentioned that I had seen the article. "Tell Bryan I say congratulations," I said.

Emily was still so little that Diane held her entirely with her right forearm, Emily's head in the crook of Diane's elbow. Diane smiled as she said, "Bryan told me he tried to recruit you, and I had to remind him that the internet isn't everyone's dream job. Believe it or not, when we first got out here, I was working full-time for the company too. But you know how people say packing a suitcase takes as much time as you leave for it? Working for a start-up is like that. You're never really finished, even if you're putting in eighteen-hour days."

"A company like that seems really different from getting your PhD in art history," I said.

At this, Diane smiled again. "Tell me about it," she said.

MY FATHER DROVE UP from Olympia for my graduation, and, separately, so did my mother and my twelve-year-old brother, Sean. We all skipped the massive ceremony in the stadium but attended the one for sociology majors, after which my mother took pictures of Sean and me before they left—my brother had a baseball game— and my father and I went out for 4 P.M. chicken fajitas. My father, who was generally unemotional, did not ask about my move to Arizona the following week but did say, as he paid the check, "Be careful of trucks on the highway. Some of the eighteen-wheelers don't signal when they're changing lanes." Before he headed back to Olympia, he dropped me off in front of the group house and handed me an envelope that I opened, after he'd driven away, to find five crisp $20 bills.

Inside, I ran into Kevin, his father, and his sister waiting for his mother to come out of the bathroom so they could get dinner at a seafood place. As soon as his father learned who I was, he invited me to join them, and, having nothing better to do, I accepted. When his mother emerged—she was a blonde who wore pale pink lipstick and a sleeveless black shirt that revealed freckled, fleshy arms—Kevin introduced us. His mother squinted at me. "*You're* Kit?"

ON MY LAST DAY of babysitting, as Sophie and I drew with chalk on the sidewalk in front of the house, she whispered, "We're having a tea party for you, but don't tell, because it's a surprise." She held her index finger to her lips.

Half an hour before I was to leave, Diane, carrying Emily, summoned Sophie and me to the kitchen, where we drank lemonade

and ate quartered peanut-butter-and-jelly sandwiches, sliced straw-
berries, and chocolate-chip cookies. They gave me a present
wrapped in tissue paper, which turned out to be a copy of Dr.
Seuss's *Oh, the Places You'll Go!*, along with a sealed envelope
that I didn't open. Then they walked me out to the front porch and
hugged me—Emily still in Diane's arm as Diane leaned forward,
Sophie repeatedly squeezing my waist with both her arms. I had
already told Sophie that I'd send her a picture of fossilized dinosaur footprints from Arizona. As I climbed onto my bike, I was
almost sure that Diane was blinking back tears, which made me
tear up too. "Bye, guys," I called as I rode away. "Thank you so
much for everything." That I never said goodbye to Bryan was un-
surprising, given that he wasn't home during the day.

The lesson I thought I'd gleaned from the Woleys—because I
was still then a person who believed that situations provided lessons, rather than just marking the passage of time—was that two
smart, dorky adults could join together and make a family, a sweet
life. With other families I'd babysat for, the messiness of their lives
was recognizable to me from my own upbringing, and always
vaguely off-putting. Then there was the way couples fell in love in
movies, beautiful women and handsome men who made witty
comments and kissed passionately. The Woleys were neither disor-
derly nor overtly sexy. They offered a framework for an aspira-
tional but perhaps attainable way of existing, a home of calm and
kindness and seclusion.

In the envelope from Diane were ten crisp twenty-dollar bills,
which is to say twice the amount that my father had given me.

IN TUCSON, THE APARTMENT that Kevin and I shared had two bedrooms, and we spent most of our first full day moving furniture
that had belonged to his deceased grandmother from a storage unit
into the apartment's empty rooms: an olive green couch and a re-
cliner, a wooden kitchen table and chairs. A high school friend of
Kevin's named Miguel helped us, and that evening, while the three

of us sat at the kitchen table eating pizza, Kevin informed me that there had been a misunderstanding and his parents wanted me to pay rent after all; they wanted $375 a month, which, he pointed out, was below market value for an apartment this size. I didn't know if the disclosure in front of a third party was a strategy on Kevin's part or just callousness.

The previous night, his parents had been grilling by their pool with friends when we arrived in town, and his mother had introduced me by saying, "And this is Kevin's little girlfriend." Though the term ought to have offered proof, tonally it had done the opposite, confusing me.

Kevin immediately began working for his dad, and I spent the days reading the Help Wanted section of the newspaper or else taking the bus to various malls and collecting job applications from stores and restaurants. On our first Saturday morning in the apartment, Kevin didn't change out of the T-shirt and boxer shorts he'd apparently slept in, not before he ate a bagel and butter, nor before playing video games in the living room for several hours. Though glimpses of him in the hall in Seattle in similar clothing had been titillating, there was an insulting absence of vanity in this prolonged version of his self-presentation, as if I might as well have been watching him floss or pee.

On my tenth day in Tucson, I got a job as a cashier at an overpriced grocery store that sold the kind of food the Woleys had purchased. To celebrate, I bought a six-pack of beer, and when I returned to the apartment, carrying it in a plastic bag, I opened the door to find Kevin's friend Miguel standing by Kevin's grandmother's couch wearing only socks, with Kevin on his knees in front of Miguel, Kevin's mouth wrapped around the head of Miguel's penis. Here, at last, was my proof. I thought then that it was proof of my own idiocy, of the fakeness of our Pangaea, and of Kevin's manipulative behavior, though with hindsight, the decisions we both made seem instead to be proof only of a kind of confusion common in one's early twenties.

It had already become clear that sharing a car was a logistical impossibility, and when, two weeks later, I moved into an apartment that I'd seen a listing for in the back of *Tucson Weekly*, I accepted $900 from Kevin for my half of the Ford Taurus and rode my bike to work. I stopped eating Corn Pops for dinner, learned to sauté vegetables, and didn't apply to law school. One day, while making small talk with a middle-aged customer, I learned that she was a speech pathologist for kids at various public schools around the city, and as she described her job, I felt a jolt of jealousy and also a foreknowledge that was unusual in my life. Within three months, I'd applied for a master's degree in speech-language pathology and audiology at the University of Arizona, and after working in the field for five years, I went back for my PhD. By the time I got a job as a professor at a not particularly well-known college in northern Illinois, it was 2008 and I was thirty-three. This is the job I still have; I'm tenured. I met my husband through a dating website, and the first time we had drinks, I drove forty minutes to a bar and grill in Rockford. Now I live in Rockford and drive forty minutes to teach.

My years in Arizona were also, of course, the years during which Bryan Woley became kind of famous, then famous, then extremely famous. Without trying, I would routinely come across articles about him or see him on TV. Early on, he was considered either a curiosity for his exuberant confidence that we'd all eventually do most of our shopping online, or else a harbinger of the death of mom-and-pop stores. In TV clips, he was the same as he'd been in their kitchen or the car, but onscreen, his animation and energy seemed unremarkable.

I had never met another famous person, and if Bryan's name came up in conversation, mentioning that I knew him felt like an obligation, almost a compulsion. Then, in the spring of my first year in the master's program, I was getting a beer from the refrigerator at a party, and through the swinging door that led to the dining room, I heard a graduate school classmate say, in what apparently was an imitation of my voice, "Oh, yeah, I know them *super-well*. When I was their nanny, he gave me rides *all* the time.

When they had their second baby, I slept in their bed." While I froze in horror in the kitchen, the woman laughed, though at least it didn't seem like she got much of a response from her listeners. It had never occurred to me that mentioning the Woleys was name-dropping; in my capacity as a fairly dull person, I thought I'd been sharing one of my few genuinely interesting tidbits. Also, I rarely lied or even exaggerated, so I wouldn't have claimed to have slept in their bed. But overhearing my classmate got me to stop telling people that I knew the Woleys—and anyway, as the years passed, did I know them? Had my knowing them expired because of time and Bryan's ascent? I had indeed sent a postcard of fossilized dinosaur footprints to Sophie, and both she and Diane wrote back—Sophie's note was two sentences of huge, intermittently backward letters about how she no longer needed her mother's help brushing her teeth—then I got a Christmas card from Diane that first year, a photo of Sophie and Emily in their yard. Then we lost touch. Sometimes back then, when I saw Bryan on the cover of a magazine, I was tempted to email Diane and not mention having seen Bryan on the cover of a magazine, to demonstrate that I wasn't obsessed with status, that I certainly didn't hope to squeeze more money out of them, but why *would* I have been reaching out?

The public view of Bryan went through a few iterations—he was kooky, he was predatory, he was prophetic, he was vindicated, he was villainous, he was respected—before, in 2017, he became the richest man in the world. By the time this happened, it had been years since I'd told anyone that I'd known the Woleys. The last person I ever told was my husband, and not until we'd been dating for months.

IF THE NEWS THAT Bryan and Diane were getting a divorce had broken, say, five years after I'd worked for them, I'm sure that I would have been devastated; I'd have thought that it undermined, or retroactively sullied, the sweetness of their family. But when I saw the headline on a news app on my phone one night, it had been more than twenty years since I'd been their babysitter. By 2018, Sophie was apparently a graduate of Harvard with a job at a museum in New York. (*This? What . . . oh, it's a dinglehopper.*) There were very few pictures online of Sophie or Emily, which surely was not an accident, but both Bryan and Diane looked better than they had in the late nineties. Bryan was now shaved bald and visibly muscular and, like Diane, never wore glasses in public; Diane remained girlishly slim, with longer, stylishly cut hair. She didn't look fake or like she'd had weird procedures done to her lips or skin; she just looked like an attractive, happy version of herself. Was it easier to age gracefully when you were a billionaire? I wouldn't know, but presumably so.

A reductive narrative had been imposed on their divorce, and that narrative certainly could have been accurate. But weren't there other plausible narratives too? Among couples I knew, divorces were, contrary to stereotype, usually initiated by the woman, as were various non-monogamous arrangements. And sometimes there really wasn't that much animosity; marriages just seemed to run their course, and even if you didn't end up divorced, it didn't necessarily mean that yours hadn't. Because the Woleys' split had some ostensibly seamy aspects that contrasted with Bryan's general orderliness, factions of the public—comedians, social media—delighted in mocking the situation. This mockery made me feel strangely, perhaps absurdly, protective of Bryan. I understood that people were making fun of him at the available point of entry, but his leaked texts, his apparent wishes to be close to another person and for another person to find him attractive? Those texts, those wishes, were ridiculous and hopeful and vulnerable and human. The reason to criticize Bryan Woley was that he kept a million blue-collar workers toiling under the same crappy conditions that blue-collar workers had always toiled under. He had it in him to revolutionize retail shopping and cloud computing and, for God's sake, space travel, but apparently he thought labor practices were fine the way they were.

* * *

ONE NIGHT AT DINNER in the third or fourth month of the pandemic, my ten-year-old son set down the fork he was using to eat lasagna and said, "I love Pangaea." Shortly before the meal, a multi-item delivery, ordered just the day before, had appeared on our front porch: a book about dragons for my son, toothpaste and a garden spade for me.

My husband and I exchanged a glance, and I said, "Well, actually—" After a pause, I said, "Pangaea is kind of bad," and at the same time my husband said, "Mom knows Bryan Woley. She babysat for his kids."

"If Pangaea is bad," my son said, "why do we buy stuff from there all the time?"

"Because it's convenient," my husband said.

"Because there's often a gap between the people we aspire to be and the people we are," I said.

"*Why* is it bad?" My son is a sensitive boy, red-haired and big-cheeked. Once, he asked me what veal was, and when I told him, he began to cry.

"Well," I said again. "Workers for Pangaea are expected to be as efficient as possible while they move around collecting the stuff people have ordered, and that can be hard on their bodies. One time, one of the warehouses got so hot that the workers were fainting. Or there were reports that they were so worried about not being fast enough that they peed in bottles instead of going into a bathroom."

My son looked aghast.

I said, "A lot of their employees work full-time but are still considered temporary, so they don't get health care benefits, and that means if they go to see a doctor, the appointment is very expensive. So then maybe they just don't go to the doctor at all."

"Mom, we should never buy anything from Pangaea again."

"On the other hand," I said, "when I knew him, Bryan Woley

was a nice guy. He wasn't a jerk. And he recently gave a hundred million dollars to food banks."

"Well, sure," my husband said. "Instead of paying taxes." As he shook Parmesan cheese onto his lasagna, my husband added, "Bryan Woley makes about three hundred million a day, so that donation is like you giving a hundred dollars to a homeless person."

"The funny thing," I said, "is that Bryan once offered me a job."

My husband snorted. "What, because of your coding prowess?"

"That was my reaction. But they were hiring people so quickly back then, and they needed to fill nontechnical roles, too."

My husband put his hands in front of his face. "I wish you hadn't just told me this."

"Why?"

"Because if you'd gotten shares of Pangaea stock in the late nineties, even if you'd just worked there for a few years, you'd be worth tens of millions of dollars."

After a few seconds, I said, "But if I'd taken that job, I'd probably never have met you, and Ian wouldn't exist."

It was hard to tell how much my husband was kidding as he said, "Who cares? You'd be the richest babysitter in the world. Instead, you're Pete Best."

"Who's Pete Best?"

"Exactly," my husband said. "He's the fifth Beatle."

THIS IS THE PART I haven't yet mentioned: The day that I saw the index card on the bulletin board outside the university career center, with the job description that Diane had written, I looked down the hall in both directions and then I removed the pin, pulled down the index card, put it in my pocket, and stuck the pin back in the board. Ten dollars an hour to look after one kid? Though I believed at the time that this act was the worst thing I'd ever done, I also didn't see how I could behave other than ruthlessly.

Almost twenty-five years later, I do worse things on a monthly and perhaps weekly basis. Recently, pulling out of a narrow parking spot at the grocery store, I sensed that I was too close to the car beside me, heard the brief grinding of metal on metal, and, without consciously deciding to—really, with just an instinct that I didn't have time to deal with this, whatever this was—kept driving. Last week, I looked out my living room window, saw a neighbor I'm not fond of, a woman in her sixties, walking past, noticed that she was wearing a cast on her left arm, and thought, *Good.* I then scolded myself, but again, that first reaction—it was so sincere. Both of these episodes would have been inconceivable when I was in college. And at this point, my most egregious crimes are probably those I rarely fault myself for: eating shrimp harvested by slave labor, wearing shirts made by children in other countries. As with buying products from Pangaea, I sort of know how such things reach me and sort of don't. I intend, as I suspect most people do, to be moral, but when in the day am I supposed to research ethical sourcing of coffee beans, and am I really expected to pay four times as much for them?

Are the Woleys good and bad in the same proportions that I am, but the vastness of their wealth makes the consequences of their choices more dramatic? That Bryan is cold-blooded in his business dealings seems hard to dispute—Pangaea has indeed destroyed not only countless mom-and-pop stores but also large corporations and tiny third-party sellers—and I don't know if this means that he once was decent and became cruel or that he was always cruel but not cruel to me, because of my proximity to his wife and children. His obsession with pleasing customers is well-documented, but does he not realize that surely some of his customers and his employees are the same people? Does he ever lie awake at night and think, *How the fuck did I arrive at this point?* Is it relevant that, in my bed in Rockford, Illinois, I often lie awake at night and think, *How the fuck did I arrive at this point?*

In the divorce settlement, Diane received forty billion dollars, which she has been giving away with notable efficiency. I doubt that either Bryan or Sophie remembers me at all, but from time to time, I wonder if Diane does; I suspect that she might, though not vividly. Then I wonder if she's ever looked me up online, which seems even less likely. When I was their babysitter, I assumed that she'd finished her dissertation by the time she gave birth to Emily, but I later learned, in one of the few-and-far-between magazine features the Woleys cooperated with, that she hadn't earned her doctorate until 2000. As far as I can tell, she never did anything with the degree, and I have no idea if the immensity of Pangaea, the immensity of being Bryan Woley's wife, precluded her ability to be anything other than a philanthropist, rendering her own goals ridiculous, almost stunty. Or maybe, at least for a while, she found satisfaction in motherhood, marriage, being the private yin to his outward yang. Or maybe she *is* other things, and it's just not visible.

Certainly not everyone who gets a PhD goes on to become a professor, and I don't know if Diane wanted to or not. In imagining that perhaps she finds her fortune burdensome, I might be letting her off far too easily; it could be that she relishes the power such wealth provides. And yet I cannot help wondering this most of all: if my life of department meetings and strip-mall takeout and a mortgage—my ordinary life—would make her jealous.

CREATIVE DIFFERENCES

The film crew flew in from New York, and the agency people flew in from L.A.; direct flights to Wichita, it turns out, do not exist from either city. Now the agency people are hanging out at the bar of their mid-level chain hotel (or this is where they were when Ben last saw them) while the film crew, accompanied by Melissa Simon, scouts locations for tomorrow's shoot.

They met Melissa at her apartment, which was an unremarkable one-bedroom—junky furniture, Indian tapestry bedspread—with many of what she confirmed were her own photos pinned to the walls. The four-person crew and Melissa then got in the rental van and, with Ben driving and Melissa in the second row, they passed the bagel place where she said she often works on her laptop during the afternoons. Melissa was enthusiastic about the idea of filming there, to the extent that Ben wondered if friends of hers own the place, and Ben was tasked with conveying that it wasn't quite the right setting. For the last hour, Melissa has been leading them around the campus of the University of Wichita, where, through the Office of Public Affairs, they've already obtained permission to film. It's an overcast afternoon in late March, and the students are on spring break.

On the second floor of a large brick building, she opens a heavy door to reveal a computer lab with dim lighting and beige curtains pulled over the windows. One lone student sits in front of a monitor, earbuds in, simultaneously editing photos on a desktop computer and watching *The Royal Tenenbaums* on a laptop computer; onscreen, Gwyneth Paltrow smokes while wearing heavy eyeliner and a fur coat. "This is where I spent most of my time as an undergrad," Melissa says. "Thrilling, right?"

In addition to Ben, who is the producer, the crew is comprised of Justin, the director; Matthias, the DP; and Ryan, the gaffer. It's unclear to Ben if Melissa knows that Justin is kind of famous; he's made two widely praised feature-length documentaries, the first about a youth orchestra in Afghanistan and the second about fracking in a small town in Virginia. If Melissa had upon shaking hands with Justin proclaimed herself a fan, it would have mildly disgusted him and, Ben is sure, he'd have retracted. But if over the next twenty-four hours it becomes apparent that she really has no idea who he is, Justin will eventually become petulant toward her, offended by her lack of deference. As with nipping in the bud the notion of filming at the bagel place, it is Ben's responsibility to discreetly convey to Melissa Justin's renown.

Melissa is walking in front of them, and whenever she glances back, Ben is struck by the prettiness of her face; whenever she turns away, he is struck by the fact that she's a lot fatter than she appeared either during the Skype calls that occurred a few weeks ago among her, him, Justin, and the agency people, or in the photos of her he's seen. She has a trim torso and disproportionately big hips, ass, and thighs. And not disproportionately big in a Kim Kardashian sexy way—big in a precursor-of-frumpy-mom way, precursor of his own mother, though Melissa is twenty-four. Ben's assessment is unconnected to any attraction or lack thereof to Melissa—he's gay—and tied strictly to aesthetic implications; Matthias will need to shoot her from the waist up. Or, given the ever-increasing fatness of Americans, and given that Melissa is the project's only Midwesterner and least famous participant, maybe they should take her fatness and, so to speak, run with it? This is a question for Nancy, the agency's broadcast producer, and Ben guesses she'll come down on the side of fat concealment. Nancy, who is fifty, tends to be overtly sexist in a way most men in 2014 no longer are.

They are walking by a storage room, with a kind of concession stand opening and shelves of photo equipment visible behind locked windows, when Justin says, "Matthias, what if we shoot her in there, with all the gear behind her? Would you be able to get enough distance to pull focus?"

"You want to shoot me in the cage?" Melissa giggles. "With, like, literally not one speck of natural light?"

"It'll look cool," Justin says. "Trust me." He says, "Hey, what's up?" to the broad-shouldered, big-bellied, black-T-shirted man with a salt-and-pepper ponytail sitting at the window, who has glanced up only fleetingly from the screen of his phone. Now the man regards them quizzically. He is perched on a stool beneath fluorescent lights, and in back of him, the equipment is stacked floor to ceiling: tripods, digital and film cameras, lenses, lighting kits.

"Clarence, I don't know if you remember me," Melissa says. "I graduated in 2012? Melissa Simon?" She gestures to the crew. "These guys are here from New York City filming a documentary that I'm part of, and they want to maybe interview me *here*."

Clarence's quizzical expression does not change.

"Ben Schneider." Ben slides a business card through the open window. "Producer. Would that be cool if we film in there? We have permission from the public affairs office."

"This is the equipment cage," Clarence says.

"No, exactly," Ben says. "And since Melissa is a photographer, it's like, hey, the subject in her natural habitat."

"We'll totally respect the gear," Justin adds. "Put everything back the way we found it."

Clarence seems, if anything, more confused. He says, "You're shooting something for the public affairs office?"

"No, we have permission from the public affairs office," Ben says. "We're making a documentary about American creativity."

Clarence then calls the public affairs office for confirmation before grudgingly allowing them to invade his domain. When the five of them have followed Justin through the door next to the concession window, Ben sees that the interior of the space is probably ten by eight feet, almost more of a closet than a room. It is, of course, better if the scope of what they're doing—taking over the room for the rest of today and all of tomorrow—dawns on Clarence slowly. But often such people are easily pacified; when Clarence gets hungry, Ben thinks, they can buy him a twelve-inch sub or whatever it is a portly Wichita Cerberus likes to eat.

The first thing that takes a long time is getting room tone, for which Justin wants to turn off the heat for the entire building (it isn't going to happen but nevertheless requires another call to the public affairs office on Ben's part, in the infinitesimal hope that his contact there will call maintenance), then Justin wants to turn off the fluorescent lights, then he wants to unplug a mini-fridge. If they can't get the heat turned off by morning, Ben assures Justin, undoubtedly they can get egg-crate foam tonight at Walmart or Home Depot. Meanwhile, Ryan is doing a lighting check, setting up an LED that Matthias says should be bounced.

Melissa stands by the door, her arms folded, watching them intently. "What will you be shooting with?" she asks.

No one responds, then Ben says, "We use a digital cinema camera called a RED Dragon."

"A Scarlet or a Raven?" Melissa asks.

Justin gives a little snort and says, "Well, la di da."

Melissa seems not to take offense. "I primarily shoot stills," she says cheerfully, "but I've played around with video."

Ben says, "It's a Raven."

As Justin and Ryan discuss whether they'll need fill light, Melissa says, "Ben, where are you from?" If she doesn't know that

Justin is famous, she does, apparently, recognize that Ben is not—that despite his producer title, he is her low-level point person. Outside her apartment, just before she climbed into the van, she made a wide-eyed, pleased expression and murmured to him, confidingly, "This is crazy!" Or maybe it's that she can tell he's gay and therefore she's more comfortable interacting with him than with his slouchily handsome, heterosexually aloof colleagues.

In the equipment room, Ben says, "I've lived in New York for fifteen years."

"Really?" Melissa says. "You're so young-looking. How old are you?"

"I'm thirty-two."

"Oh, so you're counting when you were in college? Did you go to college in New York?"

"Yes," he says. "I went to NYU."

"Did you start college when you were seventeen?"

Frequently, on the job, Ben thinks, *If I were easily annoyed, I'd probably be annoyed right now.* Aloud, calmly, he says, "No, I started college when I was eighteen. So you're right, I should have said I've lived in New York for fourteen years, not fifteen."

"Where did you grow up?"

"Delaware. A suburb of Wilmington." After a pause, he adds, "Are you from Kansas?"

She shakes her head. "Sioux City, Iowa. I've been trying to think of what to tell you guys to do while you're here." Again, she giggles. "I think maybe Wichita is a better place to live than to visit. But it *is* a great place to be an artist." There's a confidence with which she says this that Ben finds what—ridiculous? Enviable? He has for four years been working on a documentary of his own, about a blind Cuban septuagenarian in the Bronx, he's even received funding from Sundance, but would he ever casually refer to himself as an artist?

He says to Melissa, "We're here for the shoot—for you. No worries about tourist attractions."

Melissa gestures toward the other members of the crew, who

are still conferring about the LED. "Do all of them live in New York?"

"Yes," Ben says.

"And do you usually work together?" Melissa asks. "I'm guessing you're freelance?"

Freelance isn't the right term for someone of Justin's stature—he has his own production company—so, on the off chance he's listening, Ben says, "I'm freelance, but I work with these guys a lot. Just for this documentary, we've shot the footage for five of the subjects. You're our sixth."

"Who's left?" Melissa asks.

A kind of bonding often arises on sets from *not* trying hard to get to know one another, not being overtly jovial and inquisitive. The subtext is *We're all busy, we're getting this done as efficiently as possible,* but of course even so, during the hours together that aren't really all that efficient, a camaraderie organically asserts itself. Melissa's forced small talk, however—again, it's good Ben isn't easily annoyed.

He says, "You're our last subject. A film crew on the West Coast has shot the other four."

"Have you worked with Parkington before?"

"Not personally," Ben says. "No."

The reason they are here, the reason Ben is standing in Wichita, Kansas, talking to Melissa Simon, is toothpaste. Parkington is a multinational maker of personal care products that hired Kitley & Weiss—it's the K&W folks who are now drinking at the hotel—to create an internet campaign around a brand of toothpaste that has existed for seventy-two years. The campaign will feature artists—yes, in fairness to Melissa, artists—in various mediums, and Justin et al. are the ones making the documentary, or six-tenths of it, that will show the artists in their daily lives and highlight their individual talents.

Ironically, it's Justin who would be a more fitting, less surprising subject of the documentary than Melissa. The other artists are an opera singer who's the only living opera singer most Americans have heard of; a bestselling author of legal thrillers; an eleven-year-old who was nominated for a Best Supporting Actress Oscar; a maker of patchwork quilts that depict slavery narratives; a former poet laureate; a principal dancer with the New York City Ballet; a Broadway actress; and a husband-and-wife folk duo who, between them, play eleven instruments. And then there's Melissa—chubby twenty-four-year-old Midwestern Melissa. She's a photographer, which is to say that two years ago she graduated from the University of Wichita with degrees in both Early Childhood Education and Art with a Photo Media Concentration. She currently spends mornings as a preschool teacher, but since graduating, has, rather improbably, made not one but two photo series that went viral.

The first, titled *Slideshow,* featured the children—one child per photo—at the preschool where she works coming down a slide, smiling joyously. The series appeared on an obscure parenting website, then got reproduced in about a million other places. Melissa is white, and all the children in the photos are Black; as they drove from the Wichita airport to the hotel, Matthias, who himself is Black, remarked that Melissa must have taken the picture of every Black kid in Wichita, which prompted Ben to look online at the city's racial demographics (as of 2011, 72% white).

Melissa's second series, which she'd been working on prior to the posting of *Slideshow,* was titled *Body/Hair.* For a year, each time she performed any act of depilation, she documented it: tweezing her eyebrows while peering in her bathroom mirror; shaving her legs while perched on the side of the tub, her toes near the drain, partially obscured by soap suds, the blades of a candy-colored razor set against her calf; and yes, trimming her pubic hair (light brown, suitably uncomfortable to behold). In Ben's opinion, the photos were neither artful nor sexy—and he doubts a straight man would beg to differ—but worst of all, they'd been poorly color corrected. Of course, only an idiot thinks viral popularity is indicative of quality, and the series was a hit particularly among women; apparently it was the wife of the Parkington CEO who suggested Melissa for inclusion in the toothpaste campaign.

"Do you travel internationally for jobs?" Melissa is asking now. "Or do you stay in the U.S.?"

Before Ben can answer, Justin says to him, "Can you check what time sunrise is? I wonder if we should get B-roll of her walking around campus with the sun coming up, even before we shoot in here."

Simultaneously, Ben says, "Actually, the call time tomorrow is twelve-thirty," and Melissa says, "I work in the morning."

Justin gives her a look that's almost flirtatious. "You can't get the day off?" Justin's attractiveness is of the stubbly, swollen-lipped, dark-haired bed-head variety, and he is, for the first time in Melissa's presence, deploying it.

Which makes it slightly surprising when Melissa firmly says, "Unfortunately, no." Could she also be queer?

"What's your job?" Justin asks. "Want Ben to call your boss?"

"Justin," Ben says. "We can make her schedule work." As it happens, the real celebrities were more flexible with their time—the opera singer gave them two eighteen-hour days, one at the opera house and one at her apartment, *and* she cooked seafood curry for the entire crew. To Melissa, Ben says, "You have no hard out tomorrow night, correct?"

"Yes," Melissa says. "Correct." She looks at Justin. "I teach preschool."

"Oh, yeah," Justin says. "Your Mary Poppins gig. How could I forget?" Switching to his warmest voice yet, he says, "All righty. This is how we'll do it." Because conceding doesn't come easily to him, good-naturedly conceding Justin, as opposed to peevishly conceding Justin, is the most charming Justin of all. "We'll meet here at twelve-thirty. I mean, come earlier if you can. That would be awesome. But starting at twelve-thirty at the latest, we'll shoot for a couple hours in here. I'll be off-camera asking you questions. It'll be a zoo with all the K&W people, but just treat them like static. Ben will be the one running interference, and all you need to do is focus on my questions and be yourself. After the interview, we'll get some B-roll of you walking around campus, driving your car, all that good stuff. Then we'll stop back at your apartment to get you brushing your teeth, although we'll also do that in one of the bathrooms here, to keep our options open. Oh, and Ben talked to you about bringing some prints from your two series, right? We want to get close-ups of the photos with your hands."

"That sounds fine," Melissa says. "But the brushing my teeth part—you're kidding, right?"

Ben and Justin make eye contact. She wants to know if Justin is kidding? Is *she* kidding?

With deliberate calmness, Ben says, "All the artists have done it for the documentary."

Melissa looks amused, but incredulously so. "You're telling me that you filmed Beatrice Chisolm brushing her teeth? And Jack and Lulu?"

Again, Ben and Justin make eye contact; Matthias and Ryan, who were previously talking, also have gone silent and are observing the exchange, and even Clarence seems to be listening.

"Yes," Ben says. "We did."

"Dude, it's in the contract," Justin says. "Did you read the contract?"

Still seeming unpleasantly amused, Melissa says, "After I brush my teeth, do I turn to the camera and say, 'Wow! White Sparkle toothpaste sure is effective!'?"

Her sarcasm and its abruptness are both unsettling. Although Ben met her in person just over an hour ago, he's been talking to her one-on-one and during group Skype calls with the agency for six weeks. The initial Skyping was her unacknowledged audition, a means of determining how attractive and charismatic she was. Sufficiently attractive and sufficiently charismatic were the answers, at least when she was seated at a desk that obscured the lower half of her body. But during none of the exchanges did Ben see evidence of this abrasive streak.

"Seriously," Justin says. "Did you read the contract? It's all laid out."

"Yeah," Melissa says. "I read it. But it's like sixteen pages. And the language in it—I'm not a lawyer."

"Well, it's all in there, my friend," Justin says.

"You know what?" Melissa says. "I finally understand." She looks between Ben and Justin. "This is a commercial. I should have realized it. None of you have ever used the word 'commercial' with me. You keep using the word 'documentary,' you keep saying it's a documentary about creativity being underwritten by Parkington. And I'm so dumb I've believed you." She's gazing only at Justin as she says, "I didn't think you'd direct a commercial."

So she does know who Justin is. But it would seem that she doesn't know that Justin has directed commercials, for, among other products, athletic shoes, luxury cars, and a telecommunications conglomerate. It was five years ago, on a car commercial shoot, that Ben and Justin met.

Melissa glances among them. "Do you guys know how much I'm being paid for this?"

No one responds.

"Five hundred dollars," she says. "You're paying me five hundred dollars to make a commercial for a huge corporation."

"What do you think union scale is?" Justin says.

"I'm lucky to be included, right? Because I'm the one nobody's ever heard of? But throughout this whole process, ever since you first contacted me, Ben, and during the Skype calls—there was something weird about how you all acted, and only now do I realize what it was. The weirdness isn't that you were trying to get me to be in a commercial for toothpaste. The weirdness is that you were trying to get me to be in a commercial while pretending you weren't."

"Melissa," Ben says. "You're an incredibly talented photographer, and this campaign will get your name and your work in front of a global audience. If you feel like you're not being fairly compensated, I can follow up with K&W and ask for more. We aren't the ones who decided on your payment. But we definitely want you to feel good about this experience. This really is meant to be a fun, cool project celebrating artists and creativity."

Melissa laughs an ugly laugh. The question now isn't whether her previous giggly question-asking was fake but what percent fake it was. Oddly, knowing that not only is the chipper demeanor not the totality of her personality but that she employs it strategically, just as she photographs her own body strategically—it makes Ben respect and even like her more.

Slowly, she says, "I don't think I want to do this. I don't want to be in your"—she makes air quotes—"'documentary.'"

"Are you fucking kidding me?" Justin says.

"Hey," Ben says to Justin. "Why don't Melissa and I go get coffee and you guys can keep scouting?" He turns to Melissa. "Want to get coffee?"

THEY GO TO THE student center, a six-minute walk. As soon as they've parted ways with the rest of the crew, she reverts to being nice again, not acerbic. She orders green tea, and he orders a decaf espresso, and after they sit, she says, "I did read the contract. I really did. I think I even remember the sentence now. Was it something about agreeing to cooperate with reasonable promotion of the Parkington brand? Because I thought that meant I couldn't be in the documentary and then, like, slander something Parkington makes. Like I couldn't tweet that their laundry detergent sucks."

"I didn't write your contract," Ben says. "Here's what I care about. What can I do to make you feel comfortable with the shoot tomorrow?"

She is quiet, seeming to ponder the question. At last she says, "If you'd said, 'We're making a commercial for toothpaste and we want you to be in it,' I'd probably have said yes. That's the irony. It's not like I think I'm too good to sell out. But you tricked me."

"I get where you're coming from," Ben says. "But I wonder if this is partly an issue of semantics. There just aren't such clear demarcations anymore between commercial and documentary content, especially online."

She raises her eyebrows. "Really? That's really what you believe?"

"Like I said, I get where you're coming from. I don't want you to think I don't."

"Honestly, when *Slideshow* went viral, I felt uncomfortable. Should I have paid the kids whose pictures I took? But also, *I* didn't make any money. The original website that ran the photos didn't pay me, and then literally hundreds of other publications just helped themselves. I didn't know that was legal. In the end, I was paid a grand total of fifty euros from some random Dutch magazine, which came out to I think sixty-six American dollars."

"That's a huge bummer," he says. "Photo copyright these days is like the Wild West. Almost no one understands the work by people like you that goes into the images."

"I told myself, 'Melissa, just enjoy this success and attention that's probably once in a lifetime.' Then, a few months later, my shaving pictures got even more attention. And I felt weird about those, too. As a feminist, for one thing, and also I was like, has the entire world really just seen my pubes? Who will ever date me now?" When Ben laughs, she says, "I'm not joking. I know there's this idea, with social media and everything, that we all want as much attention as possible, all the time, but one of the things about my early success that's been eye-opening is that I've gotten so much attention and it doesn't feel that great. It feels strange. That's helped me realize that my goal isn't to find the biggest audience. It's to be able to keep taking pictures and to find an audience who really appreciates what I do."

My early success. An audience who really appreciates what I do. Her confidence! It's so bizarrely pure, so uncompetitive. Should Ben move to Wichita?

"Can I ask you a question?" she says. "How much is Justin getting paid for this?"

"I truly don't know. But he's not a good frame of comparison because he's directing six of the shoots for the documentary."

"But, like, what's the range? If you had to guess?"

"If you're asking if it's more than five hundred dollars, sure." If he had to guess, a hundred thousand. He considers saying ten thousand, but what if even that sounds high to her? "It's just really hard to know," he says. "Plus, he has an agent."

"I'm sure you won't tell me," she says, "but how much are you getting paid?"

"If this is about the money, we can get you more. The exposure, though—you can't put a price on that."

"At the rate I'm going, I'll be forty-five when I pay off my student loans," she says. "Literally. I calculated. And I wish I could get an MFA in photo, but then what? I'll be dead without paying off my loans."

"I have student loans," he says. "I know. It sucks." The truth is that most people in the documentary field don't. They don't seem so different from you, with their shitty apartments and their roommates and their artsy hustling, then it turns out their parents have a summer house on Martha's Vineyard (Justin), or the way they met their agent is that he was their Harvard roommate's uncle (Matthias).

Melissa says, "It's just, what you keep saying about payment and exposure—why do I have to decide between them?"

"No, right. You shouldn't. You don't." He is not entirely sure why, in this moment, he says, "For what it's worth, I'm working on a documentary, too. I'm directing one. I get the whole blood, sweat, and tears thing."

"What's yours about?"

"A Cuban guy in his seventies. He left when Castro came to power, went back to fight in the Bay of Pigs, was sent to a Cuban prison for six months after the U.S. threw all those guys under the bus, went blind due to being tortured, then he was released back to the U.S. in '62. He ends up working as a cab dispatcher, getting married, and having five sons."

"Wow."

"I'm just scared he'll die before I can finish. I need to buckle down." Quickly Ben adds, "Not to sound like an asshole. Obviously, it would be sad for his family if he died. And for him. Not just for me."

She smiles. "I knew what you meant. What's his name?"

"Diego Ruiz." Ben pauses. "A lot of the time, I'm like, why the fuck am I doing this? Making a documentary is expensive, it's a pain in the ass, I'm calling in favors from my friends. But Diego is amazing. He wears dark glasses, he has this huge belly, and he's hilarious. He's been through some of the worst things that can happen to a person, and he's warm and funny and loves his family. And for some reason he's trusting me to help tell his story. I know it sounds corny, but it's a privilege."

Divulging all this—it really wasn't calculated on Ben's part. It was true. Is this why it works? She says, "Yeah, exactly. You know in the story of Rumpelstiltskin, how the miller's daughter spins straw into gold? That's what I feel like making art is." Then she says, "If you can try to get me more money, I'd really appreciate it. But whatever. I'll be there tomorrow at twelve-thirty."

THAT NIGHT, WHEN BEN and Ryan return to the hotel from buying egg-crate foam at Walmart, a massive amount of barbecue, procured by a K&W assistant, has been laid out buffet-style in the part of the lobby where the continental breakfast will be served tomorrow morning: pulled pork, ribs, brisket, as well as coleslaw, fries, and mac and cheese. Even though the hotel's modest-sized bar is right there, the crew and the eight agency people keep drinking in the lobby after dinner, while the mac and cheese congeals and the meat grows old. The girl behind the front desk, who looks like an undergrad, does nothing to indicate they should go elsewhere.

On the plane ride out, Ben decided he'd have no more than two beers tonight, but Justin is drinking a lot, so pretty soon Ben has had four. Although Justin is married to a dark-haired, incredibly beautiful woman from Venezuela, a model, three times on location when Justin and Ben were both very drunk, Ben gave Justin blow-jobs; the third time, Justin also gave Ben a blowjob. Ben is happy to get drunk if he and Justin are going to hook up, but he doesn't want to not hook up *and* be hungover tomorrow.

He has just opened his fifth beer when Nancy, the broadcast producer, perches on the arm of the couch where he's sitting, sets a hand on his shoulder and says, "I hear our ingénue got stage fright today."

"It's under control," Ben says.

Nancy smiles tightly, though it's difficult to discern if the tightness is due to her mood or the work she's had done. "Keep it that way," she says.

But he's already received the text from Melissa; he received it at 8:56 P.M. and he just didn't know it for a half hour because he didn't feel his phone vibrate. The text says: *Ben I thought about it and I changed my mind again. I don't want to appear in the documentary/commercial/whatever. This is definite. Sorry for any confusion.*

By this point, a garrulous medical device sales rep named Randy, in town from San Antonio, Texas, has joined the gathering in the lobby, and everyone is tipsy enough to be tickled rather than annoyed. Ben walks outside to the parking lot to call Melissa. He must stand several feet from the entrance to avoid setting off the automatic doors.

"What's going on?" he says when she answers. "I got your text."

"I just feel too weird about everything," she says. "I know I wouldn't be able to relax during the shoot tomorrow and give you the footage you need."

"Let us worry about that. I appreciate your consideration, but that's our job."

"I'm not doing it," she says. "I don't want to waste more of your time." Her voice is neither tentative, as it initially was in their encounters, nor caustic, as it was later. She does in fact sound resolute, but more soberly so than angrily.

He says, "What can I do to change your mind?"

After a beat, she says, "When we were having coffee, you were convincing. You seemed like a sincerely nice person, not a condescending New Yorker who thinks it's hilarious he's in Kansas, and maybe you really are nice. But after I got home today, I was thinking about your documentary about the Cuban guy. *You* know the difference between a documentary and a commercial. And you're the person who first got in touch with me—you're the one who said from the start it was a documentary. I don't know what instructions you got from the Kitley & Weiss people, but you could have told me the truth."

"It feels like we're going in circles here," he says. "How can we move forward? We want to do right by you, Melissa."

"See, I think you might actually believe what you're saying. I think maybe you're so used to working in this fake way that you don't even recognize it. But I know you won't care if I come off looking good or bad tomorrow. All you care about is getting me to do whatever you've already decided I should do on camera."

"I can give you my word we have no interest in making you look bad."

"Your word?" She chortles.

"What if we don't film you brushing your teeth?" he says. "We just do the interview?"

It immediately occurs to him that this isn't his bargaining chip to offer, so he's a bit relieved when she says, "No."

"Well, if it makes any difference," he says, "I talked to the agency folks, and they can raise your fee to twenty-five hundred dollars." He hasn't talked to anyone yet—he's been too preoccupied with Justin and blowjobs—but he's confident he can get this amount. Possibly he could get her more, but if he gets her too much, it will emphasize how they lowballed her at first. He says, "I don't know what you pay on your student loans, but for me, that's about eight months' worth."

She's quiet again, and he can tell that it does make a difference. But it makes a difference in the sense that it's harder to turn down the additional money, not that it changes her mind. She says, "No. And I have to get up early for work, so please don't call or text me again."

OF COURSE NANCY INSISTS on calling her. First, Nancy freaks out in the lobby—she says, "It's a fucking hostage situation, and she's the terrorist"—then she goes outside with Ben to call Melissa from Ben's phone. It's almost ten o'clock and maybe forty degrees, and they're not wearing coats. At Nancy's instruction, Ben puts Melissa on speaker, though it's Nancy who's doing most of the talking.

"This isn't coastal elites trying to deceive you," Nancy says. "This is the career opportunity of a fucking lifetime dropping in your lap. Besides which, how could we have tricked you about the nature of what we're doing when you had umpteen conference calls with one of the most famous ad agencies in the world?"

Melissa says nothing.

"Honey, do you know where I grew up?" Nancy asks. "I'm from Wentzville, Missouri. I'm practically your next-door neighbor. And you know what? I may have lived in L.A. for thirty years, but I'm still Jenny from the block." Ben winces; he hopes Melissa is too young to get the reference.

"Whether you want to stay in Wichita or move to New York, L.A., or for that matter Kansas City, being part of a project of this prestige is your calling card," Nancy continues. "I'm telling you, woman to woman, Midwesterner to Midwesterner, that there's absolutely no question this exposure is in your best interest."

The silence from Melissa lasts long enough that Ben wonders if she ended the call. Then, quietly, she says, "I don't want exposure."

"Oh, for Christ's sake," Nancy says. "Do you know how many people came here for tomorrow's shoot? Thirteen. Thirteen! Do you know how much it costs to fly out that many people, for the hotel, the equipment, the man hours? And because you have cold feet, because you're too precious to be filmed sticking a goddamn toothbrush in your mouth, you think we're flushing 60K in expenses down the toilet? That's not how it works, sweetheart. You signed a contract. We'll see you tomorrow."

"No, actually—" Melissa's voice grows marginally louder. "I never signed the contract. I wasn't playing hardball. I was planning to ask you about this, Ben, because there's a line where I'm supposed to sign it, and, right under, there's a line where my agent is supposed to sign, but I don't have an agent, so I wasn't sure what to do. And I may not be a lawyer, but I know enough to know that if I didn't sign the contract—" She doesn't say the rest.

In the dark hotel parking lot, Nancy glares at Ben. Yes, this is his fuck-up. But, in his defense, getting the contract was on his to-do list for tomorrow; subjects often don't sign until the day of, and sometimes until weeks after.

"You know what you are?" Nancy says, and it's not clear if she's speaking to Melissa, Ben, or both of them. "You're an entitled little millennial piece of shit."

THE TOOTHPASTE CAMPAIGN IS an enormous, unequivocal success. Relatively few people see the full documentary, but the ninety-second montage of the artists brushing their teeth, which never airs on television, is viewed 52 million times on YouTube. Why is it so enjoyable to watch somewhat famous people brush their teeth? Ben spends a fair amount of time pondering this question (he himself watches the montage repeatedly even after his involvement with Parkington is complete) and concludes that it's because teeth-brushing is universal. It's personal but not excessively so—the participants seem like good sports rather than exhibitionists—and it's real. Using White Sparkle is of course beside the point; everyone in the video does actually brush their teeth. Even people who hire others to do mundane tasks for them, even the opera singer—such people still brush their own teeth.

That night in Wichita, after he and Nancy re-entered the hotel lobby and broke the news about Melissa's change of heart, every-

one disbanded quickly, with varying levels of irritation and out-
right rage. But it wasn't as if any of them personally lost money.
Parkington was paying K&W, and K&W was paying the crew, and
they didn't end up replacing Melissa. They just included nine subjects in the documentary instead of ten.

The two calls to Melissa from the parking lot had so thoroughly
soured the night—the whole trip—that the question of whether
Ben and Justin would hook up was rendered moot. But then, because Ben gave up on willing it to happen, it did happen after all.
As they were riding up in the elevator, Justin conveyed a kind of
unspoken sleepy-eyed receptivity that coexisted with or ran beneath his overtly expressed contempt for Melissa. But after Ben
gave him a blowjob, Justin didn't reciprocate, which wouldn't have
felt as bad if he'd never done it before; it would have felt like
standard-issue quasi-straight-guy bullshit instead of a regression of
intimacy.

Ben occasionally googles Melissa Simon. He half-expects to
hear from or about her, at the least in the form of another viral
slideshow, but a few years pass without this happening. Based on
what he can infer from LinkedIn, she does go to grad school but
not for photography—she gets a master's degree in, of all things,
business administration. And on Instagram she seems to be dating,
then married to, a tubby, smiley guy named Mikey.

Ben makes a trailer of his existing footage of Diego Ruiz to secure more funding. But after three years, when he hears from the
eldest Ruiz son that their father died a month before, Ben has shot
150 additional hours of footage and watched zero of them. Oddly,
upon learning of Diego's death, Ben feels the temptation to relay
the news to Melissa. He doesn't, though, because there's no good
reason why he would.

FOLLOW-UP

The email arrives at 4:53 P.M. on a Friday, while Janie is at the office, emptying her inbox before a five o'clock call. The subject is *New Test Result Available,* with a link that leads to a message concerning Janie's *MM MAMMOGRAM SCREENING BILAT W 3D TOMO W CAD performed on 2/2/23:*

> *FINDINGS: Bilateral screening mammogram was performed with the assistance of Computer-Aided Detection and breast tomosynthesis. The breasts are heterogeneously dense, which may obscure small masses.*
>
> *There is a mass with obscured margins in the left breast at the 8 o'clock position at anterior depth.*
>
> *The remainder of the breast tissue is unremarkable.*
>
> *IMPRESSION: ACR BI-RADS Category 0: Need Additional Imaging Evaluation*

RECOMMENDATION: Spot Tomosynthesis and Ultra-sound

As a result of the 21st Century Cures Act, all medical imaging exams are released immediately to iHealth. You may be viewing this report before our scheduling staff and your referring provider. We will attempt to contact you by phone within one business day of this report to schedule any recommended follow-up exams. If you have questions, please contact your health care provider.

Because low-level dread is often inside Janie, the first thing she thinks is, *Ah, yes, the notification of my premature death—I was expecting you.* As an affluent fifty-one-year-old white woman who lives in the suburb of Elm Grove, Wisconsin, and works on the eighteenth floor of a downtown Milwaukee high-rise, Janie sees it as plausible and fitting that breast cancer would get her; something like cholera or even diabetes would be surprising. The second thing she thinks is, *And fair enough that my breasts are unremarkable.* The third thing she thinks is, *But what in this life is not heterogeneously dense?*

No phone number is included in the email, but by poking around on the provider's website, Janie finds one for the Helen T. Kensington Breast Center. At 4:56, she reaches a grandmotherly-sounding receptionist, though it's possible the woman is no older than Janie herself. "I have an opening for Thursday," the woman says. "But, honey, you know what, I don't want you to worry that long, so I'm going to get you in Monday morning." The efficiency is not reassuring, is the opposite of reassuring, even when the receptionist adds, "This happens a lot, and most of the time, it's nothing."

After hanging up, Janie emails her assistant to reschedule the meetings she was supposed to have before ten on Monday. Then she takes a screenshot of the email and texts it to Pippa, along with the grimacing, clenched-teeth emoji. Pippa lives 1,400 miles away, in New Mexico, and they text off and on all day, every day. Pippa's last text had come in two hours prior and was *Going to have a think on it.* This was with regard to an invitation to a dinner party Pippa had received from a woman who'd just moved back to Albuquerque after several years away. Pippa told Janie she remembered that she didn't like the woman but couldn't remember why and therefore wasn't sure whether to accept or decline.

Pippa's first response to the mammogram results—*Aw fuck*—arrives in less than a minute, followed by two more:

It's probably a false alarm but if not I'll come take care of you

How you feeling dsts wise

3? Janie replies.

For more than twenty years, they have used a ranking system they refer to as "dogshit to stars," though in fact dogshit and stars encapsulate two distinct categories. It originated when Pippa and Janie were in law school and Pippa was the pet sitter for a professor's schnauzer named Buster. During a particularly notable walk, first Buster rolled in something that Pippa initially thought was dirt but that turned out to be a decomposing squirrel. Then, as Pippa scooped Buster's runny poop from the grass, her fingers broke through the plastic bag; poop smeared everywhere, including getting lodged under her nails. Then Buster bit her. Bad events have since been measured between the two women on a 1-to-5 dogshit scale. Soon after, good events got their own 1-to-5 stars scale, in honor of the two-person bachelorette trip Pippa and Janie took to Santa Fe before Janie's wedding, when one February night they floated in a hot tub on the roof of a hotel on the plaza, under the brightest stars either of them had ever seen, in twenty-five-degree weather. It was this trip that first made Pippa interested in living in New Mexico.

At her desk, Janie texts, *Trying to suspend panic until further notice*

She adds, *Did you remember why you don't like that woman?*

No and wtf, Pippa replies. *Still confused about if I should forgive since I already forgot or trust my past self's grudge*

Do Leona or Wes remember? Janie types.

Asked Leona, Wes never remembers shit like this, Pippa replies.

Janie texts, *About to get on a call*

Pippa texts back three of the straw-hat-with-green-ribbon emoji, which, in the code of their friendship—Janie no longer recalls why this is so—means *I love you.*

JANIE IS ASSISTANT GENERAL counsel for a chain of 1,200 convenience stores and gas stations located in the Midwest and California, and her call is with the manager of a store in Topeka, related to a Title VII lawsuit in which a former employee says he suffered wage loss and psychological distress because of harassment from a co-worker. Specifically, the plaintiff, whose name is Billy Bindell and who was twenty-nine during the stretch four years prior when he alleges that the harassment occurred, says that the defendant, a woman named Myrna Kent, who was then fifty-five, invited him to attend her church and also would tell him that she was praying for him. The lawyer retained by Bindell is alleging that because Kent was an assistant manager and Bindell was her subordinate, her religious references constitute harassment. Janie's initial take is that since listening to Kent's proselytizing wasn't sufficiently severe or persuasive, the claim isn't a good one. Also, Bindell is white and Kent is Black, which is better in terms of optics than the reverse would be.

Before Janie can ask even the most preliminary question, the manager, whose name is Wayne, says, "I been here eight years and never had no complaints like this before. Never once."

"Do you recall Ms. Kent raising the topic of religion with you?"

"Sure don't."

"Do you recall hearing Ms. Kent raise the topic of religion with any other employees?"

"No, ma'am. Sure don't."

"My understanding is that you regularly worked the same shifts as Ms. Kent and Mr. Bindell. Is that right?"

"People lost their damn minds in Covid is what," Wayne says. "I didn't do nothing wrong."

Janie doesn't disagree about people losing their minds, though what she says is "You haven't been accused of any wrongdoing. I apologize for not making that completely clear."

This is, of course, only the investigative phase, when she's trying to determine what happened, whether the company really is in the wrong, and how provocative the case will be if the media catches wind of it; she also needs to gather information about Bindell's job history and whether he's a serial plaintiff. In many contexts of her job, Janie finds herself asking the same essential question: What is this a story about? Not what do its participants believe, but what meaning can be ascribed to the events that demonstrably happened? Do they meet the requirements of a cognizable legal claim? And is there a discrepancy between the story the participants are telling and the actual meaning? The answer to these questions is what determines the case's path—whether the company will settle quietly and quickly, or publicly defend the case and hire local counsel in the jurisdiction where the lawsuit was filed. Despite cynicism on the part of the media and the public about such things, Janie's employer does in fact want to make things right after genuine mistakes, while not encouraging frivolous lawsuits.

She asks Wayne, "Do you recall Mr. Bindell having conflicts with Ms. Kent or with other employees?"

"She's a nice old lady who don't mean no harm."

Among the comments Kent is alleged to have made to Bindell are "When the devil pushes you down low, God lifts you up high," "You're a lost sinner, and only God can help you find your way home," and "You are held by God and loved by Jesus." In this moment, on the phone with Wayne, Janie wishes someone would tell her that *she's* held by God and loved by Jesus. Or maybe it's more that she wishes some part of her, any part of her, believed it.

She asks Wayne a few more factual questions, and he continues to be so unhelpful that, although she'd normally persist, she wraps up the conversation as quickly as possible, even if it means she'll need to try again another time. She's ready for the workday to be over.

DAVID'S CAR IS IN the garage when Janie pulls in at 6:12. As she enters the house through the back door, she can hear the giant TV in the basement blaring, which means David is running on the treadmill. She steps out of her shoes, hangs her bag and coat on hooks in the mudroom, washes her hands in the kitchen, pulls an open bottle of white wine from the refrigerator, fills a stemless glass, and walks down the carpeted basement steps drinking from it. Because of the volume of the television and the angle of the treadmill, David can't see or hear her approach, and, when she reaches the bottom step, she prepares her face; she does this even though she and David have been married since 2001 because she does it for everyone except Pippa and her sixteen-year-old son, Evan. David finally catches sight of her in his peripheral vision when she's alongside the treadmill and says, "Hey."

In greeting, Janie holds up her left hand. Over the TV, she says, "Did you talk to Evan about what time he wants to get to the fashion show?"

David uses the remote control to significantly lower the volume of the ESPN show he's been watching and says, "I think Ev's in his room." He slows the treadmill to a walk. David's face is flushed and sweaty, and because of how tall he is—6'7"—there's very little space between the top of his head and the ceiling. "I'm about to jump in the shower before I pick up Bill," David adds. "Tip-off's at seven."

Janie squints. "I thought the game was tomorrow."

David shakes his head. "Tomorrow they're in Charlotte."

"Were you under the impression I'd be driving Evan?"

David looks perplexed. "Aren't you?"

"I mean, I guess I can. Since I'm home early." Janie didn't consider, either at the office or on her drive, whether she'd tell David about the mammogram results, but now knows she won't. What is there for him to say that she can't say to herself? If she told him, depending on the level of worry Janie expressed, he'd probably forgo the game. But on her commute, Janie decided she'd take a bath after she got home, then she realized that while taking a bath, she'd have to see her own (unremarkable, heterogeneously dense, possibly cancerous) breasts, which would likely defeat the purpose of taking the bath. So she might as well distract herself by driving Evan to the fashion show—it's at his high school—then come home and watch trashy TV under a blanket.

As David slows the treadmill even more, he says, "What does it mean when a boy wears pearl earrings?"

Janie blinks. "I assume it means he thinks they look nice. Is Evan wearing pearl earrings right now?"

David nods. "Did you get them for him?"

"No." Janie can feel how David wants her to say something clarifying or reassuring about their son's choices, and she decides not to. If she dies, David will need to be able to handle this stuff. What she says is "Did you figure out why the freezer is making that noise?"

"The bad news is no, but the good news is it stopped making the noise."

Janie turns to go upstairs. "If you want to know what it means when Evan wears pearl earrings, ask him."

ON THE SECOND FLOOR, Evan is sitting on his bed, watching a TikTok video of a woman in her twenties speak effusively about how a clay facial mask that contains volcanic ash compares to a sheet mask that contains snow mushrooms. "Honey, I'm taking you to the fashion show," Janie says. "Not Dad."

Noncommittally, Evan says, "Slay."

"Have you eaten dinner?"

Evan's pearl earrings are teardrop style, not studs, so when he nods, they wobble. In addition to the earrings, he's wearing black eyeliner and fuchsia lipstick and probably several other products that are to Janie invisible, unidentifiable, or both. He's also wearing a black leather jacket with several zippers and black leather pants, an outfit he selected from the women's department at Nordstrom when they went shopping together last weekend.

"What was the protein?" she asks.

"There'll be food at school."

"What if I make you a plate of salami and cheese?" Even as she suggests it, she wonders if she got breast cancer by being a person who considers salami a reasonably healthy source of protein. Though, in point of fact, less for herself than for other people.

"Salami smells like armpits," Evan says.

"In a good or bad way?" Janie asks, and it works—Evan laughs. Janie adds, "The fashion show starts at seven-thirty, right? So let's leave here at seven."

"Slay," Evan says.

AFTER DROPPING OFF EVAN, she drives to the restaurant she ordered food from, unexpectedly finds a parking space close to the entrance, goes inside, learns her order won't be ready for another fifteen minutes, and returns to the car to wait. She listens to an eighties satellite radio station, blasting the heat in a way both David and Evan would object to. This feels like such a nice moment, a kind of cocoon of warmth and music she likes, in the dark cold Wisconsin night, that when her phone buzzes with the text telling her the food is ready, she retrieves it and eats it immediately, in the car. Is she treasuring this interlude only because she might have cancer? That she might have cancer is definitely the reason she ordered a cheeseburger instead of the quinoa bowl with seared tuna.

As soon as she's finished, she texts Pippa, *Would you say Cyndi Lauper is underrated?*

Probably, Pippa replies. *Why?*

Time after time is such a good song, Janie writes.

Are you stoned, Pippa texts, followed by the laugh-crying emoji, which Evan has tried to deter Janie from using by telling her it's millennial, to which Janie has replied that she's a decade older than the oldest millennial so whom is she supposed to be trying to convince that she's not middle-aged and dorky? Evan said in that case, she's succeeding because the word "whom" is also middle-aged and dorky.

If so, good for you, Pippa adds. *How you feeling boob-wise?*

Not stoned, Janie replies. *As for boob* . . . After brief deliberation, she selects the shrug emoji.

Pippa replies, *Getting ready to go to client if I go quiet*
But 3rd baby and don't think labor will last into tmw

Pippa didn't practice law for long and has for years been a doula.

Hope it goes well! Janie types then tosses her phone onto the passenger seat, shifts the gear from park to drive, and heads home.

SOMETIMES, AND THE THOUGHT seems more or less troubling depending on her mood, Janie thinks that she married David to amuse Pippa. But doesn't everyone make enormously consequential decisions for the slightest of reasons (and what in this life is not heterogeneously dense)? Janie met David in her last semester of law school and his last semester of business school, which they both were attending at Washington University in St. Louis. Back then, Pippa often teased Janie about her ridiculously square and conventional taste in men. Pippa had said once that Janie's ideal was a model you'd find in a department store ad insert in the Sunday newspaper. Another time she'd said that the evil quarterback in a high school movie, the one that the teen protagonist liked at first before recognizing his meanness and superficiality, was the guy Janie hoped to actually end up with.

When Pippa made these observations, Janie had no impulse to deny them; she mostly was surprised, but oddly heartened, that anyone wouldn't desire such men. Janie had been twenty-four when she met Pippa, and before Pippa, all her friends wanted the same thing—the best-looking guy they could find, the tallest guy, the one who seemed the most academically or professionally promising. It was humiliating, thrilling, and revelatory when Pippa pointed out that, apart from *tall*, all these descriptors were subjective.

When she started law school, Janie had never had a real, long-term boyfriend. In high school and college, she'd hooked up for stretches with a few guys she wasn't very into and a few guys she was very into who weren't that into her. After college, working for two years as a paralegal, she'd had her most sustained relationship, with a partner at the firm who was in his late thirties, married, and a father of three. Janie had thought he was attractive for a man so old, but she'd never hoped he'd leave his wife. She'd experienced the built-in transience of the relationship as a relief, though she'd also marveled, especially early on, at her own immorality. She'd never imagined, prior to it happening, that she could be a person complicit in infidelity.

Before she moved from Chicago to St. Louis for law school, she and the married man, whose name was Patrick, had tearfully bid each other farewell in a hotel room on Michigan, and she'd been unclear on the extent to which either of their tears were sincere. On entering law school, she reverted to the patterns of high school and college—longing for guys who eluded her, intermittently settling for the ones who showed interest.

She and David met at a thirtieth birthday party in April 1999, hosted by a married couple who both were classmates of Janie's and lived in the same building as David. In addition to being extremely tall, David, it turned out, had been the quarterback of his high school football team. (It had been a private school with only eighty people in his graduating class, not a sports powerhouse—but still.) Even more incredibly, in his youth, he had done some modeling for JCPenney. Janie and David were seated next to each other, he at the head of the table and she on his right, and she drank four gin and tonics and felt dizzy with attraction to him. But the truly miraculous part was that as the dinner wore on, as she asked him about his upbringing and his experience in B-school, first she thought his leg might be touching hers, then she was sure of it, then her leg was pressed to his from her ankle to her knee. He walked her back to her apartment, and there was a moment when they were facing each other, and he seemed to be leaning down toward her, and she blurted out, "You're so tall that I can't tell if you're trying to hug or kiss me," and he laughed and brought his head all the way in, his lips against hers, and briefly she was drunkenly ecstatic and then after a few seconds—though truly, it was more an observation than a judgment, and maybe it was a relief, because it made him less intimidating?—Janie thought, *I'm pretty sure that I'm not especially good at kissing but even I can tell that you're a bad kisser.* It felt almost like he was biting her with his lips.

Thirteen months later, at Janie and David's wedding, Pippa was the maid of honor. As Pippa and Janie waited before the ceremony in the small room near the entrance of the church, Pippa said, "How would you feel if I fucked your cousin tonight?"

"Steve? He's here with his wife and kids."

"Not Steve. Fiona."

Janie squinted. "I'm not sure that she's gay."

Pippa grinned. "I'm not sure that I am, either." She reached out and smoothed back a hair above Janie's forehead that had come loose from her chignon. "Human sexuality is a varied and delicious panoply, Janie-Jane."

Janie fake-frowned and said, "Now you tell me."

* * *

ON SATURDAY MORNING, JANIE goes to a yoga class, and afterward she decides to take a bath after all but, so as to obscure the sight of her own breasts, she dons a bikini top she hasn't worn since before Evan's birth. She already groped her left boob, found nothing (or something? No, nothing) and has reverted to her former wish to see neither the left nor right breast. Before stepping into the bath, from the speaker between her sink and David's, she starts the album of a folky pop singer that she listened to over and over during law school, both while getting dressed to go to parties on the weekend and also sometimes the next day, usually hungover and let down. When the water cools, she warms it up twice then finally climbs out, removes the bikini top, and puts on her robe.

She's doing some work at the dining room table in the afternoon, responding to an email from a member of her company's communications team regarding a case in Sacramento made messier by California's peculiar laws about how people get paid, when Evan texts her: *Can we get sushi 2nite pleeeeease. Since Dad out*

The sushi emoji follows, along with the prayer hands and the face with a line of drool emerging from its mouth. As far as she knows, Evan is somewhere in the house.

An hour ago, Janie made a chicken orzo soup that is currently simmering on the stove, but of course it's difficult to say no to an outing initiated by Evan, and it's true that she and Evan both love sushi and David doesn't. Though will David in fact be out? Where's he going?

She walks to the bottom of the staircase, which is near the front door, and yells up, "Ev?" There's no response, and the likelihood is high that he's wearing headphones, but she tries a few more times. Then she walks to the top of the basement stairs, which are off the kitchen, and yells, "David?" ESPN is, of course, blasting, and David also doesn't respond.

She returns to the dining room table, picks up her phone, and replies to Evan, *Maybe. What's your homework situation?*

Immediately, Evan texts back, *Only a lil math.* Janie sets down her phone and goes to the basement.

This time, David doesn't notice her until she's in front of him, between him and the TV screen. "Are you out again tonight?" she asks.

David holds up the remote control and mutes the TV. "Poker at Bobby's," he says. "It's in the calendar."

From time to time, Janie wonders if David is having an affair. Because of how rigidly he sees things, she doubts it, but if he is, she's not sure she can summon the requisite outrage, nor, really, can she identify with the impulse. Maybe it's just because she was so young during her own foray into adultery, but at this juncture, it seems unappealingly messy. Aloud she says, "And you're planning to have dinner at Bobby's or here?"

David shakes his head. "Pizza there." He pats his midsection and says, "Running an extra mile so I can enjoy myself. Did you order groceries yet? If you get some steaks, I'll grill them tomorrow." David grills year-round; in the winter, he covers the grill with insulating tape.

"I'll check if it's too late to add." Janie turns. "Although Evan and I are going out for sushi tonight and I also made soup, so we can do that in the next couple days, too."

On their fifth anniversary, a lifetime ago, Janie, who's a decent artist, used colored pencils to make five drawings representing their time together. The first was of them at the table at that graduate school dinner party, and Janie said as he examined the drawing, "I'd never have believed you were interested in me if not for the blatant footsy," and, affably, David said, "Ha, did you think I was playing footsy? There was nowhere else for my legs to go."

Janie was devastated by this exchange, and when she repeated it to Pippa, Pippa said, "Janie, of course he was playing footsy with you. If he couldn't keep from pushing his legs into people under tables, he'd have been charged with sexual harassment by now. The part I don't like is that that's his idea of a joke."

Now that another seventeen years have passed, what stands out to Janie is that she labored over five separate colored pencil drawings as a present for her husband. Also that she'd had the capacity to be devastated by something her husband said.

BACK AT THE DINING room table, a text from Pippa reads: *How you feeling today about boob stuff?*

Janie replies *Still* and the shrug emoji, then adds, *You all rested?* She already knows that Pippa's client gave birth to a healthy baby around four in the morning, Pippa stayed for a few more hours, then she went home to sleep.

Pippa, who never had children herself, is part of a throuple, though she likes to say she was so far ahead of the curve that she was doing it back when it was still called a ménage à trois. Once when Janie and Evan went out to Albuquerque to visit her, when Evan was in preschool, David asked how Janie planned to explain Pippa's living arrangement to their son, and Janie said, "I'll tell him that she lives with Wes and Leona like I'd tell him any other adults live together. It's not as if we usually describe what the adults he knows do in bed."

Rested-ish, Pippa replies.

But also!

I half remembered the issue with Gwen

Gwen is the woman who invited Pippa to her dinner party.

On the edge of my seat, Janie replies.

Pippa: We had an argument about Bernie Sanders spoiling 2016 election. I said he was never held accountable

Janie: Hmm. Maybe bygones?

Pippa: There's more

Pippa: Argument ended when either I told her to go fuck herself or she told me to go fuck myself . . . but I don't remember which!!!

Janie responds with three of the laugh-crying emojis.

> Pippa: Isn't it so weird what we remember and what we for-
> get?
>
> Janie: Go to the dinner party. Statute of limitations.
>
> Pippa: What year of law school did they teach us that? Can't
> remember that either
>
> Janie: I'm so glad we're going through this life together

AT THE SUSHI RESTAURANT, across from her in the booth, Evan looks at his phone so many times that Janie threatens to take it away from him, a threat she often makes, then he looks at it again, and she leans over, grabs it, and stuffs it into her bag. He is surly for about fifteen minutes, but when the food arrives, it's really good, and Evan tells her a story about his math teacher farting in class while handing back their tests and they're both laughing even as Janie says he should have sympathy for a middle-aged woman's farts.

"It sounded like a trumpet," he says.

"In that case especially," Janie says.

"Have you ever seen a close-up of an ant's face?" Evan says. "I think it's their antennae, but it looks like they have horrible eyes and fangs. It's the narstiest thing."

"I don't think I've seen that."

"I'll show you right now." He nods toward her bag, which is resting on the seat beside her. "Not gonna lie, it kind of ruined my day."

"First of all, no," she says. "I'm not giving you your phone until we're home. And second, why would I want to look at horrible fangs during this delicious dinner with my beloved child?"

"It's like a beast from a fairy tale," Evan says.

Janie shakes her head while smiling. (Let's say it's Stage 4—in that case, she wants to be one of those parents who writes exquisite letters for their kid to posthumously open every year on their birthday. Will she need to quit her job to write these letters? Will she need to quit her job anyway? If it's a lesser stage, will she not need to quit her job, but maybe she just should?)

On the car ride home, after changing the satellite radio from the eighties station to the TikTok station, Evan says, "I could give you a facial tonight if you want."

They do it in his bathroom, where all his supplies are: an eyelash spooley, whatever that is, and some eyelash growing serum; and a moisturizer with ceramides and B_3, also whatever those are, to protect Janie's skin barrier; and a lip peel. When the facial is complete, he offers to do her makeup, which she also accepts. He rubs one foundation on the bags under her eyes and a different foundation on the rest of her face; he applies a mascara to get her lashes "poppin'," as he puts it; he uses a neutral eye shadow and highlighter for her cheekbones, and lipliner, and copper lipstick.

During the proceedings, Janie sits in Evan's desk chair, which he carried into the bathroom from his bedroom, and her eyes are closed most of the time. His phone rests next to the sink, playing pop. The overall effect is soothing, and she is thinking about how delightful and funny Evan is, when he says, "Are you feeling the Elm Grove sadness?"

She opens her eyes and says, "What? No."

Once, Evan casually asked her if she was bothered by being a capitalist cog. Another time, driving past the enormous houses on Juneau Boulevard toward their merely large house, he said, "What neighborhood is this, because it's really giving Elm Grove sadness?" He wants a bohemian life, in New York or L.A., though also he's fine using her Apple Pay on his phone to buy seventy-dollar setting spray and three-hundred-dollar headphones.

In this moment, Janie says, "I'm not feeling sad. I'm feeling slay."

"Ew." Evan looks at her with both pity and affection. "That's not how people say it, and even if it was, you saying it at all is cringe."

* * *

IN LAW SCHOOL, JANIE studied at a café in the Loop where, for over
a year, she was almost certain that the guy behind the counter was
flirting with her. He was her height—5'9"—and looked to be her
age, though he was mostly bald, with a blond beard and blue eyes.
When she ordered her afternoon latte, he'd smile at her so warmly
that it was as if they shared an inside joke she didn't remember,
and she found this warmth unsettling, though less unsettling than
it would have been if she'd thought he was attractive. She learned
at some point that his name was Silas and that he was a graduate
student in Wash U's social work school. This fact alone made her
distrust her hunch that he might be interested in her, because the
social work school was something like ninety-five percent female.
If he were surrounded by all those do-gooder women in class, what
about Janie could be distinct enough to intrigue him? But in February of her third year of law school, when he was passing her latte
over the counter on a Thursday, he said, "Got any exciting plans
for the weekend?"

"Not really," Janie said.

"Have you tried Shish yet?"

This was a newly opened Middle Eastern restaurant off Delmar.
"I've heard of it," Janie said.

"I went the other day, and the baba ghanoush was out of this
world. Maybe we should go sometime." He said this as casually as
he'd said things about the weather or current events over the last
seventeen months, and Janie wasn't certain if he was asking her
out. But also, something about saying *The baba ghanoush was out
of this world* struck her as deeply embarrassing.

"Oh!" she said. "Yeah, maybe."

It occurred to her later in the day, during her Secured Transac-
tions class, that while he wasn't her type, he might be Pippa's.
Pippa liked bearded men, bald men, and short men, all of which
Silas was; as well as potbellied men, older men, and men with for-
eign accents, which Silas wasn't.

He didn't mention the restaurant the next time they saw each other, but he mentioned it the time after that, and that time Janie said it sounded fun and he asked if she was free that weekend and she said not Friday but Saturday around nine and what about a bar instead of the restaurant and he said what if they met at nine on Saturday at O'Flanagan's? Janie felt vaguely conscious of the fact that scheduling a fake date with him, a date shaped by an ulterior motive, was significantly less stressful than scheduling a real date would have been. It was like being in a play.

If everyone had had a phone back then, she might have mentioned in a text that she was bringing Pippa to the bar with her that Saturday. But very few people had phones, so she showed up with Pippa without warning. Silas seemed confused but not necessarily put off—cheerfully confused. She and Pippa sat on one side of the booth, and Silas sat on the other. They ordered a pitcher of beer and discussed movies. Pippa had hated *Saving Private Ryan*, and Silas had really liked *Shakespeare in Love* (Janie had found *Shakespeare in Love* cheesy, but both Pippa and Silas were talking so much that there wasn't an opportunity to express this), and at some point, Janie started drinking water, and Pippa and Silas kept drinking beer. Janie wondered if Silas thought a threesome was in store, or if he'd become more interested in Pippa than in her, or if none of this was sexual at all.

Around eleven, Janie said she was tired and going to head home. She felt proud and dismayed in equal measure that neither Pippa nor Silas attempted to dissuade her and was not surprised when Pippa called her at 8 A.M. the following morning to report that Silas had just left her apartment; they'd had sex three times.

Pippa and Silas continued to sleep together for a few months, until Pippa started hooking up with a professor in the Comp Lit department. During the stretch when Pippa and Silas were having sex, Janie would experience a mild sense of insult when she ordered coffee from Silas and he was as cordial as ever. Then, shortly after spring break, she met David, and she immediately stopped caring about her interactions with the short, bald barista Pippa had slept with. Right away she felt consumed, and desperately hopeful. Meeting David seemed to contain some narrative inevitability, some *life* inevitability, of the marital flavor—because it was the last weeks of grad school for both of them; because she was twenty-seven, meaning the appropriate age for an upper-middle-class American woman in 1999 to meet her husband; because of how he embodied the offhand comments Pippa had made about department store models and teen movie villains; because of how tall he was.

For all these reasons, Janie analyzed their early interactions, phone calls, and emails with great zest and agitation. One Sunday afternoon a week after they'd met, he called her, as shown on her caller ID, but did not leave a message, and she spent forty minutes discussing with Pippa whether to return the call or pretend she hadn't seen it; she ended up going with the latter but calling him that night, as if unaware he'd tried her earlier.

They hung out once a week for three weeks, they had sex the third time they hung out, and two days later, which was just a week before both of their graduation ceremonies, David and some business school friends road-tripped to Louisville to attend the Kentucky Derby. Two facts made Janie especially insecure: The first was that their last contact before he departed, which was the first contact they'd had since having sex, was an email from him saying, in its entirety, *Good to see you last night—D*. The second fact was that among the entourage of road-tripping business school students was a woman named Katherine whom Janie had heard, not from David himself, that he'd dated in the past.

On that Friday afternoon, Janie went for a run around the perimeter of Forest Park, and when she got back to the corner of Lindell and Skinker, she saw Silas walking toward her; this was the first time she'd encountered him outside the coffee shop except for the night at the bar. It was a warm, sunny spring day, and in his right hand, he was carrying a hacky sack.

"I've been meaning to ask," he said when they were a few feet apart, as if they were in the middle of a conversation, "are you moving after your graduation?"

"Yes," she said. "Back to Chicago. I take off May fifteenth." This was two weeks away; she did not, of course, know then that she'd stay in Chicago for only a year before moving to Milwaukee, where David had been hired at a wealth management firm.

"In that case," Silas said, "I guess I'd better ask now, while I still have the chance. Why did you bring a date to our date?" But his tone was teasing, flirty even, rather than accusatory. Something about Silas had always made her self-conscious, even though he wasn't that good-looking, and she had interpreted her self-consciousness as arising from what she suspected was his attraction to her, but for the first time, standing on the street corner, she wondered if it arose from her attraction to him.

Denying his supposition would have been cowardly. And Janie wasn't *not* cowardly, but due to her imminent departure from St. Louis, there didn't seem to be much point in denial.

"I thought you and Pippa would get along," she said, then added, "And I was right, wasn't I?"

"I don't know whether to feel flattered or manipulated."

"Flattered," Janie said. "Pippa is my favorite person."

Agreeably, Silas said, "She is pretty great."

There was a pause, during which the driver of a car trying to turn left on Skinker honked several times at another car, and Janie said, "I'm sorry if you felt manipulated."

He nodded toward her running clothes. "Do you have plans tonight?"

"Tonight?" she repeated. She didn't, because Pippa was taking mushrooms and watching a Miyazaki movie with another of their law school classmates, and Janie didn't do drugs.

"If you're free, why don't we grab dinner?" Silas smiled. "This time, just the two of us."

Later, Janie was unsure to what extent she said yes because she wanted to spend time with Silas and to what extent because she hoped it would lessen her preoccupation with David being in Louisville with the woman he'd dated. "Okay," she said. "But I need to take a shower."

Silas smiled again. "Not for my sake, I hope. I don't mind a little sweat."

"For my sake," Janie said. "But I could meet you in an hour?"

She returned to her apartment, showered, put on black jeans and a pale purple T-shirt, and walked to Shish, the Middle Eastern restaurant with what did turn out to be the best baba ghanoush she'd ever had, though at that point in her life she hadn't had baba ghanoush many times. Approaching Shish, she thought Silas would press her more on why she'd brought Pippa on their date months before, and she prepared a legalistic explanation. But Silas didn't mention Pippa again. From the moment she sat down, the conversation flowed. They discussed her new job, his upcoming summer internship (he had another year left in his program), the respective first concerts they'd attended, and then, more provocatively, their respective first kisses (hers at a so-called girl-boy party in sixth grade, his in seventh grade with his sister's friend Kara, who was two years older). They both drank three glasses of the same white wine, though they never ordered a bottle. As the night wore on, he touched her hand several times across the table, and then somehow, for a few seconds, they were *holding* hands? At the end of the meal, he picked up the check.

On the street, he said, "Can I walk you home?" The night had a strange and warm undercurrent, the undercurrent of being pursued. Also—this was painful to reflect on later, and she reflected on it amply—being pursued by someone actively kind.

Outside her building, which was a ten-minute walk from the restaurant, they stood a few feet apart, still talking. She was, for some reason, describing how her freshman roommate in college had pronounced "bagels" *baggles* when he said, "I really want to kiss you. Would that be okay?"

No one had ever asked, before kissing her, if they could. She said, "Okay," and he stepped forward and their lips touched. She giggled, as she always had since the age of twelve, when kissing a boy or man for the first time.

He pulled his face back a few inches, smiling, and said, "What?"

"I've never kissed anyone with a beard before."

He kissed her again, this time his tongue finding hers. Then, still in that lightly amused way, he said, "And how's it going for you? Beard-wise?"

She laughed. "It's going well." She'd have anticipated that the hair around his mouth would feel bristly, but it was soft. By contrast, David's stubble during their recent kisses had left her lips and skin chapped, even though she was pretty sure he'd shaved each of the days they'd been together.

"What if I come upstairs with you?" Silas said. "And we keep kissing?"

They ended up lying on her bed, on top of the covers, fully clothed for an extremely long time while they kept kissing. The kissing went on forever, and he softly stroked and pinched her nipples over her bra and shirt, ran his palm up the inside of her thighs, over her jeans, and then strategically rubbed his fingers around her zipper. She stuck her hands up the inside of the back of his shirt, and his skin was warm and smooth. Even though she and David had hooked up only three times and had sex once, meaning his body wasn't yet entirely familiar to her, she was conscious of Silas as a much smaller and less muscular man. Shouldn't this have been a turnoff? But she was the one who suggested they remove their shirts. After they had, he kept doing the things he'd been doing before with his fingers over her bra and zipper, until she was beside herself. She removed her bra herself and said, "We should take our pants off. Right?"

"Yes," Silas said. "We should."

A few minutes later, when her underwear was the only remaining article of clothing either of them was wearing, Janie asked, "Are we going to have sex?"

"Well," Silas said, "I'd love to have sex. But it's up to you."

"Do you have a condom?"

"Yes."

"Do you always carry one?"

"No, not always."

Janie laughed again, and Silas said, "You think it's presumptuous I brought one tonight?"

With her right hand, she gestured at the length of their almost-naked bodies. "I think it'd be hard for me to make that argument." Then she squeezed her arms around him and said, "I think it was a good idea."

He kissed her neck, then her chest, between her breasts, then he raised his head and said, "Can I go down on you?"

"Oh," she said. "I don't think I'm drunk enough."

"What does that mean?"

"Or maybe if I take a shower. I could really quickly take a shower."

"Why?"

"So that—you don't think—that I smell gross. Or—that, like, I taste gross." Even as she haltingly said this, she felt a dim awareness of how, though David had not yet tried to go down on her, she wouldn't have explained her hesitation if he had. She understood already that David preferred certain topics left unspoken, though she didn't understand—maybe not for decades—that in fact *she* wasn't a person who preferred it. She could understand why people did, but it always prevented her from feeling close to them.

"I won't think you smell or taste gross," Silas said.

"Give me two minutes. Literally two."

"Janie." Still on top of her, his head raised, he looked intently into her eyes. "Please don't take another shower. I'll like the way you smell and taste. I know I will. Do you know why?"

She shook her head.

"Because I like you."

How was she to know then that this would be the most intensely romantic moment of her life? Which is pathetic, right? But that doesn't make it untrue.

"Seriously," he said, "you'll taste great to me."

At this, she laughed overly loudly, an almost barking laugh, and he said, "Does that make you uncomfortable?"

"No." It kind of did make her uncomfortable, but uncomfortable in a good way.

His mouth at this point remained above her navel, his head hovering, and he lowered it again and kept descending and what happened next was categorically different from anything Janie experienced before or after. He was—what? Just very, very skilled at moving his tongue? At adjusting the pressure and pace and angle so that first she was breathing heavily, then she was hyperventilating, then she'd entered some sort of altered state and was basically screaming, then she knew for certain she was going to come (orgasms tended to be a hit-or-miss enterprise for her), then she had come, in his face, apparently indifferent to how she tasted or smelled, raising her hips and pressing herself against his mouth and chin and nose and grabbing his head.

For a few seconds after this commotion, when she'd resettled on the mattress and his face was essentially resting in her crotch, they both were still, then he scooted back up and was smiling very broadly and said, "That was awesome. Is it okay if I kiss you?"

Kissing at this juncture also seemed potentially gross but, given that decorum already had been suspended, did it matter? They kissed, and she said, "Where did you learn to do that?"

He laughed.

"No, really," she said.

"I guess college," he said.

"Was it your major?"

He laughed again. "It was when I had my first long-term girlfriend."

"Do you want me to . . ." Janie said, then paused, then continued—"do that to you?" He kissed her some more, then he drew back, straddling her, and said, "If I get the condom now—are you okay with that? Because that's what I want."

She nodded, and he stood, pulled the foil square from a pocket of his shorts on the floor, returned to the bed, slid it on while kneeling, and then he was inside her and they were moving together. This act was not categorically different from anything she'd previously experienced. But he made more eye contact than she was accustomed to—all this time, the lights in her bedroom had been off, but a light in the hall had been on—and she continued to rub her hands over his back, and after a couple minutes he began thrusting more forcefully, and then he went still, collapsing onto her, and she was pretty sure but not certain he'd come, and she said, "Did you—?" and he said, "Yes," and he kissed her right shoulder.

After he'd pulled out of her, he walked to the bathroom to dispose of the condom, and she climbed under the covers and he got back in bed and spooned her. They talked for a little while—this time, about how at her elementary school, if you lost a tooth, the nurse would give you a tiny plastic treasure chest to take it home in, and about how these treasure chests were one of her all-time favorite objects ever—and she could feel them both approaching sleep. But after their speaking tapered off, she became more alert while being pretty sure he'd fallen asleep. She lay there for an hour with her eyes open, feeling enormous confusion, and she considered waking him and asking him to leave. She'd do it politely, of course. But then she did fall asleep after all.

She awakened a few minutes after six, by which point a yellow morning light was showing through her thin window blinds. She still was lying with her back to Silas, and he no longer was spooning her, but their calves were touching. She shifted slightly and he rolled against her and wordlessly kissed her back twice. Which was probably the second most romantic gesture of her life, or perhaps just the most generous, immediately saving her from wondering, as she always otherwise did, if the guy regretted things or was going to be distant. In fact, it was she who turned to glance at him and said, "It was fun hanging out—and also—I'm meeting my friend Angela to run at seven—so probably—"

"Do you often run in the afternoon and again the next morning?"

"No, I really am meeting Angela," she said, and she was. "In case you think I'm not."

Silas seemed lightly amused in the same way he had when she'd brought Pippa on their date. "Okay," he said. "Although I do make great pancakes. In addition to making great coffee."

She turned over fully, and their faces were only a few inches apart, and neither of them was smiling or frowning, and maybe her life could have gone in a different direction? But also maybe not? Or maybe they just could have had morning sex, but of course she had hangups about that, too. "I bet you do make great pancakes," she said, and she squeezed one of his hands with one of hers, instead of kissing him. Within five minutes, he was gone from her apartment. They'd hugged by her door.

David returned to St. Louis the next afternoon, called her immediately, was the warmest he'd ever been—he said it would have been fun if she could have come to Louisville—and came over that night. This was the only time Janie had sex with two different men in a forty-eight-hour period, which was unremarkable by the standards of Pippa, who'd had sex with two men simultaneously.

Janie never saw Silas again—she was gone from St. Louis thirteen days later—though it vaguely occurred to her a few times that if he had her number or email, which he didn't, he'd have reached out, or that he probably knew that she knew that he'd be glad to see her if she went by the café. She did not go by the café. And certainly she never mentioned Silas to David, not then or later. She had a strong hunch that if David knew what she'd done, he'd have considered it cheating and ended their relationship.

More notable than not telling David, she didn't tell Pippa; that was how nervous, how superstitious almost, Janie was about wrecking things with David. But also the Silas interlude was just confusing. What was it a story about?

JANIE ASSUMED THAT THERE would be different machinery for the follow-up appointment at the breast center, but it's the same machine, apparently being used in a different way, and even the same room. It's a different technician—last time, it was an Asian woman who looked Janie's age, and this time, it's a white woman who looks about thirty. This tech's breath isn't shockingly bad but it's less minty than you'd expect given her proximity to patients.

When Janie was ten or so, her friend Lynn's mother, who was a real estate agent, told her and Lynn about a man in her office who'd been fired for xeroxing his butt—this was the exact terminology Lynn's mother had used. Janie and Lynn could imagine nothing more amusing or titillating than this anecdote, and they discussed it extensively. Having her tomosynthesis and ultrasound, Janie feels as if her left breast is being xeroxed—squashed against the lit-up window, with Janie holding her breath as the tech instructed, while the mass is scanned, like the sun rising in the west and setting in the east. Unlike with butt xeroxing, both Janie and the machine are upright, frozen in an awkward embrace.

The X-ray takes less than ten minutes, after which the tech waits for Janie to don her borrowed robe and leads her to an exam room, where Janie lies on the paper sheet on a padded table. She is reading emails on her phone when the doctor enters. He looks like he's about fifteen years her junior, and he's not as tall as David—few people are—but he's over six feet, with an air of both athleticism and the unearned confidence that goes along with being tall and athletic. "Dr. Larson," he says when he enters the room. "You're in luck, Jane. You have what's known as an avascular cyst. In layman's terms, just a bump. And it's benign, meaning not harmful. Benign is what you want, and malignant is what you don't want."

"Great," Janie says.

"You should come back in a year for your next mammogram and schedule the 3D kind again because of the density of your breasts. But for today, no worries. Any questions?"

"How common is an avascular cyst?"

He shrugs. "I don't have that data at my fingertips, but upward of forty percent of women have dense breast tissue so that's real common. Are we good?" Before she can answer, he says, "All right then, Jane, you take care."

Even before standing, Janie texts Pippa: *Got results already and all clear!!*

Pippa replies, *Yay!!!!!*

And then: *How you feeling now?*

Like I need to get to the office, Janie types. *But 5 dsts*

After a few seconds, she adds, *Also grateful for my health*

Pippa replies, *Yeah for real,* along with the flexed-bicep emoji, along with three of the straw-hat-with-green-ribbon emojis, and Janie replies with three straw-hat emojis of her own.

It's 9:40, and she has a thirteen-minute drive to her office and a ten o'clock meeting, but even so, as Janie returns in the robe to the changing room where she stored her shirt and jacket in a locker, as she leaves the Helen T. Kensington Breast Center, rides an elevator to the second floor, and enters the parking garage, a little of the hospital's amorphous time clings to her. She climbs into her car, presses the ignition button, starts to back out, then pulls back in and, with the car still running, texts Pippa, *Do you remember that guy Silas the barista?*

Pippa's reply comes immediately—so quickly, in fact, that Janie wonders if Pippa is simultaneously texting her about something else, which often happens. But the text is a response to Janie's question: *Yes of course, so sad*

There's something I never told you, Janie types, but then she registers the second part of Pippa's reply, deletes the words she typed, and replaces them with, *Sad why?*

Pippa replies, *You know he died right?*

Janie: What?? When? And how

Pippa: 3ish years ago? Or 5? Before pandemic

Pippa: Hit and run while he was biking

Janie: Where did he live

Pippa: Stayed in STL. Were you in touch? I never saw him after grad school, just FB friends

Janie: I was never in touch with him, not even social media

Janie: Wow

Janie: About death

Janie: That's awful

Janie: Also

Janie: There's something I never told you

Janie: I had sex with him right around the time we graduated (!!!)

Janie: After you guys had ended things

Janie: But some David overlap

Pippa sends three of the laugh-crying emojis, then: *Bravo*

Pippa: OK please tell me he went down on you bc he was an oral savant

Janie: He went down on me

Pippa sends three party-hat emojis

Pippa: Am I right

Janie: Weirdly reassured you think this because to me he was a savant but you have more expertise

Pippa: Oh no he was a savant. Best ever

Pippa: And a sweet guy too

Janie: Yeah he was sweet.

Janie: Did he become a social worker

There's a delay, then a link to his obituary arrives, which she reads quickly: He died on September 17, 2018, at the age of forty-eight. (Forty-eight!) He received a bachelor of arts from the University of Nebraska in political science and government, and a master of social work from Washington University in St. Louis. He then worked for the next twenty years with immigrant communities in St. Louis, especially unauthorized immigrants. He is survived by his wife, Stephanie, and their two children, Kyra and Pete, who were thirteen and fifteen in 2018, meaning, Janie calculates, eighteen and twenty as she reads—two and four years older than Evan. In lieu of flowers, donations could be made to the nonprofit where he was working at the time of his death.

Ugh, she texts Pippa. *Life is so sad*

True, Pippa replies.

And so confusing, Janie adds.

Also true, Pippa replies.

On a lighter note

I decided I'm going to that woman Gwen's party

To determine if I still think she should go fuck herself

Janie replies with just one laugh-crying emoji, along with *Or if she thinks you should*

WHAT IS THIS A story about?

In the parking garage, Janie turns the wrong way, away from the exit, which proves to be a surprisingly difficult mistake to reverse. (Or would it not be difficult at all, the only thing she'd need to do would be pull into an empty parking space and back out again, but some combination of inertia and momentum causes her to simply keep driving forward?) Either way: She parked on the second level, and she's soon on the third level, then the fourth, the fifth, and she's still going.

Is it a story about the randomness of good and bad fortune?

About how long she spent conflating luck and privilege?

About the consequences of building a life on a twenty-seven-year-old's status markers?

About how foolish a person would have to be to marry someone she never really enjoyed kissing?

Or perhaps it's a story about how precious it is to deeply adore two people in the world, even if neither of them is your spouse, and to share part of every day with them? Isn't this, after all, two more people than anyone is guaranteed?

At last, Janie emerges from the darkness of the parking garage's lower levels onto its roof, where she can simply make a half circle in order to begin descending back to the street. It's a cold winter morning, and she blinks several times, surprised by how bright and blue the sky is.

THE TOMORROW BOX

The email from Michael Kinnick arrived in the afternoon, while I was teaching Postcolonial Perspectives to seniors, and I saw it when I returned to my office before sixth period. Michael would be doing an event in the area the following week, he'd written, and wondered if I'd be free to get a drink. I experienced a few seconds of astonishment—I'd had so little contact with Michael since he'd become famous, and none at all for the last twenty years, that I'd assumed I was no longer a person he knew. That we apparently did still know each other prompted a somewhat embarrassing rush of pride in me, along with curiosity and a mild apprehension.

Any potential musings about the past were, however, cut short by a call from the school nurse: My daughter, Isabel, was complaining of a stomachache. As it happened, the nurse's office was about a hundred yards from the desk where I presently sat. My wife, children, and I were known as the Green Hills Academy One Car Family because that was how the four of us arrived on campus each morning, before dispersing: Isabel to a first grade classroom; her brother, Drew, to a fourth grade one; Val to the middle school building to teach biology; and I to the upper school to teach English. Green Hills was one of those third-tier K-12 private schools that considered itself second-tier, and its survival was never completely assured from one academic year to the next. It also was the school I had graduated from in 1985, when my father was the headmaster.

I texted Val to ask if she could deal with Isabel, and Val immediately texted back that she and her seventh graders were about to go collect water samples from the creek behind the athletic fields. I hurried to my AP Literature and Composition class, for which the assigned reading had been *The Metamorphosis,* and told the students to pull out a paper and pen and write a paragraph imagining the insect or animal into which they might wake one morning to find themselves transformed. Then I ran (literally) from the English and History wing to the nurse's office, which was located next to the lower school gym. The nurse's name was Sharon, and after I greeted her (her medical assessment of the situation was "No fever, so it could be something she ate"), I found Isabel lying atop a paper sheet on the vinyl-upholstered cot in the inner room.

"What's up, Coconut?" I said.

Isabel looked at me grimly—she had deep brown eyes and a thick curtain of blond bangs—and said, "We should go home." The surety of her tone made me suspicious; when truly sick, she was lethargic and compliant.

"What's the problem?" I asked.

"My stomach hurts," she said. "Can we go?" She was standing as she spoke, reaching for the enormous Spider-Man backpack that had been resting on the floor near the cot.

"I have to teach right now, and so does Mommy, so you can either stay here or come hang out in my office without me."

"Your office," she said immediately.

It was questionably appropriate to leave her unattended, but less than forty minutes remained in the school day, and she really didn't seem that sick. We said goodbye to Sharon, and as Isabel and I walked together back to the upper school, I said, "What did you have for lunch?" The cafeteria had served spaghetti, meatballs, and garlic bread; in general, the lunches, which were almost identical to those I'd eaten as a student four decades prior, were one of the ways the school's third-tier status displayed itself. Also in the Pioneer Valley, about twenty minutes away, was a first-tier K-12 school known for farm-to-table organic meals. Some teachers and students at Green Hills Academy saw this other school as our rival, but I knew the other school didn't even pay us the respect of considering the enmity mutual.

Instead of answering my question, Isabel said, "Did you know the deepest place on Earth is the Mariana Trench? It's in the Pacific Ocean."

"That sounds familiar," I said.

"Every inch of water that presses down on you weighs fifteen thousand pounds."

"Did Liberty tell you that?" Liberty was a boy in Isabel's class who shared tidbits that were often interesting, sometimes unsettling, and frequently not true: that zero was the highest number or that wearing a ring on your thumb was bad luck or that if you said the word "hell," the land beneath you would part and swallow you whole.

"He didn't make it up," Isabel said. "He showed me in a library book."

"While I teach, I'll leave my phone with you, and you can play Penguin Spree but nothing else. Okay? If you need to throw up, do it in the trash can, and if you need me, come out of my office and turn right, which is toward the cafeteria, and it's four doors down on the same side of the hall as the girls' bathroom, but only come in if you *really* need me."

Disdainfully, Isabel said, "Daddy, I know where your classroom is."

After I returned to them, my students read aloud their *Metamorphosis*-inspired paragraphs. A boy named Billy went first.

"As I swim across the swampy waters, bubbles explosively rise around me," he intoned. "For I am a hippopotamus, and I have just expelled an enormous fart."

IT WAS NEARLY FIVE-THIRTY by the time the Green Hills Academy One Car Family got home. I put water on to boil while Val pulled out the packaged lettuce; for the sake of simplicity, we have a fixed eating schedule, and Tuesdays are always hot dogs and salad. It was March, soon after spring break, and Val and I both coached lacrosse—me varsity boys, her varsity girls—meaning I'd had to find childcare for Isabel during practice. Normally, Isabel and Drew went to aftercare in the cafeteria, but at the end of AP Lit and Comp, I'd pulled aside a student named Brittany and asked if she'd mind sitting in my office and keeping an eye on Isabel. In addition to not playing a spring sport, Brittany was the one student in the four classes I taught who read for pleasure. That virtually no teenager I knew read books outside of school wasn't, admittedly, a tragedy, though it did make me worry in a nebulous way. I myself had been a high school lacrosse star named Andrew Hooke Wofford IV, but I'd also been a voracious reader, and even though I grew up to be a man who named his son Andrew Hooke Wofford V, I suspected I was much less of a jackass than I'd have been if during my adolescence I'd spent the half hour before bed watching TikTok.

Within twenty minutes of arriving home, Val, Drew, Isabel, and I were all sitting at the kitchen table, we'd gotten through petals and thorns, I was on my second hot dog, and we were deep into a debate about whether each of us would prefer to take a bath in a giant tub of tomato sauce or mashed-up avocados. Isabel and Val are extremely talkative, much more so than Drew and I are, and our dinners are the great happiness of my life. I speak the least, and—perhaps this is because I didn't get married until I was in my forties—there's never a night when I don't marvel that these are the three people I ended up with: fierce and opinionated Isabel; sensitive, considerate Drew; and funny, fearless Val, who at thirty-eight is fourteen years younger than I. By the time I was thirty, I was surprised to find myself still single—I was average in many ways, and moderately handsome, and aren't average, moderately handsome men exactly the kind who marry?—but I also couldn't picture marrying any of the women I'd dated up to that point. This continued to be true for another decade, a stretch during which I experienced intermittent confusion about whether I had unrealistic marital expectations and/or whether there might be some invisible but crucial thing wrong with me. Then I met Val and was crazy about her right away, smitten with her sporty, mischievous confidence. She had just started teaching at the prep school in New Hampshire where I worked, and given the age difference between us, I did wonder, after we began going for runs or to movies together, if I seemed to her like an old man, maybe even a mentor. She was the one who kissed me first, after we completed a twenty-mile loop in the rain on our mountain bikes.

At the kitchen table, Val said, "Avocados have what are called fatty acids and antioxidants in them, both of which are actually soothing for your skin, but tomatoes have citric and malic acids, which are irritants." She winked at me and said, "Have I ever mentioned that I wrote my master's thesis on full-body food immersion?"

After dinner, as the children were clearing the plates, I finally said to Val, "I got an email today from Michael Kinnick."

She smirked. "You mean Anus?"

From the sink, Drew looked at us with consternation and said, "Doesn't 'anus' mean—" No doubt to spare his sister, who had little interest in being spared, he didn't finish the question. The previous year, when the four of us were getting ready to go to church on Christmas, Isabel had stood at the top of the steps yelling, "Wearing tights is bullshit!" and Drew, who'd been waiting in the living room with me, had said, "Can you ask her not to swear? It's inappropriate for a kindergartener."

In the kitchen, with great urgency, Isabel said, "What does 'anus' mean? Tell me what it means!"

Matter-of-factly, Val said, "It means butthole."

Isabel's tone was one of delight as she said, "And that's some-one's *name?*"

"It's someone's nickname," I said.

"But the person doesn't know it," Val added.

"That's not very nice," Drew said, and Val looked at me archly.

"He's doing an event in Springfield, and he asked if I'd like to get together on Wednesday night when he's finished," I said.

"What does he want from you?" Val asked, and when I laughed, she said, "I mean, besides the pleasure of your company. I'm sure your rich and famous friend wants to see you, but why is he reaching out *now?*"

The same question had, of course, occurred to me. I said, "Maybe he's trying to reconnect with Camille."

Val squinted. "Through you?" Back when Michael and I had been part of the same friend group, he had had a thing for a girl named Camille, who, as it happened, had had a thing for me. Ca-mille had ended up marrying someone else, but the previous fall, after her youngest child started college, she'd filed for divorce. "Wouldn't he just get in touch with her directly?" Val was saying.

"How rich is your friend?" Drew said. "Does he have a million dollars?"

"He has many millions of dollars," I said.

"I bet he wants to buy you that car," Isabel said. The other night, she and I had looked online at Aston Martins—informationally, not acquisitionally, as an Aston Martin is not a thing we'd be able to afford.

"Don't forget to put the night you're seeing him on the calen-dar," Val said.

"Anus definitely doesn't want to buy me a car," I said. Isabel giggled, and I added, "I mean Michael."

IF YOU'D ASKED ME when I was a student at Middlebury who among my classmates was the likeliest person to become famous, it's an understatement to say I wouldn't have named Michael Kinnick. Even if you'd given me ten guesses, or a hundred, he wouldn't have crossed my mind. Middlebury wasn't big, and we were both English majors, so by the time we were seniors, we'd taken easily a half dozen classes together. If not for all that happened afterward, however, I might not have even remembered him. He came across as unremarkable and a bit awkward, but not grotesquely so. He was skinny and wore aviator glasses—not with any apparent irony or coolness—and my main actual memory is of a time when, for a British poetry survey, he and a very pretty girl named Lawrence and I were put into a small discussion group and he was talking rapidly about the "aesthetics" of Romanticism and repeatedly pronouncing it *as-tetics*. I simultaneously understood that he was trying to impress Lawrence, that she was not impressed, and that, like me, she knew he was mispronouncing the word. I rarely saw Michael outside of class. I played lacrosse, and he was a reporter for the student newspaper, and I'm tempted to say he didn't attend many parties, but maybe I just didn't notice when he did.

During my senior year, my friends James and Thatcher and I decided that after graduation, we'd move to Breckenridge, Colorado, for a year, mainly to ski, though we planned to get nominal jobs as waiters or in retail. Thatcher's parents owned a house out there that we could live in rent-free, and although I'd wondered if my own parents would object to the plan—as a school headmaster, my dad was known for waking at 3:45 A.M. in order to get a jump on the day—they didn't protest. I was considered a good kid, I'd worked hard in the classroom and in sports for almost my entire life, and I think they figured I deserved a break.

That final spring at Middlebury, shortly before graduation, Michael Kinnick approached me one day in the library. He said he'd been hired for an internship at the *Denver Post*, he'd heard I also was headed to the area, and we should connect once we both were there. Although I didn't feel enthusiasm about the possibility, it seemed unnecessary to discourage him. This was before cellphones or even email, plus Denver and Breckenridge were an hour and a half apart in good weather.

But Michael did follow up. Somehow he got the number of Thatcher's parents' house, he called, and, because this seemed easiest, I invited him to join us for a barbecue on a Saturday night in late June. After almost three weeks in town, my friends and I hadn't yet landed jobs—it turned out Breckenridge was much quieter and slower in the summer than the winter—though we'd already managed to go fly-fishing, golfing, and mountain biking. Also, I'd smoked more pot since arriving than in the previous twenty-two years.

Thatcher's parents' house was eight bedrooms, with a two-story great room and a hot tub on the massive deck facing Quandary Peak. From the deck, where the grill was located, I could see Michael park in the driveway below—he drove a white Ford hatchback—and even from that distance, something seemed different about him. The difference was confirmed as he climbed the deck staircase, holding a six-pack, and said to me, "Hey, Andy." Nodding at the others present, he said, "Hey, everyone else." In addition to Thatcher and James, whom Michael hadn't known at Middlebury, there were three girls we'd met while golfing and a friend of Thatcher's named Will who'd also grown up vacationing in Breckenridge.

Michael looked better—tanner, fitter—and carried himself with a new confidence. As he set his beer on a table, opened a can, then began shaking hands, casually introducing himself, I realized in retrospect, as soon as it wasn't there anymore, that he'd previously had a habit of saying something and waiting to see what you thought of it—if you laughed, if you agreed—as if your reaction determined his reality. That weird hesitation, that watchfulness, was gone. I also realized, when it didn't happen, that I'd been mildly nervous that James and Thatcher would think Michael was a loser and either be kind of dickish to him or razz me about having invited him to join us. While Thatcher grilled burgers and we all ate them, Michael described the articles he'd been working on for his newspaper internship: a gas line had exploded and burned down an apartment complex; a former UC Boulder basketball Hall of Famer had opened a pizza restaurant; a black bear had been spotted frolicking on the equipment at a suburban playground. The three girls—cousins named Jess and Nicole and Nicole's friend Camille, all of them just graduated from Colorado College—asked him questions and laughed at his anecdotes about conducting interviews and being edited. That is, it turned out that not only was Michael not a pain in the ass but that, living somewhere else, having an actual job and stories to tell about it, he injected a fresh energy into our group. He stayed over that night—there were, after all, plenty of bedrooms—and from that point on, the pattern of his coming to hang out with us had been established. I was more than okay with this arrangement. I probably wouldn't have put it this way at the time, but I got to feel beneficent toward Michael while also taking a kind of implicit credit for bringing a cool person into our fold.

We all did eventually get jobs, me as a so-called manny for a family with three sons under the age of six; Michael's internship with the *Post* became a permanent position. Also during this time, the girls and guys in the group hooked up in so many permutations of heterosexual coupledom that Nicole once joked about our collectively being a Love Octagon, which soon gave way to us referring to ourselves as just the Octagon. There was a time when I assumed Camille and Michael had become a couple, but once when he and I went to pick up pizza, he confided that though they'd slept in the same bed several times recently, she wouldn't do more than kiss him and had told him the previous night that she just didn't picture them together. He said, "Do you think—is there something specific that if I did it differently, she'd be more . . . ?"

He was driving, and he looked over at me and added, "I know you've had a lot of girlfriends."

"I'm not sure anyone ever knows what they're doing," I said. "Especially in the beginning."

That relationship never achieved liftoff—my non-advice, I trust, didn't help matters—and, a few months later, I was asleep for the night when Camille, whom I had never previously been physically involved with, climbed on top of me, over the covers, completely naked, and awakened me by lifting my hands and setting my palms on her bare breasts. Though I remember this night fondly, she and I never officially dated, either. There was another girl I was interested in then, someone outside the Octagon, who worked with James at the front desk of a hotel. Again, I likely wouldn't have admitted it at the time, but the fact that I still did better with girls than Michael did might have preserved my fondness for him, or maintained what I saw as an appropriate status difference.

Somewhere in the middle of all this, maybe twenty months into my time in Colorado, Michael mentioned that he'd pitched an article to a men's magazine in New York and an editor had accepted it. The article was about all the ways that Denver was becoming the next Seattle, and when it was published, he was so excited that he drove out to Breckenridge on a weeknight to show us the issue. The article took up a third of a page, including the photo of a local band. I don't remember what month it was, but it must have been cold because we had a fire going in the massive stone fireplace, and I remember being just a few feet from it as we toasted Michael, tapping our beer cans together.

I stayed in Breckenridge for three years—not one—and in the summer of 1992, I moved back East to attend law school at Vanderbilt, where, to my surprise, I lasted just one semester. I'd thought of myself as good at reading and writing, but I was alienated by the contorted formality of legal language; I also found Nashville hick, which I made the mistake of expressing to a few Southern classmates. After Christmas of that year, I didn't return to Tennessee, remaining instead at my parents' house, which was on the Green Hills Academy campus. Although I began assistant-coaching the boys' lacrosse team, that spring was a low point for me. I had thought that my time in Colorado was the preamble to my real adulthood, but for a few months there, I feared I wasn't cut out for real adulthood. Fortunately, my father connected me with a friend of his who worked at a placement firm for independent schools and helped me find a job as an English teacher at a boys' boarding school in New Hampshire called Bolton Prep. *This* was my real adulthood—it turned out that I loved teaching, that I connected easily with both the students and the other faculty members (not surprising given that independent schools were in my blood), and that the rhythms of campus felt organic. Fourteen years later, Bolton Prep was where I met Val.

A few years into my time as a teacher, Thatcher called me one Saturday in my dorm apartment—by this point, he was an analyst at a hedge fund in San Francisco—and said, "Stop whatever you're doing and get your hands on a copy of *Details* magazine."

This time, Michael's article was considerably longer—eight magazine pages—and written in the first person. In it, he recounted his dating struggles, including not losing his virginity until after graduating from college (though I hadn't known this, the detail didn't particularly surprise me, and perhaps explained some of Camille's reluctance with him) and how he'd seen a method for seducing women advertised on late-night television and ordered the instruction kit. He'd begun implementing the techniques; found them to be successful; used them for a period of several months, during which he had multiple sexual partners; experienced pride, even euphoria, that was gradually replaced with uneasiness; and ultimately admitted to himself what he'd recognized from the beginning, which was that he was using hypnosis on the women. He was suggesting dates in quiet areas of parks rather than bars; speaking to women in a calm, soothing way; encouraging them to relax their breathing and their bodies. He was now renouncing all of this, he wrote, apologizing publicly and privately to the women he'd been involved with, and starting anew. He wanted to live a life of total honesty, and if being the person he was repelled women, so be it.

When I called Thatcher back, the first thing I said was "Holy shit."

"I didn't even know hypnosis was real," Thatcher said.

"I'm not convinced it is," I said. "What if it's just him paying close attention to these women's moods, and that's what they're responding to?"

Thatcher laughed. "Is that all it takes?"

"The thing that's so weird to me," I said, "is him just letting it all hang out. Even if you take this at face value, why would anyone want to talk about their emotional crisis in public?"

All these years later, my own question seems quaint to me, and indeed, Michael was part of, or perhaps even anticipated, a kind of cultural candor that, as far as I can see, has increased exponentially. Though no one used the term then, the article went viral. Michael, who was still working for the *Denver Post,* appeared on multiple morning news and talk shows. A day or two after reading the article, I emailed him to say congratulations and was startled when he called me fifteen minutes later, surprised that he wasn't busy being famous. We chatted about what the other members of the Octagon were up to—the only person other than Michael still in Colorado was James—and Michael said that he'd been in conversations with editors at a few magazines in New York about staff positions there. If he moved to the East Coast, he said, he'd love to visit me sometime on campus. This visit never happened, though within a few weeks he'd been hired at a New York magazine as a columnist, a perch that then seemed incredible to me in its prestige.

From there, his success and cultural prominence only grew. He continued to push the total honesty thing, and it became a catchphrase for him, referred to in the column as TotalHonesty (in light of his having been both an English major and a legitimate journalist, I found the absence of a space between the two words amusing). He often appeared on TV, he wrote several books in quick succession that were marketed as life guides for men in their twenties and thirties—*TotalHonesty* was followed by *TotalPurpose, TotalHealth,* and *TotalSex*—and they were all enormous bestsellers. Within a few years, he'd left the magazine and was leading one-day seminars and weekend retreats attended by thousands. And apparently, instead of repelling women, his honesty attracted them, because he dated several actresses and models. At James's wedding, which was in 1997, Michael attended with his then-girlfriend, a woman who'd just been nominated for a Best Supporting Actress Oscar. During those years, weddings were the only time I saw Michael, and in fact Nicole's wedding on December 31, 1999, back in Breckenridge, was the last time I'd seen him in person. By then, I was accustomed to the frisson of people noticing him, murmuring about him, and when he and I were talking by the cheese table at the reception, a few other guests approached to say things like "Love your books!" or "When will you have a TV show of your own?"

I suppose that talking to him was still normal enough. In the nineties, he had a soul patch, but he wasn't some kind of gigantic asshole, wasn't an aggressive name-dropper. He'd ask me about teaching, or if I was seeing anyone—living on an isolated prep school campus in my late twenties and early thirties, I was dating less than ever—and it certainly wasn't his fault that interacting with him caused me to make unflattering comparisons between him and myself.

By then, we'd all been referring to him as Anus for years. It had started following that phone conversation I'd had with him after his first big article came out, when I'd sent an email to Camille that said, *I just spoke to Famous Amos (aka Michael), and he asked a lot about you. I think he's still carrying a torch.*

Thanks but no thanks, Camille emailed back. *I'm good with Thomas.* This was the man she later married and divorced.

Among the Octagon in diaspora, Famous Amos quickly morphed into Famous Anus and then just Anus. I don't take responsibility. I was the one who set the nickname in motion, yes, and I certainly used it, but I didn't force its evolution.

AFTER HER VISIT TO the nurse's office, Isabel seemed fine for the next few days, and then, one night around eleven o'clock, I heard her call for me. I was downstairs reading. Val usually goes to bed soon after our kids do, and I stay up in the living room, grading, then reading for class, then reading for pleasure. Even if it takes a month to get through a novel, the ritual still anchors me, the access to lives I'll never live.

Isabel's bedroom is the first one at the top of the steps, and when I entered it, she said, "My stomach hurts."

I sat on the edge of her twin bed. "The same way as before or different?"

"What if you got stuck in the Mariana Trench and you couldn't get out?"

"What if *I* did or what if a person did?"

"What if Mommy did?"

I pulled my phone from a pocket of the fleece jacket I was wearing, and after I'd typed *Mariana Trench* into it, I skimmed the results. "There's no chance that Mommy or I will go there," I said. "Only a few humans have ever been. You need incredibly complicated scientific equipment."

"Are there fish?"

I glanced again at the web page and said, "Not like we think of them. It says here maybe sea cucumbers." I clicked on a link and held my phone toward her, even though Val doesn't like for them to be exposed to screens around bedtime. But the image resembled a sweet potato with fur and antennae—it was almost cute—and I thought it would calm Isabel. She took my phone and scrutinized the photo with a serious expression.

When she looked up, she said, "When I'm a grown-up, can I still live with you and Mommy?"

"Sure."

"Are you afraid of dying because you're so old?"

If Val and Drew had been present, I might have laughed, or if it had been day instead of night. But Isabel was earnest, and I replied in that spirit. "Death is a natural part of the life cycle, and we don't need to be afraid of it," I said. "But I'm lucky that I'm very healthy, and I don't think I'll die anytime soon." She looked unconvinced, and I added, "Do you know what I do sometimes when it's time for me to sleep and my mind is thinking about things? I imagine a shoebox with the word 'Tomorrow' on the top of it, and I imagine writing what I'm worried about on a piece of paper and setting it inside the box. That way, I can think about it tomorrow, and in the meantime I can relax and go to sleep."

She still was holding my phone, and her expression was still serious, as she said, "Can I play Penguin Spree?"

"Not now," I said.

ON THE DAY I was supposed to meet Michael, I texted Camille from my office during my free second period. I typed *Having a drink tonight w/* then paused, then typed *Anus*. I added, *How are you?*

I know, she texted back.

You know from him? In the end, I had been the member of the Octagon who stayed in touch the least not just with Michael but with everyone; I'd had my kids after they all did, and I'd gotten lost in the daily busyness of life. Camille was the only one I communicated with from one year to the next, and that was on her initiative.

Yeah from him, she texted. *I'm doing OK.* She had become an interior designer and lived in Dallas, where her now-ex-husband was from. I'd once described to Val the time Camille had climbed atop me naked in the middle of the night as a high-water mark of my sex life, one I wouldn't mind Val re-creating if the moment ever presented itself, and Val had gamely done so on a few occasions. I'd also made sure to convey that, this encounter notwithstanding, I hadn't been romantically interested in Camille. Val had appeared almost insultingly unthreatened; she'd joked that if Michael had liked Camille and Camille had liked me, then by the transitive property she, Val, could be married to a world-famous life coach and writer.

I texted Camille, *I actually wondered if Anus was reaching out to me as a way to get to you.*

Like romantically? Camille added the emoji that was crying with laughter.

It's not so far-fetched, I texted. *You're both single, right?*
I don't think Anus dates women in their 50s.

Neither of us typed anything for a minute—I wondered if she was thinking about the fact that I hadn't ended up with a woman my own age, either—then she added, *Have fun tonight.*

THE PRICE OF THE seminar Michael held on the day we were meeting, I learned online, was $550, though apparently the tickets were tiered, with $800 ones allowing attendance at a bonus after-lunch talk on TotalPurpose Expanded, and $1,200 offering access to an intimate happy hour. Which, from a certain perspective, meant that, in having a drink with Michael for free, I was saving $1,200.

Michael's events were occurring at a big midlevel hotel in Springfield, but he was staying twenty minutes north, at an inn where the cheapest room cost $420 a night. I knew this because I'd looked into booking one as a surprise for Val for our tenth anniversary. I hadn't done it—she'd have been unhappy about the expense—but I supposed the figure didn't seem like much when just one seminar ticket covered the entire amount, with plenty left over.

At 9 P.M., the lobby of the inn was mostly empty, with no one sitting on the luxurious furniture or near the stone fireplace not dissimilar to the one in Thatcher's parents' house in Breckenridge; beyond the fireplace was a bar. A man behind a desk that was separate from the reception desk asked when I entered the lobby if I was a guest, and I said, "No, but I'm meeting my friend Michael Kinnick."

"Wonderful," the concierge said. "And your name is?"

"Andy Wofford."

I wondered if he was about to check with, say, Michael's assistant—and I can't lie, the humiliation would have been grimly satisfying if the concierge couldn't confirm my identity and kicked me out, the external enactment of what felt internally true—but instead the man said, "Mr. Wofford, may I get you something to drink?"

"If you've got a lager on tap, that would be great," I said. "Thanks."

Within thirty seconds, this was set on the table beside the seat I'd taken in a huge plaid armchair. I pulled out my phone and began reading *The New York Times*—I was actually a little nervous—and ten minutes later, a familiar voice said, "That guy looks a lot like Andy Wofford."

Michael was standing in front of me, not skinny now but athletically slim, wearing a white button-down shirt and tight, tapered mustard-colored pants that looked leather but probably weren't because he was a vegan. (I had worn my darkest jeans, nicest sneakers, and, under my fleece jacket, what Val mocks me for thinking is my coolest T-shirt, which has a graphic of a record on it.) I stood and said, "Hey, man, long time no see."

He hugged me for about five seconds longer than felt necessary—there's a type of man who does this, seemingly to demonstrate that he's comfortable doing so—then cocked his head and said, "Should we sit in the bar?" There did indeed seem to be an assistant-type person with him, a young woman in a pants suit who left after he said to her, without introducing me, "I'll hang out here for an hour, then text you about the charts."

In the bar, he ordered hot water with lemon—I vaguely recalled reading somewhere that he was a teetotaler—and after the waiter left, he said, "Thanks for making time to see me."

"Absolutely," I said. "Likewise. How'd it go today?"

"Really good," he said. "Really invigorating."

"How often do you do these things?" I asked.

"Less than I used to. A few years ago, I was burning the candle at both ends, and I had to pull back. Just take some time and re-group. So now I do a month of travel, a month at home, a month of travel, and so on."

"You're based in L.A.?"

"I've got a place in Malibu, kind of a beach house that's actually pretty small, so I try to decamp for my ranch in Ojai as often as possible."

This might have been a kind of East Coast provincialism, but I had never learned the geography of Southern California, and none of the place-names meant anything to me except that I suspected they were fancy. I said, "Is that like a ranch-ranch or a gentleman's ranch?"

He smiled. "Andy, I always wanted you to think of me as a gentleman." After a pause, he added, "No, but I've got a recording studio up there, and that's where I do the podcast, so I guess it's more of a gentleman's ranch. Not a whole lot of horses or cows, though the housekeeper's daughter does keep a few chickens."

Since laying eyes on him—or perhaps even since receiving his email—I'd felt a confusion about whether I was supposed to or not supposed to acknowledge his massive fame; I wished I had asked Val's advice ahead of time. In this moment, I said, "Seriously, congratulations on . . . well, everything. It's been amazing to watch from afar."

"I appreciate that, Andy." He brought his palms together and bowed his head. "Humble thanks." When he looked up, he said, "And how are you? Crazy that you're headmaster of a school now."

"No, no," I said. "I'm back at the school where my dad was the headmaster, but I'm just an English teacher."

"Ah, got it."

"It wasn't—I didn't really see administration as my path. Like, I didn't choose that. But things are good. I've got a seven-year-old daughter and a ten-year-old son, and my wife, Val, is also a teacher at the school."

Michael was nodding, gazing at me intensely. "Fabulous," he said. "It sounds like you're in a really positive space."

I chuckled. "I don't know about fabulous, but you know—not bad."

A tiny silence ensued, in which I could swear I glimpsed his gawky college self; there was some shifting of his body in the chair, some slipping of his serenely intense mask. "Can I ask you something?" he said. "And please be honest."

"Well, sure," I said. "TotalHonesty, right?" I smiled, but his expression was serious.

"Have you read any of my books?"

"You know, I've always meant to, but as an English teacher, I'm either reading Faulkner or Hurston or what have you. Or, when I get downtime, I'm more of a contemporary fiction guy."

"So no?"

"I've always been really curious," I said, and his still-somber expression seemed to reject my attempts to glide us past this awkwardness.

"Again," he said, "no wrong answer—have you ever listened to the podcast?"

"I was planning to between when you emailed me and tonight. Because I know you have millions of fans around the world, and I'm sure it's not for nothing. I'm sure it's deserved. But I lead one of those lives that's held together by duct tape and prayers. I won't bore you with the details, but I don't have a lot of time to myself these days."

He said nothing, and I said, "Remind me how long the podcast has been airing?"

"Five years."

"Well, I need to get on that, don't I? It's high time."

Soberly, he said, "I get that having young kids is consuming, but I just wonder—did I do something to offend you?"

"Oh gosh, no," I said. "Not at all."

"I've always wondered why you didn't invite me to your wedding," he said, "especially when not only was everyone else from the Octagon invited, but if I'm not mistaken, James and Thatcher were your groomsmen . . ."

If his tone had been different, I might have thought he was joking. I was so surprised that I couldn't think of what to say. Then, after a few seconds, I told the truth. "I didn't think you'd want to come. I mean, I got married so late"—it had been in 2008—"and you were just *so* famous by then."

"But everyone values their old friends."

"We hadn't been in touch for a few years, and I just figured— I don't know. I assumed you were busy or, if you came, other guests would come up to you and annoy you by asking for your autograph. And by 'other guests' I might mean my dad—he became quite a fan of yours before he passed away."

"Wasn't that my decision to make? What would or wouldn't annoy me?"

"Listen," I said. "Absolutely, if I'd known you wanted to come, I would have invited you."

"I always looked up to you," Michael said, and when I laughed, he said, "I'm serious. You were nice, and so many people at Middlebury were such snobs."

Did I agree with either part of that assessment? I wasn't sure.

"I don't know if you know this," he said, "but I was the first person in my family to go to college. I was salutatorian of my public high school in Mechanicsburg, Pennsylvania, and then I get to Middlebury, and it seemed like most of the kids already knew each other from their boarding schools. I was such a fish out of water. I didn't even know how to ski."

"For what this is worth," I said, "I'm WASPy in the technical sense, but I don't come from a lot of money. I'm a swamp Yankee."

"Compared to people who do come from a lot of money, maybe you don't," he said. "But compared to the general population— I mean, did you take out student loans?"

"No, but only because my grandfather had set aside money for my brother and sister and me for our college educations."

"You mean a trust fund," he said, and for the first time in several minutes, he was smiling, though not warmly.

"It wasn't remotely the kind of trust fund people mean when they talk about trust funds," I said, and then I heard myself and said, "Okay, point taken."

Michael was looking away as he said, "In college, it took me so long to get up to speed socially that by the time I understood the rules, it was over. That's why the way a lot of people feel about being undergrads, the sentimentality they have—that's how I feel about my time in Colorado and the Octagon. When I was in Denver and you guys were in Breckenridge, that's the time where I really experienced that closeness with others. When you become a public person, the closeness is hard to find because a lot of times people want something from you. But that period was relaxed, it was fun, my professional success was around the corner. In some ways, looking back, it's like I had a hunch it was coming. Anyway—you were my entrée into the Octagon, obviously. You gave your Andy good guy seal of approval, and that showed everyone else I was okay."

Was this TotalHonesty? Was it true? Did it matter if it was? And how might the sentiments he was expressing be affected by knowing that I and the others in the Octagon had been referring to him by a synonym for *butthole* for two decades? "That's really nice to hear," I said. "Thank you. And I'm sure everyone in my family is asleep now, but if you find yourself back in this neck of the woods, you're more than welcome to come meet my wife and kids. Better late than never, huh?"

"Apropos of the whole late-in-life dad thing, I've been talking to a surrogate," he said. "I'm guessing you know I haven't yet married or had children, but they're both on my bucket list, even if I do fatherhood solo."

He was thinking of becoming a single dad at the age of fifty-two or fifty-three? This struck me as nuts. Yes, I had a seven-year-old and a ten-year-old, but I also had a thirty-eight-year-old wife. In our first few minutes together, I'd felt a wish to write down the things Michael said that most fulfilled my expectations of him, so that I could accurately repeat them to Val—calling his seminar "invigorating," casually referring to his ranch's recording studio or his housekeeper's daughter—but then some fakeness had burned off the conversation, and this impulse had dissipated. Now he once again seemed to me like a weird famous person.

I said, "Fatherhood is something else. There's nothing quite like it."

"The way you're looking at me right now—do you think I'm crazy?"

Maybe if I'd ever read one of his books, listened to his podcast, or attended his seminar, it would have seemed worth the effort of being honest. Instead I said, "Not at all, not at all. The older I get, the less I try to pass judgment."

We chatted for twenty minutes more, mostly about the other people from the Octagon, and when he said, "I've got an early plane in the morning, but this has been great," I quickly said, "It really has." We walked out of the bar without a bill appearing. Back in the lobby proper, he hugged me once more, again for too long, and then he said, "When we first saw each other tonight, I don't know if you remember, but you said, 'Long time no see.' I just want to mention, because I suspect you're unaware, that there's a racist etymology to that phrase. Its origins are either with indigenous people or Chinese immigrants, but either way, with you being an English teacher and an educator, I thought you'd want to know."

Although I was taken aback—it seemed odd of him to say anything and doubly odd to save it for the end—I tried to sound warm as I said, "Thanks for the heads-up. Yeah, I didn't know that."

I thought of him mispronouncing the word "aesthetics" more than thirty years earlier. I wondered if, in the intervening decades, anyone had ever corrected him.

THE DRIVE BACK TO my house was eighteen minutes, the roads were empty, and the moon in the dark sky was almost full and shockingly bright.

Had that bit about "long time no see" been, as my students would have said, a flex, or had it been a kindness? What, I wondered, is an enviable life? What is a purposeful life?

Val and I sometimes joke about being downwardly mobile, but it's not a joke. Our combined salaries are less than $150,000, and we have no savings. If Green Hills Academy does close, which it's always just a few full-tuition admissions applications away from, I'm too old and too white and too male to be a desirable hire at other schools. I suspect we could get jobs somewhere, but do the four of us really want to move to a different part of the country?

At home, the house was quiet; Val had left on the light over the kitchen table. I noticed an egg-encrusted pan on the stove—Wednesday nights were omelets—and as I washed it, I thought I heard a voice upstairs. I turned off the faucet, and when I listened again, Isabel was saying, "Daddy, come here."

As I climbed the steps, I braced myself for yet another disquisition on the Mariana Trench, or perhaps some new whopper from Liberty. When I entered her darkened room, I said, "Coconut, it's pretty late."

But she seemed cheerful. She was kneeling on her bed, holding open the curtains over her window, and she said, "Daddy, look how bright the moon is tonight."

A FOR ALONE

Irene's medium, the one in which she has exhibited at galleries, is textiles, but for *Interrogating Graham / Pence* she decides to use Polaroid photos and off-white Tintoretto paper. Even though the questions will be the same for all the men, she handwrites them in black ink, because the contrast of her consistent handwriting with the men's varied handwriting will create a dialogue in which she is established as the interrogator. Before her lunch with Eddie Walsh, she writes:

Date

Name

Age

Profession

When, prior to lunch today, did you last spend time alone with a woman who is not your wife?

Are you aware of the Modesto Manifesto, also known as the Billy Graham Rule, also known as the Mike Pence Rule?

If so, what is your opinion of this rule?

When I invited you to lunch, what was your reaction?

She and Eddie are meeting at a Thai restaurant downtown. Unless it feels organically relevant, she plans to make no mention of the project until after the arrival of the check, which she will pay.

Almost thirty years ago, as undergraduates at the U, Irene and Eddie both took Introduction to Ceramics. The studio featured two potter's wheels and was open until midnight, and Irene and Eddie spent many more hours there than was necessary—not because of each other but because of the wheels. Over time, as they chatted intermittently, it emerged that both of them would have preferred majoring in studio art—Irene's major was product design and Eddie's was economics—and that neither of them had parents who would have been okay with this. Eddie had grown up on a farm in southwest Minnesota, and Irene was a dentist's daughter from St. Cloud. In the ceramics studio in 1988, a white-paint-splattered radio and cassette player sat on the sill of the huge window overlooking Twenty-first Avenue, and stuck inside the cassette slot was Cat Stevens's *Greatest Hits,* turned to side two. Though every so often a person more foolish or enterprising than Irene would attempt without success to remove it, she never tired of the songs.

She and Eddie both took more ceramics courses. After graduation, they lived in group houses two blocks apart in the Kingfield neighborhood and regularly saw each other at parties. Eddie was affable, funny, and good-looking, and always had a serious girlfriend (the third of whom, a woman named Fara, he married). Following college, Irene was hired in product development at Target and Eddie by an investment firm. Irene was twenty-five when she married Peter; they moved to Ann Arbor for him to attend medical school, then to Pittsburgh for his orthopedic surgery residency, then to San Francisco for his fellowship. By the time they moved back to Minnesota, she was thirty-five and the mother of seven-year-old twin boys. Eddie had started his own investment firm, and he and Fara had a daughter and a son and lived in a gigantic house out on Lake Minnetonka; apparently, though still affable, he had become enormously rich and successful.

Outside the Thai restaurant, Irene runs into Eddie on the sidewalk, and he hugs her warmly.

After the embrace, she says, "Thanks for meeting me," and he says, "Is everything okay?"

"Everything's fine." She rolls her eyes. "Trump-fine. Shitshow-fine."

"But—" Eddie hesitates. "You're healthy? You look good."

"Oh, God," she says. "Did you think I was sick? I'm not sick."

"No, it's great to see you. It was great to hear from you. But just—I didn't know—since it's been a few years."

"It hasn't been *that* long," Irene says. "Peter and I were at Beth's high school graduation party."

"Well, Beth just started her senior year of college," Eddie says.

So much for organic relevance. Irene says, "Do you know what the Billy Graham Rule is?"

"I don't think so."

"A few months ago, there was an article about Mike Pence that got a lot of attention that said he follows it. It's that, if you're a married man, you don't spend time alone with another woman."

"Oh, I did hear about that."

"I'm doing a mixed-media project on it. Because, after the article, there was this brouhaha among liberals about how ridiculous it is—that it's sexist, it blocks professional advancement for women, et cetera. But then I thought, How often am *I* alone with a man other than my husband? Almost never. I agree that the rule is ridiculous and sexist, yet I'm functionally living in Mike Pence's world. So I decided to conduct an experiment where I invite men I know to have lunch with me, without explanation—except that

I'm explaining everything to you now—and afterward I take their picture and ask them to fill out a questionnaire. You're my first."

"I'm glad you don't have Stage 4 breast cancer."

"That's weirdly specific." After a pause, Irene says, "Thanks, though. I'm glad, too."

They enter the restaurant, are shown to a table, and order: for her, papaya salad and fried tofu; for him, massaman curry. She looks across the table at his kind, lined face and feels a fondness for him that turns out not to be incompatible with finding their conversation boring. Is the boredom a result of the inevitable comedown following their emotional greeting or a reflection of the topics they discuss? The tuck-pointing he and Fara are having done to their house; his involvement in a fundraising campaign for the U; what they hope for from the Mueller investigation, which of course is what any Democrat hopes for from the Mueller investigation.

He insists on paying, and, because of how rich he is, she acquiesces. Before the waiter brings back Eddie's credit card, Irene reaches into her bag for the Polaroid camera and the handwritten questionnaire, which is protected inside a linen folder. He fills it out in less than a minute, then grins gamely for the camera.

As the photo slides out, he says, "Now that you mention it, I'm rarely alone with a woman who isn't Fara." Gesturing across the table, he says, "For sure, not like this. But professionally, too. I guess it's because financial planning is a male-dominated field. Where did you say your exhibit will be?"

"I'm not nearly that far along," Irene says. "I need to see how the project unfolds." Fleetingly, she wonders if he envies the fact that she's still making art or if he considers her a chump.

This is when, his expression thoughtful, he says, "I listen to a radio station when I'm driving that plays—I guess you'd call it classics. And whenever a Cat Stevens song comes on, I think of the ceramics studio."

"I know!" she says. "A Muzak version of 'Peace Train' was playing the other day at the grocery store!"

They smile at each other, and he says, "This was fun. Let's do it again soon with Fara and Peter. Fara's our designated calendar manager, so probably best if you email her."

In her car, Irene reads Eddie's answers:

Date *September 8, 2017*

Name *Edward Nicholas Walsh*

Age *49*

Profession *Co-founder, Walsh Askelson Capital Group*

When, prior to lunch today, did you last spend time alone with a woman who is not your wife? *Professionally: sometimes work with associate named Megan, albeit usually not alone. Socially: can't even remember . . . 2015? 2008? 1995?*

Are you aware of the Modesto Manifesto, also known as the Billy Graham Rule, also known as the Mike Pence Rule? *N/A*

If so, what is your opinion of this rule? *Seems weird*

When I invited you to lunch, what was your reaction? *Was worried, glad you're good!*

HER ORIGINAL PLAN WAS to have lunch with a different man every week for a year. After making a list of plausible candidates—actual friends, acquaintances from the Twin Cities art world, long-ago Target co-workers, neighbors and former neighbors, fathers of her sons' friends—she realized that fifty-two was far too ambitious. She got to twenty-one, but, when she subtracted those with whom she suspected even an hour-long lunch would be intolerably awkward, the list dropped to sixteen. Of the sixteen, two were single— one divorced, one never married—and weren't single men exempt? Another two were gay, which raised a different question: Wouldn't Irene's ability not to fall in love with them and vice versa fail to rebut the threat of omnipresent and unbridled heterosexual lust implied by the Billy Graham Rule? On the other hand, how in the year 2017 could she exclude anyone for being gay and not somehow be siding with Pence?

She gave up on scheduling the lunches at even intervals. If she could recall spending time alone with a man in the past, no matter how long ago, she put an *A* next to his name; if he was gay, she put a *G*; if he was single, she put an *S,* though she decided against contacting the single men unless not enough of the married ones panned out.

IN THE MID-2000S, AFTER Irene and her family moved back to Minneapolis, a man named Phillip was the coach of her sons' hockey team; his own son was also on the team. This was during a period when Irene decided to fight her natural aversion to group activities, and she often signed up to provide team snacks. The seven- and eight-year-old boys met three times a week. Irene didn't expect to like Phillip, which maybe made it easier to? He was extremely patient and clear when explaining to the kids the rules of hockey and his own expectations.

For lunch, they meet at a grass-fed-burger place near the suburban office where he's an insurance adjuster. She arrives first, and when he joins her she can feel immediately that he is confused but that, unlike Eddie, he will not ask why she has summoned him. Either Phillip is too reserved or they don't know each other well enough anymore. As they make small talk about how their sons are doing at college, Phillip sits stiffly, almost sideways, and doesn't smile.

This confusion is, of course, the point. And yet she can stand it for only five minutes after they order—if the artist in her is fine inducing discomfort, neither the Midwesterner nor the woman in her is. "So," she says, "did you wonder why I suggested getting together?"

"I thought there'd be other people," he says.

"Funny you should say that. Have you ever heard of the Billy Graham Rule or the Mike Pence Rule? It's that, if you're a married man, you don't spend time alone with a woman, because it's, you know, inappropriate."

At the same time, she rolls her eyes and he says, "Makes sense."

As she tries to remember if he's religious, she says, "But the rule applies across the board, personally and professionally. Don't you ever have a meeting with a colleague who's female?"

"There's a difference between talking to someone in the office and going out for a drink."

"Do you remember that I'm a visual artist? I'm doing a project about the rule and"—she pauses—"people's views on it."

"What does 'project' mean?" He's squinting grimly. "I don't want to be part of a Facebook post."

"No, it's not for Facebook. And I wouldn't include anyone without their permission. I'm taking photos and having the participants fill out a questionnaire."

"Yeah, no," he says. "I'll take a pass."

Their food arrives—a turkey burger for him, a veggie burger for her—and after the waiter walks away she says, "So, are you doing anything fun this weekend?"

This is how they get through the next twenty minutes—she is blandly inquisitive, he is standoffish—and then she says, "Regarding my project, if you agree with the premise of the Mike Pence Rule, that's interesting. It's interesting to feature some people who agree with it and some people who don't. Would you be comfortable filling out the questionnaire anonymously?"

"I'll pass on that."

"I realize I'm violating social norms here, but are you—did you—in the election—" Phillip looks at her blankly, and she says, "Are you a Trump supporter?"

"I don't care for the president's rhetoric, but Pence seems like a smart guy. Good ethics, good leadership."

Once, in the third period of a tied hockey game, Irene's son Colin scored a goal against his own team. His team lost, and afterward, while the little boys clustered off the ice and Colin blinked back tears, Phillip calmly told the team that everyone made mistakes, and what mattered wasn't any particular moment or any one game but how they played together over a whole season.

At the restaurant, she says, "I wish I thought Pence was any better, but his homophobia, his abortion restrictions, plus the way he kowtows to Trump—I find it really scary." Phillip says nothing, and she adds, "FYI, a lot of my extended family is conservative."

"Yeah, I'm not someone who argues about politics," Phillip says.

At home, on her list, she writes a *U* next to his name, for unsuccessful.

IF IRENE'S LIFE WERE a movie, it would be the third man she has lunch with who represents the breakthrough. The first two would be duds, and the third would change everything. But her life is not a movie. Still, although the third isn't life-changing, he *is* delightful. The man is Kip, her former boss at Target, now sixty-eight years old, retired, and living on White Bear Lake. He demonstrates none of Eddie's or Phillip's apparent need for justification for why he and Irene are in each other's presence. Instead he's palpably pleased to see her, and the conversation is wide-ranging: his upcoming vacation to Bermuda; their former co-workers; a six-hundred-page novel he just read, which he says left him sobbing at the end; and the very long story of a lawsuit filed by his adult niece against her sister based on the second niece's claim that their mother had given her an amethyst bracelet before her death, which the first niece said her sister had taken without permission. Irene enjoys very long stories involving lawsuits, sisters, and bracelets, and asks many follow-up questions. Is it relevant that Kip is gay? She has amended his questionnaire accordingly.

While holding up the camera, she says, "You have a tiny bit of—" She runs the tip of her tongue between her own left central and lateral incisors.

"Bless you," he says, and removes the kale remnant with his thumbnail.

Date *9/25/17*

Name *Kip*

Age *68*

Profession *Retired in 2015 as Senior Group Director at Target*

When, prior to lunch today, did you last spend time alone with a woman? *I went for a walk over the weekend with my neighbor Sheila.*

When, prior to lunch today, did you last spend time alone with a man who is not your husband? *I had dinner last week with my friend Reggie. (At Acqua, which was delicious by the way—not good for the waistline but a fantastic meal!)*

Are you aware of the Modesto Manifesto, also known as the Billy Graham Rule, also known as the Mike Pence Rule? *Pretending gay people don't exist won't make us go away. This administration is nothing but a bunch of bigots and bullies.*

If so, what is your opinion of this rule? *Utter horseshit. Give 'em hell, Irene!*

When I invited you to lunch, what was your reaction? *What a creative person you are! I'm proud to have been your mentor.*

DOMINIC AND IRENE MET five years ago, when they both had work featured in an exhibit of local artists at a gallery in Northeast; Dominic's medium is metal sculpture, usually alloy steel. They hit it off on opening night, after being cornered by a drunk gallery donor, and they began meeting every month or two for coffee. In addition to being the one Black man on Irene's list, Dominic is ten years younger, handsome, and married to a woman named Gabrielle, who's a lawyer at a big downtown firm. But Irene rarely sees him anymore. Eighteen months into their friendship, Dominic won a MacArthur Fellowship, and suddenly he was never in Minneapolis—instead he was in Miami or New Delhi or London. When they meet, at a sushi place in Uptown, Irene hasn't seen him in about a year.

The first fifteen minutes of their lunch are great. They gossip enthusiastically about the owner of the gallery where they met, who has just shared on Facebook that she's a nudist. But then they don't, as Irene had anticipated and despite her efforts, segue into discussing work. This was always Irene's favorite part of having coffee with Dominic—that they talked about the incremental progress of their art, his welding and her weaving, in such a nitty gritty way that it might have been incomprehensible to a person overhearing. This time, when she asks about his current projects, he tells her that he's having a show at a major gallery in Manhattan and also that he's looking for an assistant, if she knows anyone. He asks her nothing about what she's working on, to such a notable extent that she wonders if he believes that doing so would be bad manners, now that his success so overshadows hers.

Eventually, before taking his picture and requesting that he fill out the questionnaire, she describes *Interrogating Graham / Pence*. His expression is skeptical.

"What?" she says. "Do you think it's a horrible idea?"

"It all depends on the execution."

"Right," she says. "Of course."

"The part I'm not hearing is where it's transformative. Where's the alchemy? You have some Polaroids, some sheets of paper, and then what? That's regurgitation, not transformation."

He's not wrong. But the way he's saying it—it's both practiced and distant, like there's some invisible but enormous audience, like he's giving a TED Talk titled "Where's the Alchemy?"

Sarcastically, she says, "Thanks for the encouragement," and he says, "Hey, no one's rooting for you more than I am."

As she waits for him to complete the questionnaire, it occurs to her that she may never, after this, see him one-on-one—that he won't initiate it, and neither will she.

Date *October 4*

Name *Dominic Maxwell*

Age *39*

Profession *Artist*

When, prior to lunch today, did you last spend time alone with a woman who is not your wife? *Lunch yesterday with my agent in NY*

Are you aware of the Modesto Manifesto, also known as the Billy Graham Rule, also known as the Mike Pence Rule?

If so, what is your opinion of this rule?

When I invited you to lunch, what was your reaction? *Hang in there, Irene*

Instead of answering the second and third questions verbally, Dominic has drawn a self-portrait with one eyebrow raised, his lips pursed in scorn.

This is almost endearing enough to make her think they'll remain friends, after all.

MAN NO. 5 IS Abe, the father of a boy named Harry, who in elementary and middle school was the best friend of both of Irene's sons. Irene was unsure whether to put an *A* next to Abe's name, because she has in fact been alone with him many times, but never by design. Before their sons could drive, she stood in all seasons at her door while Abe dropped off or picked up his son at Irene's house, or she stood at Abe's door while dropping off or picking up her sons. They also stood next to each other, very much not alone— sometimes with Abe's wife, Karla—in the bleachers at ice rinks and on the sidelines of soccer fields. All of which is to say that she has no idea if she and Abe know each other well or barely.

When Abe joins her, at a chopped-salad place near his office, his eyes fill with tears as he says that he realizes Karla put Irene up to this, but that she, Irene, is a good friend to reach out. It soon emerges, in such a way that it's clear he's unaware she's learning it in this moment, that, ten days ago, in the basement of a fraternity at the University of Wisconsin, his son Harry attempted suicide. Harry has since entered an in-patient program for depression in the Twin Cities, and is also confronting an opioid addiction, of which his parents previously had no inkling. Irene has the almost overwhelming impulse to call her own sons at their colleges, both to ask if they know about Harry and to confirm that they themselves are okay.

For the duration of lunch, she murmurs unoriginal but sincere expressions of sympathy, asks if there's anything she can do, inquires about the logistical aspects of Harry's program. She eats her entire salad, and Abe eats almost none of his. She paid for both of them after they went through the line at the counter, so there's no bill to signal the end of their time together.

She retroactively decides that this was a lunch where she was checking on Abe and not just including him in *Interrogating*. Not for the first time, it occurs to her that perhaps, rather than exploring the customs of married heterosexual socializing, she is inadvertently demonstrating the isolation of modern life. As she drives home, she considers abandoning the project.

IN OCTOBER, THE #METOO movement attracts widespread attention, which means that Irene's project has become more relevant, or more unsavory, or both. She plans to explain the project up front to Jack—Man No. 6—because, of everyone who made the cut, she probably knows him the least well.

Jack and his wife, Lori, are friends of friends. Every New Year's Eve, Irene and her husband attend a dinner party held by a couple on their street named Maude and Carl, both of them political-science professors currently on sabbatical in Prague. Jack and Lori, who don't live in the neighborhood, are the other guests.

Irene sent a joint email to Maude and Carl saying that if they were in town she'd try to cajole Carl into participating in her project, and asking for Jack's email address. Carl replied, *Irene, no cajolery would be required!* Before supplying Jack's email, he described his recent visit to Prague's National Gallery. Maude replied, *Carl and I regularly get coffee or a drink one-on-one with opposite-sex colleagues in our department. Nothing untoward happens, and not only is a certain extra energy part of these encounters but that energy is important. Expecting one's spouse to supply the totality of one's mental and social stimulation is childish. On a more prosaic note, Irene, I see that the temperature in Minneapolis is dropping—could you turn our heat on to 55 degrees?*

Irene has never been in direct, individual contact with Jack, and though she has consistently enjoyed talking to him on New Year's Eve for the past five years, she has never seen him anywhere other than at her neighbors' house. He and his wife live in St. Paul, and Irene would have said he was an engineer, but she learns by googling him that he's actually a geologist at an engineering consulting firm.

She emails him and suggests meeting at a large brewery in Golden Valley that she knows is near his office. She always arrives at these lunches early, but when she walks into the restaurant he's already seated. He stands as she approaches, smiling broadly. "It was such a pleasant surprise to hear from you," he says. After a tiny hesitation, they hug.

He has ordered a beer, so she does, too; until now, the only man she drank with was Kip, with whom she had a glass of white wine.

When the waiter departs, Jack gestures to his phone, which is set facedown on the table, and says, "I just read an article about a piece of paper Einstein wrote on getting auctioned for 1.5 million dollars. Apparently he was staying at a hotel in Japan, and when he went to tip the bellboy he realized he didn't have any money, so he wrote down his thoughts about happiness on some hotel stationery and gave that to the guy."

"Hmm," Irene says. "Do I sound cynical if I say that I bet the bellboy would have preferred cash?"

Jack laughs. "That occurred to me, too, although this was right after Einstein learned he'd won the Nobel Prize."

"Then I suppose he was inhabiting his full Einsteinhood by then," Irene says. "Or close to it."

"Also, it's descendants of the bellboy who get the money from the auction. Does that mitigate things?"

"Partly, but it's still so arrogant. It's one degree away from sneezing into a tissue and giving that to someone."

Jack laughs again, takes a sip of beer, and says, "Speaking of genius types, from what I can glean on Facebook, it looks like Maude and Carl are enjoying Prague."

"Yeah, I'm in pretty close touch with Maude, because I'm their house sitter."

"Are you really?" Jack seems amused.

"Well, I have a studio above our garage, and it literally overlooks their backyard, so it's not a big deal."

"But house-sitting is a gig for a fifteen-year-old, and you're a famous artist."

"Ha," Irene says. "I wish." She raises her eyebrows jokingly. "Are you a big fan of woven textile design?"

"You've had exhibits and stuff." Jack's expression becomes self-conscious. "Yes, I've googled you. Is that weird?"

"I don't think in 2017 it's weird for anyone to google anyone else. And you're probably right that my boys would do the house-sitting if they weren't away at college. Remind me—do you still have kids at home?"

Jack nods. "Two of the three. Marisa is a sophomore at Carleton, Lacey is a junior in high school, and Annie is in sixth grade."

"Do you know what an artists' residency is?"

"I think so, but, in case I don't, why don't you tell me?"

"They're places where artists, including composers or writers, can stay for a few weeks or months and be undisturbed. They're often somewhere rural, and a chef prepares meals for you and the only expectation is that you'll be productive. This might sound kind of preposterous, but for years I planned that, when my kids went to college, I would give myself my own personal permanent residency. As in, without leaving home. I never applied for a real one because the time never seemed right, but I'd turn my entire life into, you know, the Irene T. Larsen Fellowship for Being Irene T. Larsen."

"Have you done it?"

"I'm the chef, but yes."

He raises his beer and says, "Cheers." After they've tapped their glasses, he says, "I don't know if you remember this, but last New Year's Eve you recommended a Korean documentary to me. It was about old-women sea divers."

Irene doesn't remember mentioning it, though she does remember the documentary.

He says, "I found it very interesting, if you have other recommendations."

"Well, I watch a documentary every day, so I could give you a list of my top five hundred favorites."

"Do you really?"

"Not on the weekend, but every weekday afternoon. Usually just on Netflix."

"Is it part of the Irene T. Larsen Fellowship for Being Irene T. Larsen?"

She laughs. "One of the most important parts."

Because of the surprising abundance of topics they have to discuss, there's no obvious moment to mention the project. She orders beet salad and he orders chicken salad and asks if she's a vegetarian—she is—and they talk about CSAs and a project he's been working on, on a site in northwestern Minnesota, and more of what his job entails. When the bill comes, he grabs it and says, "This is definitely my treat."

"You should let me, and I'll tell you why. Do you know what the Mike Pence Rule or the Billy Graham Rule is?"

"The men-and-women-not-being-alone thing?"

"Exactly. Which—well, my hunch is that you're not a Trump supporter—"

Jack rapidly shakes his head.

"I'm inviting men I know out for lunch and, if I'm being honest, I'm pretending to neutrally ponder the rule while really trying to highlight how dumb it is. But, at the same time, I think it's a rule a lot of straight married people unwittingly abide by."

"Oh, that's a great idea," Jack says. "That's really interesting."

Is he being sarcastic?

He continues, "I'm almost sure the last woman I saw one-on-one, before today, was a friend of my cousin Jessica who was about to move to the Twin Cities. We had coffee last spring."

"Hold that thought. If you don't mind, I have a questionnaire for you that asks about that. But was the coffee social or more of a professional networking thing?"

"She was in town to look at houses—trying to get the lay of the land on neighborhoods and schools."

"Have you seen each other since?"

"After her family moved, we had them over for dinner."

"I think what you're describing is the exception among people who don't purposely practice the rule. That you're allowed to meet with a person of the opposite sex once, and then if you see each other again it's after you've been slotted into a category, whether it's couples friends or professional acquaintances. But a married man and a married woman can't form a new, entirely social friendship."

"Wow," Jack says. "That's all so depressing. But, whatever the reason is, I'm happy to get to spend time with you. You're one of the coolest people I know."

She experiences a split second of confusion or unsteadiness before saying, "My son Arlo recently told me people don't use the word 'cool' anymore. He said everyone says 'awesome' or 'dope.' But he undermined the claim because he used the word 'cool' a few minutes later."

"In that case," Jack says, "what if I say instead that you're very witty and charming?"

She laughs. "I promise I wasn't baiting you."

"Just out of curiosity," Jack says, "what does Peter think of your project?"

"I haven't mentioned it to him yet."

Though Jack nods, she has the sense that he is taken aback.

She adds, "Not for any particular reason. I don't really discuss my art with him."

"Got it."

"Another part of the project is I'm taking a picture of each man I have lunch with. Are you okay with that?"

"I should warn you that I look silly when I smile."

As she pulls the Polaroid camera from her bag, she says, "Did someone tell you that?"

"No, but I see pictures and think, What a goofball."

Holding the camera up, her eye behind the viewfinder, she says, "You don't look silly at all." She has the impulse to say, *You look handsome.* Instead she says, "You look great."

SHE REALIZES WHILE DRIVING home that she forgot to have him fill out the questionnaire; she got distracted by talking about it and neglected to actually give it to him. She'll email him, she decides, and ask if they can meet up again for five minutes in the next few days, perhaps outside his office.

After she pulls into her garage, she checks her phone, and an email from him is waiting. She left the restaurant seventeen minutes ago, and he sent the message ten minutes ago: *Irene, it was very dope seeing you. (Did I do that right?) Let me know if you'd like to get together again. It would be an honor to offend Mike Pence's sense of decency with you anytime. Best regards, Jack.*

INSTEAD OF HER STOPPING by his office, he suggests that they meet the following afternoon at Wirth Park. As she turns in to the lot off Glenwood Avenue, he is leaning against the driver's door of his car with his arms folded. When he realizes it's her, he unfolds his arms and smiles. This time when they hug, again after a hesitation, it feels incredibly awkward. He gestures toward Wirth Lake and says, "Do you have time to walk for a bit?"

She's not wearing ideal shoes; perhaps shamefully, she took more care with her outfit than she had the previous day, and she has on heeled suede boots. "Sure," she says. "Although do you mind filling out the questionnaire now? Just so I don't forget again."

She removes the paper from the folder and passes it to him, and as he presses it against the driver's-side window he turns his head and says warmly, "Have I mentioned how impressed I am that you figured out a way to go on dates with lots of men and have it count as work?"

She hesitates, then says, "What's that supposed to mean?"

"I know you're critiquing society and all that. But you have to admit that you've found a clever loophole."

She stares at him. "That's very insulting."

"Oh, God." He looks genuinely distressed. "I was kidding. Oh, no. I'm really sorry. I just wanted to make you laugh." They're both quiet, and he adds, "Really, I'm sorry. I feel like a jerk right now." When she still says nothing—she honestly doesn't know what to say—he nods at the piece of paper and says, "What if I finish this, and while we walk I'll— There's something I want to come clean to you about. Some context."

She swallows and says, "Okay." After he passes her his completed questionnaire, she slips it into the folder and slips the folder into her bag. They head toward the pedestrian path and he says without preamble, "I've been very unhappy in my marriage for a long time. We did couples therapy, all that stuff, and I think we just have different personalities. But I can't see getting divorced with the kids still at home because—and I realize I'm not unbiased here—but I have a strong hunch that Lori would make a divorce as ugly as possible. That she'd involve our girls. Lori isn't what you'd call even-keeled, nor is she big on boundaries. There came a point about two years into couples therapy where I thought, In order to not lose my mind, I need to give up hope on improving the marriage and accept it for what it is. This might sound defeatist. But she and I were on completely different wavelengths. This was also when I thought, If I ever have the opportunity to have a different kind of relationship with someone else, I'm going to take it. Cheating on my wife isn't who I planned to be, but I just—I don't want to die without experiencing love again."

They are passing an empty beach, not looking at each other, when she says, "And did you find someone else?"

He says, "When I got your email, I thought maybe you were the person I'd been waiting for."

She stops walking, and he does, too. She is genuinely shocked. She says, "When was it that you decided you'd cheat if you could?"

"Six or seven years ago."

"And, during that time, how many people have there been?"

"None. To be honest, I've never seen any kind of opening, nothing where it even felt like a possibility. And no one I was ever that attracted to, other than very superficially. But it's not just that I got a random email from you, and it got my hopes up. It's you specifically. I'm sorry if this all sounds crazy, but there's one other part I need to mention. Do you remember the first New Year's Eve we all spent at Maude and Carl's, when we went around the table talking about what tattoos we'd get?"

Again, she does remember, but vaguely.

"People were saying things like their kids' names or a rose. I said the state of Minnesota. And then you told a story about visiting your grandmother in Ohio when you were five years old and jumping wildly on her bed, and at that exact moment an earthquake started, so when you stopped jumping the entire house around you and all the furniture were shaking. You said the tattoo you'd get would be a seismogram of that earthquake." Irene laughs, but Jack's expression is earnest. He continues, "Someone at the table said, 'You must have been afraid of your own power,' and very matter-of-factly you said, 'No, I'm just disappointed that it hasn't happened again.' I was sitting across from you, and you were wearing a dark blue dress that showed your collarbone and a silver necklace with an oval pendant or whatever those things are called, and I just was overwhelmed." He's regarding her with a great, questioning intensity.

This is all still astonishing, every part of it. She glances away before looking back at him, and he says, "But what about you? If you tell me your marriage isn't broken like mine, I wouldn't—well, I'll still feel the same about you, but I'd respect that."

After a few seconds, she says, "When I was in my twenties, I took pride in not seeing life romantically. I don't think I expected Peter to be, you know, smitten with me. We met after he'd applied to out-of-state medical schools, while he was waiting to hear which he'd been accepted by, and I married him almost for the reasons someone decides to be a foreign-exchange student. It was very important to me to not be a person who'd only ever lived in Minnesota." She smiles a little and says, "That's horrible, right?"

"Were you smitten with him?"

"It was more like we both saw each other as—reliable? Something I was naive about was how much he'd work. Even now, he works seventy-five or eighty hours a week. And when the boys were little, living in cities where we had no family, it was so hard having twins. Peter and I hadn't decided ahead of time that I'd quit my job, but it made no sense to keep it."

"What about now? Do you guys do things together? Do you sleep in the same room?"

If this is a euphemism for sex, she ignores it. She says, "Because of how much he works, he's very protective of his Sundays. We have a tandem bike, and we go out for long rides. Or, in the winter, he likes to skate on Lake of the Isles."

"Is he supportive of your art?"

"He's someone who thinks in terms of things like bone fractures. So if I say, 'I'm making a fiber installation about the 1878 mill explosion,' of course that seems kind of ridiculous to him. But he doesn't tell me *not* to make art." Jack looks appalled, and—she tells herself that she is kidding—Irene adds, "Do you still think you want to have an affair with me?"

What he says, in as undefended a way as anyone has ever said anything to her, is "I'd love to have an affair with you, if you want to have one with me."

LATER, WHEN THEY ARE having an affair, neither of them says "having an affair," nor do they use the term "cheat." In spite of the ostensible cultural consensus that what they're doing is slimy, the words they use with each other are the sweetest she's used with anyone besides her children: *My beloved. My precious darling. I adore you, I miss you, I love you so much.*

The clichés they enact are no less potent for being clichés. They meet in hotels and occasionally in one of their cars, in a secluded parking lot. They communicate via an app she had not previously heard of, which automatically deletes their messages within an hour. She becomes obsessed with her phone. She pauses *Interrogating,* even canceling the lunch she had already scheduled with a man with whom, a decade ago, she volunteered at a food bank.

She and Jack spend exponentially more time discussing their first lunch and their meeting by Wirth Lake than they spent actually having lunch or walking around the lake that day. Repeatedly, they recount what they were thinking, what they thought the other person was thinking, which of their own remarks they felt most foolish about, and which of the other person's remarks they were most enchanted by.

At first, they see each other once a week, but they grow greedier and more reckless, and once, before Christmas, it is four times in a week, and once in January it is during a weekend. (They don't have to worry about New Year's Eve at Maude and Carl's with their spouses, because Maude and Carl are in Prague until the summer.) In February, when Irene's car is rear-ended a block from the Millennium hotel on Nicollet Avenue, she thinks that is it, the jig is up, her secret joy ruined. But when, in order to explain why a loaner car from the Volvo repair place is in their garage, she tells Peter that she was in a fender bender, he doesn't ask her where, let alone why she was in that part of the city at that time; he doesn't ask her anything.

Instead the jig is up, her secret joy ruined, after Irene emails Jack an article about the auctioning of a note Albert Einstein wrote to a young female scientist. Irene gives the email the subject *Our patron saint*. The body of the email contains a link to the article and the single sentence *I can't wait to smother you with kisses on Tuesday!!* This email arrives while his laptop is open on the kitchen table, and his wife, Lori, reads it before he does and confronts him. In addition, she calls their oldest daughter at college to describe what has happened. Jack weeps while telling Irene by phone that they must end things. They both say they don't blame the other— Why did she *email* him the article? Well, because she doesn't know how to send a link on the app. But why didn't she realize emailing was a bad idea?—and they both say they'd do it again, even given how it's turned out.

Irene and Peter's understanding is that if he's home from work by eight-thirty they eat dinner together, but if he gets home after that she eats without him. At nine-fifteen, he enters the house, washes his hands, reheats the plate of moussaka she has set aside, eats it, wipes his mouth with a napkin, then says, "I got a phone call today at the hospital from Lori Deahl. Whatever you're doing, you need to knock it off immediately." Up to this point, when it comes to Peter, she has alternated between guilt and astonishment at what, for almost twenty-five years, she has settled for. That night, she feels mostly numb but also ashamed. Does Peter know about the smothering-with-kisses sentence? Does Lori and Jack's oldest daughter? For two nights, Irene sleeps on the couch in her studio, then she and Peter proceed as if nothing has happened.

She and Jack communicate a little more, and have an over-wrought conversation in his parked car, but it actually has ended. He tells her that he and Lori are re-entering couples therapy. If he wanted to leave Lori, Irene would leave Peter. But Jack has never wavered about not wanting a divorce. And, though she considers leaving Peter anyway, she decides against it. She is certain that, money-wise, he'd dispassionately and meticulously fuck her over. She would no longer have a residency, a studio, health insurance.

The spring is terrible, intolerable, the summer even more so for how lovely the weather is, the pleasant temperatures and sparkling lakes. How strange to think of Jack living his life such a short distance away, his house in St. Paul ten miles from her house, his office in Golden Valley just five. Irene keeps expecting the interlude when she met up with him two or three times a week, the exhilaration and closeness, to seem like a fever dream. But it keeps seeming real; she remembers it clearly.

Several months after their contact has ended, one late morning in her studio, she comes across the photos and questionnaires from *Interrogating*. She read Jack's responses after their walk by Wirth Lake, but she doesn't remember them, probably because she was so agitated that day.

Date *Nov 6, 2017*

Name *Jack D.*

Age *50*

Profession *Geologist*

When, prior to lunch today, did you last spend time alone with a woman who is not your wife? *As I mentioned, coffee w/ my cousin's friend last spring.*

Are you aware of the Modesto Manifesto, also known as the Billy Graham Rule, also known as the Mike Pence Rule? *Yes.*

If so, what is your opinion of this rule? *I'm not on board with it, but it would be disingenuous to pretend I don't understand the logic.*

When I invited you to lunch, what was your reaction? *I was very excited that I'd get to see you.*

She wants his questionnaire to impart some central truth, to give her closure, and, while it's nice, the niceness pales in comparison with what he said moments after filling it out—"It's you specifically"—or the many ardent declarations of devotion in the months that followed.

In early August, Maude and Carl return from their sabbatical, and, on the patio of a wine bar, Irene confesses everything to Maude. "I still have no idea," Irene says. "Does all of this officially vindicate Billy Graham and Mike Pence? Or does it mean that even a stopped clock is right twice a day?"

Maude's expression is contemplative and not scandalized. "There are, what, almost eight billion people on Earth?" she says. "It's so odd that you've decided Mike Pence either does or doesn't get to tell you how to live."

THE PATRON SAINTS OF MIDDLE AGE

After my former mother-in-law's memorial service and burial, I lasted half an hour at the reception then got in my rental car to drive to my friend Allison's house. It was nearly six in early March, and the sun was setting; spring had already arrived in St. Louis, but daylight saving wasn't until the following weekend.

I'd been unsure if I should attend the funeral—I'd been gone from St. Louis for thirteen months, Neil and I had been divorced for eleven, and this seemed like either too short or too long a stretch after which to fly back to town for such an occasion. When I'd asked Allison's advice, she'd said, "If you're on the fence, do it for Brooke's sake, to model diplomacy with Neil. And for your mother-in-law's sake. Then stay with me and give me sex advice in person."

"Okay, you're right," I said. "But in opposite order of importance."

Allison's house was a block east of the house that Neil, Brooke, and I had lived in for twenty years, after moving there when Brooke was a baby, and I purposely didn't drive down my old block. Instead I passed the turnoff for Waterman, headed east on McPherson, then went south to return to Allison's block. I parked on the street, and our other friend Cheryl opened the door of Allison's house as I carried my overnight bag up the front walk.

Cheryl said, "Are you in more of a Kleenex mood or a wine mood?" Cheryl and I had always been closer to Allison than to each other, and Cheryl and Allison also undoubtedly shared a connection around race that I didn't—both of them were Black, and I was white—but we'd all known each other for many years. When I reached the front steps, Cheryl and I hugged for longer than we would have before the pandemic, before I got divorced and moved to Cleveland, or if I hadn't just attended a funeral.

"I think Option C," I said. "Kleenex and wine."

Then Allison appeared and hugged me too and said, "The only funeral I've ever cried at was my mom's. I usually don't because I'm so prepared to."

"And then your mind decides to surprise you?"

"Or my tear ducts. How'd it go?"

I'd set my bag down just inside the front door, and I followed them both into the kitchen, which, like the rest of Allison's house, was immaculate in a way my house on Waterman had never been. And yes, she had a house cleaner, but I'd not only had a house cleaner, I'd hired the same person Allison had.

I sat on one of the two barstools by the granite island, and Cheryl sat in the other, and I said, "The first time I met Neil's parents, they took us out for dinner to an Italian restaurant on the Hill, and I ordered lemon sorbet for dessert. And literally, from that time on, his mom kept lemon sorbet on hand in their freezer for me." I smiled and teared up at the same time as I added, "And I don't actually like it very much. I'd never ordered it other than that time."

"Then welcome to never eating it again?" Cheryl said.

"His mom was always incredibly nice to me, even after the divorce. She sent me a scarf this past Christmas." I hesitated before adding, "It's not like I think getting a divorce was the wrong decision, but all day today, I felt really conscious of having gotten divorced."

"I have this"—Allison was holding up a bottle of Shiraz—"and a Sauvignon Blanc in the fridge. We're having salmon for dinner."

"I'm good with either," I said, and Cheryl said, "Same."

"Then red." One of the many qualities I liked about Allison was her decisiveness. As she pulled a corkscrew from a drawer, she added, "I still feel really conscious of being divorced around my extended family, and I did it in the nineties."

"You left work early today, right?" I said. "Thank you." As the chief marketing officer of an enormous pet food company, Allison routinely worked fourteen-hour days.

She made an almost grumpy expression, which I understood meant *Of course* and passed me a glass.

"Jess, you must know about Allison's new man, right?" Cheryl said. "The news has made its way to Cleveland?"

I could feel Allison looking at me sharply, and, in the mildest tone I could muster, I said, "I've heard. He sounds wonderful." I held up my wineglass. "It's really great to see both of you. Cheers." We all clinked.

Allison, Cheryl, and I had met when our daughters were in preschool together almost two decades prior, and we then caught up on Cheryl's daughter Mackenzie's plan to start medical school at Vanderbilt in the fall; Allison's daughter Grace's and my daughter Brooke's much less clear post-college-graduation plans and Allison's and my respective levels of concern; who was likely to be elected next governor of Missouri (a man none of us liked, replacing a different man none of us liked); where Cheryl had purchased the magenta satin blazer she was wearing; and our current menopause symptoms (night sweats for me, a recent seventeen-day period for Cheryl a week after her last period had stopped, no period at all for five months and counting for Allison).

By this point, we were sitting at Allison's dining room table eating the salmon and accompanying salad and baguette. In the kitchen was a chocolate almond bar Cheryl had brought to split for dessert, and Allison had opened the windows that overlooked Waterman. Outside, the dark spring air on the other side of the screens smelled familiar and sweet.

"Being back here," Cheryl said to me. "Mindfuck or not really?"

"The short answer is I'm hanging in there." I set down my fork. "The longer answer is, well, I have a dilemma. When we put our house on the market, Doris gave me a Saint Joseph figurine to bury in the yard. Do you guys know that tradition?" Doris was the woman who had cleaned my house and still cleaned Allison's.

Cheryl raised her eyebrows. "The patron saint of moving, right?"

"Of selling houses, actually," I said. "I'd never heard of it, but I googled it and you're supposed to follow all these very specific instructions about how deep you bury him, how you position him, how close he is to the For Sale sign. I'm not superstitious, but I figured it couldn't hurt. And it was nice of Doris, obviously."

"And clearly it works," Allison said. "The scientific proof is that your house sold quickly."

"Exactly," I said, "but I forgot to dig him up before we moved out. And probably five or six nights a week, I wake up at two in the morning in a panic—well, panicking and having hot flashes—and thinking that I need to tell the family who bought the house that Saint Joseph is still in their yard."

Both Allison and Cheryl looked perplexed. It was Allison who said, "Because?"

The answer seemed so self-evident that it was difficult to articulate. After a pause, I said, "Because Saint Joseph increases the chances that that family will move." Neither woman looked convinced, and I added, "And maybe they don't want to. Probably they don't want to. They just moved in. Their kids are really young." Allison and Cheryl still looked unconvinced, and I said, "It's fine if they get divorced because that's the right decision for them, and maybe that's what will happen in ten or twenty years. But I don't want to *cause* their divorce."

Allison smiled, and Cheryl said, "Okay, good thing you're not superstitious."

I smiled too, sheepishly. "I see your point. Anyway, I don't even remember the family's last name, but the mom's first name is Kathryn, and I was—"

"Thompson," Allison said.

"How do you know?" I asked.

"I met them at the block party."

"When I wake up in the middle of the night, I compose emails to her in my head explaining the situation. But maybe we should just go right now and I'll dig it up? I didn't bury it as deeply as you're supposed to, and I think I remember exactly where."

Allison and Cheryl exchanged a look, and Cheryl said, "Jess, no Black woman in her right mind is going to root around in some strangers' yard, let alone after dark."

"Ah, right." I winced. "Sorry." I experienced a flare-up of embarrassment about my own cluelessness, which was something I'd felt intermittently over the years. But I'd learned enough to know not to belabor it.

"You go ahead, though," Cheryl said. "Don't let us stop you."

"I mean, it's probably not a good idea for me, either," I said. "I don't think of people in U City as gun owners, but who even knows anymore. Anyway, that's my answer to how it feels being back here."

"No offense," Cheryl said warmly, "but if you think you're responsible for that family's fate, you're seriously overestimating your own power."

"And Saint Joseph's," Allison added.

IN THE FALL OF 2005, two weeks into the school year, when my daughter Brooke was three, she came home from preschool one Monday afternoon with a picture book titled *Pretzels Are for Biting.* "Do we bite our friends?" one page asked, before providing the answer: "No! We bite pretzels." The friends one didn't bite were brightly dressed, and all the foods one did bite were at least reasonably healthy: bananas and carrots, pizza and tacos. That evening, I received an email from the class's lead teacher conveying that it had been a good day in the Sycamore Room, reminding all parents to check their child's cubby to confirm that it contained a change of clothes, and informing us that although one of the Sycamore friends had been learning when it was appropriate to use his teeth, she was sure that discussing the book that we all could find a copy of in our child's backpack would be helpful for everyone. (Brooke's backpack was pale blue, with pink butterflies on it, and her name stitched in purple, and it was so small that she needed a bigger one by first grade. But I've never been able to get rid of it, and I took it with me when I moved to Cleveland.)

When I saw the teacher's email, I was on my laptop in the den. We'd eaten an early dinner, and Neil was watching a baseball game on TV while Brooke balanced on her hands and knees lining up her stuffed animals in a row. I asked if someone in her class had been biting other kids, and matter-of-factly she said, "Hugo, but he only bites girls."

"Does he bite you?" I asked.

"Yes," she said.

"Where?"

"My ponytail."

I looked in confusion at Neil and said to Brooke, "He put your ponytail in his mouth?"

Brooke gazed at me intently and said, "Is flying carpets real?"

"Did he bite you one time or more than one time?" I asked.

She held up four fingers and said, "Two times."

"Did he do it for the first time today? Or before today?"

She shrugged.

"You're asking really leading questions," Neil said.

"Maybe," I said, "but I don't like the sound of this."

"It seems like the school has it under control."

"I wish flying carpets were real," I said to Brooke. "But they're only in books and movies."

In the morning, I awakened to an email from a woman named Allison Carter: *Hi fellow Sycamore moms of daughters, just touching base about Ms. Tara's biting email yesterday. The child in question has now bitten my daughter, Grace, three times, including breaking the skin twice, and I'm concerned that the school is not taking this seriously enough. Grace mentioned that the student bites girls, not other boys, and if I'm reading the class list correctly, there are four girls in the class (Grace and your daughters) and eight boys. I'm going to speak directly to Ms. Tara but want to check in before I do and see if any of you have other information.*

After a few more emails back and forth—Cheryl, one of the other mothers, said she thought it was her daughter Mackenzie who'd been bitten first, and it had happened the previous Thursday—we scheduled dinner at a sushi restaurant in the Central West End for that very night. I'm embarrassed to admit that when I walked into the restaurant and saw two Black women sitting at a table, it didn't occur to me that they were two of the three mothers I'd been emailing. As I explained to the hostess that I was meeting three people but it looked like I was the first to arrive, one of the two women held up her hand and called, "Jess? I'm Grace's mom, Allison." At the time, I wondered how Allison recognized me, and, for that matter, how she subsequently recognized Lauren, who was the other white mom; Lauren's daughter's name was Lily. Later, Allison told me that she'd not only googled us but that it had been deliberate on her part to get the white mothers involved because she assumed it would make the teachers more responsive.

What she said then, after Lauren arrived, was "I thought it would help the school better understand our concern if we convey to them that we've connected with each other."

"Meaning don't put the onus on us to ensure that our daughters don't get bitten," Cheryl said. "Pretzels are for biting, my ass."

"Do we know how many times it's happened?" I asked. "I haven't had any luck getting a clear answer out of Brooke."

Allison pulled from a maroon leather handbag her BlackBerry and four sheets of paper that featured the grid for September 2005, with the three dates that Grace had been bitten already marked—typed—with her name and the location on her body.

"Is it weird to say I feel like my private detective dreams are coming true?" Lauren said.

"It's a little weird," Allison said, and we all laughed.

"Speaking of," Cheryl said, "I looked up Hugo's parents, and I'll give you one guess what his dad does."

"Cannibal?" I suggested.

"Pretty sure that's not a paying job, but close."

"I already know so I'll abstain," Allison said.

"Lawyer?" Lauren said.

"Solid guess but wrong," Cheryl said. "Any more tries?"

"Chef?" I said.

"So close." Cheryl was smirking. "He's a dentist."

We all laughed some more, and I said, "Really?" and she said, "His clinic is in Rock Hill."

"Yeah, I think I might not go to him," I said, and we started laughing again before returning to the business of how to communicate with the school. Half an hour later, a white woman who looked to be about sixty stopped at our table on her way out of the restaurant and said, "I just want to say how lovely it is to see you all having such fun together." I didn't see the comment as particularly meaningful until it happened again, this time with another white woman who looked about fifty, the third time the four Sycamore moms had dinner together. By then, we'd set up a monthly dinner that was partly social and partly an effort to keep tabs on what was happening in our daughters' classroom. That second time, the woman said, "I just want to say what a lovely group of friends you are." Being congratulated by other white women for public multiracial socializing happened semi-regularly after that, and though it was a novelty to me, it apparently wasn't to Allison or Cheryl. As Cheryl said after yet another of these moments, "If there was an Asian woman with us, then they'd really get excited. It would be like a tampon commercial coming to life."

The biting had stopped by October. Allison's, Cheryl's, and my daughters all enrolled in Flynn Park for kindergarten, and we continued to have occasional dinners, with a rotating handful of other mothers. Otherwise, I saw Allison frequently and Cheryl rarely except at school events. Lauren's daughter switched to private school, and within a couple years, we'd all lost touch with her. But St. Louis is small, and I ran into her about a decade later, in the shoe section of the Nordstrom at the Galleria. Both our daughters had their driver's permits by then. "It's almost enough to make you nostalgic for Hugo, huh?" Lauren said.

CHERYL LEFT AFTER THE dessert. Allison started to load the dishwasher—I offered, and she said, "No, because you won't do it how I like it"—but she did let me dry the salad bowl and the salmon platter after she'd handwashed them.

Then I poured both of us another glass of wine and said, "Okay, update me."

I'd learned early on, back when our daughters were in preschool, that Allison had adopted Grace on her own. But we'd been friends for a few years before she mentioned her brief marriage. The wedding had occurred when she and the guy were seniors at Kansas State University, they'd known each other from a bible study group, the marriage had lasted eight months, and the guy had then moved to San Francisco and begun dating men.

Both before and after hearing this story, which Allison hadn't told in detail and I hadn't pried about, I'd wondered if she was gay, too, or would have been if she'd been born a little later, or if perhaps she was asexual. If she'd dated during the time we'd been friends, I hadn't known about it. I'd always assumed both that she got hit on regularly and that she was intimidating to some prospective partners—in addition to having a high-power job, she was pretty and charming—and I'd also assumed that if she wasn't dating, it was by choice. At the same time, I knew, of course, that my being unaware of something didn't mean it wasn't happening.

And then, a little after 10 P.M. a month before, she'd sent a text that said, *OK not sure how else to say this but I need sex advice*
Honored you think I'm qualified! I wrote back. *Go on . . .*
Can I call you, she replied.

She had, she told me by phone, just been on a second date, though she hadn't known for sure until the second date that the first date also had been a date. The man was named Henrik, he was German but had worked as a vice president of a telecommunications company in St. Louis for a decade, and they'd met on the board of a hunger-relief nonprofit. Henrik was my age (forty-nine, or two years younger than Allison), and he was the divorced father of one son who lived in Brooklyn and another who lived in Berlin. Twenty-four hours prior to her texting me, they'd made out in his parked car in front of her house.

"That all sounds fantastic," I said. "Congratulations."

"Yeah, there's a tiny problem," she said. "I don't think I know how to have sex."

Because she didn't sound like she was joking, I tried to keep the amusement out of my voice. I said, "In what sense?"

"Freddy—my ex-husband—we tried a few times and it was terrible. I wish I could say comically terrible but maybe just terrible. I think he was disgusted by being with a woman, and even finding out later that he was gay, it didn't erase those experiences."

"I'm so sorry. And—" I tried to think of how to ask the question tactfully. "Have you been involved with anyone since?"

"It was such a relief when our marriage ended that I really didn't want to deal with that for years. This was a long time ago, too, but once, as an experiment, I thought I should see if one-night stands were for me. So I tried and the answer was no."

"And just to be clear, you want to have sex with Henrik?"

"I think so."

"Have you talked about it with him?"

"Lord, no."

I laughed. "Why is that so far-fetched?"

"Because of the awkwardness. He was very straightforward about his interest, but even so—no."

"How was he straightforward about his interest?"

"Well." She hesitated. "At dinner, he said, 'I find you very attractive and want to date you. Would you like to date me?'"

"Can I just say I love that kind of man? I wish they were all like that. What did you say?"

"I said I'd consider it."

"Ha, he must be on pins and needles. But fair."

"I was caught off guard. Then I was embarrassed for being caught off guard because there we were at The Crossing, drinking wine, and there was a candle in the middle of the table."

"Okay, this is what I think. Henrik sounds wonderful and promising. I think you can tell him you want to take it slow without going into details if you don't want to. And I think the physical stuff will happen naturally. You're great at everything you do so I assume you'll be great at sex, too, if you're with a partner who's worthy of you. But also if you're looking for techniques there are plenty of books and podcasts and videos out there. Honestly, in my experience, most men aren't that picky. But for your own comfort that might help."

Over the phone, she took a deep breath then exhaled. "Thank you."

"Consider me on call," I said. "Willing and ready to serve at any moment. But I do have one question. Just out of curiosity, why me?"

She laughed. "There are two reasons, and neither of these will sound like a compliment, even though they sort of are."

"I can't wait."

"This is your word, not mine, but you've mentioned being a slut several times."

"Wait, have I really?"

"Years ago, on one of our walks, you said that you'd been a big slut in college."

"True," I said, "although I don't remember announcing it." After we'd learned we lived a block apart, occasionally Allison and I had taken walks on Saturday mornings, while Neil would make pancakes for both girls. By middle school, our daughters were no longer close, but Allison and I took walks every few Saturdays at 8 A.M. sharp. I always walked to her house and then we headed toward the park.

"You said it in passing, but I took note," she said. "The second time was that dinner right before you moved. Cheryl asked if you thought you'd ever get married again and you said maybe eventually but for now you were looking forward to going back to your slutty ways."

"Okay, I think I do remember that. I guess we're supposed to retire the term, huh?"

"Or use it celebratorily."

"Well, I'm not offended yet," I said. "What's the other reason?"

"You know how some people's life is so perfect that they probably forgot what it's like to freak out about something you should have stopped freaking out about when you were in high school?"

This seemed to be a reference to Cheryl, who was a nurse anesthetist married to a radiologist and the mother of three high-achieving children; her family's Christmas card, which was always a professionally taken photo of them in color-coordinated sweaters, arrived without exception on the Friday after Thanksgiving. And she still hand-addressed them!

On the phone with Allison, I laughed. "Yeah, I have heard that some people are perfect," I said. "And I'm okay not being one of them."

In the four weeks since that conversation, Allison and I had spoken only once, but she'd texted every few days with questions that were a mix of clinically specific and endearingly girlish (she asked the kind of questions I'd once thought my daughter would, before I'd realized that my daughter would never voluntarily ask me about sex). The texts also served as progress reports of a kind:

When you kiss and the other person puts his mouth over yours do you move your mouth or just let your mouth be covered?

Or:

If a mouth is going around an erection do you think the lips should be covering the teeth but otherwise the mouth is as tight as possible around the shaft or not necessarily?

To the first question, I had replied *What do you want to do?* and she had replied *I don't know!*

To the second, I had replied, *Hmm I think teeth have a bad rap but can sometimes add pleasing contrast when used with care?*

Then I'd added, *Remember what Dr. Spock said? "Trust yourself, you know more than you think you do."*

I realize he wasn't talking about blowjobs.

In Allison's kitchen—I was sitting on a barstool again, and she was standing between the refrigerator and the island—she said, "As a matter of fact, we decided to have sex this week. He got tested for, you know, that whole panel, and he's negative."

I sensed she wouldn't like it if I were overly enthused, so I simply said, "Great."

But her brow was furrowed. "There's more, though. He knows it's been a while for me. Like a long, long while. And it seemed like he was fine with it, but then we had a weird conversation. Have you ever used handcuffs?"

"Not recently, but yes."

"Do you own them?"

I squinted. "I don't think so? Because I'd have found them in the move? Neil and I played around with scarves at some point, years and years ago, but I'm almost sure we didn't have real handcuffs. Oh, you know who I used handcuffs with is my grad school boyfriend Marcus. He kept them in a drawer in his nightstand."

"So that sounds normal to you?"

"Well, I'm not sure that my doing something makes it normal, but I don't think that it's extreme. I take it Henrik owns handcuffs?"

She nodded.

"And are you not comfortable with using them or with him having them or what?"

"I don't morally disapprove. I just don't see how a man who owns handcuffs could be satisfied with"—she made a circle in front of her torso with her right hand—"a middle-aged quasi-virgin."

I was pretty sure this was the most self-effacing comment I'd ever heard Allison make. I'd noticed over time that neither she nor Cheryl insulted themselves in the reflexive, somewhat disingenuous way my white friends did; Allison and Cheryl didn't use self-criticism as a bid for either praise or bonding. At some point in my late thirties, I had, while barely being aware of it, begun cracking jokes about aging—saying that I was "hagged out" or turning into an old lady or a dinosaur. On one of our Saturday morning walks, I told Allison that I officially had so much gray hair that I could no longer pluck it without risking bald spots, and she said, "If you don't want gray hair, why not dye it?" I'd said, "I might, but that makes me feel like I have one foot in the grave." Lightly, casually even, Allison said, "Yeah, only white women are afraid of getting old." It was not an exaggeration to say that this observation had radically reordered many of my beliefs, and not just about aging and gender.

Sitting at Allison's granite island, I said, "You think if Henrik owns handcuffs, it means he's intimidatingly experienced or too BDSM-ish for you or what?"

"Potentially both," she said. "Plus accustomed to a certain level of proficiency."

"But this isn't an annual job review. Proficiency in sex is subjective. You guys have done pretty much everything other than penetration, right?"

She nodded.

"What matters is chemistry, not proficiency. You feel like you're both having a good time when you're hooking up?"

"As long as I can get out of my own head, we have a great time."

"And getting out of your head will probably become easier and easier. Did Henrik show you his handcuffs or just mention them?"

"At one point, he held both my wrists above my head, and it made me ask. I know it's a thing. But I was surprised when the answer was yes."

"Did you like the way he held your wrists?"

Her expression was thoughtful. "I didn't dislike it. Although that part got overshadowed by the handcuffs discussion."

"Do you know if he has other bondage-type stuff?"

"I asked, and no. And he said he can take it or leave it with the handcuffs. But I just—I don't know—I got spooked."

"The thing that I keep hearing is that the two of you really enjoy each other. He's nice, he's into you, and he isn't concerned about the fact that you don't have a ton of sexual experience. And it sounds like he's being honest with you about where he is. There's nothing you've said that sets off alarms for me. No red flags, as our daughters might say. Or beige flags."

Allison shook her head. "I can't even imagine telling Grace. She thinks I'm a nun."

"One, you don't need to rush it, and two, I bet she'll handle it just fine. Sorry, but I really don't see any remaining obstacles. I think you and Henrik are good to go all the way."

She smiled wryly. "It probably won't end up being this week because he has a work trip to New York tomorrow. But maybe next week."

"Wait." I winced. "Were you planning to have sex with him to-night? And I messed it up by staying with you?"

"It's been three decades. Another few days won't hurt."

"I'm so sorry. You can go have sex. Seriously. I can stay here by myself."

"Absolutely not." Allison was frowning. "Your mother-in-law

died. And anyway, when it happens, we'll have sex here. I have much nicer sheets."

"I can go stay in a hotel!"

"Also absolutely not. So how was it seeing Neil today?"

"Did I tell you he asked me to tell Brooke that he wasn't involved with Simone before our divorce? This was a few months ago." Simone was the new girlfriend of my ex-husband, and she was ten years my junior (meaning thank goodness I had learned to stop berating myself for aging). "He and I were completely cordial today, and I left the reception as soon as I felt like I could without being rude. And now I get to see you while also unfortunately depriving you of sex."

"Is Brooke staying with Neil?"

I nodded. "She and I had lunch before the memorial service, and that was great."

"Why couldn't Neil tell her himself that he and Simone didn't have an affair?"

"Exactly. But I humored him." I took the last sip from my wineglass. "I think he thought if he told Brooke, it would seem suspicious. And it seemed like she believed me, but her main reaction was 'Ew, gross.' Like she didn't want to hear about it either way."

Allison gestured at my glass and said, "Should I open another?"

Because she'd already switched to water, I shook my head. "I assume you know this, but the first time any two people have sex it usually isn't as good as it will be eventually. I bet Henrik is nervous, too. And it's very normal for men our age to have erection issues. You shouldn't take it personally if he does. Henrik sounds fantastic, but I just want to make sure you're not expecting fireworks."

"I'm not expecting fireworks."

"Am I being condescending?"

"A tiny bit but you know what? It's warranted." She smiled a shy smile. "Although there haven't been erection issues so far."

"Well, bravo, Henrik."

"I know this isn't penetration, but he does this thing where he tells me to, well"—even though we were the only people in the house, she lowered her voice to a whisper—"hold his dick and rub the tip of it against my clitoris the way I want, so he'll know how I like it."

"Oh, Allison." I literally teared up, just as I had when I'd admitted I'd never really enjoyed lemon sorbet. "I'm so happy for you," I said.

NEIL AND I HAD rarely fought, but there had been moments in our marriage that were like abrupt clouds over a sunny picnic. Once, at a ten-person dinner party, it occurred to me that if we were attending as strangers rather than as spouses, we'd likely find each other to be the eighth or ninth most interesting person at the table. Or the TV shows we watched together—left to my own devices, I'd have watched reality trash, and left to his own devices, he'd have watched crime dramas. We watched mediocre sci-fi series as a compromise, which seemed like a metaphor, but it also seemed like figuring out what it was a metaphor for would be unwise.

Up until the evening it occurred to me that we should get a divorce, though, it had never occurred to me that we might. Neil had gained ten or fifteen pounds during the pandemic—who didn't?—and decided in early 2022 to join a running group. Right away, he was very into it, sharing details of pacing and elevation. He met up at 6 A.M. with seven or eight other people every weekday and for a longer run on Sunday afternoons. He'd never signed up for any form of social media, but he downloaded an app that allowed him to post a graphic of each day's run, to which his fellow runners could respond with affirming emojis or words.

I'm not being mocking here—we all need to get through each day somehow and there are far more destructive habits than jogging and tracking your jogs. He described his runs, and his fellow runners, with greater specificity than I considered necessary, but I was glad that he'd found a new interest. He signed up to run a half-marathon in the fall, and the night before, I joined him at a pasta dinner at the home of some of his running buddies I'd heard about but not previously met. From the minute we entered the hosts' house—it belonged to a husband and wife in Creve Coeur—I observed a version of my husband I had never seen in our twenty-four years together. He was talkative and boisterous and was apparently considered hilarious by others, as well as a wise dispenser of advice. He was palpably alive and happy. The previous month, he'd grown a white goatee, and I suddenly understood that his goatee was tied to his new running identity.

This is not a story about my husband having an affair—he didn't—but while standing on the back deck of this couple's house, I watched from ten feet away as Neil chatted with a woman named Simone and I understood in a lurching sort of way, from his body language and expressions, that he was in love with her; that the attraction was mutual; that he himself didn't necessarily know he was in love with her; and that it was extremely unlikely he would cheat on me, both because he wouldn't be able to admit to himself that he was in love with Simone and because even if he did, he wouldn't want to be a man who cheated.

There are, of course, many reactions I could have had. Perhaps the most generous would have been to be happy for him, to maintain our life together while encouraging him to wring all the probably platonic joy he could from running and his new community. And part of me thinks this *was* my reaction, except for the maintaining-our-life-together part. Because what I also thought was, *Wait, you have the capacity for this kind of exuberance? Do I? I think I do, but not in our status quo, and I always assumed we'd tread water in our status quo until one of us dies. But if you're pursuing your bliss, maybe I want to pursue mine, too.*

The life I really wanted did not, as it happened, feature anything thrilling or exotic: not skydiving or salsa dancing or pastry-making lessons in Paris. The thing I wanted the most was to move back to Cleveland, where I hadn't lived since I'd left for college, and to buy a small house in the same neighborhood as my two sisters. Our parents were no longer living, but on the weekend I wanted to go to Michaels to buy yarn with my older sister, and to make soup with my younger sister. I wanted to be part of the monthly dinners with our cousins and to see my nieces and nephews and I wanted my own daughter, who was at DePaul in Chicago, to visit my side of the family more than every other year. Because I was a high school guidance counselor, I could live anywhere; it was because of Neil, and *his* family, that we'd always lived in St. Louis.

On the deck of some strangers, while my husband told an apparently side-splitting anecdote to Simone, I had the belated and destabilizing realization that in believing what I most wanted was unavailable, I'd been using an extremely narrow definition of availability.

A few days later, I talked to Neil not about Simone specifically but about the general stagnation of our lives. In the next conversation, I raised the idea of separating, and he said it seemed like I was throwing out the baby with the bathwater. But in our third conversation, by which point I was having doubts, he seemed more convinced of the wisdom of separating than I was. I asked if he'd consider moving to Cleveland with me, and he said no, and he asked if I'd consider moving to Cleveland part-time and staying married, and I said no. Five months later, after downloading all the paperwork, we went together to file our Certificate of Dissolution of Marriage on the third floor of the county courthouse. Then we stood outside and I cried on the sidewalk and Neil hugged me, then we went to a barbecue restaurant for lunch and ate pulled pork sandwiches and coleslaw.

Of course I second-guessed myself. I'd done so when telling Brooke, and I did it when filling out the part of the form at my new PCP's office in Cleveland that asked for my emergency contact. I didn't do it at Thanksgiving, though, which I co-hosted with my younger sister, in a house filled with seventeen of my relatives, including Brooke. I bickered more with my younger sister than I'd anticipated, but I loved making soup with her on the weekend, and

I loved going to Michaels with my older sister when she went to buy yarn. And I actively didn't miss parts of my life with Neil that I hadn't realized I would actively not miss, like hoisting our bizarrely heavy fake Christmas tree up the basement steps together, and eating on a weekly basis at his favorite Mexican restaurant. On the other hand, early on, Neil and I had established a rule that whenever either of us encountered a baked good that included rhubarb, we always should buy it—rhubarb was unusual enough, and we both loved the taste—and sometimes in Cleveland, when I spotted a rhubarb pastry in the glass case at a café, or even just saw it listed as an ingredient in a cocktail on a menu, I'd avert my eyes so as not to be gripped by sadness.

Three months after I'd moved away, Neil told me by text that he'd started dating a woman in the running group named Simone and reminded me that she and I had enjoyed meeting each other at that pasta dinner before the half-marathon. *Good for you!* I texted back. *I joined Bumble, have a date tonight with an electrician.* Then I realized I'd mixed up men from the app—there were a lot of them—and added, as if it mattered, *Wait no a veterinarian.*

IN ALLISON'S GUEST ROOM, I awakened at ten after three in the morning—ten after four back in Cleveland—and lay there for a while, not reaching for my phone because what would I be looking for? Though I did realize I'd failed to check in for my flight back to Cleveland, which would be departing at 9:55 A.M.

Hi there Kathryn, I thought, *I hope you're enjoying the house!* It was strange to be thinking of these words a block from the house in question. *At the risk of sounding ridiculous, just wanted to mention*

Hi Kathryn, I just want to give a little heads-up

Hi Kathryn, not sure if you're aware of the custom of

Then I thought, *Fuck it,* and I pushed off the covers, went to use the bathroom, and before I could ruminate anymore, pulled a jacket over my nightgown and let myself out the front door of Allison's house. She had an alarm system, but I could see from the green light on the panel's keypad that she hadn't set it.

Outside, it was about sixty degrees and very dark. It took eight minutes to walk between Allison's house and the house that had once been mine. How many times had I made this walk after parting ways with Allison on a Saturday morning? Definitely hundreds. I knew the trees and the yards, the pitch and cracks of individual sidewalk squares, the houses and many of their sleeping residents. In fact, it was in the yard of the Kohlmann family, whom I'd lived four doors down from and who had triplets—were they two now? Or maybe three?—that I spied among quite a few other scattered toys a plastic spade, like a child would use at the beach along with a bucket. How serendipitous this felt, perhaps like a sign of encouragement from Saint Joseph himself.

A brick walkway led to my old house, and two steps led from the sidewalk to the brick walkway. As you faced the house, a black wrought-iron railing stood to the steps' right. On the lawn was a lilac tree that Brooke and Grace had long ago used as base in games of tag, and to the left of the steps was a mulched flowerbed. I'd buried Saint Joseph in the mulch by the steps.

All the lights in the house were off. I'd steeled myself for the new owners to have made some painful change—they'd have cut down the tree or gotten rid of the porch swing—but things either looked the same or it was too dark to tell what was different.

I almost could stay on the sidewalk, off the property, as I bent and pressed the tip of the spade to the mulch. Immediately, it occurred to me that perhaps having found the spade was not lucky but unlucky because if I hadn't, I'd have recognized the futility of digging; I'd have realized there was no way I'd find Saint Joseph with just my fingers, whereas this way I was able to delude myself. When what I was likelier to find, I suspected as I began to displace the mulch, was worms or insects.

I could smell the lilac blossoms, and I could hear a dog barking in the distance. Was digging like this a gesture of altruism on my part? An enactment of my white privilege? Or perhaps even proof that I, like a few people I knew, had in the time during and since the pandemic journeyed into some kind of emotional instability, with one questionable decision begetting another. Though maybe the pandemic was indistinguishable from all the other ways that middle age could unmoor a person. Then I thought, no. I thought, maybe on altruism and maybe on white privilege, but no on instability. I might be exercising peculiar judgment in this moment, but I have my reasons for doing so. Not everyone who knows me needs to agree with my choices. Among the gifts Allison had given me years before when she'd said "Only white women are afraid of getting old" was the reminder, at a time when I'd needed it, of just how many cultural narratives were optional rather than compulsory. Though, admittedly, to my amusement or dismay or amused dismay, when I'd once quoted the line back to Allison, she'd laughed and said, "That definitely sounds like the kind of flippant thing I'd say."

"Flippant?" I repeated. "It was profound. It helped me remember that anyone who gets to old age is lucky."

She laughed again. "But you know that of course Black women are afraid of getting old, don't you?"

I had dug no more than two inches into the mulch when the plastic shovel hit—something. Maybe a rock, maybe just an extra-large chunk of mulch, maybe Saint Joseph. And maybe Kathryn, wholly unknown-to-me Kathryn, did in fact need my protection from life's upheavals, or maybe she'd be okay either way, she'd figure things out and make a home for herself on Waterman Avenue and find her friends. Maybe she already had.

GIRAFFE AND FLAMINGO

There was a tiny kind of story my mother told when I was growing up, less a narrative than a few colorful facts. Sometimes she was sharing a tidbit about her own experiences and sometimes about those of a person she knew or even a stranger. Such anecdotes, I believed, were intended to be interesting rather than instructional; they were the sort of things you carry around inside you not because you've chosen to but just because you haven't forgotten them.

In 1953, when she was seven years old, a boy in her grade celebrated his birthday by inviting other kids to a movie theater to watch a Disney nature documentary about the desert. Midway through, when a big tortoise got flipped over on its shell and couldn't right itself, the birthday boy cried so hard that his mother had to take him home.

When my mother was sixteen, she became friends with a rich girl in her class. Before a dinner at the girl's house, the family served cantaloupe wrapped in prosciutto as an appetizer. My mother had barely ever encountered an appetizer, had never seen prosciutto, and believed she was eating raw meat. She was too shy to inquire if this was the case, and was surprised by how tasty she found it.

When she was twenty, having not previously been on a plane, she arranged to spend the second semester of her junior year studying in Paris and living in an extra room in the flat of an older couple. Though my mother had studied French for years, she was nervous about her ability to make herself understood, and as she flew across the Atlantic, in her head she practiced the information she planned to convey on arriving. When the older couple met her at the airport, she worried they'd assume she'd brought only a carry-on, and she wanted them to know she'd also checked a suit-case. *J'ai besoin de trouver ma valise,* she said silently as the plane bumped over the dark ocean and a man she didn't know snored in the seat beside her. *J'ai besoin de trouver ma valise.* For decades, and for no reason she could discern, the sentence still echoed in my mother's brain on a daily basis.

I don't recall making the decision to mimic this anecdote-sharing habit after I had children. I guess I just saw it as normal in a way my husband didn't. I told my own kids about how all through grade school a girl named Jessica and I vied to be the best friend of a girl named Carlee and that in fifth grade, one night when both Jessica and I were sleeping over at Carlee's house, all three of us in sleeping bags on the bedroom floor, I awakened to find Jessica throwing up on my head. I told them that while I didn't think this act was completely intentional on Jessica's part, I also didn't think it was completely unintentional.

I told them that as a teenager I babysat for brothers who had bright red hair, and that their mother said that up until giving birth for the first time, she'd had bright red hair, too, but as soon as the first boy was born, her hair began to grow in a faded shade closer to brown than red, and it never reverted to its former flaming color.

I told them that my grandmother's next-door neighbor had a lapdog named Pearl who would eat only from her owner's hand. I told them that once my family had gone to St. Petersburg, Florida, for vacation and at the end, my brother, their uncle Bill, had announced that he'd forgotten his toothbrush at home and hadn't brushed his teeth in a week. And then, shortly after we moved from the East Coast to the Midwest, I told my children that when I was a senior in college, my roommate and I had lived on a hall in a dorm with six male athletes, and over time, five of the athletes fell in love with my roommate. I told my children this as we sat in a booth in a diner, at four o'clock on a Tuesday, after I'd met them at the bus stop and taken them straight to dinner. I took them out for early dinners at least once a week, before my husband got home from work and I left for my evening concert.

I said, "I've been thinking about this recently because one of the athletes was named John Olney, and everyone called him by his last name."

The neighborhood my family had moved to a month before was called Olneyville. Though I didn't say so to my kids, it had given me pause when the real estate agent first mentioned it while showing us the house. I wasn't under the impression John Olney had ties to the area, but his surname just had such unpleasant associations for me. By the time the agent told us the neighborhood's name, however, my husband and I had already decided we liked the house. Not surprisingly, it was much bigger and nicer than what we could afford on the East Coast and was within walking distance of a shopping district with both fancy and casual restaurants, a farmers' market on Sunday mornings, and the kind of artsy shops that sell handmade jewelry and funny magnets. After we moved, I'd realized Olneyville was one of those neighborhoods that takes a self-conscious, underdoggish pride in itself, located as it was in a Rust Belt city whose glory was considered by anyone who didn't live there to be in the distant past. But if you resided in Olneyville—especially as opposed to the city's western suburbs, which were filled with McMansions and Republicans—you probably believed that the city was having a renaissance and that you were part of it.

The reason my family had moved was that I'd been hired to be the principal violist in the symphony orchestra, which, thanks to the Rust Belt city's illustrious past, was one of the top-ranked orchestras in the country. My husband, Travis, worked as a marketing project manager and didn't particularly want to move, but the promotion doubled my salary. Given the state of our finances, it was hard for Travis to protest.

In the diner, I said to my children, "Besides being known for its music school, my college was known for its sports teams. But before my senior year, I'd never lived in a dorm with any athletes. And the bathrooms in that dorm were coed, so we were *really* living close together. Do you know what 'coed' means?"

"Can I get a milkshake?" Sophie asked. Both of my children were across from me: Elliot, who was ten and had just started fifth grade, and Sophie, who was eight and had just started second.

"You can split one," I said.

Elliot glanced at his sister and said, "Chocolate?"

She nodded.

"'Coed' means boys and girls together," I said.

"And theys and thems," Sophie added.

"I didn't know anyone who identified as nonbinary in college, but I'm sure they were there," I said. "At the time, it seemed very weird to me to share a bathroom with boys because I'd never done it before."

Elliot said, "If five of the athletes fell in love with your roommate, who fell in love with you?"

I laughed. "No one. And I was a little insulted at the time, but now it seems like a long time ago."

"Dad is the one who fell in love with you," Sophie said.

I hesitated for a split second before saying, "Well, that was later."

TO SAY THEY'D FALLEN in love with Chloe had been, on my part, euphemistic or perhaps exaggerated. But clearly they found her attractive, and I understood why. She was slim and had long, wavy blond hair and blue eyes, like an angel in a Renaissance painting. I, meanwhile, had eczema behind my ears and on the inside of my elbows, and one front tooth that very slightly overlapped the other.

Three of the athletes were soccer players, and three were swimmers. At a dorm party just a few days into the semester, after Chloe and a soccer player named Tim had both had a few beers, he asked if she wanted to take a walk, and, under an enormous beech tree that was a campus landmark, they made out. When they returned to the dorm, he invited her to hang out in his room, and she declined. As she climbed into her bed well after midnight, she whispered to me, "Dormcest," then shook her head. "What was I thinking?" The next afternoon, Tim knocked on our door to see if she'd like to get coffee, and she accepted in order to take the opportunity to tell him that she didn't anticipate anything more occurring between them. That was that. Tim was very quiet—I almost never talked to him the entire year—and he didn't pressure her.

The next to fall in love with her, so to speak, was a swimmer named Mike. Once, around eleven o'clock at night, a little awkwardly, Mike and I were brushing our teeth side by side. It was just the eight of us—Chloe and me and the six athletes—who used our hall's bathroom, which was rectangular. When you entered, there was a urinal on the left, then the two sinks, a toilet inside a stall on the right, and, against the far wall, two showers.

After he'd spat into the sink, Mike said, "Hey, can I ask you something?"

I said, "Okay."

"Does Chloe have a boyfriend?"

Although I knew the answer was no, I said, "I don't think so."

"Yeah, cool," he said. "Just wondering. Because she's hot."

When I repeated to Chloe what Mike had asked—as, presumably, he'd intended for me to do—she shook her head, rolled her eyes, and exhaled, as if this were all an irritation. Chloe and I had joined the same chamber music ensemble as freshmen—she played the flute—and her talent and hard work were so self-evident that I was surprised when I first heard another conservatory student say that the reason the professor went easy on Chloe in a studio class was that he wanted to fuck her. I imagine such insinuations contributed at least somewhat to the fact that by the time we were seniors, Chloe wasn't planning to try to get an orchestra job after graduation; instead she was hoping to stay on campus for a fifth year, earn a master's degree in education, and become an elementary school music teacher. I was careful not to belittle this choice, and perhaps she was equally careful not to remind me—it wasn't necessary—that just a tiny fraction of students graduating from music conservatories were ever hired by orchestras. The number thrown around was 5 percent, and once after a recital, a cellist with a unibrow had told me it was statistically harder than getting into Harvard Medical School.

Chloe never dated Mike, who'd asked me about her while we brushed our teeth, but by October she and another soccer player named Sean were a couple. Sean was the roommate of quiet Tim, whom Chloe had kissed under the beech tree, but Tim had begun dating a volleyball player who lived off campus, and he stayed most nights with her, thereby allowing Chloe and Sean privacy in Sean's bed. Sean and Chloe dated for real, into the spring, and during the first few weeks it seemed weird to barely see her anymore, especially when she was just across the hall. But I was practicing up to ten hours a day at the music building, so it wasn't necessarily that she was never in our room; it was that she was never in our room when I was there, at night. I sometimes thought of her saying "Dormcest" and making a face after kissing Tim, and I thought about how the prohibition apparently hadn't been on intra-dorm dating but rather on Tim himself. To me, Tim, Mike, Sean, and also a swimmer named David seemed virtually interchangeable: brown-haired and handsome and fit and distant, like younger versions of an FBI agent in a movie. They were not talkative, or at least not talkative with me. The outliers were Alex, a swimmer who was the only one of the athletes who was actively nice—he always greeted me by name and smiled—and whose handsomeness was marginally less generic in that his brown hair was curly, and Olney, who was a soccer player and, as I soon decided, a jerk.

The swimmers attended practice most mornings and occasionally in the afternoons, and the soccer players attended practice most afternoons, and they all got rowdily drunk on Friday nights, in other locations, then staggered back to the dorm. A few times early in the year, I entered the bathroom to either pee or brush my teeth, and one of them was standing right there at the urinal, and I was overwhelmed with panic and confusion and proceeded to do the thing I'd been planning to do while feeling deeply uncomfortable about their proximity; and a few times early in the year, I entered the bathroom and one of the athletes was in the closed stall, and I could see male feet, either bare or in shoes, and I could smell shit, and then I backed out of the bathroom wordlessly. I soon developed a habit of pausing outside the bathroom door, listening, and entering only when I heard nothing.

It was, of course, unthinkable for *me* to poop in the presence of any of the athletes. This didn't feel like a decision or even a reaction to cultural constructs of gender or decorum; it felt nonnegotiable, like gravity. In the past, sharing bathrooms with a bunch of girls hadn't been my favorite part of dorm life but also hadn't been something I gave much thought to. Now, each morning, I awakened at six forty-five when, through the walls, I heard the swimmers' alarm clocks go off, and I waited for the swimmers to leave for practice. I went into the bathroom, peed, and washed my hands. I returned to my room with an extra paper towel. I ate an orange I'd procured from the cafeteria the previous night for this purpose, sitting on my unmade bed, the orange's juices dripping onto the paper towel. I drank a glass of water; and fifteen minutes later, I returned to the bathroom to poop, still before anyone else on the hall woke. When I was finished, I felt a relief so extreme it was almost giddy; it was almost happiness. I could then shower, dress, and walk the three-quarters of a mile to the music building without worrying about any of this for another twenty-four hours.

And then, one morning a few days before Halloween, while I was mid-poop, the bathroom door opened and someone entered. There was a crack of space next to the stall door, and through it I saw a red T-shirt and a sliver of John Olney. My only notable interaction with Olney had been at about three o'clock in the morning the previous Saturday, after the athletes had returned from wherever they went to drink. On the other side of the wall against which my bed was set, they were in Olney and Mike's room, shouting and laughing and throwing something around that sounded like, but probably wasn't, a chair. I was performing in an orchestra concert the next afternoon, and after about ten minutes, during which the noise didn't decrease, I got out of bed, went into the hall wearing the T-shirt and shorts I slept in, knocked on their door, opened it, and, squinting into the light, said, "Hi, guys. Can you be more quiet?"

Four of them were in the room, and Olney looked at me, grinned, and said, "Fuuuuck you!"

"Hey, man," Alex said to him. Alex was the curly-haired nice one. To me, he said, "Sorry, Emily. We'll keep it down."

But after I returned to my bed, Olney was louder than before, and I didn't try to intervene again.

Four days later, in the toilet stall, I froze. It was safe to assume the entire bathroom smelled like shit, my shit. My face flushed, and my heart began thudding. I was waiting, but for what? Wasn't *he* waiting to use the toilet? If I waited long enough, might he exit without doing so? A minute passed, then another minute. The bathroom was totally silent. Neither of us spoke. Did he know I was the one in there? Could he sense my discomfort?

Finally, even though I wasn't finished, I also knew I couldn't keep going. I stood, wiped, flushed, and emerged from the stall to find Olney smirking. "Jesus Christ," he said. "What'd you eat?"

I washed my hands without speaking or even looking at him.

The next morning, when I heard the swimmers leave for practice, I went through my peeing-then-eating-an-orange routine, but when I had to poop, I walked past the staircase leading from the second floor to the first, to the far side of the hall, where another coed bathroom was located. This one was also quiet at such an early hour, and I began to use it every morning. This altered habit worked for two weeks, until one day when I came out of that bathroom and Olney was at the top of the steps, about to descend them. He and I made eye contact, he smirked, and neither of us said a word. The next morning, I was in the stall in that other bathroom when he entered and stood by the urinal, perhaps eight feet from where I sat. Had he been listening or even looked out the door of his room to check when I passed by? An odd thing to think of now is that for nine months, John Olney and I slept just a few inches apart, albeit separated by a wall.

Once more, I stopped pooping before I was actually finished, wiped, flushed, emerged from the stall, and washed my hands while he stood there. I never again pooped in the dorm between November and May. Instead, after the swimmers left in the morning, I changed into my terry-cloth bathrobe; went into the bathroom closer to my room, carrying the plastic bucket that held my shampoo and other toiletries; immediately took a shower; and peed standing up, with my feet apart over the shower drain. I was conscious in a way I wasn't when I peed into a toilet that the pee that came out after sleep was a dark yellow, sour-smelling gush. I also brushed my teeth in the shower. Then I returned to my room, dressed, and left for the music building. In the building's atrium, I ate my orange, then I gulped from a water fountain. In the fifteen or so minutes while I waited for my bowels to be stimulated, I read an article or two from that week's issue of *Newsweek* magazine. When it was time, I walked to a bathroom in the farthest corner of the basement and pooped. I maintained this ritual on weekends, too, because it was easier.

After a few days of the new pattern, when I emerged from the dorm shower wearing the robe I'd hung on a hook just outside the shower curtain, Olney was standing with his back to the sink, his arms folded. I startled and he laughed, but it wasn't exactly a triumphant laugh. It may even have been a defensive laugh. "I'm not gonna rape you," he said. "Don't flatter yourself."

As it happened, assault had never occurred to me. I intuitively understood that what Olney was doing was supposed to be un-traceable, unprovable, unspeakable—that if I tried to mention it, to describe it to another person, it would render me ridiculous. Dorm bathrooms were, after all, communal spaces.

And yet, as we looked at each other, I wondered if we'd reached a stalemate. He'd succeeded in driving me out of the dorm to empty my bowels. But I'd succeeded in finding an alternative. If he stood in the bathroom while I made some smelly shit, there was a shame that, however illogically, affixed itself to me; I was the one befoul-ing the situation. But lurking outside the shower was creepy in a way where the creepiness affixed to *him,* and I think we realized this in the same moment. There was, of course, a general psycho-logical recognition between us or else he could never have played this game with me. He couldn't have played it with a girl who didn't already, at a certain level, consider herself disgusting.

In March, I flew to New York and auditioned for the Chamber Music Society of Lincoln Center's young artists program, which was my dream position. Auditions occurred only every three years, and if accepted, I'd play at Alice Tully and tour the world with the most respected musicians. When I got back to campus, I entered my dorm room at 10 P.M., carrying my duffel bag, and found Chloe sitting up in bed, sobbing. *She's jealous of my audition,* I thought, and then she said, "Sean and I broke up."

"Oh," I said. "Why?"

She shook her head vaguely. "We're just not on the same page."

There were only six weeks left before our graduation, and I thought maybe Chloe and I would start spending time together again, eating M&M's at 11 P.M. and gossiping about other conser-vatory students, as we'd done in earlier years, but she and Sean proceeded to get back together and break up again a few more times, and she and I barely spoke, even when we were in the room at the same time. The night before our graduation ceremony, after both our families had already arrived and were staying in nearby hotels, I entered the room and saw the back of a pale, naked male body pumping up and down on Chloe's bed, heard panting, and assumed it was Sean. Somewhat surprisingly, I'd never before walked in on them in the act, but it felt as if all bets were off now, all norms set aside—most of our belongings were in boxes, and everyone was dispersing. I was retreating from the room when the naked male turned his head and smirked at me, and I saw that it wasn't Sean. It was Olney. Under normal circumstances, I'd have experienced some combination of revulsion and jealousy— revulsion because I loathed him and jealousy because of the way other people seemed to just find themselves having sex, almost by mistake—but I didn't really care. And I didn't care because of something that had happened a few days prior.

I'd been hurrying out of the room when I'd almost collided with Olney, who'd been exiting his room. Our bodies hadn't touched, but my instrument case had banged his thigh, and he'd said, "What the hell?"

Usually, I kept my viola in a locker in the music building, but I'd brought it back to the dorm the previous night because I'd needed to change its strings. I said nothing, and Olney glared and said, "You think you're so fucking talented with your stupid fucking violin."

Probably, even then and without much effort, Olney could have reduced me to tears. He could have said that I was ugly or repulsive, that no one would ever want to date me, that he and his friends had never understood why Chloe lived with such a loser. But, whether by chance or error, he had tried to insult me on the one front where I was impervious. It wasn't just that I thought I was so fucking talented. I *knew* I was so fucking talented. I did not know what my professional future held; I was still waiting to hear from the Chamber Music Society about my audition. After graduation, I'd get in my parents' car and ride home with them. I'd gig while continuing to try out, over the coming months and maybe years, for permanent positions with orchestras in various cities. If I could save up enough money, I'd move to New York without a job. But I knew I had what was required—not just pure talent, which Chloe had, but also the determination, the swagger even. I knew, as much as such a thing was knowable, that I'd be in the 5 percent. And I also suddenly knew that whatever being a college soccer player had provided John Olney with, it was ending; it wasn't transferrable.

I looked him in the eye and said, "It's not a violin. It's a viola."

MY HUSBAND AND I had established a system of bribery—I won't go into the tedious details—in which our children could, every six weeks or so, "earn" a toy or other item based on doing their chores and homework without complaining. That fall, after we'd moved, I walked with Elliot one Saturday morning to the shopping district a few blocks from our house to a store called Giraffe and Flamingo, which sold the manga trading cards and comic books he liked, along with artisanal wooden dolls, and anti-Trump pins, and belt buckles and bracelets made out of old license plates. As Elliot examined the comics, I looked at T-shirts hanging from a rack. They were organic cotton, cost between twenty-two and twenty-six dollars each, and featured the word OLNEYVILLE in various fonts, along with half-ironic slogans:

If you lived here, you'd be home by now.

Quirky since 1796.

Progress & Prosperity (& Paczki)

There also were a few shirts with the area code of the city, and a few with the shape of the state, and some random shirts with images of Vietnamese chili-garlic sauce.

How profoundly arbitrary life is, I thought, which, of course, was the opposite of a profound thought.

* * *

ON CONCERT NIGHTS, I usually got home from the hall around ten-thirty, after Travis and the kids were asleep, and I stayed downstairs for a while. I often poured a glass of wine and sat in the living room with all the lights off, scrolling on my phone. It wasn't long after I'd looked through the rack of Olneyville T-shirts that I returned home with a headache. We'd performed the songs of ABBA that night, the kind of pop-cultural pandering that's been the norm with symphonies for years now, and though I actually liked ABBA as a listener, I hated the charts—the music was boring, and the drum set was too loud.

In my dark living room, on my phone, I googled John Olney and found nothing, or nothing for the John Olney I'd gone to college with, though links existed for other men with his name. I then googled Chloe and, after a few false starts, started reading her Facebook posts, which weren't private. We hadn't kept in touch, though three years after our graduation I'd heard through a mutual friend that she was marrying David—that is, she was marrying one of the athletes from our hall, one of the two she hadn't "dated" during our senior year. I hadn't been invited to the wedding, and I wouldn't have gone if I had been; it was the same month that, after auditioning for the second time, I joined the Chamber Music Society. I couldn't help wondering if the athletes, all those guys who'd kissed or aspired to kiss her, had served as groomsmen.

Sitting in my living room, I discovered that she appeared to be married to Alex—not David, one of the generic ones, but the curly-haired athlete, the only athlete who'd been nice. Had I been confused, and had Alex been the one she'd married years earlier, or was it possible she'd married David at one point, then later married Alex? My curiosity got the better of me, and right then, via Facebook, I sent her a message.

I know it's been forever, I wrote. *But I have to confess I just looked you up and . . . are you married to Alex who lived on our hall?*

Within ten minutes, she had written back: *Wow Emily it's great to hear from you!! Yes, after my divorce from David (yep, also from our hall) and Alex's divorce from his first wife, Alex and I found each other again, now doing the "blended family" thing. Um . . . dormcest? :) Congrats on all your success!*

That's amazing, I wrote back. *Is Alex still friends with the other guys?* The truth was that her congratulations weren't that gratifying. I was accustomed to my success; I knew it was of a nichey variety, and sometimes I secretly was more surprised that I'd gotten my eczema under control than that I was a principal in an orchestra.

They take an annual ski trip, Chloe wrote. *Or most of them do, I don't know if you know but John Olney has had a lot of health problems, was diagnosed with ALS about a year ago and is already confined to a wheelchair. Very sad.*

Oh wow I didn't know that, I wrote. My heart began beating more quickly. *Where does he live?*

In Phoenix, no wife and kids, she wrote. *He was a ladies' man for so long but never settled down, I wish he had now (for his sake).*

In the Facebook photos, Chloe was plump rather than slim but still very pretty. Apparently she enjoyed gardening, belonged to a book club, and had recently participated in a 10K run/walk to raise money for a park conservancy. Her children and stepchildren were teenagers, and blond like her. There was nothing to suggest that she taught music or even still played it, but that didn't mean she didn't, and, either way, I wasn't going to ask. *She seems kind,* I thought. I had, I understood now, felt let down by her our senior year—I felt she had chosen the athletes over me, and without hesitation. It wasn't as if this brief exchange of messages made me see her all that differently, but it made me suspect that *she* saw the dissolution of our friendship differently. I also suspected that she didn't see herself as the heroine of a fairy tale in which six out of six men fell in love with her—that this was only the way I perceived things.

Good for you for marrying Alex, I wrote. *He was always the nicest and cutest of all of them.*

One of the surprises of adulthood has been that, as the years pass, it has become less rather than more clear to me whether I'm a good or bad person. Learning that John Olney had ALS certainly didn't make me feel gleeful; it was deeply depressing. But as I finished my wine, set the glass in the sink, and walked up the steps to the second floor, I became aware of a blooming internal admiration for myself for *not* feeling glee, and, really, I wasn't so sure this self-regard was any less reprehensible.

IN FAIRNESS TO TRAVIS, I mentioned it at a bad time—just after he'd returned from walking our kids to the bus stop the next morning and before he drove to work. I was putting the breakfast dishes in the dishwasher, and I turned off the faucet and said, "Did I ever tell you about John Olney?"

He looked up from his phone and said, "Who?"

"A guy who lived on my hall my senior year of college who was a huge asshole. In general, I mean, but also to me specifically. I heard from my college roommate last night that he has ALS."

"That sucks," Travis said.

It sucked that a guy in college had been an asshole to me? That the guy now was experiencing serious health problems? Both? But already it didn't seem worth asking, and to think of describing the entire situation, the bathroom stalls, made me preemptively tired. Sometimes the ways in which the lines of communication had gradually broken down between my husband and me seemed specific to us—our opposing work schedules, which made us both feel like single parents—and more often they seemed so common as to be clichés. Most musicians I knew were married to other musicians, which had its own pitfalls—uneven success, the difficulty of finding two orchestral positions in the same place—but also offered the advantage of both members of the couple speaking a shorthand. Among musicians married to civilians, the civilians tended to worship the musicians. Travis had never worshipped me. We'd met because he was friends with my neighbor in New York, which is to say he'd met me as a person rather than as a musician. I hadn't thought adulation was something I wanted or needed; I had thought companionship sufficed. But I'd failed to anticipate how calamitous the standard erosion of affection over time could be when you started with a modicum as opposed to an abundance.

In our kitchen, I said, "Have you ever noticed those Olneyville T-shirts at Giraffe and Flamingo? I'm wondering if I should send him one."

Travis squinted. "Why?"

"Because of Olneyville and his last name is Olney."

"So?"

"Do you know which one ALS is? Apparently, he can't walk anymore. So maybe if he's isolated, it would be nice for him to get a present. And just, you know, the name coincidence."

Travis shrugged. "Do what you want, but I wouldn't." I thought the next thing he was going to say was *Because he was an asshole to you.* Instead he said, "I don't think an adult man really wants a T-shirt with his name on it."

THE NEXT AFTERNOON, WHEN I took Elliot and Sophie out for our four o'clock dinner, I said, "Do you remember when I told you about all the boys who fell in love with my roommate in college?"

"They didn't *all* fall in love with her," Sophie said. "One of them didn't."

"I was wrong about that," I said. "The one I thought never fell in love with her is now her husband."

In a slightly perturbed voice, Elliot said, "Mom, I think if they'd known you better, at least one of them would have fallen in love with you."

I smiled. "I promise I'm not upset. I don't think I had much in common with any of them. But I learned something else, and I'm curious to get advice on this from both of you. Of those six boys, one was a jerk to me, but I just found out he's sick with a serious disease. His name is John Olney, so I was thinking maybe I should get him an Olneyville T-shirt to say, 'I'm sorry you're sick.'"

"They sell Olneyville T-shirts at Giraffe and Flamingo," Sophie said.

"Exactly. Those are the ones I meant."

"How was he a jerk?" asked Elliot.

"Well—" I paused. In addition to not knowing if I was a good or bad person, I wasn't sure if I was a good or bad mother. I wanted the things I told my children to be enlightening, not burdensome. "Do you remember that the bathrooms in my dorm were coed? There was only one stall in the bathroom, and John Olney would wait until he knew I was using it to poop, then stand outside it to try to make me feel embarrassed or intimidated."

It seemed highly plausible that the mention of poop would make one or both of my kids laugh, but neither of them did. Sophie said with outrage, "That's so rude!"

"But why did he do that?" Elliot asked.

How strange it was to realize that this topic was not unspeakable, though I'd never have guessed, when it was happening, how long it would take me to speak of it or in whom I'd ultimately confide. Slowly, I said, "I don't really know why. Some people just have meanness inside of them, and they enjoy unleashing it on other people. And maybe he decided to unleash it on me because, being an athlete and being male, he was considered cooler or more popular than I was, and he knew he could get away with it. Other people have unhappiness inside them, and they want to get rid of it, and it comes out as meanness."

"*I'm* popular and I'm not mean," Sophie said.

Elliot said, "You sound conceited."

"I'm glad you're not mean," I said. "Both of you. I don't know if I should send John Olney a shirt or not because . . . well, I haven't seen him for more than twenty years. Maybe it's nice if I do, but maybe it's—do you guys know what the word 'gloating' means?"

They both shook their heads.

"It's feeling pleased with yourself at someone else's expense," I said. "Maybe if I sent him an Olneyville T-shirt, I'd be telling myself that I was being a nice person, but really I'd be saying, 'Look how well my life turned out. Look at my great job; look at my great children. Too bad things aren't very good for you.'"

"I don't think you should send it to him," Elliot said. "Because of that."

"I think you *should* send him a T-shirt," Sophie said. "Because he's sick and it might cheer him up."

Unexpectedly, I felt my eyes well with tears. My children were so thoughtful! I loved them so much! Though Elliot and Sophie consider me a frequent crier—I cry when the contestants on game shows cry, usually after they just won a lot of money, or when one of the songs from Mahler's Rückert-Lieder comes on the radio—I decided to spare them my tears this time. I blinked twice, swallowed, and said, "Do you both know what you want to order?"

HOW DID I THINK for so long that the tidbits my mother shared didn't contain lessons? I see in retrospect that they were nothing *but* lessons.

As you make your way through the world, you will feel bewildered, appalled, and charmed by other people.

In the real version of all our days, as opposed to the version we publicly present, there are many undignified moments.

The circumstances that distress you and the circumstances that distress someone else might not overlap in the slightest.

In situations that make you nervous, do your best and proceed; others before you have also been nervous.

I still, as it happens, have not decided whether to send John Olney a shirt.

J'ai besoin de trouver ma valise, I think as I scramble eggs for my children or as I drive alone in the evening to the symphony hall. *J'ai besoin de trouver ma valise.* Across continents and decades, the sentence now echoes in my head, too. And I recognize in a way that I once didn't that my mother must have told an abridged version of certain stories, a superficial account meant to protect me or herself. She spent an entire semester in France. What happened *after* she found her suitcase? But my mother is no longer living, so I cannot ask.

THE HUG

It's a Sunday afternoon in July and they're sitting in the back-yard when Daphne tells Rob that her long-ago ex-boyfriend will be in town on Wednesday. Rob is reading the opinion section of the newspaper, Daphne has just set down the arts section, and she says it offhandedly, in a way that initially gives Rob the impression that Theo happens to be passing through St. Louis.

"Obviously, he won't come inside the house," she says. "I assume we'll just catch up out here."

"If he's here for dinner, I can grill."

"We haven't nailed down the timing yet, but great. I was thinking about if there's anyone else from college to invite, and I realized I'm the last one still here from my friend group. Isn't that weird?"

"It's a testament to your stability."

"Or my boringness. By the way, I think it'd be nice if I give Theo a hug. I hope that's okay with you."

Rob, who is in a lounge chair across the table from Daphne's chair, squints at her. "It would be nice?"

"He said he hasn't touched another person for four months. He's clearly having a hard time."

"And that's your responsibility?"

"Actually, yes," Daphne says. "In the sense that I'm a human being and he's a human being and we're all part of the brotherhood of man."

"Hmm," Rob says. "That's an interesting way to describe the guy you almost married."

Daphne's expression is more perplexed than concerned. "Are you acting like this because of jealousy or germs?"

They have been quarantining since Saturday, March 14, when they discussed it all day and decided against attending the fiftieth-birthday potluck for their friend Leah, and that's the last date on the calendar Rob can remember with clarity. As a freelance web designer, Rob has worked from home for more than a decade; Daphne usually goes to an office but has been able to do her job, which is payroll and accounting for a nonprofit, remotely. At first, everyone they knew was also quarantining—they live in the racially diverse and left-leaning neighborhood of Tower Grove South—but the protests in early June seemed to break the seal and now they see their neighbors hosting parties, or playdates where kids go in and out of each other's houses. And these are their fellow liberals, not the Missourians who made news over Memorial Day weekend by cramming into seedy-looking resort pools a few hours away. Meanwhile, Rob and Daphne's only child, Olivia, who is a junior at the University of Minnesota, has remained in the off-campus apartment she shares with two friends, finishing her spring classes remotely and volunteering at a canned good and diaper distribution center and, in her down time, cooking vegan meals that she texts photos of to Daphne and Rob because neither of them is on Instagram.

Rob has not yet answered Daphne's question when she adds, "Theo's driving, if that makes you feel better. He's not getting on a plane."

"He still lives in Montana?"

Daphne nods.

"And Bozeman must be, what, thirty hours by car." Rob pulls

out his phone, checks, and when he sees that it's closer to twenty hours, does not correct himself. "So he stops six or seven times, and I assume he plans to stay overnight in a hotel."

"I'm not saying it's risk-free, but I know he's being incredibly careful. He's actually kind of a hypochondriac."

"Why is he traveling now anyway?"

Daphne shrugs. "He's lonely."

"Wait, he's coming to see you?"

"He's going on a road trip. Here first, and then on to New Hampshire to visit his cousin."

"Hell," Rob says in a fakely high-spirited tone, "in that case, why don't we join him? We could all rent an RV together."

"If this reassures you, we'll wear masks if we hug."

"You've certainly given a lot of thought to this long, soulful embrace."

"There's nothing romantic about the situation. Theo is a person in pain."

"Are you saying he's suicidal?"

"If he was, would it make hugging him okay? I don't think he's suicidal, although I'm sure he's clinically depressed."

"Everyone is clinically depressed right now," Rob says.

Daphne stands. "I'm going to put the recycling out," she says. "Do I have your blessing to do that?" He doesn't respond, and she adds, "I'm confident hugging Theo is lower risk than a haircut." The comparison is not a coincidence; Rob got his first haircut of quarantine last week, at a place that took his temperature before he entered, maintained distance between clients, and had so-called enhanced cleaning protocols.

"Here's the thing," Rob says. "When your father and step-mother came to visit, you didn't want to hug them." This was in June, on Father's Day, after they'd driven from Jefferson City for an outdoor lunch.

"Of course I wanted to," Daphne says.

"Well, you didn't do it. The fact that this is what you want to take a chance on, after we've been so careful—that Theo's what you want to take a chance on—forgive me if that raises some questions."

THE TRUTH IS THAT Rob is not clinically depressed. He's doing . . . better than usual? Indeed, he's lost eight pounds since March. In the past, he'd have a couple of beers or a glass or two of wine each night, and he decided, as a pandemic experiment, to restrict his drinking to weekends. He started taking a pre-dinner walk, in lieu of the pickup basketball game of middle-aged men he used to erratically join. For years, Daphne has been the one who plans their social life, and though they now occasionally have distanced drinks (for him, sparkling water if it's during the week) in their yard or someone else's, it's with one of two other couples they've known forever. That the more arbitrary get-togethers he used to find himself part of have fallen by the wayside—the first birthday of the child of one of Daphne's co-workers or the restaurant dinners with a group of six, half of whose names he'd get to the end of the night without having fully registered—is such a relief that he understands he never enjoyed them. He actively misses Olivia in a way he hasn't in the two years since she left for college, wishes she were around to accompany him on a walk or to do a puzzle with. But the reality is that she's probably happier with her peers.

In their Craftsman brick house, which is neither large nor tiny, Rob and Daphne have developed a routine that prevents being in each other's presence all the time. She wakes before he does and does yoga in the backyard; she is finishing a smoothie when he enters the kitchen, showered, to make coffee. Early on, they ate lunch together, then, and he's pretty sure this was intentional, they began staggering their lunches. He eats a peanut butter sandwich and an apple around noon, then she comes in a few minutes after one—he's long gone by then—and eats a mug of sauerkraut with a dollop of either sour cream or Thousand Island dressing on top. He finds this meal repulsive, akin to consuming a mug of nothing but relish or jelly, though actually more disgusting than either of those would be. In the beginning, he couldn't identify the memory evoked by the smell of the sauerkraut, but eventually, with repeated exposure, realized it was from Olivia's babyhood, when she'd awaken on some mornings with diapers so soaked with urine, so bulging and heavy and warm, that they seemed almost alive. The first time Rob saw Daphne eating her mug of sauerkraut, he said, "You're having that straight?" and she said something about probiotics, and he dropped the subject.

Rob does not, in general, find Daphne disgusting. After twenty-two years of marriage, she looks much as she did when they met, except now her hair is gray: a petite woman with a pixie cut and piercing blue eyes who favors flats, black slacks, and short-sleeved pastel sweaters. Every day, she wears small gold hoop earrings given to her by her parents at her college graduation; a thin gold necklace with Olivia's name carved into the pendant; and her plain gold wedding band. When Daphne's hair began to turn gray about ten years ago, she asked once if he wished she would dye it and he said truthfully that he didn't care. They still have sex, which feels like either proof that their marriage remains intact, the reason their marriage remains intact, or both. Just as they agreed without discussion to a schedule of eating only dinner together during quarantine, they have for many years without discussing it had intercourse after going to bed every Saturday night—no more and no less. When Rob hears that a couple they know is divorcing, this habit is always the first thing he thinks of, as a form of reassurance. Then he thinks about a conversation he had the night before their wedding in 1998. As he and his groomsmen were leaving the church to go to the rehearsal dinner, his cousin Nils, who was a few years younger, leaned over and whispered to Rob, "You're really ready to swear off getting laid by anyone else for the rest of your life?"

Rob replied, "I'm just glad I'll be getting laid for the rest of my life." He can still remember Nils's expression, which turned from jocular to a little sheepish. Rob thought, and still thinks, that he'd accidentally said something perfect in that moment, not because he was trying to be clever but because it was true.

AT DINNER ON MONDAY, Daphne says, "I've listened to your concerns, and five or six days after Theo visits, I'll get tested. Until then, I'll sleep in Olivia's room, and I'm happy to wear a mask when you and I are together in the house."

"Jesus," Rob says. "You really want to hug this guy, huh?"

"The chances of getting Covid from him are very low. I'd be taking the precautions for your peace of mind."

"Or you could just not have your passionate embrace."

Rob grilled chicken thighs and zucchini, and as Daphne cuts into her chicken, her nostrils flare in irritation. But her voice is calm as she says, "Is it possible that you don't care if I hug Theo but you drew a line in the sand and now you feel like you have to defend it?"

"Is it possible that you're still carrying a torch for your ex and trying to conceal it by pretending to be worried about his mental health?"

She looks at Rob directly, her blue eyes intense. "I'm not still carrying a torch for Theo," she says, "but would you like to discuss your fear that I am?"

After hesitating for only a split second—Daphne has been in therapy, but Rob never has, and this feels like a moment where that discrepancy is manifesting itself in an annoying manner—Rob says, "As a matter of fact, I wouldn't, although maybe it's a discussion you should have with yourself." Even to his own ear, however, he sounds petulant. Plus, he has long suspected that if Daphne nurses any private crush, it's on a co-worker named Mark, a man who seems to Rob unremarkable physically and intellectually but in whose presence, at retirement or holiday parties, Daphne has always giggled atypically. Rob doesn't think anything has ever

happened between Daphne and Mark, more that Mark is not ridiculous in the vague way that Theo is.

Daphne dated Theo when they were undergraduates at Washington University and for a few years after. In college, Theo was the
star of several plays, and people thought he might become a professional actor, but he never did; perhaps not unrelatedly, Theo is
from a wealthy family in Chicago, and, as far as Rob knows, he's
barely held a real job in the last three decades. When Daphne and
Theo were twenty-four, she accidentally got pregnant, even though
she was on the Pill, and, although she's pro-choice, she felt ready
to have a baby. She thought she and Theo should get married and
become parents. Theo wanted her to have an abortion—he was
nice about it, not bullying, Daphne emphasized in describing this
time to Rob—but then, before they reached a resolution, she mis-
carried. Their subsequent breakup was mutual. The tenor of their
relationship had changed, and though they weren't angry at each
other, they'd both learned things about the other that made it impossible to stay together. Daphne's description to Rob of these
events was matter-of-fact rather than distraught, as if she were re-
counting a breakup in which she had not been directly involved.

The year after the miscarriage, Daphne and Rob met at an Ok-
toberfest pub crawl organized by a mutual friend. While Theo
wasn't invited to Rob and Daphne's wedding, he returned to St.
Louis for a few other weddings around that time. Before meeting
Theo in 1999, Rob felt some combination of nervous and mildly
hostile, but when Daphne introduced the two men, Theo held out
both of his pointer fingers and thumbs like revolvers and said, "I
challenge you to a duel!" Then he stepped forward and hugged
Rob—the irony of this gesture is not, in retrospect, lost on Rob—
and said, "Only kidding, man. I've heard a ton of good things
about you." At some point later in the evening, on the dance floor,
Theo pulled off his jacket, tie, and shirt to reveal a massive black
octopus tattoo sprawled across his back—this was before massive
tattoos were commonplace—and watching from the sidelines, Rob

had to admit, if only to himself, that there was something goofily endearing about Theo.

As far as Rob knows, Daphne's contact with her ex over the last twenty-plus years has been infrequent, perhaps an annual email or two and a Christmas card. Theo didn't marry until he was in his forties and divorced just two years later, but he always sent a Christmas card, usually a photo of himself in some faraway location: in front of a temple in Bali or a pyramid outside Cairo; feeding a koala bear at a sanctuary near Melbourne. More than once, Rob was compelled to mock these cards—besides the ostentatious travel, wasn't the point of photo Christmas cards to show friends what your children looked like?—and Daphne would defend Theo but not very vigorously. After Olivia was born, Theo had sent them baby cowboy boots (cowgirl boots?) that probably would have fit Olivia for about a month, well before she could walk, and that Rob is certain she never wore.

But what if this interpretation of Theo as a sweet, distant fool is a misread on Rob's part? Or what if it once was accurate but, now that the world has been turned upside down, a wealthy fool from the past looks more enticing?

Carefully, Rob says, "I trust you. Of course I trust you. But given that there's not much difference between hugging him and not hugging him, how about not doing it?"

From across the kitchen table, Daphne furrows her brow. "If there's not much difference, why are you making such a big deal of it?"

The anger he experiences in this moment is surprisingly visceral, an immediate heat in his face and neck. "Then can't you just not because I asked you and I'm your husband?"

"Touch deprivation is a real thing," Daphne says. "You can google it."

"For fuck's sake," Rob says. "Let him hire a prostitute."

Daphne has just taken a bite of chicken, which she chews and swallows. When she speaks, her tone is pensive rather than defiant. She says, "It's interesting, because before 2016, I think I might have felt like I needed your permission for this. I'd have preemptively given you the power to tell me I couldn't do it, or maybe I'd have bought into some idea that it wasn't allowed in a marriage. But, as despicable as Trump is, he's made me see that so many of the things I thought people couldn't do were just things people usually don't do. They're just norms. They aren't laws."

What's Rob supposed to say to this? Congratulations on your feminist awakening? Fuck you? What he says is "Comparing me to Trump is a pretty low blow."

"No," she says calmly. "In this scenario, I'm Trump."

ON TUESDAY, THEY'RE NOT not talking, but they don't talk very much. At dinner, as if by agreement, they both avoid the topic of Theo, whose visit, assuming it's still happening, is less than twenty-four hours away. Instead they talk about the antiracist book Daphne is reading for her upcoming Zoom book club, then about two restaurants that have just permanently closed (one of them is where they ate a six-course meal on their twentieth wedding anniversary), then about who Biden will select as his vice presidential candidate and when. After dinner, they watch the first two episodes of a show about a female detective investigating the murder of a sixteen-year-old girl in South Dakota, a show Rob heard is good that Daphne said she's willing to start though she suspects it's probably too dark for her. As the credits roll on the second episode, and a haunting violin melody plays, she says, "Yeah, I can't do any more of that." She stands and, as usually happens, she goes upstairs to use the bathroom while he starts the dishwasher and switches off the lights.

Their room is dark when he joins her in bed, and he can't tell based on her breathing if she's awake or asleep. Within a few minutes, her breathing becomes louder and he realizes she probably was awake before but is asleep now. She is lying on her stomach, her face turned away from him, and, beneath the covers, he reaches out, pushes up the hem of her nightgown, then pushes down the waistband of her underwear. He runs his palm back and forth over her bare backside. This is never the way sex starts between them—also, it's Tuesday night, not Saturday—and the sound she soon makes is one he has never heard, not in what must be well over a thousand couplings. She is . . . purring? Instead of flipping over and facing him, she rolls onto her left side and backs into him. Neither of them speaks for the entire encounter. Is this not impressively hot? Are they not keeping things exciting?

But late the next morning, while he is working in his basement office, she comes down and says, "I've decided to meet Theo in Forest Park, and I'm going to pick up sandwiches first from Fattore's. Do you want me to pick up something for you and drop it off here?"

In the brief amount of time it took for her to start and finish those sentences, he thought she was about to invite him to join her and Theo, and he planned to proudly decline. Realizing this was not the offer she was making, he hesitates for a second or two. Then he says, "I've tried to make it very clear what I want, and it's not a sandwich."

BUT ACTUALLY, IT'S ALSO a sandwich? Or at least, a little absurdly, her mention of Fattore's gave him a craving for their corned beef, and a half hour after he saw the wheels of Daphne's car recede through the basement window, he calls in to place an order of his own. The temperature today is in the high eighties—not bad for St. Louis—and after he's procured the sandwich, he eats it in the backyard, washing it down with a beer from the refrigerator because why not?

After he's finished, he returns to the basement. He's creating a website for a new client, a real estate agent who left a big company to work for herself and who told him, contrary to what he'd have imagined, that many people are buying and selling houses during the pandemic. But it's difficult to concentrate, and he decides to take his afternoon walk a few hours early. The loop around Tower

Grove Park typically takes him about an hour—a podcast or audiobook seems too ambitious today given his distracted state so he listens to Bruce Springsteen—and when he's finished, instead of heading home immediately, he sits on a bench off Magnolia Avenue and texts Olivia. *Hi honey,* he writes. *How's everything going?*

Three minutes elapse before she texts, *R u ok dad?*

Wondering if Daphne has mentioned to their daughter the recent conflict, he types, *Good overall. How are you?*

But u never text me during day

Is he really such a creature of habit?

Two more texts from her arrive: *Did mom tell u what I told her about donations?*

Local mutual aid societies way better than big orgs that spend a lot on marketing

He texts back, *Have you cooked anything interesting lately?*

The three dots of her reply appear, then disappear, then don't reappear. After a minute, he stands and walks home.

DAPHNE LEFT FOR FATTORE'S around eleven-thirty and when he gets back to the house, three hours have passed and she hasn't returned. He goes inside, uses the bathroom, drinks a glass of water, and is setting the glass in the dishwasher and trying to decide on his next move—Work work? Yard work? Shower?—when Daphne enters the house through the back door.

The first thing he notices is that she's not wearing a mask. Before Rob can remark on this oversight, as per her suggested protocol after seeing Theo, she says, "I didn't hug him." Though it's not that hot outside, she seems spacey, almost dazed.

He's genuinely surprised. After a few seconds, he says, "Well, I appreciate that."

"I didn't not hug him for you."

He has the impulse to reply sarcastically, though she didn't speak in a sarcastic way. And she continues to sound bewildered as she says, "It wasn't because I had second thoughts. I would have hugged him. But he obviously didn't want to hug me. The really stupid part of this argument you and I have been having is that Theo and I had never discussed hugging. It wasn't a plan we came up with together ahead of time. I'd just assumed that he'd want to because he's a touchy-feely person and because he'd mentioned his lack of contact with other people. And I thought it would seem cavalier if I told you after the fact. It would be more respectful to give you a heads-up beforehand. And then it turned into a whole thing. But it was very clear that the idea of our hugging had never crossed Theo's mind. He wanted us to be ten feet apart instead of six, and I'd taken those chairs we used to sit in at Olivia's soccer games, but he wouldn't sit on one. He used a towel from his car."

Rob isn't sure if he's joking or not as he says, "You could have told me it was because you had second thoughts."

She looks at him intently, focusing on his face for the first time since she entered the house. "You'd have preferred that I lie?"

"I'd have preferred that you did have second thoughts."

In the ensuing quiet, the sink drips twice and a neighbor's dog barks. Then, reverting to that subdued, spacey tone, she says, "I really don't have romantic feelings for Theo. I certainly don't wish I'd married him. He's so flaky. But the same thing that would have made him terrible to be married to, his neediness and his neuroses— there's something endearing about that in small doses. And before seeing him, I was thinking, well, he's very in touch with his emotions. So we'll have a connection, we'll reflect together on how strange life is during the pandemic. Instead, he delivered this two-hour monologue and asked me literally nothing. I know he's been on his own and I'm sympathetic to that, but first it was a tirade about processed meat—after he'd texted me that he wanted a salami sandwich—and then it was his dispute with his neighbor in Bozeman who uses tons of lawn chemicals and then it was about how Democrats are as complicit as Republicans and how we as Americans should take our cue from Scandinavian countries who are so much happier because they embrace the outdoor lifestyle and just on and on and on. I felt like I was a trash can that he was dumping words into. If I met him today, if he were the friend of a friend, I'd think he was self-centered and boring and just weird."

In a ratio Rob is unsure of, though it's probably about ten to one, this information is gratifying and depressing. "I'm sorry," he says. After a pause, he adds, "Would you like to talk to me about how life is strange during the pandemic?"

Her laughter then is disturbingly bitter.

"I wasn't kidding," he says.

Her expression is hard to read as she says, "You know what I sometimes wish? I wish that either I liked you too much to eat sauerkraut around you or you liked me too much to find it gross that I do."

He is both amused and mildly insulted, and it's in this spirit that he says, "We don't need to like each other. We love each other." It occurs to him that he might have just uttered another true and perfect rejoinder like the one he made all those years ago to his cousin Nils, but when he glances at her for confirmation, he realizes he didn't.

"Oh, Rob." If she doesn't sound angry, she also doesn't sound amused. Possibly but not definitely, she sounds sad. If he were a different kind of husband, a different kind of person, he'd ask what's inside those two words. That he doesn't ask isn't because he doesn't care.

He says, "Come here." But he is the one who walks toward her. He slides his arms around her ribs, below her armpits, pulls her body into his, and squeezes her torso. There are a few seconds where she is simply standing there, neither resisting nor responding. Abruptly, he realizes that they don't really embrace much apart from sex. He's pretty sure they used to, a long time ago.

Of course he cares. But he doesn't think asking what she means by *Oh, Rob* will lead them to a better place. Engaging with a fleeting emotion doesn't necessarily serve a purpose.

Several more seconds pass. The sink continues dripping. Finally, she raises both her arms and he feels them tighten around him. She hugs him back.

LOST BUT NOT FORGOTTEN

I suppose it was because my thirtieth Ault reunion was coming up (my thirtieth!) that I found myself thinking again about my encounter with Bryce Finley. This was the one boarding school story I'd never told. Not to Martha or anybody else at Ault, not to the friends I made in college or after, not to my husband when I got married. Over the years, I regularly recalled what had happened—especially, for obvious reasons, in 2003—but still I never told anyone.

At first I didn't tell because I didn't know if I'd be describing something magical or humiliating. Then because it seemed private, and the privacy of it didn't seem to be mine. And finally I didn't tell because I wasn't confident I could depict the events properly, without setting them up for misinterpretation. But maybe I am using three justifications to say the same thing.

At last, on the other side of my reunion, I've told not one but two people. No doubt it was in part the milestone of three decades that prompted my disclosure—surely, by any measure, the statute of limitations had passed.

At this point, Ault is both in my bloodstream and a negligible part of my daily existence. To be sure, it shaped many of my life-long habits and preferences: a fondness for fleece jackets and white button-down shirts; a sentimental attachment to the hymn "Jerusalem" and all the Christmas ones from the Service of Lessons and Carols; my subconscious sense that it's morally wrong not to exercise every day, even as I consciously find this notion ridiculous at best and probably downright repugnant; and my pronunciation of certain words, so the first syllable of "deliver" rhymes not with *he,* as my mother said it, but with *huh,* as my classmates at Ault said it. Having spent most of my adulthood back in the Midwest, I'm occasionally asked where my accent is from, and rarely does it feel appropriate to say, *It's the accent of a middle-class girl from Indiana who went to a fancy Massachusetts boarding school.* What I say instead, brightly, is *I'm not sure!*

For a long time, I thought it was hard to explain Ault succinctly, but eventually I realized that it was merely hard to explain it honestly. And the explanation that was both succinct and honest is: *As a boarding school student, I always felt that I was implicitly apologizing for not being sufficiently rich and preppy and privileged. In all the years since I graduated, I've been reckoning with just how rich, preppy, and privileged I am.*

I KNEW, OF COURSE, that Bryce Finley had attended Ault and that if he'd graduated, he'd have done so eight years before my arrival. After Martha and I were assigned a room in Ahmed's, I learned that we lived in the room that had once been his, back when Ahmed's had been Frederick's, a boys' dorm run by a physics teacher named Mr. Frederick. In advance of the reunion weekend in the spring of my sophomore year, it occurred to me that Bryce Finley might appear on campus because it was his tenth, but it also occurred to me that he might not because he'd never graduated, and because he was a celebrity. When I pored over old yearbooks, I always lingered on the page for his senior class where the names and photos of the students who'd left Ault without graduating were listed. In his photo, he looked much as he did later—extremely good-looking—except so young and so tiny that it was almost possible to believe his youth and tinyness had rendered his good looks invisible to his Ault contemporaries. The yearbook page was black and white, which meant you couldn't tell how deeply brown his eyes were, but you certainly could see that his lower lip was considerably fuller than his upper one and that he had high cheekbones and long light hair pulled into a ponytail at the base of his neck—a masculine ponytail, I thought, because that helped me understand his clear sex appeal even when he'd been fourteen or fifteen. I failed to recognize that his androgyny, then and certainly later, *was* his sex appeal. The way I knew he'd been tiny as an Ault student was that in the photo, in loose khaki pants and a loose untucked button-down shirt, Bryce Finley, who was white, was standing next to a Black student in an Ault football uniform who appeared to be a foot and a half taller. The football player was looking to the side and down, and Bryce Finley was looking to the side and up. I knew from cross-referencing other photos that the football player was named Jordan Carmichael, that he'd been a year ahead of Bryce Finley, and that they'd both lived in Frederick's when Bryce was a sophomore. This photo was unlabeled, as were the three other candid shots of students on the page. The page's only words were *Lost But Not Forgotten* across the top, then a list of four names in alphabetical order by surname; Bryce Finley's was second.

After leaving Ault, Bryce Finley had, as I knew from my diligent consumption of celebrity magazines, attended a private school in his hometown of Denver for his senior year, then enrolled at USC but never graduated from there, either. By the time he was twenty, the band for which he'd become the lead singer, Formica Dream, had appeared on both *Saturday Night Live* and the cover of *Rolling Stone*. In the years since, they'd played Wolf Trap, Red Rocks, and Madison Square Garden; in fact, I knew of the existence of Wolf Trap and Red Rocks only because of reading about Formica Dream playing there.

All of which was to say that I had no idea if it was realistic or preposterous to anticipate catching a glimpse of Bryce Finley as he entered the enormous white tent set up on the circle for the weekend, where alumni ate lunch Saturday and posed on the bleachers for their class photo, which would later appear in the Ault quarterly. (On Saturday night, when the alums dispersed to individual class dinners, the tent would open for a few hours to current students for a dance, and I wouldn't attend.) Or perhaps I'd see Bryce Finley cheering on the sidelines of the boys' lacrosse game on Saturday afternoon, or—this seemed least likely—attending the chapel service on Sunday.

Everyone at Ault knew that Bryce Finley was an alum, and people who lived in Ahmed's dorm knew he'd once lived there, and I assumed that almost nobody else gave thought to whether he'd attend his ten-year reunion. It was the kind of news that would spread quickly if he actually arrived on campus, but few people would devote anticipatory attention to it.

But at Saturday lunch in the dining hall, over lukewarm lasagna, Dede announced that she'd heard that Bryce Finley was at that very moment en route to Ault from a show in Germany, on a plane about to land in Boston. She'd learned this information by asking two women wearing the thick white nametags also used at parents' weekend, accented with the Ault crest, affixed to their shirts with tiny gold safety pins; the class year after their handwritten names was Bryce Finley's year, Dede reported, and I could tell she was especially gratified to mention that one of them had referred to him as "Bry." (To just directly ask people what you wanted to know—where did Dede find the nerve?)

It was a sunny mid-May day, and my JV lacrosse game was on a lower field at one-fifteen. I understood that there was no chance a celebrity would attend a JV girls' game, or, for that matter, a varsity girls' game. Thus, when my game ended—we'd lost 4 to 2, and I'd played for one minute just before halftime and three more at the end—instead of taking a shower in the gym, which also was crowded with alums who'd just attended the induction ceremony for the Ault Athletic Hall of Fame, I hurried to the boys' varsity lacrosse game to look around.

Bryce Finley was far from the only famous graduate of Ault, and not even the only potential distinguished graduate at that weekend's reunion, though surely he was the only one who would plausibly show up in snakeskin pants. A congressman from Maine was there for his twenty-fifth reunion, and an ancient-seeming television broadcaster was there for his fortieth. I knew their names but would have recognized neither of them even if they'd been standing next to me when I'd grabbed two brownies and two lemon bars from the refreshment table at the athletic induction ceremony, wrapped the treats in a napkin that also featured the Ault crest, and stuffed them in the pocket of my lacrosse skirt.

At the boys' game, I saw no sign of Bryce Finley, even when I systematically scanned both sides of the field, even when I walked around the field's perimeter. Perhaps I should mention here that I wasn't a particular fan of Formica Dream's music. Yes, there was their huge and irresistible hit "She's So Down on Me," a peppy number in which Bryce Finley's falsetto, over a synthesizer, acoustic guitar, and drums, either belied the ostensibly downbeat title, turned it into a double entendre, or both. The scenario in the lyrics was some combination of intriguing and daunting to me, but in general I didn't like synth-pop nearly as much as I liked, say, Bob Dylan. Formica Dream's melodies and lyrics felt polished and superficial, nodding to the kinds of despair and longing and lust that filled me without truly embodying them.

At the same time, my fascination with celebrities was so intrinsic to my daily functioning that it was like my spleen. Where did it come from? What did it do? It supported my existence; it helped me tolerate the world. Also, Ault's past and present proximity to the semi- and fully-famous was a way of both contextualizing the school and affirming its status to people back in South Bend, including my immediate and extended family members; it reinforced their idea of what boarding school was in ways that were pleasing to me and probably pleasing and a little disgusting to them, by which I might mean doubly pleasing. Did my own fixation with celebrities also arise from their beauty, their status, the frequent soap opera drama of their lives, the occasional tawdriness? Yeah. Sure. All of that.

And so I'd stayed for the entire boys' lacrosse game, eventually standing just close enough to a throng of other not especially popular girls in my class that I hoped it made me invisible without presuming their friendship, and Bryce Finley had never materialized. Then there wasn't much to do but return to my dorm room, eat one brownie and one lemon bar, then the other brownie, then the other lemon bar, then go to dinner with Martha, walk back to the dorm with her, and chat with her while she primped for the dance. When I expressed my disappointment at Bryce Finley's absence, and my irritation with Dede for spreading false rumors at lunch, Martha said, "But, like, what did you want from seeing him? Were you going to ask for his autograph?"

I considered this. "Only if other people did," I said. "And if it didn't seem like he minded." Martha was leaning close to the mirror above her bureau, pulling the skin on her left cheek downward with her right fingertips to apply eyeliner, and I added, "I just want to feast my eyes on him."

She laughed. "There's something about him that reminds me of my grandma's cat."

"His whiskers?" I suggested. "His tail?"

"It's right here." She lifted her hand off her left cheek and ran the fingertips of both her hands alongside, though not actually touching, her earlobes down to her mouth. "The narrowness of his face maybe. Or his cheekbones."

After Martha left, I took off my bra and put on my flannel pajama bottoms and a royal blue T-shirt. In the bathroom, I used the toilet, washed my hands and face, and brushed my teeth. Back in the room, I considered doing the reading for my history class and instead picked up the latest issue of *Time*; Martha's aunt had given her a subscription.

I was lying in bed reading an article about Raisa Gorbachev

when I heard a knock. Before I could even say "Come in," the door opened and a slim, short man with feathered blond hair, wearing bleached jeans and a silky red button-down shirt, entered the room. Astonishingly, thrillingly, terrifyingly, it was Bryce Finley. He was by himself.

His demeanor made me fairly sure he hadn't noticed my presence. After close to a full minute of unself-consciously looking up and around, as you might upon entering a small rustic church, he leaned over Martha's bureau, which was close to the door, and lifted a peach-colored grosgrain ribbon-trimmed picture frame that contained a photo of her and her brother on a sailboat.

"Hi," I said, and he startled. But he did so a little theatrically, making me wonder if he'd known all along I was there. When he looked at me directly, his eyes were indeed that deep brown, and his lips were indeed pillowy.

"Yo!" he said. "I'm not a creep, I swear. I just used to live in this room." His tone was cheerful, and though I had no firsthand experience with drugs of any kind, it occurred to me, based on a looseness in his voice, that he might be under the influence of some.

"I know," I said.

He seemed to take this tacit acknowledgment that I recognized him as an invitation and stepped forward. Other than during visitation, which was the two-hour period three nights a week that a boy or girl could enter the other's dorm room, provided they kept at least three of their four feet on the floor, socializing was not supposed to happen like this; if a boy were caught in a girl's room outside the approved time, the offense was punishable by a day of in-school suspension and subsequent probation. This meant it happened several times a year and then its particulars were announced at roll call by the headmaster: "Early on Sunday morning, a female junior was discovered in the room of a male junior, in violation of visitation rules. The consequences of this violation are . . ." Within a minute or two of the conclusion of roll call, everyone knew not only that it had been Cornelius Fleming and Franny Martin but that at the moment of discovery, they'd both been naked and he'd had two fingers inside her (I wondered, of course, which two).

How unimaginable, how humiliating and marvelous, it would be if it were announced at roll call that a male alum was caught in the room of a female sophomore. But *was* Bryce Finley being in my room an offense? A dad could come into a room, as could a brother, though usually a warning went out first if the brother was a teenager.

"As a matter of fact," Bryce Finley said, "you're in my bed. Like Goldilocks."

"You mean I'm Goldilocks or you are?" I asked, and he laughed. I'd been trying to understand the analogy, not to make a joke, and I was delighted that I'd accidentally been clever.

"Exactly," he said, and then abruptly he'd crossed the room and I wondered if he was going to lie down next to me, or on me, or if he was going to rape me, or if it would be sex and not rape because maybe I wanted it? Who wouldn't want sex with a hot celebrity? Would we then fall in love? (You have to remember: I'd never kissed a boy, and I'd certainly never kissed a man.)

My body buzzed with the array of alarming and exhilarating possibilities, even after Bryce Finley had laid down not on my bed but on Martha's. In a recent fit of "redecorating," we'd taken apart our bunk beds, and her bed was set at a perpendicular angle to mine, so that every night her feet and my head were close together and my feet and her head were far apart. In the seconds of his greatest proximity to me, I had smelled cigarettes on Bryce Finley, which I found slightly disgusting before remembering his status.

Except for my arms and the issue of *Time,* I was, from the collarbone down, covered by my flowered comforter; Bryce Finley was on top of Martha's flowered comforter, his head on her pillow. He looked at the ceiling for a few seconds, then pointed and said, "I used to have a Prince poster up there."

"Oh," I said.

"The albums everyone knows are *Purple Rain* and *1999,* right?

But the really genius one is *Sign o' the Times*. There's nothing that dude can't do. No genre, no instrument. Someone told me he knows how to play twenty-five different instruments. You know how many I can play?" He turned onto his side, folded Martha's pillow in half, and gazed toward me, which I knew he was doing because I was craning my neck to gaze toward him. About six feet separated us.

After a pause, I said, "No. I don't know."

"Two," he said. "Guitar and keyboard."

"I like guitars," I said. "And keyboards."

In a tiny way, he either smiled or smirked. "What's your name?"

"Lee," I said.

He seemed to analyze this information as if it were meaningful, in a way a sober person probably wouldn't have. At last, he gestured over his shoulder with his right thumb and said, "Do you ever go out on that porch?"

It wasn't really a porch, it was the roof over the entrance of Ahmed's, but I knew what he meant. "Yes, but not that much," I said. "We did more in the beginning of the year."

"We used to go out there and smoke," he said. "Not weed. Just cigarettes. Does Mr. Cooper still have that big fucking slobbery Saint Bernard?"

Hesitantly, I said, "I don't think anyone named Mr. Cooper teaches at Ault."

"No?" he said. "What about Mrs. Tilly?"

"I've heard of her," I said. "There's a prize named after her. But she's not here anymore either."

"She ran the infirmary. Sweet old lady. One of the only people who was truly nice at this place." He rolled onto his back again. "I'm not even sure why I'm here. At the reunion, I mean. I was miserable as a student. I was telling my drummer about coming back and he was like, 'Why, man? You couldn't pay me enough.' He went to public school in Oklahoma and he's like, 'Why the fuck would you voluntarily go to a reunion?' And I was like, 'Fair question, but there's something about Ault that's hard to get out of your system.'"

After a few seconds, I said, "I'm not that happy here, but I can picture missing it after I'm gone." Not that he'd know, but this was an uncharacteristically candid admission on my part, nothing I'd ever reveal to anyone other than Martha and maybe not even to her. She'd think that saying *I'm not that happy here* was negative and unnecessary.

Bryce Finley and I both were quiet, and then he said, "Want to go out on the porch?"

Why had I put on my pajamas so early? Why had I removed my bra?

I said, "Now?"

THE SO-CALLED CLASS AGENT responsible for encouraging everyone from my year at Ault to attend our thirtieth reunion was Dede— Dede Faber née Schwartz, my frenemy and freshman roommate, along with Sin-Jun. Dede and I unexpectedly stayed in touch during college via the then-newfangled medium of email. After graduating from Penn, Dede had attended Columbia Law School and married another lawyer, named Bill. In fact, I'd been in her wedding and so had Aspeth Montgomery, and in a development which once might have struck me as far-fetched but seemed unremarkable by the time it happened, Aspeth and I had on a Saturday in June in the late nineties worn identical teal bridesmaid dresses on the porch of a country club in Scarsdale. Dede had eventually had three kids while becoming a partner at a big firm. She presently lived on the Upper West Side, and I stayed in her guest room every few years when I was in New York.

That January prior to our thirtieth reunion, she sent out an email reminding all of us that the reunion would be in May and including a link to Ault's website. In March, she sent another email, a similar one except that this time she included a list of the names of people who'd registered—at that point, just fourteen out of our class of eighty, and I wasn't among them. (I'd go in the end, of course, I always went to the five-year reunions, less because of sentimentality than because of a curiosity undiminished by the evidence provided at previous reunions that there wasn't much to be curious about. My classmates, or at least the thirty to fifty percent who also attended reunions, had grown up to be mostly thin, well-dressed, well-mannered, and, in more than a few cases, disorientingly boring. I'm not sure they were actually more boring than the average adult, but it surprised me more, because of how much I'd once cared what they thought of me. They, too, it turned out, led with discussions about their kids' sports teams, their trips to Telluride and Paris, and the mild winter.)

The other thing that differentiated Dede's second reunion email from her first one was that she included everyone's email addresses on it, except for the handful of classmates who'd managed the feat of evading the alumni office; these were the people who were truly lost but not forgotten. By the time I clicked on the original email around eleven in the morning Central time, a robust conversation was unfolding:

The first response, from Devin Billinger: *For Christ's sake Dede have you ever heard of bcc*

From Darden Pittard: *Dude, chill, not like we can't find each other's info in the online directory.*

From Jasdip Chowdhury: *Like Ault will ever let any of us out of their sight for fundraising reason$$$, they're better than the CIA at tracking people.*

From Dede: *For Christ's sake, Devin, I did it on purpose so those of us who've already registered can gently nudge and encourage our friends to also attend! Plus I need a headcount for the lobster dinner on Sat.*

From John Brindley: *How many 48 year old douches does it take to organize a reunion?*

From Phoebe Ordway: *Phoebe Ordway wishes she could leave the chat*

From Devin: *Who you calling a douche Brindley*

From Clara O'Hallahan: *Have you guys read Consider the Lobster by David Foster Wallace? I will not be in attendance because I'll be on a silent meditation that weekend, but I suspect the book will make you rethink Saturday's menu.*

Even before seeing the chain, which I did not participate in, I'd received a text from Dede that read *Okay Clara then pack a vegan granola bar for your retreat and STFU!!* It was later in the day that I received an email from my classmate Jeff Oltiss:

Hi Lee, Jeff Oltiss here. Hope it's okay that I'm reaching out after seeing your email on Dede's not bcc list:) Not sure if you remember me and not sure I'll make it to the reunion, but I have followed your career from afar (I live in Princeton, NJ) and just wanted to say congrats on what sounds like great work. In recent years, I have made a point of giving back to my community, as Ault espoused (admittedly, the town of Princeton doesn't need much help from me, but I've become very involved with an organization in Trenton that helps students from low income backgrounds apply to and stay in college). I confess if I had it to do over, instead of going into finance, I'd choose a career that directly addresses the social inequity that I think is at the root of so much of the current national discord. Anyway, I hope the last, er, 30 years have treated you well.

Best,
Jeff

There were several unexpected aspects to this email. The first was that, although I had thought a lot about Ault in my adulthood, I had given minimal thought over the years to Jeff Oltiss. In fact, I only ever recalled him with regard to one moment: the parents' weekend in the fall of our junior year when, after dinner, parked near the chapel, my father had ordered me to get out of the back seat of the car and slapped me across the face. Jeff happened to be walking by, and even though it was dark out, I knew he'd seen the incident because we made eye contact. His expression had been muted, nonreactive. This was very Ault-like, of course, very adolescent and boyish. But insofar as he'd revealed any emotion, I always had the sense he'd felt compassion more than scorn. In the twenty months before Jeff and I graduated, we'd made eye contact many more times, in the science wing and the dining hall, and had never spoken.

Another unexpected aspect of the email was that, while I felt enormous gratitude for my job and my life, I didn't have the kind of career people usually "followed." I was the director of a nonprofit that had been created—as it happened, by me—to teach art classes in federal prisons but had expanded into providing other, mostly financial services, such as depositing money into inmates' commissary accounts or covering gas or other forms of transportation so families could travel to see their incarcerated loved one. I'd arrived at this job circuitously, as many people arrive at work they feel is a calling.

At the University of Michigan, I'd majored in art and art history, which my father had taken as evidence of Ault's elitist influence on me—that I'd choose a major so impractical, so pretentious. Prior to graduating, I'd interviewed at a firm that placed teachers in independent schools, "independent" being the euphemism that such schools have long preferred to "private." I knew only three worlds then: my childhood world in South Bend, the rarefied setting of Ault, and the college town of Ann Arbor. The rarefied world was the one that I was most drawn to, or so I thought. I was hired as a high school art teacher at a K-12 school in Chicago and moved into an apartment in Andersonville with a friend of a friend when I was twenty-two. At first I liked the job—the camaraderie with the other teachers, the bright-eyed articulate students, the bustling and only quietly luxe environment—but by my second year, it had already started to seem repetitive. Also, the same thing that drew me to such a place repelled me from it. These kids were all so lucky that no matter how hard I tried, my presence didn't really matter; if I wasn't their teacher, someone else energetic and industrious, with access to first-rate supplies, would be.

Around this time, I read an article in *The Tribune* about a poetry writing class taught inside a prison in Marion, Illinois. I wondered if something similar could exist with art classes but did nothing about it for three years. At that point, I quit my teaching job and moved back to Ann Arbor for a guy I'd known as an undergrad, who was still at the university getting his PhD. As it turned out, the relationship fizzled almost immediately—this was devastating at the time—but I found a job in the education programs at the university's art museum, where I learned how nonprofits worked. Three years after that, shortly before I turned thirty, I taught my first acrylic and watercolor painting class to inmates at FCI Milan, a low-security prison for men located twenty minutes south of the university campus.

Then eighteen years passed, as they do, and I was the executive director of an organization with nine full-time and two part-time employees and twenty-three volunteer art teachers. Intermittently, we'd receive media attention, and I assumed that Jeff had stumbled onto an article in a regional publication, perhaps because we followed each other on Facebook. But when I checked, we didn't follow each other; he didn't have a Facebook account that I could find, though I did track down photos of him from a couple years prior on what appeared to be a cousin's page, in Rome, wearing a navy blue polo shirt. Some were group photos, with a woman—the apparent cousin, whose name was Sandy Oltiss—and a man and Jeff and then varying assortments of the next generation, four or five of them who all looked to be in their teens. If Jeff presently had a wife, she could have been the one taking the pictures, but she was never shown. And if Jeff himself were a person whose existence had no bearing on yours, you'd probably find his appearance to be average, even generic, for a white guy of his age and background. But if you were the kind of person who'd spent your entire life scrutinizing others, and certainly if you'd spent your formative years on the campus of a New England boarding school, you might notice that he was an unostentatiously but extremely preppily handsome man: He had closely cut gray hair, blue eyes, a warm smile, and the fit physique of a person who did things like run, bike, and ski, probably in places like Martha's Vineyard and Park City. I also found a photo of him on the website of a private equity firm headquartered in Manhattan, at which he was a vice president of investor relations, and a few more pictures of him on the website of the organization in Trenton he'd mentioned, of which he was the current board president. In the nonprofit photos, he wore a white oxford cloth shirt and smiled, and in the private equity firm photo, he wore a gray suit, pale blue shirt, and darker blue tie and also smiled but grimly, or perhaps I was projecting the grimness onto him. While working at a private equity firm was a job I struggled to have much respect for at this point, the fact was that a not inconsiderable number of my Ault classmates, males included, had only briefly, or never at all, held what would be widely defined as real jobs. Some handled "family investments," and maybe this was a real thing, but it had always sounded to me like getting paid to count your own money.

Hi Jeff, I wrote back half an hour later. *So nice to hear from you and thanks for the kind words about IncARTcerated, which has been amazingly rewarding. (I admit that I wish I could change the name, partly because we do a lot in addition to art classes and partly just because it's so corny, but it seems that the toothpaste left the tube on that one back in the early aughts.) Anyway, why aren't you going to the reunion? Lee*

Lee, great to hear back from you, he replied within five minutes. *That Friday night is the eightieth birthday of my former mother-in-law, and even though my ex-wife and I aren't still married, we're amicable and I continue to have a good relationship with her family. Also my kids, now ages twenty, nineteen, and sixteen, will be there, and they can be so elusive these days! But maybe I should figure out a way to attend the festivities Saturday, especially since I've never been to an Ault reunion. Are you planning to go?*

So, as I'd suspected, he wasn't currently married. My next question was whether he already knew I, too, was divorced.

I wrote, *I'm also on good terms with my ex-husband and his family, though not quite to the "attend his mom's 80th birthday" level. Maybe more like the "include her on my Christmas card list" level? Anyway, I got divorced four years ago. You? And my daughters are a bit younger than your kids, now twelve and fifteen. I've been to every single one of our five-year reunions! I feel a little embarrassed about this. I always go in thinking I'll conquer my Ault demons by facing them, then when I'm back there, honestly, it's mostly little ham and brie sandwiches and small talk and I almost forget the demons, at least for the weekend. Maybe that's the point of reunions?*

Ha! Jeff wrote back. *If I'd known I could vanquish Ault demons and eat little sandwiches at the same time, I'd have returned years ago. I don't think you should feel at all embarrassed about having attended all the reunions, and for that matter, I don't think you should feel embarrassed about the name of your organization. Sure, a little punny, but also memorable! I've been divorced for almost seven years. A tough life experience that I also think was for the best.*

We exchanged three more emails each that day, and the last one I sent was at around eight at night: *About to go quiz my younger daughter for her history test but fun catching up today. Let me know if you do decide to go to the reunion. You should! (How else will you find out all the details of Devin's newfound love of pickleball?)*

By this point, I suspected that Jeff would attend. I also knew that if I let it, our emailing could probably escalate in a way that would be enjoyable and maybe misleading; I'd done the whole middle-aged dating app thing, and been mildly burned more than once by my own tendency toward frenzied early texting in the absence of confirmed in-person chemistry. And I was pretty sure that Jeff, too, was wondering if maybe there'd be something between us. I didn't really know why me, or if he was also putting out feel-

ers with other women from our class, but while once such questions would have agitated me, they didn't anymore. There was a
kind of proof and clarity I'd required not just in my adolescence
but well into my adulthood that I recognized retroactively as a ced-
ing of the ground rules to others, as if ground rules definitively
existed, as if this sort of thing were not always a murky collabora-
tion. Also, I'd learned that while it was hard and rare to truly connect with anyone, sometimes some men were attracted to me. I'd
accepted this the way other people seemed to accept the existence
of a god—rather than asking why or searching for evidence, I tried
to simply take reassurance and comfort in the unexpected glim-
mers indicating that it was so.

TO GET ONTO THE roof, Bryce Finley and I had to climb out the window next to Martha's bed. He'd been the one to open it, and as he
got onto his knees, he neither removed his shoes, which were black
Vans, nor took care to avoid letting the soles touch Martha's comforter. Observing silently, I felt a pang of disloyalty to my roommate. As Bryce Finley raised the window and the screen, I took the
opportunity to pop out from under the covers and grab an Ault
sweatshirt from the bottom drawer of my bureau. I pulled it on,
along with some socks I'd left on the floor. He hopped outside,
onto the porch, in a graceful way that made me think of Martha's
grandmother's cat, and I followed.

The roof was a modest eight-by-eight feet, and he stood close
enough to the edge to make me nervous. In the hope of modeling
more prudent behavior, I sat, my knees raised and my elbows set
against my kneecaps. After a few seconds he sat too, then reclined,
propped on his forearms as if at the beach. We were side by side,
less than a foot apart, and while it was far from pitch-black out—
there was the light from my dorm room, along with a streetlamp
twenty yards away, the old-fashioned kind that made Ault seem
like a movie set as much as a functioning school—the general darkness made me less self-conscious than I'd normally have been in

this proximity to a handsome male celebrity. Or at least less self-conscious about my skin and breath and decision not to shower after my afternoon game, though then again, did a person need to shower after 240 seconds of lacrosse?

I'd been in Bryce Finley's presence for about five minutes total—five bewildering, insane, delicious minutes—and this was the point when my confusion over whether I did or didn't want witnesses crystallized. Meaning not that I knew what I wanted, but that I clearly knew I didn't know, or that I wanted both. I wanted this to be private, and I wanted everyone to hear about it. I wanted it to be my Ault claim to fame, I wanted my own fame by proxy, and I wanted to protect the interaction forever because surely this was the most exciting thing that would happen to me?

We were on the third floor. A dance studio occupied the first floor, then above that were our common room and the Ahmed family's apartment, and above that were the rooms for the eighteen of us who lived in the dorm's singles, doubles, and triples. A pedestrian path ran along the front of the building, which meant students, teachers, alumni, and their spouses or families intermittently passed by about thirty-five feet below us. The temperature had reached the mid-seventies during the day and fallen ten degrees after dark, the smell of mown grass and dogwood blossoms hung in the air, and music from the dance under the tent was audible, songs like "Up on Cripple Creek" by The Band and "You Be Illin'" by Run-DMC.

Bryce Finley pointed at the sky, against which countless stars glittered. "Whenever I came out here," he said, "I used to think about, like, what if the sky wasn't a sky and instead it was a planetarium? And the moon was a skylight?" He was speaking at a normal volume, and my own sense that we should be whispering meant, perhaps, that I ultimately came down on the side of keeping this encounter private. Also, did planetariums have skylights?

"Which is weird," he continued, "because usually I have this pet peeve of when people compare nature to not-natural stuff. Like the sun looked like a basketball, or the lake looked like a mirror.

Shouldn't it be the other way around? The mirror looked like a lake."

I pondered this observation, unsure whether I agreed. I'll add, though, that in the thirty-plus years since this night, whenever someone says, for example, that the sunset looks like CGI, I think of Bryce Finley.

"The stars are so bright here," he was saying. "Not like in L.A."

"I've never been to California," I said.

"It's because of how polluted it is," he said. "Because of the traffic. It's crazy, man. If you're trying to get from Hollywood to Venice Beach at rush hour, it could take you ninety minutes easy."

This casual, factual utterance of the word "Hollywood"—it was almost more than I could bear. And yet, while there were many things I didn't know about how best to interact with a handsome male, an adult man, a famous person, or any combination thereof, I somehow did know I ought not to ask him questions *about* his celebrity—that it would be annoying or hayseedish or just boring if I said, *What was it like when you were on SNL?*

I was rummaging around in my brain for what I could say (something about his trip over from Germany?) when he said, "Sometimes I feel like I was never a real Ault student, you know what I mean? Because I got spring-cleaned."

He turned his head to the left and when we made eye contact, I had the sense that while it didn't particularly matter who I was, my presence did matter—that this was a conversation he wanted to have and it was better that I'd been in the room than it would have been if I hadn't. (Am I parsing this all too much? Of course I am.) I blurted out, "I don't feel like a real Ault student, either. I'm from Indiana, and my life before I came here—I hardly even knew what lacrosse was."

"I grew up outside Denver," he said. "Which other kids would act like was the American frontier, but I'm from the 'burbs like they are. Just not the 'burbs of Boston." He shook his head. "'Spring-cleaned' is such a brutal euphemism. Have some balls and call it what it is. 'You're unwelcome here.'" He wasn't wrong.

"Spring-cleaning" was also a misnomer in that it happened during the summer, and it was when the administration informed a student they weren't invited back in the fall not because the student had broken a rule that was grounds for expulsion but because they just weren't the "right fit" for Ault. "And they did it after my junior year," Bryce Finley was saying, "which, like, do it before that or don't do it at all. Don't do it when a person has one year left. My dad was furious, and he threatened to call lawyers, but I was like, whatever. It was such a fuck-you from the school, and why does anyone want to be in a place they're not wanted? But maybe I should have fought back."

I strongly, passionately did not want to be spring-cleaned. Most complaints a person could make about Ault were understandable to me, and also why would anyone ever want to be anywhere else? Aloud, I simply said, "Yeah."

"And is that what made me, you know, chase fame? Proving to Ault, hey, you underestimated me? You thought I was disposable? Well, look at me now. But the problem is that fame is a mirage, too. You just feel lonely in a different way."

Even then, at fifteen, I knew this wasn't an original sentiment. But to hear it expressed by a beautiful man experiencing it first-hand, on a lovely spring night—of course I was moved. He'd looked away, out toward the circle, but he looked back at me, and this time the eye contact contained an intensity I was unaccustomed to. Then, to my astonishment, tears welled up and slipped over his eyelids and down both his cheeks.

"Jesus Christ." He wiped his eyes roughly with the backs of his thumbs. "I don't know what's wrong with me."

"No," I said. "Nothing." He didn't respond, and, more vehemently, I said, "There's nothing wrong with you." I wondered, and it was incredible to wonder, should I kiss him? Surely not. But maybe? Tentatively, I reached out my hand, held it in the air for a few seconds, then touched his shoulder.

* * *

THE WHITE REUNION TENT on the circle gave it the aesthetic of a preppy wedding, but, really, the whole weekend was a bit wedding-like: the smaller Friday night gathering that was maybe missable or maybe would lay the groundwork for the next two days, connecting you to your weekend sidekicks; on Saturday, a combination of events meant to evoke nostalgia, elicit donations, or both; on Sunday, a coda in the form of chapel and brunch. You could run the students' cross-country route, or climb to the top of the chapel tower and ring the bells. Mostly, you could encounter hundreds of sentimental rich people wearing expensive clothes.

Martha picked me up at 4 P.M. Friday at Arrivals at Logan, a gesture whose generosity felt like it was of the past. Over text, I'd written, *Won't the Friday afternoon traffic be bad,* and she'd replied, *More time for us to visit!*

But my plane had landed early, and the traffic hadn't been that bad, and before five-thirty we'd turned in to a parking lot down the street from the suburban bar and grill where Dede had reserved a private room for our class. Dede had decided this location would be more of a draw than the all-alumni Friday dinner. For our first fifteen years of reunions, there'd been a cliquishness around the Friday night gathering, or gatherings, because there'd been the general one on campus and an exclusive one elsewhere, spearheaded by Aspeth. At our fifth reunion I hadn't even known about the smaller off-campus one; at our tenth I'd been invited because Martha had been, and this of course felt like progress; and at our fifteenth, I'd known about it but not been invited, which felt like backsliding. But by our twentieth, people seemed too mellowed by the years, or just too tired, to go to the trouble of excluding each other. Or maybe it was that Aspeth had married an enormously rich man in his sixties, moved to Sydney with him, and stopped attending Ault reunions.

After pulling into a parking space, lowering both our windows, and turning off the engine, Martha looked over at me and said, "I have something to tell you."

I assumed she was about to say that she was having an affair, getting a divorce, or both—we were, after all, forty-eight, in the prime years for such things—but instead she said, "I've been getting Botox." Apparently in some kind of demonstration, she widened her eyes and flared her nostrils. "Are you horrified?"

"Why would I be horrified?"

"Because it's superficial and I'm supposed to be the kind of person who's above that. Or, I don't know, because it's literal poison." Martha was the head of the classics department at Boston College, married for twenty years to a physics professor at Harvard named Mike, and the mother of sixteen-year-old twins who were very good at tennis.

"I think you get to make your own choices," I said. "And believe it or not, people in Michigan get Botox, too. I'm not shocked."

"But you never would, would you?"

It was hard to explain why I wouldn't. It wasn't a lack of vanity. It was more that there was a way I understood myself that had felt entrapping in adolescence but liberating as I got older, a version of wherever you go, there you are. If I'd still be me with Botox, why bother with the Botox? "I probably wouldn't," I said, "but I'm a huge hypocrite in other ways. Isn't the best any of us can hope for to be endearingly hypocritical?"

Martha laughed uproariously and said, "Oh, Lee, it's fantastic to see you. You're always such a breath of fresh air."

Thirty-three and a half years on, I still didn't quite understand why Martha was so fond of me at the same time that she made me feel like a stock she'd bought low. Another part of my life at Ault and my life later that I found difficult to reconcile was that I'd felt profoundly socially inept there and yet it turned out in the years afterward I was not only socially competent but in many cases I was more than competent—I was sometimes charming!—and also that my competence was probably built on my adolescent ineptitude. To win people over, as I'd learned as a teenager by doing the opposite, you just had to be easygoing and mostly upbeat, to not complain (unless wittily), to not overly care or reveal, to roll with where a conversation went. It was helpful to ask questions but not intrusive or meaningful ones. It also was helpful to know when to stop asking questions.

Not unrelatedly, it turned out that a significant part of being the executive director of a nonprofit was fundraising and that I was extremely good at fundraising. I was rarely intimidated around even the richest prospective donors because, compared to Ault people, they were more like kind of rich than *rich* rich. But there also was some balance I intuitively knew to strike among the wealthy of warmth and familiarity with a non-toadying deference. I understood their world, I got them, the dressing on this endive salad was delicious, that throw pillow in the shape of a yellow Lab was so hilarious, I'd been to Block Island, oh, sure, for a friend's thirtieth birthday, but I'd stayed in the *tiniest* hotel room and the soap had given me a rash, haha. In this way, over years, I persuaded affluent progressives to donate millions of dollars to incarcerated people and their families.

I also made the decision early on, after once hitting up Martha for a donation—she gave a thousand dollars, and we were thirty-one at the time—that I wouldn't try to fundraise with my Ault classmates. I just couldn't. It felt too close to asking them for money for myself.

In her car, her sensibly Martha-ish Volvo crossover, Martha said, "You think Cross is coming tonight?"

"I know this is hard to believe," I said, "but any remaining lust in my heart for Cross is for the Cross from a million years ago. Not current Cross. But also no. He never comes Friday night. He's too busy being important." Like Jeff Oltiss, Cross had gone into finance and had a vague yet fancy-sounding job title, but he was based in Boston rather than New York. Dede had told me he was the number-three person at his firm, which employed two thousand people worldwide. Cross was also the co-chair of Ault's current five-year capital campaign seeking to raise four hundred million dollars, meaning in yet another of the absurd plot twists of time, I sometimes received alum-wide emails about the importance of funding Ault's enduring commitment to academic rigor and ethical integrity from the person on whom I'd learned to give blow-jobs.

I wondered about mentioning my email exchange with Jeff Oltiss to Martha and didn't. After no contact since that day in March, I'd heard from Jeff the preceding Monday: *I'm coming to the reunion!* he'd written. *Outside chance I'll be there Friday night, definitely by Saturday lunch. Save a ham and brie sandwich for me?*

I'd replied, *Great and I look forward to reconnecting!*

The reason I was reluctant to mention him to Martha wasn't exactly that I thought I'd curse the possibility of something between us; it was that mentioning him felt premature. There would be more information available instantaneously when Jeff and I saw each other in person.

After examining ourselves in the sun-visor mirrors of her car, Martha and I entered the restaurant and made our way to the private room in the back and there were only five people there: Dede and Darden and Darden's wife, Rochelle, and two guys I'd almost never spoken to, Pete Birney and Fritz Huff. I felt both an instinctive panic and also an awareness that there was no reason to be nervous, that if I met these exact same people at a fundraiser or dinner party, I wouldn't be remotely anxious. Dede murmured, "I think Fritz is literally, unironically wearing Drakkar Noir" as she embraced me, and Darden was one of those excellent huggers, and soon I was drinking a glass of white wine while Pete and I discussed how different Ault would have been if social media and smartphones had existed when we were there, and already nine more people had arrived. Then Dickie O'Doherty approached Pete and obviously didn't recognize me and I held my hand over my heart and said "Lee Fiora," and Dickie nodded agreeably while looking just as baffled. I said, "I'm going to get another glass of wine. Can I get either of you one?" and Dickie held up a glass of sparkling water and said, "Nah, sober for three years now."

I was almost finished with my second glass of wine, long into a conversation with Darden and Martha about their respective kitchen renovations—Darden's family had had to move out of his house for his—and feeling deep affection for both of them while also thinking, *This really is incredibly tedious and do they talk this unself-consciously in front of everyone or just in front of other Ault people or do they only socialize with other people who can afford massive kitchen renovations?* and then someone set their hand on the small of my back and I think I knew, even before I turned. When I did turn, a good-looking man a few inches taller than me, with gray hair and blue eyes and a warm smile, said, "Lee, it's me, Jeff. Jeff Oltiss."

We both hesitated infinitesimally—he already had a beer in his left hand—and then we leaned in and kissed each other's cheeks just once. There are a fair number of habits that preppy men have that I no longer find endearing, if I ever did—smugness, resource hoarding—but, on occasion, a preppy man with good manners and beer on his breath can still make me weak in the knees.

"Hi, Jeff Oltiss," I said. "Welcome to your thirtieth reunion."

"Hi, Lee Fiora," he said. "It's good to be here."

We eyed each other for a few seconds, then Darden said, "Oltiss? Hey, man, great to see you," and they heartily shook hands, and Jeff heartily shook hands with Martha, too—they didn't kiss. Then Darden said, "Jeff, we're discussing kitchen renovations from hell, and I don't know if you've been in the market for a Sub-Zero refrigerator lately but if there's the slightest chance you'll want one in the next calendar year, can I recommend getting on a wait list now? Like, put down that beer and sign up in this very moment?" Everyone laughed energetically.

At the soonest possible opportunity, while Martha was conveying to Darden what she considered the pros and cons of a kitchen island sink, I turned to Jeff and said, "I thought you probably weren't coming until—because of—I hope your mother-in-law—"

He looked amused. "You hope my mother-in-law didn't kick the bucket? Is that what you hope? She's alive and well, but I appreciate that." He glanced at his smartwatch. "The birthday is underway at this very moment. I just decided that after waiting so long to come back to Ault, I shouldn't be half-assed about it." After a pause, he added, "Also, she's my ex-mother-in-law."

Because maybe the comment was flirtatious, but maybe it wasn't flirtatious at all, I didn't acknowledge it. "How'd the drive go?"

"Trafficky but uneventful. I binged a podcast about the Cold War. So who here do I need to avoid? And will Devin preemptively share his pickleball triumphs or are there special questions I should ask to get him to open up?"

"I think he'll be pretty forthcoming," I said.

The way Jeff had touched my back before we'd even spoken, the immediate air of amusement between us, how enticing his combination of familiarity and unfamiliarity were—this all made it seem as if we just needed to catch up to knowing each other as well as it felt like we eventually would and then the real fun could start. But of course I'd been delusional, delusionally hopeful, plenty of times.

And then I took a sip of wine and said, "This is probably incredibly weird for me to bring up, but do you remember parents' weekend our junior year?"

His demeanor shifted, there was some recalibration from festive to serious, and I thought, *Oops.* But when he spoke, his voice was thoughtful.

"Not only do I remember it," he said, "but I think it's tied to why you and I are standing here now." He paused, and Darden and Martha laughingly greeted our classmate Oliver Amunsen, and neither Jeff nor I acknowledged Oliver. "I'm trying to think of how to explain this," Jeff said.

We looked at each other for a beat longer than normal, and I said, "I'm getting nervous."

He shook his head. "You don't need to. When we were at Ault, you and I were both pretty quiet, right? And the only class we had together was sophomore English with Ms. Moray?"

"I once cut her hair," I said. "Which is strange enough. But the even stranger part is that she let it count for extra credit. She gave me an A."

He laughed. "Of all the sort of lawless or intra-judicial things that happened during our era of boarding school, that seems like one of the more innocent ones. But yes, definitely strange. Anyway, in that class I thought you seemed maybe shy and smart and sometimes sad. I wouldn't have said I knew you well, but then again, we all saw each other constantly. I could swear we were both standing by the bagel-toasting machine the time Amy Dennaker put a piece of bacon through and it caught on fire."

"Oh my God, you're right," I said. "I still think she's lucky she didn't burn down the dining hall."

"Back to what happened with your dad—do you remember that we made eye contact?"

"Yes," I said. "I remember."

"I knew that you were horrified that I'd seen it. In the next few days, I wanted to find a way to tell you that it was okay—that it didn't make me think anything was wrong with you, that I wasn't going to tell anyone. I looked for an opportunity, and one morning in the mail room, I tried to approach you, and you looked at me with an expression of just total panic and walked in the other direction."

Briefly, I closed my eyes. "That sounds about right," I said. And maybe it was some trick of time or suggestion but as I opened them, I felt as if I could recall the interaction, how I'd been on the way to a math class in which I knew there'd be a quiz, and to sense that Jeff might say something about my father and then have to take a math quiz had just been too much; both happening would be unbearable.

"So I decided, okay, I won't bother her," Jeff said. "But by then, even though it had only been a few days, I'd gotten in the habit of looking for you. And I kind of kept doing that until we graduated the next spring." He paused again before adding, "Looking for you."

"Hmm," I said. "Like you wished we could be friends or like you wondered if you should report my dad to child protective services?"

"Well, first of all, I don't think I thought in terms of whether your dad was abusive or not abusive. It was a different time, right? I probably perceived him as—I hope this isn't disrespectful, but—clearly not the nicest guy? If that's what he'd do when people might see, what would he do when they wouldn't? But again, I think there was a lot more of all of that back then."

"Yeah," I said. "My dad wasn't the nicest guy." He had died a decade earlier. At his best, he had been warm and mocking, and at his worst, he had been mean and mocking.

"As for wishing we could be friends," Jeff said, "I'm not sure 'friends' is the right word. There was this wool sweater you had that was huge on you and I thought you looked really cute in it."

Jeff! I thought. *Where were you all this time?* Aloud I said, "I know exactly which one you mean, and actually it belonged to Martha's dad. Who was a dad of the non-asshole variety." It occurred to me that my saying her name might draw Martha's attention, but she and Darden were deep into a debate about chrome versus stainless steel cabinet handles. I said, "It's so strange hearing all this because I always felt unremarkable at Ault. I knew I'd never be the smartest or prettiest, but the one thing I was was watchful. But it sounds like you were more watchful."

"Selectively. Don't forget that I thought you were cute." We then made an intense kind of eye contact, a kind I'd made with very few men in my entire life, which was followed by a shivery feeling in my heart, and I wondered if something was really going to happen between Jeff and me. Not like reunion sex in a hotel room but like becoming part of each other's lives.

I took a deep breath and said, "The truth is that I don't remember if I thought you were cute. I mean, I'm sure you were! Who isn't cute when they're in high school? In their awkward, grumpy, messy way? But you definitely grew up to be very cute."

"Yeah?" Jeff smiled a bit sheepishly, and also extremely endearingly. "I'm glad to hear that you think so." Then he set his right hand on my left forearm, above the silk fabric of the forest green blouse my older daughter had helped me select, along with my clothes for Saturday. He said, "And you stayed cute."

I looked sheepishly back at him, and neither of us said anything, and this, fortunately or unfortunately, was when Maria Oldega hurled herself into the lopsided square formed by me, Jeff, Martha, and Darden and said, "Holy shit, you guys, how is it possible we graduated from high school thirty fucking years ago?"

For the next two hours, I wasn't alone in conversation again with Jeff, though I never stopped feeling that heightened awareness of where he was. And then we ended up outside the restaurant in a group of seven or eight people discussing the logistics of who was going to their suburban houses and who had rooms at the Hyatt near Ault's campus, which was newly built and apparently the preferred locale of parents of current students, displacing the now-aging Sheraton that I'd once considered fancy. "Where are you staying?" I asked Jeff. It was the first direct thing I'd said to him since we'd each declared how cute the other was two hours before.

"An Airbnb in Raymond. I tried to make a reservation at the Hyatt, but it was all booked by people who had the sense to plan ahead."

"Yeah, for a rare treat, I was one of those people. So see you tomorrow? I assume you'll be at eight A.M. roll call?"

He laughed. "My Ault nostalgia isn't quite that intense. But hey, maybe I'll text you when I get to campus in the morning?" He pulled his phone from his pocket.

"Sure, I'll give you my number," I said, and I hoped my tone sounded as light as his.

Back in the hotel room I was sharing with Martha, I had a hard time falling asleep and woke up before six, meaning before five Central time. I felt around in the dark for a bag of pretzels I'd stuck in my bag at the Detroit airport and tried to eat them as quietly as possible. After a minute, Martha said in a normal voice, not whispering or disoriented at all, "You sound like a mouse."

"Martha, I think maybe Jeff and I are about to fall madly in love!" I blurted out.

"Wait." Just in that one word—Martha and I knew each other so well—I could hear her amusement and affection. "Jeff *Oltiss*?"

ONE AFTERNOON IN AUGUST 2003, at a strip mall in Ann Arbor, after buying IncARTcerated supplies at a huge chain crafts store— mostly paint, paintbrushes, and ten-inch-by-ten-inch canvases— I set it all in the trunk of my car then went into a café and ordered an iced coffee. As the woman at the register handed my change to me, she said, "Did you hear that Bryce Finley overdosed?"

"He what?" I said.

The woman looked close to my age, which was thirty, and she had short red hair and a nose ring. I'm not sure there's a purpose in my analyzing her emotions, and especially in analyzing them retroactively, but: I think she was genuinely sad and also a bit energized. She was, perhaps, trying not to smile as she said, "They found his body in a hotel room."

Something turned in my stomach. "You mean he overdosed fatally?" I said.

She leaned toward me and whispered, "I heard he was bi."

He'd been staying at a hotel in Santa Monica, and the eventual ruling was combined drug intoxication, believed to be accidental, which I was relieved to learn. Among the substances found in his system were cocaine, marijuana, benzodiazepines, and amphetamines.

After leaving the café that afternoon, I called my fiancé, Dan, from the parking lot. I'd acquired my first cellphone that summer, a thin blue flip phone. When Dan answered, I said, "Bryce Finley died!" and Dan said, "Bryce who?" and I said, "The lead singer of Formica Dream?" and Dan said, "Oh, I hate that song."

"Do you remember he went to my boarding school?" I spoke of Ault infrequently enough that, even with the man I'd marry, this was how I referred to it. Without waiting for a response, I said, "He died of a drug overdose. Today, a few hours ago."

"That's a bummer," Dan said.

I opened my mouth to say—what? *When I was a sophomore and he was on campus for his tenth reunion, he came into my room.* And? And I didn't know; I still didn't know. Instead I said, "I met him once."

"Cool," Dan said. "Although his music still sucks. Hey, I have a meeting now, but want to get Thai for dinner?"

I should say that I loved Thai food; for years, Old Siam was my favorite restaurant, and also I'm glad I married Dan because for almost a decade we made each other's daily lives better—we did until we didn't—and because we had the kids we had. In a way, to describe that marriage is like describing having gone to boarding school. Is there an infinite amount to share, or does a sentence or two suffice? I guess it depends who you're telling the story to.

These are some of the details about Bryce Finley that I didn't tell the man who would, two months later, become my husband and fourteen years after that become my ex-husband, though none were facts I learned from interacting with Bryce Finley. I knew them from continuing to follow him in the news: that in 1995, he acquired two pet chinchillas he named Humpty and Dumpty; that at a concert in Barcelona in 1999, he welcomed a twenty-two-year-old guy named Shawn onstage to propose to his girlfriend, and then, after she accepted, serenaded the couple with "She's So Down on Me," which remained Formica Dream's most popular song; that at a 2002 awards ceremony, he got to sing a duet with Prince.

IT WAS AFTER TEN by the time Martha and I arrived on campus on Saturday morning, following a brisk walk on a trail behind the Hyatt, egg sandwiches in the lobby, and leisurely showers. At Ault, we registered and affixed the thick white nametags with the Ault crest on them to our shirts using tiny gold safety pins. We ended up in the new library, which was seven years old, eating cranberry orange muffins and listening to Cross speak into a microphone behind a podium about how, in order for Ault to continue to lead and inspire students at the level of excellence it had embodied for over a century, we all needed to do our part to get over the four-hundred-million-dollar finish line.

The truth was that when I'd been hired as a teacher in Chicago, I'd been hoping to be hired at a school in Boston because I'd heard Cross was staying there after Harvard. There had been a hold he had on my imagination that had taken a long time to loosen, either in spite or because of not seeing him in the ten years after we graduated. And then there he was at our fifteenth reunion, a bald but still quite handsome father of two with a pretty wife who, like him, had gone to business school. With a one-armed hug, he greeted me succinctly and neutrally, in a way that stung and then, at last, set me free. He was just so distant and impenetrable, and I'd had such an appetite for so many years for boys and men who weren't particularly kind or warm or interested in me, but at last I saw this for the waste that it was. Perhaps it's not a coincidence that I was married by then to a man who was somewhat kind and warm and interested, which had been the most I'd believed I could ask for or expect.

Observing Cross at our reunion, as he earnestly dropped phrases like *community values* and *in-kind gifts* and *estate plans*, I thought that I could have done better, high-school-hookup-wise, but I could have done worse, too. I had wanted Cross so badly, and if I'd never quite had him in any secure or public way, I'd experienced a lot of lust and a little bit of the satisfaction of lust. And then Jeff was beside me again and he murmured in my right ear, "If I have to listen to another minute of this, my brain is going to short-circuit. Want to get out of here?"

I whispered back, "I thought you'd never ask."

We went out some back doors that I wasn't entirely sure wouldn't set off an alarm until we were on the other side—I'd said nothing to Martha and I knew she'd understand—and we were then behind the new library, and Jeff gestured to the left and said, "What if we walk down to the boathouse?"

The boathouse was a mile away, and it was about seventy degrees out, with cottony clouds dotting a cerulean sky; it had poured rain at our twenty-fifth reunion, but this day seemed like it might be perfect. "I'd love to," I said. I crumpled the napkin I'd taken with the cranberry orange muffin, a napkin that also featured the Ault crest, and stuffed it into the pocket of the jeans I was wearing. (For my Saturday outfit, my older daughter had chosen dark jeans, a white and blue nautical-stripe sweater, and white sneakers. "Not too try-hard," she'd said.) As Jeff and I began walking, I said, "I kind of would have guessed that you were a disciple of the church of the capital campaign. But since I don't actually read the annual report, I can't say for sure."

"Ha!" Jeff said. "I do give to the annual fund, but it's not much these days."

"More or less than five million a year?" To joke about money on the campus of Ault felt pleasingly risqué, and I wondered if this was what it was like for those seniors who lit a cigarette right after the graduation ceremony ended.

"For some mysterious reason, in the years leading up to when I thought my own children might apply here, my donations got bigger," Jeff said. "Then they never even applied, but also I had a kind of awakening."

"How so?"

"I've learned a lot from all three of my kids. How can you not, right? Mostly lessons in how little you know. But my middle child, my son Liam, has really challenged me to think about things like systemic racism, social inequality, inherited wealth, all of that. He's nineteen now and very smart, but he had a terrible time in school, lots of anxiety and depression from a young age, and he always asked questions about what you might call our family lifestyle. Why did five of us need an eight-bedroom house? If that guy outside the grocery store was asking for money, and I had money in my wallet, why wouldn't I give him some? Why did his mother and I donate to the symphony instead of to people who needed housing? I'd give reflexive answers, but the thing is, when he pressed me, he was often right. I'd wondered these things, too, when I was his age, and then I'd gotten on the track I'd gotten on and just become busy enough getting through each day to ignore the existential questions." Jeff glanced at me and said, "How's that for some lighthearted Saturday morning banter?"

"No, it's interesting," I said. "So he convinced you to decrease your donations to Ault?"

"To anywhere that has a huge endowment, or caters to people who are already privileged, or both. He's not in college now. He wanted to switch from private to public school, and we let him do it junior year of high school. Now he lives in a group house in Philadelphia and works at a food pantry and I hope he'll go to college, but for the time being he doesn't want to. Once a month we have brunch at a vegan diner, and he tells me another book to read and we talk about it the next time."

"Did he influence you in terms of that organization in Trenton you're involved in?"

"Yes."

"And how is he mood-wise?"

"Stable. Which is fantastic. What about your kids? You said you have daughters?"

"They're great," I said. "I mean, they're giant pains in the ass, I worry about them all the time, and they make fun of me all the time. But they're hilarious."

"What are their names?"

"The fifteen-year-old is Carter, and the twelve-year-old is Clayton. Meaning I gave my daughters extremely boarding schoolish names without telling my ex that's what we were doing. But I had to compensate somehow for having been named Lee Fiora. They'll never go to boarding school, but sometimes it's hard to shake your own teenage idea of what's cool and glamorous, even after you start a nonprofit."

"Well, for the record," Jeff said, "I think Lee Fiora is a lovely name." He stopped walking, so I stopped, too, and we faced each other and his expression became so focused that, even though it was ten-twenty in the morning, I wondered if he was going to kiss me. Instead he said, "Do *you* give to the annual fund?"

"Not never," I said. "But not usually. And a nominal amount. On the one hand, I was given a scholarship and in spite of my best efforts at self-sabotage, I did receive an excellent education. On the other hand, have you ever heard those jokes about the Ivies, like Columbia is a real estate company that holds classes, or Harvard is a hedge fund with students? I feel like Ault is a privilege perpetuator that, I don't know, serves tater tots in the dining hall. Do you think tater tots are still served in the dining hall?"

"Hard to know." He was still looking at me intensely and then he said, "Do you know what I do for a living?"

"Yes."

"And do you see me the way I see Cross?"

I laughed. "Yes and no."

"Do you know what I'm asking?"

"I think so. I mean, I assume you're rich, but by most people's definition, so am I. My ex-husband is general counsel for a utility company. He didn't grow up with money, and obviously we're not still married, but I have a nice house. I've dedicated my professional life to trying to improve America's fucked-up carceral system a tiny bit, *and* I buy organic apples."

Jeff was quiet for a few seconds, and then he said, "It's also the pandemic that caused introspection, I'm sure, but I want the rest of my life to be—not completely different, but different. I want to take early retirement in the next couple years, and I want to give away most of my assets, and I want to live more deliberately, in line with my values. I'm still figuring out what those values are, how closely aligned they are with Liam's. But I don't want to sleepwalk, or to play pickleball for four hours a day. And I want to spend time with people whose company I really enjoy."

"Great," I said. "You should definitely do all of that." I wasn't entirely sure if he was flirting, articulating a mission statement, or both. Also, even in that moment, I was thinking how an Ault person would say *assets,* while a normal person would just say *money.*

"I want to make a donation to your organization. I already decided that. But this"—he pointed at himself, then at me, then back at himself—"I want to hang out with you and I guess what I'm saying is that I hope you want to hang out with me. Socially or whatever. But you don't need to spend time with me this weekend in order for me to make a donation."

I smiled. He didn't seem that neurotic, but he didn't, thank goodness, seem completely not neurotic. I said, "I'm not spending time with you in order for you to make a donation."

I'D LEARNED TO EAT lobster one summer when I visited Martha's family, but it wasn't something I'd done many times since; at most, I ordered a lobster roll at a restaurant every few years when I was in Boston or New York. Which is to say I wouldn't have *chosen* to eat lobster around my former classmates, due to the mess and the smell, which I of course feared would cling inordinately to me, and I definitely wouldn't have around a man I wanted to find me attractive. But lobster was on the menu, and there we all were on Saturday night, at one long picnic table covered in disposable red-and-white-checked cloths, thirty-nine of us counting the handful of spouses, cracking the claws, extracting the fanlike tail of meat, chewing on the skinny legs. Little white bits dotted the back of my hands and the inside of my wrists, and the briny scent was everywhere. Our class was eating in the backyard of a French teacher who lived on campus, and Dede gave a two-minute speech, and Jeff was sitting four people down on the same side of the picnic table as me, so I couldn't see him. Over and under all the conversations, both the ones I participated in and the ones I didn't, I felt the anticipation of when we'd next find each other.

And then it was nine o'clock, nine-twenty, the catering staff was putting everything away and various classmates started to leave, especially the ones who lived around Boston. There was a plan to gather in the lobby of the Hyatt, and I could not pretend to be surprised that there was then a subplan in which Jeff and I would walk with Dede to the faculty house where the fortieth reunion was taking place so that she could give the key to the French teacher's house to a member of the alumni office, then Jeff would drive both Dede and me to the hotel. "And that won't inconvenience you?" I disingenuously asked him. "If you're staying at an Airbnb?"

He said, "No, because I'd go hang out at the Hyatt tonight anyway if that's what everyone else is doing."

The other faculty house was on the far side of campus, and on our way back to the parking lot behind the dining hall, where Jeff had left his car, we were passing the chapel when Dede said, "Can we pop in for two seconds? That's the one thing I didn't have time to do today, and I've always loved when it's empty."

"I didn't know that about you," I said. "See how much we all still have to learn?"

But the chapel was locked—we tried a side entrance, too—and then we returned to the front and stood by the steps talking about how many of our classmates' anecdotes over the weekend had revolved around rule-breaking hijinks (overturning vending machines, climbing through pipes) and how none of us had ever broken almost any rules.

"Besides smoking," Dede said. "And a little vodka now and again." She lightly kicked my calf with her high-heeled sandal. "And besides the ten thousand times you broke visitation with Cross."

"Not ten thousand," I said. "I assure you."

We were about a hundred feet from the tent on the circle, which had by this point been taken over by the current students, who were dancing to songs I was familiar with because of my daughters. The students looked, from this vantage point, like a sort of amoeba, sometimes shout-singing along with the words, and lights were flashing, and we kept talking for a while. Jeff was the first one to sit down on the chapel steps. Then I sat beside him, and Dede sat on my other side.

As students, during morning chapel, we'd all tossed our backpacks onto the stone patio and retrieved them after, literally hundreds of backpacks, with no thought for security. Similarly, none of the dorm room doors had had locks. I knew there were key cards now, but I didn't know if students still left their backpacks unattended.

Jeff gestured toward the activity under the white tent and said, "Do you think we should tell them?"

"Tell them what?" Dede asked.

I said, "That they'll blink and thirty years will pass? That even though most of them probably feel like underdogs, they're not, and that even though all of them probably feel like their lives haven't started, they'll look back on Ault as this singularly intense time and place?"

"Don't stop," Jeff said. "You're on a roll."

I laughed. "That might be all I have."

"Of course you can go to boarding school and still be an underdog," Dede said.

"Can you?" I said.

"*Most* of us were underdogs," she said. "Think about it. About ten people in our class were royalty, and the rest of us were—"

When she hesitated, I suggested, "Peasants?"

"I know you're joking, but kind of," she said. "And I know you always saw me as being in with Aspeth and Cross and those guys"—it would have been small, and possibly still injurious to her even after all this time, to clarify that I'd seen her more as *wanting* to be in with Aspeth and Cross and those guys—"but I secretly felt out of place because of being Jewish. There was definitely anti-Semitism here. Once in biology Mr. Kelly said that Hollywood is run by Jews. Or when I told Horton my first choice was Penn, she was like, 'You mean the Jew-niversity of Pennsylv-asia?'"

"Classy," I said. "A twofer. Did you know Cross is half Jewish?"

Dede shook her head. "The wrong half. His dad's side."

"At the risk of sounding competitive," Jeff said, "I secretly felt out of place because my parents enrolled me at Ault while they were going through an incredibly ugly divorce. You know that stereotype of why kids get shipped off to boarding school? But I didn't know anyone else it was true for. It seemed like most kids had grown up around Massachusetts in these happy families, and their parents came on the weekend to cheer at their soccer games. My parents both lived a twenty-five-minute drive from campus, and I didn't even go home for some long weekends."

"Okay, fine," I said. "I was out of place because I was from Indiana. Even other people in the Midwest look down on Indiana! Also I was out of place because I got a scholarship."

"It's weird to think that wasn't a source of pride," Jeff said. "Like, that's how much Ault wanted you to enroll."

"At the time, I felt like not coming from a rich family was either a personal or moral failure." I glanced at Dede, who was on my right. "Maybe this gets to your point, Dede, but I think almost everyone who ever went to Ault feels like there's an asterisk by their name that explains why they weren't a real Ault student. But it's so silly. We all were Ault students. Don't tell me you guys can't see that now."

"Wait," Dede said. "You of all people are telling me not to hold on to my boarding school insecurities and grudges?"

"Haha," I said. "But seriously—" As we'd sat there, a kind of mental whorling had been occurring in my mind, the coalescence of disparate fragments, and in this instant, I understood what they were. I said, "I assume you guys remember who Bryce Finley was?"

"RIP you beautiful man," Dede said. "Seriously, he was the reason I went to Ault over Grant Academy."

I turned to Jeff. "Do you remember Bryce Finley?"

"Of course." In a startlingly good falsetto, he sang the refrain from "She's So Down on Me."

"Damn, Oltiss," Dede said.

I said, "Sophomore year, the room in Ahmed's that Martha and I lived in had been his."

"I knew," Dede said, "and I was so jealous."

"Do you remember that our sophomore year was his tenth reunion?" I said. "On Saturday night—I guess thirty-two years ago almost to the minute—I was in bed around nine P.M., like the dork I was, and he came by the room."

"No fucking way," Dede said. "By himself or with an entourage?"

"By himself. I was in my pajamas reading a magazine. But it gets weirder." I paused. Was it hard to decide how to present the information because at some point I'd truly thought I'd never tell anyone or because after waiting so long I wanted to tell it perfectly?

"Please tell me he wasn't a predator," Dede said. "I don't think I can stand another fallen idol. Although if he was a predator, I guess that means he wasn't gay." The rumors about Bryce Finley's sexuality had started when I was in college, after he and his drummer had been photographed by a paparazzo sharing a hammock in Hawaii, both of them nude.

"He wasn't a predator," I said. "I doubt he even knew Ahmed's had become a girls' dorm. Either way, he probably assumed the room would be empty."

"Maybe he intentionally went into what he thought was a boys' dorm," Jeff said, and both Dede and I were silent.

At last I said, "I have to admit I never considered that."

"He probably knew by the time he got to your room, though," Dede said. "Girls' dorms had a different vibe."

"Don't say because they smelled so good and were so clean," I said.

She laughed. "They were marginally less bad-smelling. And had more female detritus."

"Anyway," I said, "I think Bryce Finley was maybe high, and he started chatting with me, then he laid down in Martha's bed."

"Oh my God," Dede said. "I hope Martha never washed those sheets."

Again, I hesitated. "I didn't tell her. I've never told any of this to anyone."

I felt Jeff looking at me and when I looked to my left, he said, "This is such an honor," and it seemed like maybe he wasn't kidding.

"Why didn't you?" Dede asked.

"Because it was confusing and also because it turned embarrassing."

"Then I can't wait."

"Did you ever come in my room sophomore year? It had that little roof over the entrance to the dorm. You can almost see it from here." I gestured in that direction.

"I know the roof you mean," Jeff said.

"Bryce Finley suggests we go out on it. For old times' sake, because he'd hung out there when he lived in the room. So we do, and he starts talking about stuff very similar to what both of you were just saying, about how he felt like he hadn't been a real Ault student. In his case, it was because he'd been spring-cleaned. Which is ironic, Dede, since you're saying you went to Ault partly because he had. Then he was talking about loneliness and fame, and he started crying. Literally crying. I'm not exaggerating."

"Is that the embarrassing part?" Dede said. "I was thinking you'd be the embarrassing one."

I laughed. "Of course I was the embarrassing one."

We all were quiet, and a song with a heavy bass throbbed from the tent. I knew Dede and Jeff were waiting.

"He turned and looked at me, and he really was very attractive in a very androgynous way. Almost like he'd been designed in a lab to be dreamy to a nervous fifteen-year-old. He and I probably weighed the same amount. If he'd been six-foot-three or had a beard or big muscles, I'm sure I'd have been terrified. I *was* terrified to some extent. But there was something, I don't know, Peter Pan-ish about him."

Jeff said, "Lee, are you stalling?"

Disbelievingly, Dede said, "Did Bryce Finley *kiss* you?"

"Not exactly." I covered my face with both my palms, and from behind them I said, "I kissed him."

"No!" Dede shouted and her voice was both stunned and ebullient. Jeff was laughing. Dede said, "Like a peck on the cheek or for real?"

"Somewhere in between." It was only after saying this that I dropped my hands. "It was the first time I'd ever kissed anyone! I tried to copy what I'd seen in movies, but I had no idea what I was doing. Like I lean in, I put my lips on his lips and, I don't know, go for it." Anticipating what Dede would ask next, I said, "No tongue. And I'm still not sure, but I think he did kiss me back. Just for a few seconds. And maybe it was instinct on his part, or pity, but there was this, I don't know, very brief sweetness. Then he pulled back and said, 'Oh hey. Hey, no. I shouldn't do that.'"

"He was right," Jeff said.

"Well, he probably had no interest in kissing me," I said, "but he also didn't want to humiliate me."

"He probably did want to kiss you," Jeff said, "and he knew he shouldn't because he was an adult man and you were a girl in high school." I looked to my left again, at Jeff's face less than a foot from my own, and maybe it was the topic of kissing, but I again had that swoony premonition not just that he and I would kiss— before long, maybe that night—but that we'd have a whole future. How extraordinary this was, how surprising yet inevitable. "Also," he said, "if that's the embarrassing part, I don't think it's embarrassing. He opened up to you, and you were nice and tried to connect with him."

"I tried to connect with him using my lips," I said. "I mean, thank you for absolving me. Immediately afterward, what made me cringe was that I was this totally inexperienced dork making a move on a celebrity. But the reason I cringe in retrospect is that on some level I kissed him so that I could tell people I had. This was very muddled in my mind, and I never told anyone until tonight.

But I kissed him for the same reason someone now would want a selfie. So I could prove that I'd met him by extracting something from him."

"I think that's okay," Jeff said. "It's human."

"I can't fucking believe you kissed Bryce Finley," Dede said. "So then what?"

"We stayed out on the roof maybe five minutes more. It seemed like he recovered from his sadness, or maybe he just was worried that if he confided more, I'd try to take his pants off. Inside my head, I was like, *Holy fucking shit, what have I done? Was that awesome or shameful?*"

"It was awesome," Dede said.

"It was funny," Jeff said.

"Eventually, Bryce says his friends are probably wondering where he is. We climb back inside, and he leaves. I think he said, 'Take care' as he took off." Describing it, I was transported backward in time: the way the dorm had smelled, the weight of the door as it clicked shut after Bryce, how a spring night had felt when I was fifteen. "I was jumping out of my skin, so eager to tell Martha that I almost went to the dance to find her. But I was scared I'd run into him again. And then the minutes tick by, and by the time it's curfew, this confusion had settled over me. You both know that Martha is the best, but maybe I feared she'd be too sensible about the whole thing. She'd say something calmly devastating, like, 'Well, if Bryce Finley was under the influence, he's probably already forgotten what happened.' And part of me wanted to hold on to a fantasy that he'd been like, 'Who is that irresistible fifteen-year-old in the Ault sweatshirt and no bra? I shall be haunted by her forever.' "

"I'm sure he was charmed by you," Jeff said. "How could he not have been?"

Dede then elbowed me, and when I looked at her, her expression was some blend of inquiring and amused, which I understood to be her way of saying, *What the hell is going on with you and Jeff and do we want this?* I shook my head about a millimeter, which was my way of saying, *I'm not discussing it with you now, even nonverbally.*

To both of them I said, "In all seriousness, I think one of my problems at Ault was that I tried too hard to learn lessons. I didn't recognize how much of the time life is just random. And often the lesson I thought I was learning was the wrong one. So I probably thought the essential takeaway of my encounter with Bryce Finley was that I wasn't very good at kissing. And then in the future, I was only more nervous."

Dede groaned. "I have one of those. In the spring of our senior year, I hooked up with Devin a few times. And he once said to me, 'You're not that pretty, but you have a smoking hot body, and it's okay, because you can't fuck a face.'"

"Wow," I said. "What an asshole."

"Be that as it may, I took every part of that mindset with me into college. I'm not that pretty, but I have a smoking hot body, and it's okay because you can't fuck a face."

"First of all, you were gorgeous then and you're gorgeous now," I said. "In addition to having a smoking hot body. And second, you can most definitely fuck a face." As I said it, I wondered if I'd feel that bristling male disapproval, the particular WASPy strain of it, from Jeff. Perhaps it was even a test on my part, because I knew I was blunt. This may have been the single biggest difference between my teenage self and my middle-aged self: that I'd once been roiling with thoughts and opinions and yearnings that I suspected were strange or shameful or simply inexpressible, and therefore didn't express them. As I got older, it wasn't the thoughts and opinions and yearnings that went away; only, over time, their suppression. But in this moment, both Jeff and Dede laughed very hard.

(Later, Jeff told me, "I already wanted to have sex with you, but it made me really, really want to."

"So you could fuck my face or so I could fuck yours?" I asked.

"Because I thought having sex with you would be fun and exciting and honest. And I was right." We had this conversation in my bed in Ann Arbor, on the third day of the first time he came to visit me, which was three weeks after our reunion. He was lying on his back, and I was lying on my side with my head on his chest, and he was playing with my hair. He added, "And so both of us could fuck each other's faces." When I laughed, he said, "I swear that I don't usually use the word like that but I'm making an exception because it's a special occasion, and I thought you'd like it.")

On the chapel steps, I turned to him and said, "What offhand comment did someone at Ault make that's been tormenting you since the late eighties or early nineties?"

"In my second week at Ault, on the bus to a soccer game against St. Gregory's, this junior named Bret Deacon said to me, 'You tie your shoes like a kindergartener.'"

"How does a kindergartener tie their shoes?" I asked.

"I wondered the same thing. I think it had to do with making two loops instead of one. Just to be clear, this wasn't my worst moment at Ault. There was the whole culture of roughhousing or hazing in the boys' dorms. But that bus ride was so early in my Ault experience, and Bret said it in such a hostile way, just sneering at me, over nothing. Why did he care how I tied my shoes? I realized that I needed to be on very high alert all the time."

"Maybe Devin learned to be an asshole from Bret Deacon," I said.

"Did you change the way you tie your shoes?" Dede asked.

"No, but I still think of Bret saying that every time I do it."

"That's awful," I said. "Should we hold a ceremony to banish Bret from your consciousness?"

"I think this conversation is the ceremony," Jeff said, and then he moved his right hand so that his pinky touched the pinky on my left hand. I felt that seizing of my heart, a sensation I'd experienced a few times a year as a teenager and less as I grew older, that arose from a wild hope that my life could be, if only intermittently, exactly as I wished. As I curled my pinky around Jeff's, I thought, *It's going to happen, and it's going to be so, so good.*

"On that note," Dede said, "should we be on our merry way?"

"I suppose we should," Jeff said.

Also later, he said it occurred to him to offer his car to Dede so she could drive back to the hotel and we could keep sitting there and talking. He said, "I'd been waiting thirty years to hang out with you." Now we joke that when we get married—neither of us is in a hurry, and I'm not even sure we will, but it amuses us to talk about it—we'll ask Dede to be our officiant. After we'd dated long-distance for two years, and his younger son had started college, Jeff did quit his job, though he still does some consulting, and he moved into my house in Ann Arbor.

I realize, of course, that there are not particularly romantic reasons why Jeff and I are drawn to each other. There's the novelty, the discovery, of how we sort of didn't know each other blended with the comfort of so many shared frames of reference. Much of the familiarity between us is, undeniably, socioeconomic. He's always lived in a different income bracket than I have, and at certain moments, like when he reveals he's never eaten at Perkins, I'm reminded that our backgrounds overlap without being identical. But these are minor differences. There's an essential recognition.

At the same time, that he is now my life partner cannot be entirely attributed to the facts that we attended the same boarding school and both were divorced at our thirtieth reunion. It's that he's him and I'm me, that we just really like each other in all the ordinary ways. We like going for walks together at Nichols Arboretum on the weekend, texting each other when we're apart, cooking dinner together, watching TV together; we like talking about the big and small things that are bothering or amusing us. He attends my older daughter's basketball games and my younger daughter's clarinet recitals, and he FaceTimes with his kids from the kitchen. When my daughters are at their dad's house, Jeff and I like taking off each other's clothes. If I'm right that all of this is ordinary, I'm enormously grateful for it; our ordinary life, our closeness, is thrilling to me. Though my best friend in Ann Arbor merely rolled her eyes when I told her, "You don't know what an accomplishment it is that I got an Ault boy to move to Michigan for me. It's like I'm Wallis Simpson."

On that night of our reunion, Dede stood first, then Jeff and I also stood and our pinkies separated at some indefinite moment. But I wasn't nervous that I had ruined things; I wasn't even worried anymore about how much I smelled like lobster, or how much he did. We walked toward the pedestrian path and turned onto it. On the circle, under the tent, the song playing was a megahit from more than a decade earlier by an Australian singer older than me. I hadn't realized it still got listened to, at least by teenagers. But the students were dancing enthusiastically, a thrumming mass of exuberance, and I ached a little at their youth and the badness of the world they'd be inheriting, even with their unreasonable advantages; I ached for the group activities I hadn't taken part in when I was their age, the fun I hadn't allowed myself. Surely, in dorm rooms all over campus, current students were not taking part and not having fun, but nevertheless inexorably becoming themselves.

Dede and Jeff and I made a left, away from the circle, away from the teenagers we had and hadn't been, and went to join our classmates.

ACKNOWLEDGMENTS

I'm so grateful to the following people . . .

My editor, Jennifer Hershey; my agent, Claudia Ballard; and my publicist, Maria Braeckel. Working with the three of you is a joy and a privilege.

My wonderful larger team at Random House, including Andy Ward, Susan Corcoran, Rachel Rokicki, Windy Dorresteyn, Alison Rich, Madison Dettlinger, Wendy Wong, Peter Dyer, Paolo Pepe, Robbin Schiff, Elizabeth Eno, Cassie Gonzales, Greg Mollica, Kelly Chian, and Lawrence Krauser.

My equally wonderful team at WME, including Anna DeRoy, Tracy Fisher, Suzanne Gluck, Fiona Baird, and Oma Naraine.

My excellent British publisher, Transworld: Jane Lawson, Patsy Irwin, Milly Reid, Hannah Winter, Sara Roberts, and Georgie Bewes.

The editors of the publications that first published some of these stories, whose thoughtful feedback helped me improve them: Willing Davidson, Heidi Pitlor, Tyler Cabot, Scott Stossel, Jen Gann, Leigh Haber, Michelle Hart, and Laura Battle.

My early readers and detail-providers, many of whom are also beloved friends and some of whom are family members: Susanna Daniel, Erin O. White, V.V. Ganeshananthan, Sally Franson, Essie Chambers, Matt Klam, Aminatou Sow, Ariel Levy, Tolani Akinola, Sheena MJ Cooke, Emily Jeanne Miller, Dessa, Lewis Robinson, Nick Arvin, William C. Taylor, Will McGrath, Jeff Brockmann, Jim Mahoney, Jeff Gleason, Meegan Hollywood, Beth Guterman Chu, Aisha Sultan, Rebecca Hollander-Blumoff, Julius Ramsay, Alex Donn, Lindsay Sloane, Afabwaje Kurian, Dawnie Walton, Kari Forde Anderson, Karma Hughes, Ellen Battistelli, Tiernan Sittenfeld, Jo Sittenfeld, P.G. Sittenfeld, Sarah Sittenfeld, and Thad Russell.

My classmates in the Groton Form of 1993—thank you for the generosity you've shown toward my writing, and its many creative liberties, since we were teenagers.

Finally, my love and appreciation go to the three humans and one small beast who live in a house with me and who see on a daily basis the messy way that books are written.

ABOUT THE AUTHOR

CURTIS SITTENFELD'S *New York Times* bestselling books have been translated into thirty languages and twice selected as Reese's Book Club picks. They include the novels *Prep, American Wife, Eligible, Rodham,* and *Romantic Comedy,* and the story collection *You Think It, I'll Say It.* Sittenfeld's stories have appeared in *The New Yorker, The Atlantic,* and *The Best American Short Stories,* of which she was the 2020 guest editor. She lives with her family in Minneapolis.

curtissittenfeld.com
Facebook.com/curtissittenfeldbooks
Instagram: @csittenfeld

ABOUT THE TYPE

This book was set in Sabon, a typeface designed by the well-known German typographer Jan Tschichold (1902–74). Sabon's design is based upon the original letterforms of sixteenth-century French type designer Claude Garamond and was created specifically to be used for three sources: foundry type for hand composition, Linotype, and Monotype. Tschichold named his typeface for the famous Frankfurt typefounder Jacques Sabon (c. 1520–80).